Strings on a Shadow Puppet

T. L. Evans

Strings on a Shadow Puppet

The Tale of the HMS Hunter

This is a work of fiction. All characters and events portrayed in this book are fictional and any resemblances to real people or incidents is purely coincidental.

First Printing 2013

ISBN-10: 0988543605
ISBN-13: 978-0988543607

DEDICATION

To Elisa,
the source of my love and courage

ACKNOWLEDGMENTS

One cannot help but sound like an Academy Awards speech when one acknowledges those who have helped in the creation of a book, especially when it is one's first novel. Even so, there are many who really do deserve a huge amount of credit for the help they have given.

Firstly there is Dr. Stephen G. Hague, whose intellect, imagination and friendship helped to inspire so much of this novel. Without him, this book would never have been written, nor would the world it describes have been so rich…or dark.

Equally to blame is the incomparable Jojo Jensen: writer, artist and remarkable voice talent. Not only did her superior editing turn a rambling amateur book into the novel you see before you, but it was she who convinced me to enter the blogesphere and pushed me to the eventual publication of this book in its present form. How many versions of this novel did you read Jojo? Even you must have lost count. Thank you, thank you, thank you.

Then, there are the Wordos: that cunning group of writers who pen their craft and help lesser writers to become professional. Jerry, Kathy, Nina, John, Grá, Stephen, Dave, and so many others it is hard to remember played a role in helping me get over some of my foibles, but a special thanks goes to Rhiannon Rasmussen-Silverstein, whose comments on my early chapters let me discover where this novel began (there were three previous starting chapters).

Finally, and foremost, in the spirit that *le Roi* enters last, my greatest thanks goes to Carmen Elisa Oquendo Cifuentes, without whose help, support and love I would be nothing. She not only put up with me while writing this book, but before that even… what would I do without you?

PRELUDE

Alex's body slumped in the chair like an exhausted boxer between bouts; eyes closed, a small drip of saliva touching the side of his mouth. His mind, however, was keenly focused on the VR simulation he was jacked into. It was a recording of the kind of recent event that he was a sad expert in. He took in every detail, but did not try to interact with the proceedings. It wasn't that kind of sim.

As in the real world, Alex's virtual avatar was tall and well built with the tell tale prismatic eyes that revealed his genetically modified background: wheels of color that told of his mandellan descent. He wore the double breasted black uniform of the Sophyan Imperial Navy, and around its high collar were the two golden laurel leaves denoting his rank and status.

His dark hair did not move in the breeze that shuffled scraps of paper across the asphalt, nor did he try to dodge the ball that was thrown through his form. He was too busy taking in the other details. The red-brick façade of the school, the hand crafted leaf patterns in the iron gates, the way the last of the children ran through the doors as the bell sounded. Once they were all inside, the attendant, a sentient alien with a long central carapace and slowly undulating ambulatory organs made its way across the forecourt, picking up items that the children left behind with its hand-like suckers.

The explosion ripped through Andres Academy, hurling steel, concrete and glass through the elite school; spreading a fiery cloud of smoke into the air. Alex ducked involuntarily as a block of burning debris flew through his avatar. Had it been real he would have been as dead as the sophant was, crushed by the detritus of the blast.

A grey cloud of dust settled over the street, while torn metal and tiny limbs fell scattered across the once fine court yard. When the rumbling ended and the last crashes of the collapsing building shook, there was a moment of silence that stretched beyond reason. A brick fell, a glass pane shattered. The first frightened sobs were followed by screams of horror and pain. Not all the cries were human, nor were all the body parts.

Fires flickered in the background. A small child, human, walked out from a gutted classroom, still holding the hand of a playmate who was not so lucky. The bellows of a Larquianne sounded loudly over that of its surviving classmates. It crawled out from beneath a pile of rubble, using its three forearms to pull itself free. Its black fur was matted with blood, and its bottom half was missing. Its cries soon quieted to a whimper, then faded all together.

Sirens approached quickly, and wheels screeched to a halt as rescue workers raced from their vehicles. Had Alex actually been there, he might have been able to stop them. Such a horror had never happened on this world before, and they weren't ready for the second blast. It was worse than the first. It contained airborne nanotech devices that worked on the nervous system. The screams of the rescue workers drowned out those of the children. The broadcast began immediately after the second detonation.

"The ability to control one's own future is not a privilege, it's a right!" The image of the figure who spoke was carried across all the comms channels by a hacker signal. It was an extreme ectomorph, tall and ultra thin, with slanted eyes, swirling dotted tattoos, an extended cranium and high curling hair. Alex recognized the image was a stylized human.

"The ability to select one's own government," it continued, "is not a privilege, it's a right. Democracy is the only form of government that ensures these privileges remain rights, inalienable human rights. Rights that cannot be controlled by the privileged few, nor shared with bug-eyes, slimies or others whose alien ways corrupt human society! I am the Dalang, Speaker of the Wayang Liberation Front, and this is not the last you will hear from me! Long live the Federalist Revolution!"

Alex jacked out, he did not need to see anymore. Once more in the real world, he wiped the drool from his chin and looked at the two men who stared at him from across the well appointed library. He blinked, taking in the anachronistic leather bound volumes, the fine antique furniture and the elegant fireplace with ornate Billanoban carvings. He drew himself straight in the chair, and looked at his audience once more.

"The other two attacks included the hijacking of a star liner and a pirate raid," the first man said. He was a well built man with golden skin and almond eyes, and clearly held authority in the room.

"Seem familiar?" the second, older man asked. He had silver hair and a hawkish nose. His eyes were locked on Alex.

"The rhetoric is different," Alex said in the calm plummy tones of the long entitled and highly educated upper class. His jaw was clenched tightly, the muscles in his cheeks worked beneath the skin.

"The methods are identical," the first man said. His voice as aristocratic as Alex's.

Alex stood and walked across the room, his hands behind his back. He looked out the window at the terraformed nature that lay beyond. He didn't notice any of it.

"This is your chance, Alex. Your chance to set things right." The second man leaned forward with a knowing smile. "You can get the people who were behind the *Silver Slipper*."

Alex turned and looked at them both, as if considering what they had to say. Yet they already knew his answer and so did Alex.

PART I

The Legacies of Command

CHAPTER 1

Fran's PAD sounded a single harsh beep as she walked through the double hatched bulkhead. The map she followed vanished from the display and was replaced by flashing red letters: *You Have Entered A Restricted Zone.* She frowned and looked back the way she had come. A long metal corridor with occasional hatches and a twisting maze of pipes, ducts and wires along the ceiling stretched behind her. It was identical to the one that stretched before her.

"Oh... shoot," Fran said.

She looked despairingly at her PAD. The map was gone. Her brown eyes glanced down the corridor searching for some sign or landmark. There was none. Her frown deepened, but still no lines formed on her young face. Her stomach tightened with nerves, and her ponytail bobbed as she turned to look up and down the hall.

"How am I supposed to find my ship if they block out the stupid map?" But she knew the answer. She was supposed to have downloaded the directions into her implants, only she didn't have any implants. Fran was a natural.

The *HMS Résolut*, flagship of the 12th Fleet, was a dreadnaught. It wasn't the largest class of vessel in the

Imperial Navy, but it was damn close. Coming in at well over a million tons, its enormous spherical bulk was filled with gangways and corridors that twisted their way through the various engines, weapons systems and personnel compartments which all looked the same to Fran. Somewhere in that mess was the stealth ship *Hunter*, to which she should be reporting.

"This is Able Technician Francis Maria Harpur to *Résolut* Control System." Fran held the PAD to her mouth and eyed the ceiling. "Request directions to *HMS Hunter*."

"*HMS Hunter* is located in Launch Bay Five," a calm androgynous said.

"And where is Launch Bay Five?" Fran's voice was almost desperate. She wanted to find her way to *Hunter* before a security detail found her. She was embarrassed enough as it was, being delivered to her new home under guard would just be too much.

"You have entered a Restricted Zone, that information is not available."

"Great," Fran said to herself. Two minutes ago she'd been in an overcrowded hall filled with people who she could ask. Now? No one.

Had she known she was supposed to rendezvous with her new ship onboard a Dreadnaught, she would have memorized the *Résolut*'s deck plans, but did they tell her? No, that would have made life too easy. All she'd known was she'd been assigned to the prestigious Advanced Reconnaissance and Assault Group of Ripper's Raiders, and she'd be serving on the *HMS Hunter*. She'd spent weeks studying the layout and designs of the small *Spectre* Class Reconnaissance and Assault vessel, but now had no way to find it within the bulk of the warship that it was docked in.

"Great way to start your new career in Naval Intelligence, girl. Get lost before you even report to the ARAG. Great, just great."

She tried to swallow back a belch and failed. Brushing the loose strands of her long dark hair from her eyes, she cast a one last glance in the direction she had come from before continuing the way she had been headed. "What other way could it be?"

She followed the long corridor, occasionally adjusting the straps on the duffel she carried on her back. Her tiny frame made the pack look enormous, though it really only carried a toiletry kit, a few changes of cloths and the most essential of her gear. The rest of her stuff was being taken directly to the *Hunter* from the transport ship she'd arrived on.

"Why couldn't they have taken me along with it?" She muttered as she continued walking down the corridor, "or given me a map I could download onto my PAD? But nooo, that's not secure. I could lose a PAD, you can't loose implants, no sir. God forbid you don't have implants. I mean, who wouldn't want implants? Who wouldn't want thousands of tiny nanobots crawling around your nervous system like so many little spiders weaving a web. Who wouldn't want a microscopic network wired straight into your nervous system? Who wouldn't want to be constantly logged in like a cyberjunkie and… now what?"

The corridor had come to a junction in a small hexagonal room, where in addition to the new hallway it crossed, a set of ladder-like stairs headed up and down. There were no signs, no indicators. Her gut whined and gurgled. Her PAD flashed with red letters: *You Are In A Restricted Area!*

"No shit," she said, looking in each of the six directions, "Well think, you're supposed to report to the *Hunter*, right? Which is part of the ARAG, so it's gonna be in a restricted zone… so you can't be far off can you? It's supposed to be docked in Launch Bay Five right? So a launch bay has gotta be near the outer hull. On a dreadnaught, that means down."

She smiled to herself, proud of her reasoning, and started down the steep stairs backwards so that her pack didn't pull her off balance. She kept going until the stairs ended. Other than the fact that there were no downward stairs, the junction was identical to the one she had started in; not to mention the other seven she had passed through in her climb. Looking around, she sighed.

Sinner reached awkwardly over the table as he adjusted the torque on the hydrogen flow modulator with a gentle twist of his screwdriver. Scattered about him were the tools of his official trade: a combination of equipment that spanned the tech-level scale from simple hand tools to nanotech manipulators and field inhibitors. To the uninitiated the visual effect was total disarray, but each served its purpose and was placed in a precise location where Sinner could readily reach it without looking.

The fact that this clutter dominated the *Hunter*'s mess-lounge, the stealth ship's only communal living space, was also precisely calculated. Built for reconnaissance and clandestine ops, she was not a large ship. For her size the crew accommodation was generous, but the functions of her mission did not leave much room for comfort. The four meter by five meter multipurpose mess-lounge not only served as the sole eating, recreation and fraternization area on the ship, it did so for both the officers and the enlisted men. At the moment relaxation would have proven difficult, for while all the retractable tables and chairs were extended, every centimeter was covered by varying pieces of the ship's engineering section; each placed by Sinner in premeditated disarray.

Set in the center of the chaos, he tinkered with the engine components on both macro and microscopic scales. Like the room, he was dressed with pre-calculated disorder on the edge of insubordination. The sleeves of his slightly wrinkled black jumpsuit were rolled up to the three silver chevrons and two bottom rockers of his rank. His salt-and-pepper hair was cut close and his middle aged face shaved smooth. Only one of his jack-ports was obvious, the one on his wrist. It was a utilitarian grey that disguised its cutting edge functionality as a cheap low tech implant.

He winced slightly as he tweaked the flow modulator, trying to judge the proper torque based upon the feel of his hand and his considerable experience. Such adjustments were crude, but he would make the finer adjustments using the sonic manipulator and microfilament restrictors later when he could spare the time and concentration. At the moment his attentions remained elsewhere as he rode the nanobots working within the mixing chamber of the injector unit. He allowed the images being broadcast to him from the microscopic robots to be superimposed on his regular vision, occasionally minimizing the view of the robots into a small window while he looked more closely at the work in his hands.

For the most part, he did not interfere with their pre-programmed behavior. Instead he observed and only controlled them remotely when necessary. He did not enjoy riding nanobots as much as he did their macro-sized cousins. It was too much like hard work to direct the thousands of tiny robots at once and the sensation of their microscopic perspective was disorienting. Still, he did his job, occasionally making changes that added to his plan for the flow regulator rather than following the manufacturer's specs. Thus far, those changes had increased engine efficiency by two-point-three percent. He smiled when he saw it increase another point one percent.

Gradually, as each of the nanobots finished their job, Sinner ordered them to self destruct and dutifully observed as they did, ensuring none could malfunction or could be hacked in combat and used against them. Sinner made one more adjustment by hand to the modulator and ran the diagnostics. He had increased the efficiency by five-point-two-four-three percent. Pleased with himself, Sinner saved the recorded list of his actions, and considered which task to perform next.

"Ah fuck, Sinner!" Gunny Chrom's voice sounded as she entered the room, "You know there's a reason why you're not supposed to work in the fucking lounge!"

I guess that answers that question, Sinner thought. He closed out his virtual windows and suppressed a smile.

"Crap, Chief," Corporal Bowman said as he trailed into the room behind her, "I was going to buy you a beer, but as there's no place to drink it."

"Keep your pants on," Sinner answered and began collecting his tools, "I'm just finishing up."

"Yeah? Well we just finished fifteen hours of joint training ops and were looking forward to a chance to kick back." Gunnery Sergeant Andrea Chrom glared at the ship's engineer. "But since you turned the lounge into a workshop again...."

Sinner smiled at her in a not-quite-apologetic manner. He stood and moved some of his gear off a sofa. Marine to the core, Chrom did not smile back. With dark brown skin, prominent high cheekbones, and full lips, she was a beautiful woman. Sinner always thought he might have made a try for Chrom if she wasn't such a hard-assed killer. Then again, he also wouldn't have liked or respected her as much. Sinner would take a crewmate he could rely on over a nice piece of fluff any day.

"Look, I gotta get the ship back up to specs don't I?" Sinner asked.

"You've got a whole goddamned engineering section for that," Chrom said, unceremoniously dumping some of Sinner's gear on the floor.

"Have you looked in engineering lately?" Sinner asked, "Not a lot of space when the fusion chamber is propped open."

"You goddamned pussy-assed Navy boys think you're the only ones with a job to do on the ships," Chrom said, "In case you haven't noticed, there're some Marine Recons around here with a job to do too."

"I didn't notice," Sinner answered, "At least, I didn't noticed you doin' any work."

"Very funny you goddamned prole-sav," Bowman said, tossing Chrom a beer, "but I seem to recall having pulled you're ass out of the fire when the Skipper and Warrant Duffy bought it."

"You got me there," Sinner said. He cleared the most comfortable of the loungers and gestured for them to take a seat.

"Meet your new Tech yet?" Chrom asked. She put her feet on a table and kicked some of his tools on the floor.

Sinner glared at her, then bent over to pick up the gear. "No, hasn't checked in yet. But I've seen her specs. Looks alright."

"Her?" Bowman asked, sitting up and taking interest. He was average height, muscular and very well cut, but he never wore clothing to show it off. He kept his light brown hair to regulation length and his uniform as neat and pressed as his duties allowed. Ed Bowman was thoroughly Marine.

"Keep your friggin' hands to yourself, Corporal."

"Aw, you're no fun," Bowman said, mock pouting as he leaned back on the lounger, "I just like a bit of a mix in the crew. Keeps things interesting. I'd love it if we got a sophant."

"A sentient non-human in the Raiders?" Sinner said, "That'll be the day."

"This new kid better be more than alright," Chrom said, bringing the topic back to the crewmate, "Ripper's Raiders is the best fleet in the Navy, and the ARAG is the best unit in the fleet. Alright will get her dead. Maybe us too."

"She's young," Sinner said with a shrug, "but her file says she's bright and shows some talent."

"But?"

"But she's a natural."

"Bigot," Bowman said with a smirk.

"Don't get me wrong," Sinner replied, "there's a place for naturals, even on a ship, but with as much crap as we got going down here? I'd prefer someone with at least some implants backing me up in engineering. Besides, she hasn't seen any combat."

"Great. More fresh meat," Chrom said. She and Bowman exchanged a meaningful look.

"Speaking of fresh meat," Sinner said, deciding to initiate his second project, "you hear anything about the new Tactical Officer? I understand he's supposed to be one of you jar-heads."

Bowman popped the air seal on his beer and sucked on the tube. Chrom just shook her head.

"What?" Sinner stopped clearing his equipment and looked at them.

"You really haven't heard?" Bowman asked, "You and Samantha the Super-Spook must be losing your touch."

"That's Lieutenant Smith to you, Corporal," Sinner said, pointing a finger at Bowman, "And funny enough, our XO has more important things to do than chase gossip."

"Don't get all jealous, Chief," Bowman said, his hands held up defensively, "I ain't moving in on–"

"Stow it, Bowman," Chrom said.

Bowman shrugged, but let it drop.

"What is it, Gunny?" Sinner asked, turning to Chrom, "I would've thought that having a marine as the ship's troop commander would suit you. Isn't he Force Recon?"

"He's not even a marine," Chrom said with a look of disgust on her face, "I talked to Bernsie earlier today, and he tells me that someone's decided to play politics with our lives."

"What do you mean?"

"You heard that some Army puke will be cross-training with Force Recon, right?" Chrom said with a tone of disgust.

"No friggin' way."

"Yes friggin' way." Bowman took another sip of his beer.

"Crap." Sinner leaned against the table. "That's some fucked up shit."

"You ain't joking," Chrom replied, "Our new TOMO is an Army officer, full officer mind you, not a Warrant Officer like Duffy was. Major Bernse got saddled with him and given a direct order to put him into action."

"So he chooses us?"

"Told me the mission was important, but he could rely on us to get it done even with a political chump serving as Tactical Ops and Marine Officer."

"Shit, it ain't like Van Trappini to let some politico into the ARAG," Sinner said, but his mind was on the new captain.

"Well it sure as hell don't sound like Bernsie." Chrom took a swig of her beer.

"Or the Admiral for that matter," Bowman added.

"Naw, I can see the Admiral doing it."

"What?" Bowman said with surprise, "You criticizing the Ripper? I thought you Navy pussies turned to dust or something if you said something bad about the heroic Admiral Rippavitch."

"The Ripper's a great man, don't get me wrong," Sinner said, "but even if it ain't official, he's head of the Hegemonists. He plays politics. Someone's got to look at the big picture."

"See? What I tell you?" Chrom said, "Even the best Navies are still basically pussies."

"You got a name yet?"

"Leftenant Rascoine Lord D'Ascoine," Chrom answered with flair.

"You're kiddin' right?" Sinner asked, "Razza Dazza D'Ascoine? The guy with the statue in the entrance hall to the Senate? The one they made the Sim of the Week about?"

"The one and only."

"Fuck me," Sinner said.

"No thank you." Chrom crushed the empty and threw it into the recycler.

The information began to percolate in the back of Sinner's brain. *I'll have to let Samantha know, ASAP.*

"How about the mission?" Chrom asked, "Any news on that?"

"Counter-insurgency, Alterande Sector," Sinner said.

"Offing more Feddie bastards, that's what I like to hear."

"What about the CO?" Bowman asked, "Any idea who it is?"

"Nope," Sinner lied.

CHAPTER 2

Fran stood with her face pressed against the window. Below her in the docking bay marked with a large red number five was the ship she knew had to be hers. It was smaller than most of the other craft and clearly not as well armed, but there was no mistaking the *HMS Hunter* for anything but a weapon of war. It had the distinctive wedge shape and sharply set angles that made it immediately recognizable as a *Spectre* class stealth ship. Its camo-capable hull was set to a solid light absorbing matte black with no visible markings. It made the *Hunter* resemble some ancient flint or obsidian arrowhead, but the ship's armament and electronic warfare equipment made it far more dangerous than any lithic tool.

Fran didn't notice how her breath steamed the window until it clouded her vision. Even then she ignored it, staring at her new home, noting how its wings were unfolded into atmospheric mode. That gave the ship a bat-like appearance that was too cool. What was more, Fran knew that as slick as it looked, the ship was in fact even more remarkable in its function. Though she'd never seen a *Spectre* class ship before, Fran knew the vessel inside and out. Its strangely angled hull made it hard to pick up on sensors. Combined with its capacity for low-observable propulsion, that stealth design was perfect for lurking behind enemy lines and striking unseen at larger and better armed vessels. She also knew that if necessary the ship could give up its stealth in favor of the high-g acceleration. Even though it only had two triple mounted laser turrets and a single missile launcher, if used properly it could take any warship in the docking bay.

It was also the ideal ship for recon and intelligence missions. The mixture of sensor and surveillance arrays she saw being fitted in its modular bay suggested that was to be their mission. She couldn't wait to start.

"Assuming I can ever get down there."

Her eyes scanned along the edge of the bay. There were a dozen different airlocks and cargo doors leading into it, but how she might get to any of them remained a mystery. She frowned.

The sound of footsteps sent a sudden panic through her. *Marines!* She felt the sting of tears at the corner of her eyes and fought them off. "Great, just great. Not only are you going to get found by Security, you're going to cry. Won't that be a brilliant first impression?"

She considered fleeing, but there were only two doors, and she had come from one of them.

"How stupid would it look if I tried to run from the Marines? It's not like I'm doing anything wrong. I just got lost."

Taking a deep breath, she decided to take the embarrassment and waited for the security detail to arrive. But the tall dark skinned man who stepped out wasn't a Marine, he was worse, a flight officer. He was dressed in the finely made black uniform, with two gold laurel leaves at his collar denoting him as both a lieutenant and a hierarch. She came to attention as the blush worked its way up her neck.

"What are you doing here, Able Technician?" the lieutenant asked, but far from being officious, the man seemed friendly, or at least amused.

"To be honest, sir, I'm trying to get to that ship down there," Fran said, relief welling up in her, "but I got totally lost."

"You can't really get there from here," the officer said, "but if your set your incomms to channel fourteen, the ship's network should show you the way."

"I can't, sir," Fran said, "I'm a natural. I don't have any implants."

"A complete natural?" the man asked, blinking in disbelief, "no implants at all?"

"Yes, sir." Fran felt her color rise once more.

"Well then, you're completely screwed."

Before she could say anything else, the officer turned and continued on his way. Jaw open, Fran stared after him as his footfalls faded uncaringly down the hall.

She felt the sting in the corner of her eyes as they once more began to water. "Oh great. Now I really am gonna cry. That's really kick ass of you isn't it? Gah, how could I ever think I could be part of the ARAG of the 12th Fleet?"

Fran closed her eyes, and fought the tears. They started to roll down her cheeks all the same. She sniffled in a deep breath, and looked up in hopes of regaining control. It didn't help. She stomped her foot, bit her lip, then suddenly grew still. Her eyes narrowing, she looked back up to the deckhead. The tears stopped as she studied the labyrinthine pipes, comm lines and ducting above her. Dropping her pack she climbed up an access ladder and read the printing on the sides of the cables and conduits that ran through the ship's innards. A slow cunning smile replaced the despair.

"I'll show you who's screwed."

She dropped onto the deck, shouldered her pack and headed back the way she had come. Walking with a greater certainty, she kept her eyes on the trail of piping that led her on her way. After five paces, her smile broadened, and a bounce returned to her step. Turning a corner, she walked straight into a wall of Marines.

Samantha stepped past the marine guards at the security station, aware that their eyes followed her with more than a professional appraisal. She ignored it and walked on, making her way through the series of dimly lit compartments of the *HMS Résolut*'s Command Deck. Like most battleships of her weight, the dreadnaught combined elements of tradition and style into her design, particularly in those sections primarily populated by officers. Brass and real teak veneer covered the otherwise functional handrails; decorative motifs were engraved on the structural bulkheads. To Samantha, they served as irritating reminders of class and power worked into the very fabric of the warship.

Lieutenant Samantha Smith was tall and blonde, with a powerful build and the striking beauty of a mandellan. She wore the high collared black uniform of the Imperial Navy, but unlike most officers in 12th Fleet, the insignia was the silver of a commoner. On her shoulder was the hand stitched arrowhead patch of the *HMS Hunter*. Her skin was a subtle tan, though only two weeks before it had been dark brown. A few more weeks in space and it would settle into a rosy pale as the melatonin adjusted to meet the level best suited for the ambient light. That, if nothing else, was a sure sign that the mandellans should be counted among The Made, even if no one wanted to admit it in public.

She stepped by another set of marines and entered the calm blue lighting of the Fleet Strategic Information Center. Small clusters of ornately decorated command chairs were centered on holographic operations stations. These were spread through the hall like billiards tables in a gentleman's club and enlisted men passed between them like waiters. The golden laurels that noted most of the staff officers' social status only intensified the impression of masters and servants.

"What's the Ice Maiden doing here?" Lieutenant Xiang-Delasantos asked in a stage whisper.

"Get used to it," the response was issued by another officer in a similar falsely hushed tone, "The Ripper's Pet Egalitist is a common sight in SIC."

After two years the comments seldom bothered her. Samantha had grown used to the fact that her fellow officers did not care for her, or her politics. She was never anything but polite and professional to them, but that was irrelevant. She knew from her years of studying sophontology that people resent those who they admire, but cannot win over. Physical attraction made things worse.

She stepped up to the door to the Admiral's Quarters and the Chief Petty Officer who guarded the door to the Admiral's quarters smiled with genuine warmth. The senior NCO's in the fleet tended to have a very different opinion of Samantha than their superiors did.

"Is the Admiral available?" she asked.

"Hold on a moment and I'll check for you ma'am," the CPO answered. He looked down to the left for a moment, then nodded. "Please go in."

If the SIC looked like a gentleman's club, the Admiral's Suite looked like the library in a stately home. Real wood panels lined the bulkheads and genuine paintings of pastoral scenes were securely fastened to them. Plush furniture was positioned about in a comfortable setting, with a faux fireplace on one side. At the far end, the double sliding doors that led to the Admiral's office were open.

The Ripper sat behind an ornately carved desk speaking to the air as he waved Samantha in. As she entered, she noted the holographic image of some Imperial hierarch or another standing in the center of the office. She stopped at the edge of camera range and leaned against the paneling with her arms crossed.

"No Minister, I can assure you that won't be a concern," Admiral Lord Rippavitch said in the kind and personal tones he was known for. He cut a striking and powerful figure. The black of his flag officer's uniform was highlighted by the double row of golden laurels at the collar. His chestnut hair was touched with grey, and his eyes, like Samantha's, bore the polychrome trademarks of a mandellan. He kept his skin at a stylish golden brown tone through the intentional use of UV light.

"We could use your presence in the chamber on this vote, Ben," the hierarch's holograph said, "You may not officially be the Head of the Opposition at the moment, but everyone still thinks of you as such."

"I appreciate that, Jaro," the Admiral said, "but I have my duties to the Fleet. We are entering the preparation phase for our next action cruise, and I'm afraid the safety of Sophyan space outweighs the need for my vote on the bill. I proxied my vote to my daughter, I'm sure you'll win this."

"But Ben-yi, your presence, the presence of the heroic Ripper in the Senatorial Chamber, it's worth ten times your votes," the hierarch said.

"You're too kind."

"It has nothing to do with kindness, Admiral," the man continued. His pleading tone made Samantha recognize him as the Minister for Arts, "I need the Hegemonists votes, and without you there I may not get them."

"I've made it clear in my press releases where I stand," the Admiral said, "I've sent high grade AI avatars to key members of the party, and my daughter is an excellent orator in her own right. Besides, I've arranged for the D'Ascoine's to support my stance, our stance, in both votes."

That explains what Sinner told me about our new TOMO. Samantha thought.

"Well having a Great House on board will certainly help, but will it be enough? I have put a great deal into…."

"I'm sorry, Jaro, I have to go," the Admiral said cutting the man off, "There is an officer here that needs to speak to me. Now, good bye and good luck."

"That was a high quality avatar," Samantha said once the image was gone. The Ripper looked at her in expectant silence for a moment. She came to an "at ease" stance.

"It wasn't an avatar," the Admiral said, his expression softening as he waved her into a chair, "the Minister is in system."

"And you didn't grant him a private audience?" Samantha asked. She took her seat, keeping her attention on the Admiral's gestures. A slight smile, his shoulders relaxed, a patient amusement in his voice; the Ripper was in a paternalistic mood.

"I don't want to encourage him," the Admiral said shaking his head, "I support the new funding to the arts bill, but really, there are priorities. My duties in counter-insurgency outweighs any art funding. Jaro's proposal won't have any trouble passing. Octavious has spoken in favor of it. With both the Emperor's backing and mine, it will hardly fail."

"If the vote is secured why does he want you there?" Samantha asked, but she was more interested in the mind-frame that the question would put him in than in the answer.

"Gods, sometimes I forget how sheltered from politics your father kept you." The Admiral shook his head. "Jaro is lobbying to be Minister of the Interior when Senator Tuatoa retires. If he can get both myself and the Emperor to support him in person before the Senate, it will make a very powerful statement. Now, Samantha, how can I help you?"

"I managed to get the information we discussed from one of my sources," Samantha said, passing him an encrypted data crystal, "and since Captain Van Trappini is away from the fleet, I thought I'd better deliver it to you directly."

"Summarize it." The Ripper took the file.

"Despite the last report from the 253rd, there're now only three main insurgency groups working the Alterande Sector, down from five." Samantha adjusted herself in the leather chair. "Those led by the Voice, the People's Front, and a new group, the Wayang."

"Interesting." The Ripper leaned back in his chair. "Factional fighting?"

"Mergers. The Wayang are absorbing the others, centralizing a great deal of the terror network."

"That could be a problem."

"It seems they have a particularly good leader, calls himself the Dalang. Substandard rhetoric, but he runs their operations with military precision and is very good with the money. Their cells are particularly ruthless and I suspect that they're a lot deeper into criminal enterprises than we've seen before. Details are in the report."

"Thank you," the Ripper said, a small frown touched his brow and his eyes narrowed. She had obviously set something churning in his mind, and hoped he would not dismiss her before she came to the real purpose of her visit. Still, she knew better than to interrupt him when he was plotting.

"Can I offer you a drink?" he asked to her relief. She had maintained the audience.

"A spiced coffee would be welcome." Samantha's smile was deliberately bright, a practiced mirror of her teenaged innocence. A moment later a simple cylindrical servant drone brought her a hot and sweet black coffee flavored with cinnamon and nutmeg. She sipped it and smiled as she looked at the Ripper. Her mind focused on her private agenda, she rubbed her forefinger over the scarred cuticle of her thumb as she tried to read his mood.

"Can I ask you a question, sir?" she asked, her head tilted, intentionally mimicking those of adolescence again.

"Of course, Sammy." the Admiral answered. He had not called her Sammy since she had joined the fleet.

"Why did you assign Lieutenant Commander Fotheringday to command the *Hunter*?"

"I have my reasons." His response was light and friendly, but she noticed he didn't seem surprised that she knew the classified information. "Did you want the command yourself?"

"That's neither here nor there," Samantha said, covering one hand with the other and hiding her thumb from view.

"I'm just curious why you would assign the son of one of your chief political rivals to command a ship inside the ARAG? I can understand why you might let him into the fleet, but inside Intelligence?"

"I believe he would be particularly useful on this mission, especially in light of what you've brought me on this Dalang character. I assume that regardless of whether or not you were cleared, you've managed to see his CV? His record in counter-insurgency stands for itself."

"Those parts of his career that are on record shine, but there are some years missing that raise a few questions."

"You've been doing your homework." The Admiral's smile faded.

"I'm concerned about my other operations," Samantha said. Leaning forward, her eyes narrowed and her voice took on an edge, "Our initiatives, my contacts, they could all be compromised if…"

"I know the dangers, Lieutenant."

"With all due respect, sir, I'm not sure you do. The networks are…"

"Don't presume to tell me about the importance of issues within my own command, Lieutenant."

Samantha opened her mouth to argue, then closed her eyes and leaned back in her seat. *Shit.*

"This isn't the bloody Astrographic Service, Samantha. You're in the Navy now. We have a chain of command and a need-to-know-basis, especially in Intelligence."

"Sorry, sir," she said as meekly as she could muster. She'd done it again, ignored her training, let her guard down and gotten carried away with her emotions. It took a concerted effort to avoid picking the ragged edge of her cuticle. "I was out of line."

"I'm an Admiral, a Senator and the former Head of both the Hegemonists and the Opposition. Do you really think I don't know what's at stake?"

"Of course you do, sir." She felt her index finger plucking at her thumb. Flecks of red appeared.

Looking down at her hands and swallowing her natural tendencies, she did what she had been trained to do. She forced the silence to linger. Eventually, what she had learned from a doctorate in sophontology, years of exploring different cultures, and her more recent work in Naval Intelligence seemed to pay off.

"Damn it, Samantha," the Ripper said. Another awkward silence followed. "As Head of the Egalitists, your father was not only my one time ally, he was a friend. After his murder, when you came to me asking to transfer into the fleet, I agreed. I'd hoped it would give you closure."

"I know," Samantha whispered. She knew the Ripper had been good to her, even considering his ulterior motives.

"Since then you've shown you could make a damn good officer, but you must learn your place. You've been in the ARAG for two years now Sammy. It's time you behaved like it."

Staring at her hands, Samantha watched the trickle of blood seep from the scar tissue by the side of her thumbnail. Lifting her eyes to the Admiral, she replied, "I'll do better, sir."

CHAPTER 3

Lights flashed and strobed in time to the music. Alyiar could feel the rhythm in his chest as he walked around the edge of the dance floor. His eyes studied the erotically writhing forms of the young hierarchs, seeking out the wealthiest and spotting those who protected them. The dance floor was the center of the club, a series of huge circular sunken stages filled with bodies and lit by lasers and synchronized lights. The rest of the nightclub was a darkened array of bars and corner nooks; hardly secluded, but more private than the dance arena where the sons and the daughters of the ruling classes displayed themselves. It was in those more darkened corners that the threats would lurk, the body-guards and rent-a-cops meant to look after the burgeoning young elite. Alyiar noted each one, recording their faces and locations, but he didn't focus on it. He simply passed the info on to those who would later neutralize the threats. Tonight, security was not his assignment.

Inside his mind a silent chime went off. It was almost time to put on his game face. He moved into position, his eyes lighting upon Bolyiacov doing the same. No matter what features she wore, Alyiar always recognized her. A sleepy smile passed over her face, showing that she had made him as well. He pretended to ignore her and got to his post: a darkened spot overlooking the dance floor.

Hovering over the dance floor was the image of the musician dressed in glitter and little else; a holographic singer undulating her belly and waving her arms with the movements of a marionetteer. Below her, the half naked men and women moved as if tied to unseen strings. Some leaped high into the air, spun and came down meters away. Displays made possible by cybernetics, genetic mods or muscle grafts – playthings for the ultra rich.

The dancers were beautiful, at least, the humans were. Modified by knife or test tube, they were stylishly perfect to a point that disgusted Alyiar. The fact that, for the moment, he shared that perfection was irrelevant. He would change in a few moments.

Only the sophants stood out as different, and there were not many of them. A few slimies and a couple of bugeyes, just enough for diversity's sake. One kept drawing his eyes, the great furry form of the child of Senator Futhmoarthen stood a full meter taller than its dance companion. Red-brown hair flowing wildly as it danced, it was bipedal, but if it had any arms Alyiar couldn't make them out. Other than hair and legs, the only feature that he could see were the rows of eyes that descended in tri-lateral symmetry.

Elsewhere another sophant scuttled like a meter wide crab, occasionally popping up and down into his view with its ludicrous movements. Alyiar couldn't make out if it was an encoutersuit or its natural form. He set a predictor to note the creature's likely continued positions.

Alyiar felt the vibration he'd been waiting for. A dull rumble in the distance went unnoticed by the celebrants, but caused a series of subtle movements among the private security. Bolyiacov would no doubt have been watching for the signs in others that Alyiar ignored, the tells that would give away the security that had managed to remain unnoticed. Alyiar didn't care. He had made his marks already and now it was game time.

Even as the sound wave from the far off bomb shook the darkened windows, Alyiar was transforming. His face stretched like rubber, his features moving from the innocuously beautiful to the stylized bizarre. As subdermal nano- and micro-tech activated, his skull lengthened, his hair grew, his eyes stretched and slanted to an unnatural angle. Swirling lines and dotted patterns formed on his skin, his limbs grew as his telescoping bones gave him ectomorphic proportions. From underneath his sleeves pistols were launched into each hand, and he was not alone. Others, including Bolyiacov, had similarly transformed and moved out from the shadows.

Gunshots rang out through the nightclub as he and his fellow transforming revolutionaries stepped into view. Screams sounded, bodies fell. The staccato sound of a machine gun came from the direction of the front door. Someone had tried to be a hero. Wylde would have taken care of them. In the center of the dance floor Rubo had taken form: a Wayang Stalker like himself, long hair curling into a spiral above his elongated stylized head. Alyiar chuckled when he recognized their leader; he had made him out to be a prime target.

"Quiet!" Rubo shouted, submachine guns in each hand, "Everyone get feckin' down on the ground now!"

"Wallets! Jewelry!" Hastings said, moving through the crowd with a bag.

Here and there a man or a woman fell, body guards singled out by Bolyiacov's deadly aim. Alyiar kept his eyes open for new threats. His targets were already marked and mapped to be taken at the end, kidnapped and ransomed for more money than the average citizen made in a lifetime. In the ghettos Alyiar could only have dreamed of the kind of wealth as they would make in this attack, and this was only one cell making a single raid. The earlier bombs, one in the Army barracks, one at Imperial Hospital, would have signaled a dozen such attacks in the city. Banks, markets, bars and private residences would be cleaned out tonight.

That money would help to fund further attacks, after passing a percentage on to the Dalang to help fund the revolution against the Imperialists who had stolen Sophyan culture.

CHAPTER 4

Wearing a forced smile, Alex cast his polychrome eyes about his living room and wondered how many of these people he actually knew. Aristocrats and meritarchs, nobles and elected elites, theocrats, technocrats, and countless other forms of the Imperial Hierarchs drank and mingled with each other as they weaved their way through his town house. Thrown in among them were more than a spattering of others who were not members of the Imperial upper class. Some were Alex's friends and colleagues, officers in the Imperial military and Astrographic Services, others were academics with whom he had attended graduate school; but most were celebutants whose main purpose was to see and be seen by the good and the great. One of the most notable of the actual notables was missing, however, and it was the only person Alex truly wanted to see.

It was twenty-three hundred hours, well beyond the point by which a man of his father's caliber would make a fashionably late entrance. Alex felt that painful tug of hope that he would appear. *It is hope, not despair, that is the great curse of humanity*, he thought before turning his attentions back to the party.

Alex hated such events, but he had been brought up far too well to let it show. Only the occasional narrowing of his eyes hinted that he was ill at ease. He knew, of course, that his eyes were his most striking feature, even if they did speak of his not-quite-natural heritage. They were the eyes of a mandellan, marked by the radial lines within the irises that shifted colors as light caught them at different angles. Some people claimed that the eyes were hypnotic, and put the success of the mandellan lords down to such mesmerization. Others suggest their genetically manipulated intelligence. Alex thought it was more likely due to upbringing, one that kept him at the door greeting late comers despite the fact that arriving at this hour was gauche.

He wished that he had not let Sally talk him into having the party. He had other things to attend to: the duties of his new command, details about his mission, the need to spend time with his new girlfriend. Yet Sally had insisted a party was necessary, and he supposed that she knew best.

He looked around the room for her, but saw no sign of the ginger and auburn locks. *If she's going to make me endure this sort of thing, I wish she'd stay by my side and fend off these…*

"Alex! So good to see you!" a gaunt young woman with clear signs of body sculpting said as she approached with a skeletal smile.

"And you," he said with a warm smile and offered his hand. He had no idea who she was. "I hope that you're enjoying yourself."

"Just got here, but it seems a marvelous party."

"You are too kind. I see you do not have a drink though. Where is the servodrone? I told Mergatroid to have it meet the guests with drinks. I am so sorry."

"Oh, it's no worry."

"Well, there is an old fashioned bar out in the garden and they are serving a delightful pinot selasi."

"Really? I'll have to make certain I try it. It's been long time since I…"

Alex gave a mental command that opened his address-book subroutine. It immediately updated his query to the house's information network, identifying those individuals he knew. A fog of information ascended into his vision as colored labels began to hover about the celebrants, categorizing them as friends, colleagues, rivals, and the like; each displayed with the number of times they had met or otherwise interacted.

'Gla'chung Phique' (Propername: Harriet Siun-Ray Gla'chung) – never met, multiple mutual acquaintances. Reporter with the Segontium Herald – Specialties: cultural news, social pages, celebrity…

That was enough. It was time he extracted himself from this particular operation. With an immediate command to his personal house management program, Mergatroid, he instigated a small accident in the opposite corner. A tinkle of glass and a few nervous laughs told him that it had worked.

"Oh dear," he said, "I had best see what that was. Please excuse me?"

Even as she gave her reluctant consent, he escaped and made his way to a quiet corner. It wasn't that he was completely opposed to parties or get-togethers, but as a whole Alex would rather have spent a quiet evening with friends than a loud one with strangers. All the same, he knew Sally was correct. His place in society required that they celebrate his long awaited promotion to Lieutenant Commander. He only wished that his father would have joined him. Checking the household logs, Alex noted that there was still no sign of the Old Man. He closed his eyes and released a long slow sigh.

The good March Warden of Sandwythe had been furious when Alex had told him that he was to join Ripper's Raiders. Even his politically powerful father had been unable to keep the resulting argument out of the gossip pages. Considering the dangers involved with his upcoming missions, Alex wished that his father had been able to overlook it, or that he could have explained it better. He would hate for their last words to have been in anger. But what was to be done? Duty called and so did the opportunity that it represented. This assignment meant more to him than having his own command. It would allow him to finish what was begun with the *Silver Slipper*, to find the Linking Agent and clean some of the blood off his conscience. Besides, in the long run, his posting would help the Emperor.

So despite the fact that he should be celebrating, Alex skulked in the corner, grateful for the brief respite and hoping for notification that his father had arrived. Roving debutants and minor officials drifted by, dressed in varying styles of haute-culture. Some of the styles suited Alex's sense of aesthetic, but most were tacky.

Why did we invite these people? He wondered before returning to his surveillance and analysis of the room.

He watched the great tendrilled form of the Baron Th'kong bladder its way towards the Duke of Yeovil, noting with regret how few sentient aliens were present. Though the different non-human races of the Empire were greatly outnumbered by humanity, they were still members of society. As such he wanted to ensure that they would feel welcome in his home. He suspected such xenophillic thoughts would not go down terribly well in the rest of the 12th Fleet, but there was only so far Alex was willing to go for the price of duty. Bigotry was one line he was not willing to cross. As far as Alex was concerned, Sophant Rights was the keystone of the Empire. It had even united the Emperor and the late President Smith of Meridothia, and indeed divided the Egalitists from their natural pro-democracy allies the Federalists.

Alex clenched his jaw as memories of Federalist atrocities came back to him. The guerrilla raids against military targets, terrorist campaigns that killed indiscriminately, and the general persecution of sentient aliens. This was how the one time political party claimed to support their beliefs, through armed opposition and terrorist assaults, through smuggling and piracy. Federalists were criminals who justified themselves in the name of democracy.

His mind went to the recent attacks, and the bomb at the Andres Academy. He recognized the patterns, not the message, but the methods. Hijacking, piracy, kidnapping, and attacks against children. It was just like before. There was only one difference: the latest attacks in the Alterande Sector were far better organized than those used in Archon. There were fewer assaults against military targets, but they were better executed and exceptionally well planned. The rest of the attacks targeted civilians, and were ruthless by even Federalist standards.

"You're grinding your teeth." Sally's voice brought him back to the party. She stood next to him, a reproachful look in her large deep blue eyes. Brushing a stray strand of her long, striking red-blonde hair behind her ear, there was a sympathetic kindness in her face.

"I was worried," he said, casting his eye over her smooth lightly freckled skin with a smile he didn't try to hide. She wore a glittering green evening dress that accented her slim athletic build and long white legs. "You abandoned me, I thought you might not come back"

"As if," she said, "This is your night. You should be mingling, not hiding in the corner."

"Just a small respite," Alex said, looking into her deep blue eyes, "Besides, what kind of impression will I make if my gorgeous new girlfriend is off gallivanting about the party while I am stuck at the door?"

"I was trying to keep your guests entertained." Sally smirked in response, "Not easy considering how stuffy you can be."

"Years of training, my dear."

"Alex?" a voice from his past came from behind.

Alex turned and saw a familiar smiling face that he recognized with mixed emotions. The man was clad in a very stylish, form fitting royal purple velvet jacket, cut to the waist to mimic a Naval flight jacket. It lacked the high collar of an Imperial uniform, but showed the five laurel leafs curving around its wide lapels. About his neck he wore an embroidered cravat pinned with his noble diamond. This time, Alex had no need to check his identity.

"Richie," Alex said with a warm smile, "How delightful to see you."

"And you, Alex, and you. You are looking quite dapper this evening. Congratulations on the promotion. It was long over due."

"I could say the same. I see you're a full Commander. Congratulations."

"Upon retirement I'm afraid. I finally decided to return to my family's business, which has, I must admit, been doing very well. Very well indeed."

"I am delighted to hear it," Alex said, "Please, allow me. Lady Sally Simbletyne, I have the honor of introducing you to Sir Richard Al-Escobar, Baronet of Cameron and my line-commander out on the Attallic Main for what? Two years?"

"At least, if you include both the mission you undertook with the Marines and everything that happened with the *Silver Slipper*."

"Indeed," Alex said with a smooth ease that he didn't feel, "Sir Richard was the senior Intelligence officer for the *HMS Stoker*'s Cruiser Group."

"And Alex was my diligent second in command," Sir Richard said. His smile looked slightly forced.

"I'm delighted to meet you," Sally said. She offered her hand. Al-Escobar took it and bowed.

"Sir Richard, this is my… girlfriend?"

"Unless you are proposing something more permanent," Sally said with a coy smile, then turned to Sir Richard, "We've only been going out for a few weeks."

"Girlfriend then," Alex said, "Lady Charlotte Luanne Drusilla Sally Simbletyne of Khyber-Puq."

"I am honored to make your acquaintance, m'Lady," Al-Escobar said.

Alex smiled, feeling both pleased and a sense of slight unease at the presence of his former commander. He had no misgivings about the man himself. Richie had been an excellent intelligence officer and superb CO. Indeed, he felt a collegial friendship with the man, whose loyalty through the difficult times had been truly helpful. His presence however, reminded Alex of the black event that had so severely scarred him. Alex knew he owed Al-Escobar nothing but gratitude. In any other circumstances he would have been delighted to see the man.

"You say the business is doing well?" Alex said, "Shipping isn't it?"

"Shipping is our main focus, but Cameron-Inglesie Distributors has expanded into a range of services. We've acquired a series of mining and production facilities. The diversification is, in fact, doing extremely well. It's why I needed to resign. Too much of a fortune at risk to leave to one's proxies."

"That is good news," Alex said, "Especially considering how close your systems are to the Corridor and the terrorist activities that have been going on there."

"We've been mercifully free of too much pirate or terrorist activity."

"I would have thought you would be a prime target."

"It does worry me and forces us to invest a great deal in our security forces. I even made certain to poach a few good men from the ranks of the 117th. Kyle Hammond among them."

"That was a very clever move," Alex said, "Kyle was an excellent officer with a natural aptitude for mathematics and navigation."

"I recalled your compliments of him. He's doing very well in my fleet," Sir Richard said, "And yourself? Still in the service I see, and from what I hear you've transferred over the 12th. Counter insurgency was always your specialty. Intelligence I assume."

"No. Line Officer," Alex lied. One did not announce that one was a member of the Advanced Reconnaissance and Assault Group to anyone who was not previously approved for such knowledge. Even a former CO.

"Excellent," Sir Richard said with a knowing nod, "and how does the Lady Simbetyne fill her days?"

"I've been competing in the Kalldedrian," she said, shifting the topic with the ease and comfort of a socialite. Alex was grateful. He had no desire to lie to his former commander regardless of regulations, and even less of a desire to rehash the events of their mutual past. He was quickly diverted from such thoughts by the bubbly and delightful tales that Sally wove as she described her triumphs and failures on the sporting circuit.

Alex was amused by the almost airheaded way in which she conversed in public. It served as stark contrast to the more concentrated conversations they shared when alone. He relaxed and allowed himself to be distracted by the slightly flirtatious glances she gave him.

It did not take long for them to be interrupted and Alex was quickly drawn back to the realm of social networking. From time to time, he was able to split away from the crowd and chat with his fellow officers or some old friend from his graduate school days. For the most part, however, he remained cornered by those who wanted to be seen to be talking to him rather than those he wished to talk to.

"Able Technician Francis Harpur, reporting for duty," Fran said, standing at attention.

"No shit." the Chief Petty Officer eyeballed Fran like a of piece of waste. He was middling height and middling build, with close cropped graying hair that was clearly not quite as thick as it had once been. A dozen fiber-optic cables ran under his skin, connecting him to the *Hunter*'s main control panel which he obviously ran remotely. Around him a swarm of drones responded to his commands. He was a Wirehead, a serious cyborg who didn't try to hide it. He addressed the Marine who had brought her to the ship. "Where'd they find her?"

A birdlike robot turned to look at her, its stance mimicked the CPO's. Fran swallowed another belch. This one tasted like the lunch she'd had three days ago.

"Wandering around deck seventy-five, junction forty-three," the Marine who had introduced himself as Corporal Bowman said, "Pretty close to home huh, Sinner?"

"And that goes to show why us Navies are better than you Jarheads," the CPO said, "Even a natural Able Technician can get by one of your damned security patrols."

Fran had assumed that her new immediate superior would have implants, almost everyone off of her homeworld did, but this guy was a technophile. It was bad enough to be a natural with most people, but with a Wirehead as her direct line manager? Her stomach did a backflip.

"Sure, sure," Bowman said, "Now pay up."

The Chief gave a hard look to the Marine's outstretched palm, and by the look on Corporal Bowman's face, Fran guessed that somewhere in cyberspace credits were exchanged. *At least he doesn't have all his jacks chromed up or anything.*

She took advantage of their distraction to grab a quick glance around the main engine compartment. Compared to the frigate she had last been assigned to, the space was tiny. Gunmetal grey girders and a rainbow of color coded conduits and cables ran along every surface. A few hung unconnected from the wall. Fran noted where some scorch marks and metal pitting had been cleaned from the surfaces. Two workstations sat on opposite sides of the three meter wide space, with an open gee-couch set in front of each. The junior engineer's was empty, but a half built plasma injector took up the entire seating area.

Unusually, the huge round door to the main reactor was open, blocking off more than half the working space. Staring at it, she wondered what kind of action the ship had seen to require repairs to the fusion rockets. Then she realized that she was being watched. The security camera above the orifice twisted and focused in on her while the birdlike observation drone shifted its feet. She turned to find Bowman the Marine and the Wirehead CPO staring at her. She swallowed hard and came back to attention.

"I guess I'll leave you in the hands of what passes as our Chief Engineer," Bowman said through a chuckle, "Catch you later, Sinner."

The Chief Petty Officer nodded in response, but didn't take his eyes off Fran. They looked so real she wondered if they were fully electronic or if there were just automated receptors built into his retina. He said nothing for a long time, just stared at her like she was a freak.

"So, you got to within a hundred meters of the ship, huh?" he said. With a small click the wires running from him to the ship suddenly disconnected, some withdrawing into the walls, others snaking back under his skin. Fran jumped, but the Chief ignored it. Once withdrawn, there was no hint that the cables even existed; he almost looked like a natural.

"How'd you manage it?" he asked.

She opened her mouth to answer, but a low deep belch sounded out instead. Fran turned beat red.

"Very lady like." Sinner said.

"I'm so sorry I…"

"Answer the question."

Fran dropped her head and thought she would die. "I followed the AR5 conduits."

"I never had much of a use for ladies."

Looking up, Fran saw that he was smiling broadly. "Following the AR5s to a launching bay was good thinking. Plus you made Bowman's Marine buddies look bad. Anyone who can do that is okay by me. Let me give you a tour of your new home."

"I shouldn't have drank so much," Sally said.

"You were having fun," Alex said through a smirk.

The sun had risen and the last guests left. Sally leaned heavily on the door jam as Alex drew the curtains in his bedroom. It was going to be a sweltering day.

"If I were really a good girlfriend I'd have stayed sober, focused on having as much sex as possible before you shipped out for who knows how long."

"A good girlfriend would have just relaxed and enjoyed herself so we have as much fun as possible before I leave."

"I'm going to meet you in Lai-Jung," she said resolutely.

Alex slipped her into a comfortable nightgown. "And what would you say makes you think that I am going to the Lai-Jung system?"

"Oh that's obvious," Sally slurred, "I'd just lie and tell them that I figured it out by reading the newspapers. Where else would the best counter-inshurvenshy Officer in the Navy be going?"

"Any number of places my dear. Now just go to sleep would you?"

As Alex laid her on the satin sheets, the cocktails in Sally's system gave her little choice but to comply. Alex did not take long to join her, brushing his teeth and splashing a touch of water on his face. There was, however, one last task that he wanted to perform. After he had turned off the lights and lay in bed, he opened a window in his mind and allowed himself one final peek at the household log. It confirmed what he already knew; Lord Henry Fotheringday had never made an appearance.

CHAPTER 5

"Pass me the A-four lens tuner, would ya?" Sinner asked from under the Engineering console.

Samantha picked the tool from its holder and put it into his waiting hand. She sat crossed legged on the floor of Engineering, while Sinner's legs stuck out from under a workstation. Around them lay a chaotic spread of tools. On the top of the console a fist-sized robot that was mostly lenses and microphones waddled to the edge and looked at her.

"What about this D'Ascoine Character?" Sinner asked.

"He's just what he seems," Samantha said to the robot with a shrug, "the privileged third child of a powerful hierarch out to make a name for himself. Bernse stuck him with us because he knew we could still get the job done with him on board. Of course that was before we got the new CO."

"And how 'bout our dodgy new captain, you get anything new on him?" Sinner asked. A thump and a half-heard curse sounded from under the console. The lens-bot shuffled its position.

"Not a lot more than we had before," she said, "but I did get a name from one of my sources: the *Silver Slipper*. A liner of some sorts that disappeared out on the Attallic Main during the new CO's time there. I cross ran it with some of Fred's people at INI and something's distinctly not right about the whole thing."

"I tell ya, he's here to scrape up dirt on the Ripper."

"Using the son of the 'Author of Empire' to infiltrate the Emperor's number one rival's fleet is a pretty poor choice of spies."

"Double bluff."

"Maybe. What did you get?"

"A bit more than you," Sinner said. He slipped out from under the console and flipped a switch. Nothing happened. Muttering curses under his breath, he crawled back under the table.

"Right towards the end of the missing period in his record," he said, "Fotheringday made a series of bank transfers from his personal accounts, and I'm talking huge amounts, all sent to nobodies. Real nobodies, you know? Giant trust funds set up, about a hundred of them, but gods know why. It didn't leave a lot in his savings."

"Bribes? Money to buy silence?"

"That's my way of thinking. Can you power-up the holo-display?"

Samantha reached up and put her hand on the console. Buttons and readouts immediately appeared on its surface, while slightly fuzzy images hovered above it. The robot turned around on the surface, its lenses adjusting rapidly in and out.

"You're still out of focus. About three degrees."

"Frick." The console went dead again. The robot turned back to face her.

"You have names?" Samantha asked.

"They're in the file. Any luck with the records you nabbed from fleet Personnel?"

The console lit up once more. This time the images were clear, but twice as large as they should be. Samantha reached up and adjusted the display. The holographs reduced to their proper size. The robot looked them up and down before doing a pirouette.

"Yes and no."

"What do you mean?" Sinner pulled himself out from under the table and wiped his hands on his trousers.

"I mean that up to the point of redacted records, the Intel unit of the *Stoker*'s Cruiser Group is thought of as pretty high class, but afterwards? The Officer-In-Charge, Lieutenant Commander Sir Richard Al-Escobar, was transferred over to the 253rd where he was stationed in a post below his rank doing some pretty low level desk jockey stuff. The same was true of quite a few other promising characters. All were transferred out of the unit at almost exactly the same time: all into obscurity. Even the guy serving as his Exec disappears off to a System-boat Tender."

"Sounds like a cover up."

"The question is, of what?" Samantha said, "I'd like you to customize some cracker programs for use on the records division. I want something that can break open high clearance seals."

"You're gonna try to lift files from INI aren't you?" Sinner leaned back and crossed his arms.

"I'd like to be ready, just in case."

"That'll get us into the kinda shit that even the Admiral can't shield us from."

"Only if we're caught," Samantha said with a smile.

Closing his eyes, Sinner looked away, but nodded in compliance.

"I tell you, Sinner," she said quietly, "Either Fotheringday was out on some really black op or there was some sort of incident that was hushed up. Either that…."

"Or what?" Sinner asked, giving her a sidelong glare.

"Or you're right and he's being sent here to set up the Ripper."

"Great, either our new captain is an incompetent, or a mole." Sinner picked up his tools.

Fran sat staring, not quite able to believe where she was. The lights were dim and the air was hazy. Out-of-date songs with a slow heavy beat sounded in the background. The central stage, or service table or whatever it was, was lit by multi-colored lights. There, a man and woman licked their lips and undulated to the music. Some of the customers had gone out of their way to ensure they got the front row treatment at the promenade-bar, but Corporal Bowman had led Fran to a more distant, darkened booth with a good view. For that, and that alone, she was grateful.

A slick, glistening waitress put a cold beer and pink alchopop on the table. Bowman smiled and slipped her an extra five credits. Funny enough, it didn't seem to be the bare breasts that really caught his attention, but rather the long shapely legs and thong covered bottom.

"I can't believe you brought me to a strip club," Fran said, shooting him a glowering look.

"What?" Bowman shrugged. "I thought it would be fun to get out, you know? Just the two of us, the junior most of the crew. Let off some steam, have a few laughs. I mean, this is our last port of call before we ship out. Who knows when we'll be back in a system?"

"This wasn't exactly what I thought you…."

"And now it's time for tonight's special event!" a loud announcement interrupted, "It's Amateur Night!"

Raising an inquisitive eyebrow at Fran, Bowman leered and gave an inviting smile. Fran's jaw dropped, and for a moment, a look of disgust passed over her face. She closed her eyes and looked away before glaring back at the marine corporal. His smile turned into a smirk.

"You're hazing me," Fran said. Her eyes suddenly narrowed as realization dawned, "You're like, totally putting me on aren't you?"

Bowman laughed out loud and slapped the table. Fran let lose a sigh of relief.

"You should have seen your face!" Bowman finally managed through the laughs, "You looked so - horrified!"

"Shocked and appalled is more like it," Fran said, turning red with embarrassment as she smiled, "You are so mean."

"Oh God, I couldn't help it," Bowman said. He wiped the tears of laughter from his eyes, "You're just so, wholesome. I had to see how you'd respond."

"Very funny," Fran said, smiling in earnest, "I'm gonna get you back you know."

"I'm counting on it."

On the stage a man got up and started to disrobe with one of the dancers. Groans came from the audience. A female customer joined him and the groans stopped. Fran stared in horrified fascination. Bowman's laugh returned her attention to him.

"So this whole night out was a joke?" she asked.

"Well, this part was. A joke and a test, you Navy types can sometimes get pretty far up your own asses."

"And you marines can be jerks."

"How many marines you actually serve with?"

"Well, none," Fran said, rattling the ice in her drink, "Two now I guess. How many navies you…"

"Lots," Bowman said, and looked around to see if anyone could hear him, "Look, in the uh, the unit, they like to keep things pretty integrated. Lots of joint ops between you flyboys and Marine Force Recon. Lots of cross training too, they say it keeps us one big happy family. It also means we got a lot of overlap in case of injury. But on the *Hunter*? We take it to a whole new level. We've got a crew of seven, including the CO. There's no room for anybody who isn't filling at least two roles. So you got your Navy pu… puppies like you doing what ever shit you do."

"You mean like keep the ship running?"

"Whatever. And then you got hard-ass marines like Gunny Chrom and me acting as ships gunners, sensor ops and professional ship troops. But if we get into a boarding action you can bet your butt you're gonna be holding a gun right by my side."

"Great," Fran said, hiding her fear in a sarcastic tone. She knew that she had accepted an assignment in an elite unit, but she had been so excited at being asked that she hadn't really considered what that meant. Sitting across from this battle hardened marine made her think about the danger. Her stomach rumbled.

"You'll be fine," Bowman said with a sincere smile, "I'll look after you."

"Thanks," Fran said, but Bowman held her gaze with a look that wasn't that of a professional soldier, nor a sexual predator. It was filled with encouragement and camaraderie, like she'd expect out of the big brother she'd never had. Fran nodded and blushed as deeply as if he'd just made a pass. Maybe more so.

CHAPTER 6

Alex stood with his hands behind his back; a lone officer staring out of the view port of transport's Observation Lounge. He was dressed in his Shipboard Office-Duty Uniform; a high collared, double breasted two piece that was less functional than the duty jumpsuit of a line officer, but far more impressive in its façade. To that end, Alex supposed it was functional, but he wore it because it was what protocol regulations suggested.

Out the viewport was a field of stars. He could not yet see the growing fleet with his naked eye, so he watched the ships gather via the window he had opened on his Mind's-Up Display. Small dots appeared as each new ship jumped to the edge of the system. A single blip was shortly joined by a second contact, then four others. A trickle of new arrivals soon became a steady stream as different elements of the 12th Fleet came into system. As larger contacts appeared, he would occasionally zoom in on them: opening a second window in his mind's eye to try to make out the ship type based on tonnage and sensor signals before they broadcast their identity. He seldom could, but did it as a mental exercise as he contemplated his forthcoming missions.

The armada had already surpassed the size of most normal fleets, and yet not even half of its ships had arrived. The 12th, Ripper's Raiders as it were, had more vessels in it than any other fleet in the Navy, but they were all small. Indeed, there were only two capital ships within the Raiders: a light carrier and the flag ship *Résolut*. Most of the rest were corvettes, cutters and escort ships. They were the types of vessels that could never stand up to a true battle on the line, but were more than a match for the kind of blockade runners and pirate ships used by the Federalist insurgents. Their vastly lower price tag allowed the Ripper to mount a much larger patrol sweep of problem systems while still allowing small targeted actions. It was a good arrangement, and Alex diligently noted every ship's ID as it appeared in system.

Behind him, he heard the door swish open.

"Any sign of her yet?" D'Ascoine asked in his ever jovial tone.

"Not yet," Alex said, turning to his soon-to-be third in command.

Leftenant Rascoine Lord D'Ascoine sauntered towards him, still in the green and black uniform of a member of the Assault Forces of the Imperial Army. Alex had already had words with him about wearing his Duty Reds, but the Leftenant claimed his Marine service gear had been accidentally stowed in the Transport's hold. Alex suspected that Razza had done so intentionally, wanting to keep the well tailored attire of the Army Special Forces on as long as possible.

Alex could see the point. Dressed as he was, Rascoine Lord D'Ascoine cut almost as dashing an image in person as he did in the media. Cold grey eyes, perfectly trimmed van dyke and a devilish smile, he came across as self-assured, perhaps even cocky; yet from all accounts he was a brave man, perhaps even a hero. In Alex's experience, however, there were two types of heroes: those who took calculated risks and those who were reckless. Alex hoped that D'Ascoine was the former.

"Damn," Razza said, "I was hoping to get things going, eh?"

"Indeed, but patience is a virtue, Leftenant, especially in the Navy. Even combat is a slow process in space."

"That's why I chose the Ranger-Dragoons, old boy, none of this lollygagging around waiting for vectors and alignments. No sir, bags of smoke and straight down the middle, that's the Army way."

Alex laughed and shook his head. They had met when the Army Officer had come onboard the transport on the second week of his transit. Though they had never been introduced, they knew many of the same people. It did not take long for the two of them to determine that Razza would be serving as Alex's Tactical Operations and Marine Officer. Exactly why he was being saddled with an Army Officer to fill one of the most crucial combat roles in his command remained a mystery. He suspected that even the full mission brief would not answer that question, but that did not stop him from speculating. Considering the power of the D'Ascoine family, the conclusion seemed obvious, but Alex hoped he was wrong and that it had to do with the man's abilities and courage under fire.

Kyle Hammond half-sat on one of five small containers that remained in the middle of the enormous empty cargo bay. His open eyes moved as if in REM as he used his implants to compare the cargo manifests from different ships to a variety of navigational charts. He would occasionally open an overlay with the latest Naval patrol routes noted on it and adjust his numbers accordingly. It had been a long time since he'd left the service, but if Hammond learned anything during those years, it was to be excessively precise in checking records. He'd certainly seen what could happen if you weren't.

The bay was immense and dimly lit, with great metal arches casting odd shadows across the flat floor and sliding airlocks that could be opened to space, had the ship not been within a starport. The bay was one of seven, each far too large to hold the small batch of cargo he had kept behind specifically for Sir Richard.

A sudden clang and thud echoed through the hall, causing him to return to the real world and cast his eyes to the half open door between the different ship's holds. He held his breath as silence swallowed up the distant noise, but released it when he heard the soft ticking that soon followed. He knew the sound, the pace, and the echoes too well to be worried.

The fine, handcrafted shoes sounded a tattoo as they passed through the empty cargo bays between them. The pace was steady, firm and self assured. Hammond chuckled to himself as he listened to its approach, but kept his eyes on the hatch. It squealed as it was pushed fully open.

"That should really be looked at," Sir Richard said in a playful tone. As ever, he was dressed with exquisite care in the finest charcoal business suit available.

"I'm not the captain," Hammond replied, his own tone falsely mimicking the cheer of the CEO. It was typical of a hierarch, even one such as Sir Richard, that he wouldn't recognize how even a jovial comment by one's boss could send waves of concern through an employee.

"Good to see you, Kyle," Sir Richard said as he approached with an extended hand.

Hammond shifted to his feet and took three steps to meet the newcomer and take his hand, "You too."

"How did it go?" the former Naval Intelligence Officer asked.

"By the numbers. We transferred the cargos all the way down the main, picking up about three dozen new shipments and making a forty-two point three percent profit en route."

"Net or gross?"

"Net."

"Is that before or after taking into account the complimentary food shipment we sent to the refugees on

Intigun IV?" Sir Richard sauntered around the crates, eyeing them from every angle.

"You noticed?" Hammond said with forced bemusement, "I hadn't thought you paid that close attention."

"I always pay attention when it comes to funds," Sir Richard said, his voice a tad more serious, "We're not a charity, Kyle. We're underdogs in a hostile market and the cost of that gesture, humanitarian as it was, is far more than the price of the food. It means that holds which could have been filled with profitable goods were…"

"After," Hammond said, holding up his hands defensively, "I logged the rations as a Marketing Expense, which was legitimate. Those people will view us in a better light, and that will keep some of the real hardcore bastards off our asses."

"I suppose we can deduct it from taxes as well. Forty percent you say?"

"Forty-two point three."

"That is excellent." Sir Richard smiled, then began tapping his toe against the edge of the crates. "Did it do any good?"

"People ate who couldn't have otherwise."

Sir Richard nodded, lifting the edge of one of the containers. The dark red bottles within glittered. "A twenty-seven vintage? That'll turn a tidy profit. Now, I have the new deployment data for Listun Ferrigus. The Ferrigus Main will make some prime pickings just about the time that you're due to deliver the shipments."

"Good. Very good." Hammond checked the manifests and patrol routes once more. "We can work that easily. It will give us time to pick up some of that new cargo from the Atrucans and move it down the Corridor Main in say… … say… twelve, twenty-four… about thirty-six weeks max."

"Just what I thought," he picked up one of the bottles and looked at its label distracted, "I'm almost tempted to hold on to one of these."

"Oh by the way," Sir Richard continued, putting the bottle back in the crate, "Guess who's just been assigned to the ARAG of the 12th Fleet? The newly promoted Lieutenant Commander Lord Fotheringday."

"You must be joking," Hammond said, a confused frown on his brow, "Alex? Serving with the Raiders? After the *Silver Slipper*?"

"Apparently nepotism knows no bounds."

"Typical," Hammond shook his head as he slammed the lid of the container down. The sound echoed through the all-but-empty hold. He punched the autoseal button and the container hissed. Leaning against the cargo he froze, his eyes narrowing as he turned to his employer and Alex's former CO.

CHAPTER 7

"So, I thought I was totally at fault, but when the review of the sim came, I wasn't blamed at all," Fran said. She was crouched in the access hatch to the mixing chamber of *Hunter*'s primary fusion engine. With three of the panels open, there was a slight tangle of wires and conduits exposed as she made the fine adjustments to the flow. Inside the mixing chamber itself the Chief stood handing her tools and checking on her work. No pressure.

"Let me guess," Sinner said, passing her a point-five-nine hand-regulator, "When you over-wrote the protocols, you didn't think about the readout programs."

"You read my review file," Fran said with a mocking pout as she accepted the tool.

"No kid, it's a school girl error. You were workin' on the fly, made the new adjustment without alterin' the specs and the injector let too much hydrogen into the fusion furnace. Result? A classic unequal flow of hydrogen that causes the failure of the magnetic containment field, and you and your crew end up at the simulated center of a small short lived star."

Fran made tiny movements with her tool, checking the results of each gesture on her PAD's readout. She cocked her head and frowned for a brief moment before tuning the knob on the side of the clear plastic visor she wore. The Heads-Up image projected on the wrap around lens rotated, she smiled.

"I was expecting to get dragged through the shit for it, I mean, even if my idea was good," she said, "I still screwed it up. But Lieutenant Commander Murtang didn't see it like that. He said he was impressed with my solutions. Could you pass me a three-oh-five please?"

"So you end up posted with the 12th," Sinner said, passing her a three-oh-seven.

Fran accepted the tool, looked at it and frowned. She turned her confused look to the Chief, who already had a three-oh-five in his hand waiting. He winked and handed her the correct tool. Fran glowered at him before returning to her adjustments. The Chief chuckled as he turned his back to her and fiddled with something inside the chamber.

A clunk sounded from the upper deck where Lieutenant Smith was fitting the surveillance-satellite module. A part of Fran wished she was working with the Lieutenant, even though the thought of it made her stomach rumble. Fran had been impressed with the Ship's XO from the moment she set eyes on her. Smith was tall, beautiful, and walked with a grace and strength that reminded Fran of a jungle cat. She liked Smith instantly, and wanted the Lieutenant to like her in return.

She wasn't so certain about her new Chief Petty Officer, however. It was more than his occasional testing of her skills: that was to be expected of any NCO. At first Sinner had struck her as more than a little rough around the edges – shady even. He had seemed to be the kind of person that her parents used to warn her about, like he was always on the make. Still, Lieutenant Smith gave the Chief a good deal of respect. The two clearly had a close relationship, and that made Fran want Sinner to respect her as well.

"Hey, Jackless-wonder, turn on the four-four-five mag level would 'cha?" Sinner asked over his shoulder. Ignoring the insult, Fran complied with a quick series of adjustments. A high pitched hum sounded in the chamber.

As the Chief finally began to relax around Fran, she realized that he was in fact one of those people that her parents had warned her about. He was also smart, patient and extremely good at his job. In the few days she had been under his command, she had learned more about engineering than she had since she'd signed up.

"Push it up another two," Sinner said. Fran grabbed a large laser-based device from the tool kit and worked on the open panel at her feet.

"Ya' know the problem with these shipyard engineers?" Sinner said as he craned his position to access a more difficult part of the chamber, "They follow these specs that were written by companies trying to avoid being sued, and then try to make it impossible to adjust it 'cuz they think they know better."

"But aren't the specs they use designed to keep us safe?" The high pitched hum became a whine. She turned to look behind her. Outside of the vault-like hatch, in the engineering compartment, she could just make out the data on the readout from her workstation. She watched the numbers change as she manually adjusted the feeds.

"Sweetheart, if we was gonna play it safe, we wouldn't be in the friggin' Navy, and certainly not in the Raiders."

"I guess, but…" Fran was interrupted as a black officer's uniform, touched with a noble's gold appeared at the entrance to the access hatch.

"Officer on the dec-" Fran started jumping to her feet, but only got to a half hunched over position before cracking her head against the low arch of the fusion chamber's access gangway. The force with which she hit the bulkhead nearly knocked her back onto the deck. Tears welled up in her eyes. A hand grabbed her elbow and steadied her.

"As you were," the officer said, his rich plumy tones warm and slightly bemused, "Are you alright?"

"Yes, sir," Fran said wincing and unconsciously moving her hand to the top of her head, "I'm sorry, sir, I…"

"No need to apologize, Able Technician, I appreciate the enthusiasm."

"Thank you, sir," she said, opening her eyes for the first time and seeing the officer who stood next to her. He was tall, dressed in a ship-duty office dress uniform that accentuated his broad shoulders and narrow waist. His hair was dark, his smile a warm mix of amusement and concern, but it was his eyes that really caught Fran's attention: shimmering wheels of color. Despite her pain, Fran felt her breath taken away by the handsome features, she felt a nervous tingle inside, and became even more conscious of the foolish image she must have made on this man. Her stomach rumbled.

"Are you certain you are alright?" he asked, "That was quite a crack you took on your head."

"I'll be fine, sir," Fran responded.

"Very well, but if you feel any effects, do report to the medic first thing."

"I will, sir."

"I take it you are the ranking engineer, Chief?" the officer said, looking into the mixing chamber where Sinner laid down his tools to greet the officer.

"I am, sir," Sinner replied, "Chief Petty Officer Sinclair, sir."

"I am Lieutenant Commander Fotheringday, the new CO, and this is our Tactical Operations and Marine Officer, Leftenant D'Ascoine," Alex said gesturing to the man in green and black behind him. Fran had not noticed the other officer until that moment. She cast him a glance, but her attention returned immediately to the warm handsome Commander in front of her. She suppressed a belch.

"Welcome to the *Hunter*, sirs," the Chief said in the most formal tone Fran had ever heard out of him.

"Thank you, Chief. Is the Executive Officer on board?"

"Yes, sir, she's in the modular bay area, seeing to the fitting of the bay unit. Comms are down since we opened the power plant, but I am certain I could…"

"No need to disturb what you are doing, I will go and find her myself. Get a chance to see the ship a bit. Carry on." The CO said before moving out of the confined space of the engine rooms.

"Tell me," the officer in green said as he took the CO's place in the hatch, "What's the present state of the weapons systems?"

"They're off line right now, sir, but in general they check out fairly well."

"Have the synchronization systems all been checked?" D'Ascoine asked, plowing into a wide series of questions on the status of the ship's defenses.

Fran could tell that Sinner was growing agitated. He had been in the middle of his work, and he was always slightly impatient with any interruption to his concentration. This time, however, Fran suspected that his irritation was compounded by the fact that the Leftenant's questions prevented him from warning Lieutenant Smith that the CO was onboard. The Army officer's perfunctory and condescending manner didn't help. Sinner was a professional, however, and while his answers came in an increasingly brusque manner, he didn't even come close to insubordination.

Unable to help, or send a message through implants, Fran nursed her aching head and felt herself sinking slowly into embarrassment. All she had wanted was to look like a professional to her new CO, and now he would think she was an idiot. Her gut twisted painfully.

Alex passed forward through the *Hunter*. Though he had studied her basic design, it was rewarding to walk about her and see her in the flesh. Moving from the heavily shielded bulkheads of the aft engineering compartments, Alex passed the hatches that led to armory and drill range in five steps before walking through the mess/lounge with its carpeting and holowalls strategically placed between the girder-like struts and supports that arched along the ceiling and bulkheads. He ducked through an airtight hatch, passed by the four hatches that led to the crew quarters and cycled through the armored airlock that divided the centrally placed habitation zones from the forward facing command decks. He smiled as he stepped out into the trapezoidal chamber crammed full of displays and controls and lit by a dull red light.

Though *Hunter* was too small to have a proper Tactical Operations Center, her cramped Gunnery Control Center was a model of combat efficiency. Three gel filled g-couches dominated the room: one that was forward and faced aft, two that were aft and faced forward. Set centrally between them was a holographic display unit that would project tactical and other information to supplement the 2D, 3D and implant-direct interfaces that filled the coffin like gunners couches. It was from here that D'Ascoine and his gunners would control the firepower of the warship. Alex suppressed his impulse to linger in the combat center and climbed the gangway ladder that led to his destination: the bridge.

Despite the nomenclature that suggested the kind of large command center used on most warships, the bridge of *Spectre* class vessels were little more than cockpits. Two large g-couches faced forward, surrounded by interactive monitors, hovering dynamic holograms, and i/o jacks which hung ready for direct interface. In front of the twinned Pilot and NavCom stations was the transparent forward observation port. Its armored shielding open, it formed the most primitive of their views into the world outside the ship. The variety of diagrams, images and other projected heads-up displays that scrolled across it demonstrated just how redundant a window was in the modern world. Sometimes, however, redundancy had its purpose as well.

Alex felt a nostalgic thrill. Not long ago he had doubted he would ever command a bridge of any size again. Yet here he was, like a captain-pilot of the space ships of old, he looked at the station where he would be spending the majority of the next two years.

"Sinner?" a woman's voice came from behind him, "Could you pass me the L3-4 splicer? This stupid comms-connector is the wrong configuration for our input devices."

Alex turned around and saw the backside of a woman dressed in a khaki flight suit crouching at the airlock hatch to the modular bay hold that lay behind the bridge. She was obviously engrossed in her work, struggling to ensure the satellite surveillance module, or SATSURMOD, was properly fitted in the hold. Scattered about her were a variety of electronic manipulators, mechanical fitting tools, and handheld display feeds that were used in guaranteeing electronic compatibility and proper configurations.

"I suppose that is one of the drawbacks of having different contractors supply different elements of the same ship," Alex responded as he passed her the tool. She looked back as she took it, a tiny frown of confusion on her brow was quickly followed by a glimmer of embarrassed realization.

"I'm sorry, sir," the woman said as she untangled herself from the awkward crouching position, "I hadn't known you were on board."

The woman slid through the narrow circular hatch and gracefully unfolded herself to fully stand. She was a tall woman with a remarkable figure: strong broad shoulders, a narrow waist and shapely hips. Her blond hair was pulled back into a pony tail, her skin was pale but touched with a slightly rosy tone and after a moment it became clear to Alex that she was in fact quite striking. Despite the fact that she had no stripes of rank on her tan sleeves, Alex noted the badge on her chest and two silver laurel leaves on her lapels identifying her rank as a Lieutenant. He surmised that this must be his XO. As she stiffened to attention, Alex's gaze came to her face and met her large almond shaped eyes: eyes that were as polychromatic as his own.

He cocked an eyebrow, surprised that he didn't recognize her. There were only so many mandellans, about four hundred or so in the whole Empire, and while he had not met all of them, he was at least familiar with most on some level. He was still pondering this when he noted the disparity between the silver of her laurels of rank and her implied status as a mandellan. His eyebrows raised in response. *Her insignia should be gold.*

Alex didn't have much time for such champagne-reformers at the best of times, but someone who blatantly ignored a dress code that was designed to assist others in immediately recognizing the rank and status of those they spoke to was even more grating. Such displays of social position in addition to military rank had been introduced during the days of the Republic in order to ensure that political games of intrigue were not unwittingly played out during military operations. Failure to live by such regulations was not only a failure to follow general orders, but also complicated the social and political interactions on-board a ship. It allowed officers and enlisted personnel to make social blunders that could have real consequences for those who were not part of the elite. For the moment, however, he hid his irritation at the meaningless gesture. There were other matters that needed to be dealt with first.

"Lieutenant Commander Raiden Alexander Parviz Fotheringday, reporting for duty," Alex said.

"Lieutenant Samantha Smith, Ships' XO," the woman said before stiffly coming to attention. As she did, Alex noted the slightest eye motion; she was accessing files through her implants.

Checking my ID against security, Alex thought, *Well, at least she's follows proper security protocol.*

"Welcome aboard, sir," she said with a slight smile as she slipped back to an 'as-you-were' stance, "I'm sorry we didn't have a proper welcome for you. I hadn't known you'd arrived and..."

"To be honest, Lieutenant, I'm much happier to see that you've started fitting her out," Alex said.

"I thought it was best to make certain she was ready to get underway as soon as possible," she said, brushing a stray hair behind her ear.

"Excellent."

Alex forced a natural seeming smile as he noted a slightly withdrawn element in his XO's manner. It was more than the expected conservative responses of an officer in front of an unknown CO. There was something else, something he could not quite put his finger on. He wondered if this was the first sign of the kind of 'inter-mandellan tensions' that were so infamous between members of their stock. He decided that perhaps it was time to ever-so-slightly press the issue of his command – and her wardrobe.

"That's an unusual uniform," he said, a touch of jovial inquisitiveness to his tone.

"Ah... It's my old uniform from the Astrographic Service, sir," she said as she stiffened and showed the hint of a wince. Glancing down at her outfit with what seemed to be self-consciousness, she continued, "I find its configuration is a bit better suited for working on ships... more pockets in the right places. If I had known you were coming on board..."

"No you were quite right. Practicalities first, eh?" he responded, *well that addresses the outfit.* Something in her response, however, triggered his more subtle intelligence training and told him not to press her for the moment. He felt he was missing something. It was only then that other elements in what she said hit home.

"You were in the IAS?" he asked. He wondered if he had been given any experienced Naval Officers.

"Yes, sir," she responded, fidgeting with her fingers. "I served in Astrographics for about seven years before transferring to INI and the Raiders about… three years ago now."

"Excellent," Alex said with a false enthusiasm. He had hoped for someone with a bit more experience as his second-in-command, particularly since his TOMO was a novice to both naval and marine operations. Still, there might be advantages to having someone from the IAS onboard, especially if she had been more than an explorer. Perhaps she had even been one of their intelligence operatives. That could be useful.

"Well," he said trying to keep both his speculations and his worries from his mind, "I suppose as we are both on the bridge, this is as good a time as any to transfer the command. Shall we?"

With that, Alex handed over the symbolic letters of command and they began the long laborious process of admin and security protocols that officially transferred command. A hundred metabolic scans, fifty directly fed passwords and countless hand performed signatures later, the *Hunter* was his.

CHAPTER 8

Alyiar looked at the others as he fastened his belt. Rubo was checking in on the rest of the teams as was only appropriate, but the others were more than a little irritating. Wylde was agitated and ranting and Bolyiacov was baiting him, probably out of boredom. Same as it ever was. Alyiar shook his head and returned to prepping.

For the past two weeks he had been a child: cute and smiling with mocha latte skin and a musical laugh, he had become part of the background of the ship as they scoped it out. Now, at last, they were acting. He checked his skin tight voose suit once more before adjusting his belt and wrist packs. Closing his eyes, he started to focus, accessing his body control system.

"You ready?" Rubo asked, wearing the skin of a Lantinarra high roller. Luxurious black skin stretched over high cheekbones and body sculpted muscles. His perfectly fitting white suit dripped of new money. The white gold bracelet displayed he was married, the tri-colored baubles spoke of his three non-existent children.

Alyiar nodded. He felt the soft vibrations of the star-lounger beneath his feet, heard the quiet hush of air as it made its ways through the ducts. He triple checked the non-reflective pistols at his wrists.

"I don't even get why we're making this run," Wylde said. He was clad as daughter number one, aged fifteen. Dressed in a miniskirt and bows, only the submachine gun in his hands looked out of place. Alyiar shot him a glare, Rubo ignored him.

"For the money maybe?" Bolyiacov said. She was draped across the lounge, eyes hidden by mirrored wraparounds, the bracelet on her left wrist matched Rubo's exactly. Other than that, she was wearing her "haute-culture-number-four" form again. She was getting lazy and petulant; that happened from time to time.

"I thought orders had come down from the Great Mother herself that we were to lay off commerce raiding," Wylde said, "Only hit political and military targets."

"The Dalang said go for the money," Bolyiacov said without opening her eyes, "So here we are."

The other members of the cell were dispersed elsewhere through the ship, some pretending to be tied to the family, most of them not. Rubo had taken the prime comfy role for himself, again. He set himself up as a high stakes gambler in the first class section of the ship, chosen Bolyiacov as his addict and alcoholic wife and Alyiar as his number one son. The six room suite was perfectly excessive in the style of rich-but-not-quite-hierarch. Rubo played the role of someone-with-something-to-prove to a tee, probably because it wasn't much of a stretch.

Alyiar took a deep breath and looked up with angelic brown eyes at the drone-access duct. Even in his tiny state he wasn't going to fit.

"But if the Federalist Council wants…" Wylde said.

"We take orders from the Dalang," Rubo said, his voice petulant as his eyes suddenly focused on the room rather than whatever he had been watching through his implants, "and he has a lot more direct line of communication to the Council than you do."

"It just seems like this is all petty theft shit," Wylde said, but his voice sounded more submissive.

"Hijacking ain't petty, boyo," Bolyiacov said without moving, "It's what's gonna make us rich."

"I didn't join this to get rich, it's about returning power to the people and…"

"You think this is about getting rich?" Alyiar couldn't take it anymore. He lost his temper. "This is about making a real difference! Not just killing soldiers, but hurting the system. It's like the Dalang said, you fight the Army and what do you really accomplish, huh? You kill soldiers, who in the end are basically just ordinary citizens right? Misguided, trapped in the mentality of the Imperial, but just people like you and me. You target the money, and you hit the hierarchs, make them pay where it hurts, in the economy!"

Bolyiacov looked up at him, the first movement she had made in twenty minutes. She shook her head as if he were fundamentally misguided, then returned to her empty stare.

"I know the party line," Wylde argued, "but I still say that the Regulars do make a difference. When I was running with Hectoro's people…"

"You were just feeding the system!" Alyiar said, his child's form making him look like he was throwing a tantrum, "You were putting more money into the hands of the companies that supplied the military. Money for bullets, money for bombs, money for all that shit. Money that came from the taxpayers and went into the hierarch's pockets. You steal a ship filled with cargo? You're taking money from them! You sell that ship and the cargo on the black market or to the Atrucans or somewhere off in the fringe and you undercut the price of…."

"Drop the feckin' politics, and take your positions would 'jha?" Rubo said, looking at them with bored irritation.

Alyiar nodded, feeling a mixture of anger and shame. Wylde grumbled as he went to the door, but Bolyiacov remained as she was for a moment longer, before finally dragging herself off the lounger and readying for combat.

"*Is everyone in place?*" Rubo sent his scrambled and coded broadcast on the preselect channel. The responses came back positive.

"*Then we are a go,*" Rubo said, "*Wylde, feed security the loop.*"

Alyiar didn't wait to see if it was successful. He put on his game face and shifted his body. As his rib cage closed in its circumference, it lengthened ever so slightly to allow space for his organs. He felt his shoulder blades fold up, his pelvis dislocate and tent towards the front to narrow. His skull became longer and thinner as it took on the mask of The Wayang Stalkers Freedom Cell. The intricate curving tattoos of their public face were the only part of the change that didn't hurt like hell. By the time he was done, Rubo had already removed the access panel. Bolyiacov held a military issue FAP-117 handgun at the ready, Rubo a PPL-110.

Alyiar held nothing. Instead, he reached up above his head and telescoped his long bones and spinal spacers so that he grew long and thin. His hands on the edge of the repair drone access port, he locked his biomechanical grip, and telescoped his body back to child size. He disappeared into the ducting and began to make his way towards the bridge of the star liner. Slithering like an earthworm, he stretched, grasped, and collapsed his way through the body tight space though the thousands of meters worth of access tunnels designed to be no larger than a cat.

"That's an unusual uniform," Samantha muttered as she walked into her quarters. She knew, of course, what her new CO had meant: it doesn't speak of your rank and status above everyone else.

She had run through her first meeting with the new captain a hundred times, and each replay irked her more and more. Standing in his neatly pressed, gold marked office duty tunic, her new captain seemed every inch the elitist Imperial hierarch, condescending to any who was not of his own social position. His comment about her uniform confirmed the stereotype.

Samantha knew she had been out of uniform, but she had been working, trying to complete at least some of the thousand things that needed to be done before the ship was able to leave dock. The fact that she knew that her new Commanding Officer was likely to show up that morning was irrelevant. Her old Imperial Astrographic flightsuit was just more functional when it came to doing manual labor and she had things to do!

Besides, she thought, *he could have signaled ahead. Let us know he was coming, given us a chance to make a good first impression, but no! He had to surprise us… as if we wouldn't figure out what* that *was about.*

It was the kind of formulaic crap that she had come to expect from hierarchs, particularly Pro-Imperialists. Catch the crew off guard, put the officers in their place, make certain everyone knew who was in charge. She should have expected as much from the son of the Author-of-Empire.

Looking at the timer illuminated on the wall, she stripped off the well-worn comfort of her IAS uniform and the Vacuum-Wear Under-Suit or "voose-suit" that she wore beneath it and stepped into the fresher unit that stood in the corner. Bathing was the only time ship-board personnel were allowed to be without some form of vacuum protective gear on.

You would've thought that after two years of serving with Hegemonists, I would have gotten used to the concept of elitism, but now they give me a whole new level. Sometimes I swear it's me that the Ripper is testing.

"Sauna-shower program four," she said, picking at her cuticles as the unit heated up with steam. Seconds later, a hard spray of hot water massaged her tense muscles. The fresher units on board allowed for a variety of cultural cleaning methods: sand, water, oil, t'zing and any variety of others that gave the shipboard personnel some sense of comfort while on duty. It was one of the benefits of Imperial service that had been inherited from the Sophyan Confederal Republic's service before it: they valued the psychological welfare of their crews. At the moment, Samantha's psychology needed every aid she could get.

At least he did seem genuinely pleased that I was putting the ship's preparations first, she thought as the moist heat helped her to relax, *assuming that it wasn't all an act. Assuming that he isn't just trying to infiltrate us, find some dirt on me, or the fleet, or the Admiral.*

She placed her face in the stream and ran her fingers through her shoulder length hair. The warmth of the water allowed more than her muscles to loosen up. Gradually her irritation faded and was replaced by curiosity and intrigue.

She thought about the redacted elements of Fotheringday's record and how that tied into what Sinner had found. The payoffs to nobodies in the Archon sector, his subsequent assignment to duties well below his standing: morale officer, customs agent.

Were you investigating something? Are you still? Are you a mole, a screw up or just another self-serving aristocrat salvaging your career by serving in the most decorated fleet in the Navy?

If she had just managed to finish fitting out the ship by the time the CO reported in, she would have made a positive impression. Unfortunately, there were too many details that needed attending to. She couldn't complete them all; at least, not while stealing files from the records office.

What was I thinking? she asked herself as she began to lather her hair, *I knew he could show up at anytime. First impressions! Stupid. Here I am, trying to keep an eye on him and the first thing I do is piss him off! Brilliant, just brilliant.*

Her hands moved to her body, spreading the soap to her arm pits. She'd worked for a decade with informants; first learning about human and alien cultures as a sophontologist, then as an Intelligence officer, weaseling information out of sources and confidents. She smoothed the suds over her shoulder, arms and thighs.

"You're just a freakin' genius, Sammy."

She rinsed, and the warm water and steam continued to relax her muscles and clear her mind. She thought about her irritation. She thought about what the IAS uniform meant to her. She thought about the comfort she got from wearing it. The need for that comfort that she sometimes, no, often felt.

Why is it greater now? Is it the new assignment? The prospect of danger? She doubted that was it. Her life as an explorer in the IAS had been dangerous enough. Since joining the Navy two years ago she had received two commendations and regularly faced even greater threats whose nature would never allow a medal. It wasn't the danger: it was the assignment and the Commander.

He was the son of the man who was the key in the consolidation of power that turned the Sophyan Confederal Republic into the Sophyan Empire. She was going to be obeying someone whose father's political victory had ended her father's career, and more. She wondered how her Dad would have felt about it. What he would have said about her working with a Fotheringday?

Nothing. He would have had me judge Alex Fotheringday for his own sins, not for those of his father. She turned off the shower and stood for a moment, staring at nothing. She shook her head and tried to focus on the upcoming meeting, and the status of the ship.

Stepping from the fresher unit, she dried herself off before pulling a clean black voose-suit from her berthing unit. Slipping her foot into one leg of the one piece skin tight outfit, she felt the cool satiny smoothness of the material allow her leg to slide effortlessly to the outfit's integral foot. Pulling the rest of the suit up with similar ease, she adjusted the groin to properly position the waste disposal areas of the suit, before slipping her arms into the torso portion of the outfit.

Mind you, it's not exactly like what I saw in him set my worries at ease, but he didn't press the issue… and I was out of uniform.

She secured her breasts into the customized extra support harness she had placed into her own personal uniforms.

Samantha had always found the substantial extra-expense well worth the added comfort and support it gave. Yet it was more than the customizing that she enjoyed about her voose suits. They reminded her of her early childhood on board the IAS exploration vessels, a golden period spent with her mother. A time filled with the fascination of learning and the warmth of love.

She thought of her mother, and wondered how she would feel. Not just about her working for an elitist and speciest like Rippavitch, but about the fact that Samantha had left the Astrographic. Her Mom had been so proud that she'd gotten her doctorate, that she'd made Project Manager so young.

The timer on the wall drove out her reflections. She needed to meet with her new CO, regardless of her feelings towards him. As she adjusted and plugged the voose-suit's built-in monofilament i/o jacks into her own implanted cybernetic systems, the outfit warmed to her ambient body temperature and she forgot that she was clad at all. Looking at her old khaki astrographic uniform, with its efficiently placed clips and pockets, Samantha withstood the temptation to put it back on. Instead she withdrew the neatly folded and far more elegant black Naval Officer flightsuit. Despite the fact that she had spent almost three years in the Navy, Samantha was not yet truly comfortable with her role in the military, and still preferred her identity as an explorer. Regardless of her service record, she had never envisioned herself as a soldier: a warrior perhaps, avenger without a doubt, but a soldier? No.

She sighed, and was about to put on the one piece uniform of the life she now served when the door to her cabin opened and an officer dressed in Army Ranger greens walked in. He was good looking, and very well put out, with a single gold laurel leaf around the high collar of what was clearly a designer made Army uniform. Taking one step forward he smiled and opened his mouth as if to speak before stopping dead in his tracks and blatantly staring at her. She watched as his eyes traveled over her as his initial surprise turned into a leering appraisal.

"Close the door," she said without trying to hide her irritation.

"Pardon?" he responded, but his eyes lingered on her figure instead of rising to her face.

"Close the door, Leftenant," she ordered.

"Sorry, of course," the army officer responded stepping in and finally offering her his hand, "First Leftenant Rascoine Lord D'Ascoine. I'll be serving as Tactical Operations and Marine Officer."

"Yes," Samantha replied. As she shook his hand her voice was only slightly less hostile, "Lieutenant Samantha Smith, XO."

"Delighted," D'Ascoine said with a broad charming smile while he plainly continued to get discreet glimpses of her figure, "Quarter's are a bit cramped."

"That's life in the Navy," she said, and returned to putting on her naval flight suit, *I think they just got a lot more cramped.*

"Well then, which is your bunk?"

"My berth is the one on the aft bulkhead. The other is yours. You're required to sleep with the outer hatch closed, in case of decompression."

"Yes, yes of course… berth," D'Ascoine said with a smile. Now that she was in her flight suit and fastening the double-breasted front, his attention had drifted over to the berth unit, "So they haven't delivered my things yet?"

"Not that I'm aware," she replied and looking in the mirror she adjusted her uniform, trying to ensure that it looked professional.

"I don't suppose you could talk to someone about that, eh?"

"Excuse me?" Samantha turned slowly around to face him. Surely he was not asking his superior officer to fetch his things?

"I'm not quite sure who would I speak to about it and the Skipper…" His eyes ran across his own uniform.

"I've always carried my own gear to quarters. Now, if you don't mind Leftenant, I've got a meeting with the captain."

"Oh, right then," D'Ascoine said, looking just a touch disappointed, "Duty calls. I suppose we'll have plenty of time to get to know one another."

"That we will," Samantha replied, trying to hide her irritation with a weary smile. She grabbed a PAD and paused in front of the mirror for a moment to give one last look to her hair.

"By the way," D'Ascoine said, appearing in the reflection behind her. He spoke as if addressing her ass, his smile both lecherous and condescending. "What's with the silver, eh old girl? Did you loose your real laurels in the wash?"

Arms filled with the new TOMO's array of baggage, Fran and Bowman came to a stop in front of the Officer's Quarters. Fran put down some of the bags and went to ring the buzzer when the sound of hell's fury came from behind the door. Fran's finger froze just before she pushed the button. She gave a confused look to Bowman. His face mirrored her own.

Inside the cabin, she could hear Lieutenant Smith's voice as it tore into whoever was closeted inside with her. It made Fran's blood run cold. She couldn't hear exactly what was being said, but she knew if the XO's fury was ever directed at her, she would have withered and died on the spot. Confused, she stared at the button, then moved as if to push it.

"Are you out of your fucking mind?" Bowman asked.

"But the TOMO is expecting his…"

"Just leave them here and high-tail it," Bowman said, already piling the luggage by the door, "Believe me, you don't want to go in there now."

Fran looked uncertainly at the door, but the sound of the XO's voice quickly made her decide that Bowman was right. The two of them neatly piled Leftenant D'Ascoine's belongings in the hall, before making a hasty retreat to the other end of the ship. Just as they were getting to engineering, they heard another outburst, this one coming from outside the Officer's Quarters. From the sounds of it, it seemed that Lieutenant Smith had tripped over the pile of belongings as she stormed out of the cabin.

CHAPTER 9

The bridge was round and of reasonable size. The work stations were all set facing the central holographic space below the drone-ducting where Alyiar now lurked. His body was twisted in a 120 degree angle as he waited for the signal. The crew were completely unaware of the single filament camera he had slipped through the tiny hole he had cut. They simply worked at their stations, providing luxury transport to the wealthy members of society. Alyiar sneered. The coded signal followed shortly.

Alyiar blew the access panel and slipped snakelike out of the repair drone ducting. Fingers locked on the edge, his arms brachiated as he twisted, slithered, then dropped into the center of the holographic display. The bridge crew of the star liner were looking up from their work as the pistols came to his hands. They were still staring blankly when he opened fire. His guns were on full automatic. He could hear other gunshots ringing out elsewhere on the ship.

Stars and navigational icons hovered in his vision, but he ignored them as he spun slowly, letting his bullets tear through man and machine alike. He saw the brain casing of a four armed sophant explode as his rounds tore into its fragile form. It had been a bipedal thing, and its uniform made it look like it might have been the First Mate. Alyiar was glad it died before Rubo got a hold of it. Rubo hated bug-eyes of any kind.

Alyiar ran out of ammo before he ran out of targets, but one of the two remaining crewmembers was still in shock. He went for the other. Flipping his biomechanical body across a console, he sent his feet crashing into the man's chest. He heard ribs crack as he landed, but crushed the man's skull in his hand, just in case.

Across the bridge, the other crewmember, a woman, had finally begun to react. Alyiar's implants tracked her movement; vectors interpolated across his vision showing she was heading for the weapons wrack. Chipping up his responses another notch, he reloaded his gun before she made it half way. A spray of bullets riddled her body. The bridge was now his.

Alyiar turned to the ship-wide monitors that lined the walls. He saw at once that the cargo bay had been taken, but team two was still in a heavy fire-fight in engineering and a team of four security guards were heading for Rubo, Bolyiacov and Wylde. Looking around for the manual controls, Alyiar saw that he had destroyed them in his shooting spree.

"Fuck," he muttered. He hated direct interfacing, too many chances for viruses and too many bad memories.

He walked over to the engineering station, unplugged the i/o jack of the corpse there, and placed his hand over the receptacle port. A thin interface cable wormed out of his wrist and writhed its way to the i/o port, trying to find the opening. It slipped in the hole, activating his interface. Launching the viruses written by the Dalang himself, Alyiar took control of the ship's environmental controls.

In his mind's eye, he rode the security cameras first person, and watched as the blast doors slammed shut in some compartments and opened in others. Making certain where his own people were, he opened the airlocks. Explosive decompression followed.

Passengers and crew were torn away from their positions along with anything else that wasn't fastened down. Many erupted violently as they were exposed to vacuum, most simply flew out of the ship or froze solid before their softest tissues had a chance to explode. Only the combat in engineering continued, and even there it was only a matter of seconds before the crew there surrendered. Alyiar watched as they kneeled on the floor, hands on their heads.

"*Feck, Alyiar*!" Rubo's voice came through his implants, "*There were a lot of profitable kidnapping targets you just blew into space.*"

"*Sorry. There were nasties headed your way.*"

"*Next time see if you can be more discriminating.*"

Gun shots rang out from engineering.

As Alex suspected, the *Hunter*'s Captain's Quarters was a room much like the other crew cabins; a three by four meter compartment dominated by a large berth module. Unlike the other crews' quarters, however, this room only had one such unit: no captain was expected to share his accommodation on any Imperial Naval vessel. Even so, the berthing unit was no more luxurious than any of the others on board. It was a sealable module the width of a double-width bed that one could crawl into. Shutting a cupboard like door could give its occupant some privacy and allowed it to serve as a refuge in case of ship-wide decompression.

Across from the berth, where the other cabins would have had a second unit fitted, Alex saw a medium sized desk with a large body-forming chair behind it and two occasional chairs in front: the Captain's office suite. An anachronism, its prime purpose was as a reminder of social order. To Alex, it also served as a perfect place to display his personal items, particularly the holo-display of Sally.

Deciding that unpacking could wait, he sat in the comfortable work chair behind the desk and downloaded the files he had long been hoping to review. The mission details would not officially be available to him until after their first jump, but now that he had officially taken command of the ship he could at least read the personnel records. He called up the crew's files and floating holographic images appeared before him. Pushing the others aside with a dismissive gesture, he touched the hovering icon of his Executive Officer. Two rotating images of her materialized before him, one a bust and the other a full body figure image. A text window opened in his minds-eye:

Smith, Samantha J. Lieutenant, INI 12th Fleet. Serial Number: LAMONT 271-20B-2966-607-729-6706. DOB: 003 IC (859 SCRC). Homeworld: Meridothia, Merido Sector, Imperial Core. Mother: Dr. K'Tow Lin-Wu, Senior Principal Investigator (O6) IAS – deceased. Father: Smith, John A., President of Meridothia (ret.), and Senator for the Republic of Meridothia (SCR) (ret.) – deceased. Born in the capital of....

"Oh bloody hell..." Alex cursed softly as he leaned back in the form fitting chair. He should have known: she wasn't a hierarch reformer.

There were not many mandellans in the Empire, and only two individuals had ever turned down the status of hierarch. Both had been mandellans, and both had been leaders of the prodemocracy movement within the Empire's predecessor, the Sophyan Confederal Republic.

Cursing, he pressed the palms of his hands into his forehead before pulling his fingers through his hair. "You call yourself a bloody historian: she even has her father's nose."

The Pre-Imperial Opposition had consisted of three political parties: the Federalists, the Egalitists and the Hegemonists. Each had been led by a particularly charismatic mandellan. Two of them had been the dissenters that refused to participate in the new order once the Emperor, and his father, had won the day.

The Leader of the Federalist Party, Eleanor of Allevi, took her followers into exile even before they had lost the Senatorial vote for Imperialization. Transforming a legal political movement into agents of insurgency, she became the Great Mother of the Federalists, dedicated to overthrowing the Empire by whatever means possible. Thirty years later, she continued to lead a generation of terrorists who had never known anything but armed insurrection. Clearly no child of hers would be serving in the ARAG of Ripper's Raiders.

Wearing silver instead of gold, Alex thought leaning heavily on the desk and closing his eyes, *who the bloody hell did you think she would be?*

The other dissenter was President John Smith of Meridothia, Leader of the Egalitist Party and, apparently, the father of his Executive Officer. In contrast to Allevi, her one time ally Smith resigned his positions when his democratic home world voted in favor of imperializing the interstellar union. Though Meridothia had remained a democracy in terms of its own self-governance and had wanted him to stay in post, Smith said that he could not in good faith remain as that world's leader. Yet neither could he support Eleanor's civil war.

"Democracy cannot be forced upon a people at the point of gun or with the threat of a bomb!" Smith's resignation speech sounded in Alex's mind, "We must strive and struggle to return to democracy through legal means. One cannot spread egalitarianism through fear and death! Those who democratically reject democracy have a right to do so; just as we have the right to tell them they are wrong and try to convince them of that fact. Our stance, our beliefs, our future lies in peaceful persuasion, not totalitarian terrorism!"

The Federalists had called him a traitor and thirty years later he was killed at the hands of pirates who some say were in their employ. His call for reconciliation had made him a sacrifice on the "Altar of Freedom."

And now his daughter is serving in a counter-insurgency fleet. Revenge no doubt, but what is Rippavitch getting from it? Alex's polychrome eyes narrowed. According to his father, and to

Sally for that matter, the Admiral never did anything without an ulterior motive.

Checking the dates, he noted that the attack on President Smith's ship occurred some six months before Samantha requested a transfer from the Astrographic Service to the Imperial Navy. Her request was granted quickly and she had not been assigned to just any fleet, but the one dedicated solely to the campaign against terrorism. The fleet led by the final member of the political triumvirate that had opposed Imperialization: Admiral Lord Li-Yu Benjamin Rippavitch.

Alex leaned back in his chair and tightened his jaw. Around him, the holographic images and files drifted aimlessly across the room. "How do you fit into the Ripper's little schemes, eh, Lieutenant Smith?"

The Ripper was the only member of the Opposition Alliance to accept a position as Hierarch. The on-again-off-again Leader of the Hegemonists, Rippavitch was not an advocate of democracy, but rather an outspoken proponent of hegemony and opponent of Sentient's Rights.

The anti-Imperialization alliance had been wholly political in its nature, formed to oppose rather than promote. In contrast to the democratic reformers, the Hegemonists were conservatives who had wanted the Sophyan Confederal Republic to remain the Oligarchy it was. Rule by an educated elite remained the central position for the Hegemonists as they continued to call for decentralization and a return to confederation.

"I do not quite get it." Alex slowly swiveled his chair as drifting images lost their focus and bled into the walls. "No vote in the Senate; no real role in politics at all. Why are you here?"

His jaw tightened as his mind ran down through different avenues of how her presence affected his missions. Egalitist icons, Hegemonist leaders, Federalist terrorists and somewhere in the middle of it lay Alex, the Dalang and the bloody *Silver Slipper*. How did his new XO fit in?

The door chimed. Alex sat up in his chair and the images that drifted through his cabin snapped back into place. Opening a window in his mind's eye, he saw Lieutenant Smith standing at the door. With a wave of his hand, the hovering files disappeared and were replaced by star charts and tactical displays.

"Come in," he said with warmth.

CHAPTER 10

The darkened cockpit-cum-bridge of the *HMS Hunter* was filled with an array of hovering holodynamic images and icons. Streams of data flowed across monitors and vector displays were projected on the HUD of the forward viewport. Strapped into her gee-couch, Samantha used a combination of the holocontrols, the i/o of her implants, and the manual backup keyboards and joysticks to run the ship's navigation, communication and sensor systems. To her side, Lieutenant Commander Fotheringday did the same with the helm. Each flicked switches, gave mental commands and manipulated interactive holographs as if they were practicing some ancient martial art.

A taxi drone pulled the *Hunter* across the flight deck, towards the airlocked elevator floor that would cast it out into space. As it did, Samantha was both amused and somewhat pleased to see that Fotheringday kept the forward view port open and used it to maneuver the ship. He frequently strained to look out through the armored window with his own eyes at the progress of the ship. Many pilots, particularly those among the officer class, relied completely on their cybernetics to pilot their ships. Slumping in their chairs and directly interfacing with the ship, they would see a computer interpolated universe and use mental commands alone to control their vessels. Fotheringday, however, seemed to want to see things with his own less accurate, but perhaps more reliable eyes.

"Something amusing, Lieutenant?" he asked as he spared a glance in her direction. She couldn't tell if the look in his eyes was condescension or humor.

"No, sir."

"Never trust one source of information when others are available, eh?" he said as if to answer a question.

"A good policy," Samantha replied.

As he returned to the pre-launch, she realized he was mocking himself. She opened her mouth to comment on it, but thought better and returned to her duties. With a man as pompous as the Captain, it was best to play him slowly.

Once the *Hunter* was in place, the drone released it and sped away as yellow warning lights flashed through the empty docking bay. Fotheringday ran through a final pre-flight check with the crew while Samantha spoke to the *Résolut*'s CIC. On the dashboard between them, a simple green light appeared as the voice from flight control confirmed what it told.

"We have a clear to begin launch sequence at your command, sir," Samantha said.

"Very well then, Lieutenant. All hands this is the Captain, stand by to begin launch sequence."

"Conn, this is Engineering," Sinner's voice sounded over the speakers, "All ship's systems are reporting nominal and ready to go."

"Engineering, Conn, check," Fotheringday responded.

"Conn, this is Gunnery Control," D'Ascoine said, "Weapons systems are reporting nominal. All systems are locked on safety and standing by."

"Gunnery Control, Conn, check."

"We have three green lights and are cleared to launch at your command sir," Samantha said, relaying the latest message from CIC.

"Very well. *HMS Résolut* this is the *HMS Hunter.* We are ready for launch."

"*Hunter*, this is *Résolut.* We are initiating launch sequence in four… three… two… one."

There was a sudden jolt as the elevator-airlock released its clamps. A vibration ran through the ship as they descended into the floor of the docking bay. As soon as they were below the deck, the enormous inner airlock door slid shut over them, sealing with a thunderous bang. A hiss sounded as the air was sucked from the chamber, gradually fading to silence before another shudder ran through the ship. The elevator door tilted and the *Hunter* began to roll forward towards its edge. With a gesture to the holocontrols, Fotheringday fired the maneuvering thrusters and increased their speed until the ship dropped from the angled platform and moved away from the great rotating sphere that was the fleet's flagship.

Stars and blackness greeted them.

They drifted for ten meters before the CO made another flowing hand gesture and Samantha felt the soft acceleration as the *Hunter* engaged its reaction drive. The vessel quickly picked up speed and moved away from the huge battleship from which it had launched. Samantha checked on the gradually increasing distance, noting the parabola of their path compared to the ever accelerating *Résolut.* Even if they had tried, the *Hunter*'s stealthiest drive could never keep pace with the constant firepower of the *Résolut*'s thirty fusion rockets. Designed for discretion rather than speed, reaction drives were hard to spot, but far from the fastest form of propulsion. Still, combined with the geometry of the absorptive hull, Samantha knew the *Hunter* would soon vanish from the fleet's sensors; at least until they fired up their own fusion rockets.

"Two minutes to safe distance," Samantha reported.

"Thank you, Lieutenant."

Looking through her implants at the space about the ship, Samantha saw the rest of the fleet spread out around them.

Even compared to the small patrol ships, cutters, and corvettes, the *Hunter* was tiny. Next to a frigate or destroyer she was insignificant. Though *Hunter*'s small size gave her less firepower, it also gave her greater stealth. Given the nature of the ARAG's overall mission, Samantha would have taken her ship against any of smaller warships available, and most of the larger one's.

"We're at a safe distance," Samantha reported as she dropped out of cyber-reality, "No other ships in our burn zone."

"Thank you, Lieutenant," Fotheringday responded, passing his hands around the holographic controls, "All hands this is the Captain, stand by to engage fusion engines on my mark.... four, three, two, one.... Mark!"

At once Samantha sank into the gel of her gee couch as the fusion rockets were opened and engaged. A new vibration filled the ship as their acceleration increased four fold. Soon they passed the other ships, overtaking the *Résolut* and moving out of formation with the armada. With fusion rockets firing, the *Hunter* was no longer invisible. Instead a sword of light cut from behind her, small in comparison to many of the ships around them, but still bright enough to be seen by the naked eye from across the system.

"Lieutenant Smith," Fotheringday said, "Please plot our course."

"Aye aye, sir," Samantha replied, readying herself for the process.

"*Samantha A4-Nav-Survey Program,*" she thought, giving a mental command, "*Initiate navigation program and project a Temporal Grid.*"

Around her, the bridge, the ship and all elements of the real world vanished. Instead, she floated in space, her avatar's body clad in the comfortable uniform of an IAS investigator. Stars shone all around her. Here and there text and images gave information about the different stars or the presence of varying ships that moved within sensor range. Soon a host of data hovered where the bright fusion engines of the 12th Fleet blazed, and in the distance other icons representing far off system gun boats and merchant ships also appeared.

At the center of it all, Samantha's drifting form marked the spot where the *Hunter* now stood. With a gesture like a conductor, she summoned the great arcs and lines of the astrographic program. Concentric spheres of vector arcs and rays stretching off into the impossible distance. She floated at the vertex of all the projected meridians, at the relativistic center-now axis of her universe. She studied the graph of space-time projected around her, each line telling the relative distance of different key stellar bodies and how long ago the light from those objects had been emitted or reflected.

As a long range scouting vessel they were capable of creating an Essar-Rosenthal field strong enough to travel 0.423 parsecs in a single instant jump; further than most military and all but a handful of civilian ships. The *Hunter* could travel three parsecs in a week, or the average stellar distance between two adjacent star systems in between two to three days. Yet their fuel capacity was still limited, and they were forced to follow strings of stars that allowed them to refuel at gas giants and water worlds. A miscalculation in navigation could leave a ship stranded too far away from any source of fuel. More than one ship had ended its days as a hulk whose radioed distress call only arrived to the nearest population center years or even centuries too late. To Samantha, however, navigation was more than a process of calculation: it was one of discovery and personal pride.

She was happy as she meticulously plotted their course. Adding data from other ships, Naval, Astrographic and even merchant vessels, Samantha developed a complex series of overlapping images of space-time. She examined variations in the different ships' records on a case by case basis, removing those due to sloppy navigational practices, and searching for those caused by unidentified natural phenomena.

Though examples of bad navigation irritated her, she was delighted each time she came across a naturally occurring anomaly. In her spare time, she often tried to determine the possible causes of such irregularities in the data. To date, she had successfully identified two escaped planetary bodies and one large gas cloud. It wasn't as rewarding as discovering new cultures, but it was fun all the same and helped improve interstellar navigational charts.

Today, however, Samantha was pleasantly surprised to see that one record that normally did not match the others had been corrected by someone else. Data taken from the Inglesie system was always .044 percent off the projected values when observed from inside the system. It was an extremely minor variance, one that on its own would not cause any navigational difficulties; even Samantha had never been tempted to explore its causes. Yet her compulsion for perfection always made her seek it out and remove the anomalous readings. To her surprise, however, she found that data from one of the other ships in the Raiders, the *HMS Aramus*, did not show the expected anomalies in the readings. Someone must have identified the source of the anomaly and made the corrections.

Somebody is even more anal retentive than I am, she thought as she tagged the Inglesie record to be reviewed later and went on to examine the other anomalous readings. As she did, she idly wondered why that information had not yet spread through the fleets, or the IAS for that matter. *I guess some people are more interested in making the corrections than getting credit for them.*

When Samantha had satisfied her own personal definition of good protocol, she checked the information again, and finally generated a Bradley projection. It took a moment of intense computation, but eventually the image responded by warping and twisting as it moved and amalgamated the different datasets. Gradually the hundreds of different projections merged into a single three-dimensional representation of space. Gone now were the spider-web projections and light-cones measuring relativistic space-time, replaced by a simple, box-grid that spread between the stars. Samantha knew it was technically inaccurate, but it did create an image that a human mind could more readily perceive. She quickly traced a path along the map before checking her figures yet again and setting in the course.

Dropping out the Navigation program, Samantha was once more in the cockpit. To her side, she was surprised to find Fotheringday staring at her with one eyebrow cocked and a look of slightly bemused expectation on his face.

"Course plotted and set sir," Samantha said, curious but ignoring the stare.

"Any momentum corrections?" the CO asked, after slight pause.

"No, sir," Samantha responded, after quickly double checking the monitors in front of her, "We're ready to go."

"Very well, Lieutenant," Fotheringday said, and opened up a holowindow to check the figures himself.

As if you might find a mistake? She thought.

"Excellent," Fotheringday said with another nod, "Conn to Engineering, this is the Captain speaking. Charge her up, Chief. It is time for us to bug out."

PART II

Command, Control and Communication

CHAPTER 11

Alyiar scanned the downport, looking for signs of a trap or a set up. Behind him Rubo was logged into the comm-nets doing business closing the sale of the liner they had taken, using the information they downloaded from it to set up other strikes against the same company, and sending that intel around the Wayang. All about them the busy planet-side starport served to hide their activities. The deafening sounds of cargo vessels taking off and landing, the constant clatter of containers being loaded and unloaded, the myriad communications being broadcast across all channels, not to mention the scrambling and white noise devices in the suitcase comms unit that Rubo used; all went to make it impossible to understand what was being said.

Even so, caution was the trademark of the Wayang network, especially the Stalkers. Dressed as deckhands Alyiar and the others kept a close eye out for trouble. Thus far he had seen nothing more suspicious than some kid well on his way to being a cyberjunkie leaning up against a pile of cargo crates in a different landing zone. Head bobbing in time to some unheard soundtrack, the boy seemed oblivious to world around him. Alyiar suppressed a shudder as the memory of desire ran through him.

"You alright?" Bolyiacov asked. She had changed clothing into that of a standard shiphand, but still wore her blonde haired Haute-culture number four form. She was getting lazy, but Alyiar was hardly in the mood to point it out.

"There but for the Graces…" he muttered, nodding at the kid. Even now, over two years later, he felt the pavlovian response, the desire to return to the virtual worlds. Only his dedication to the Cause stopped him.

Bolyiacov shrugged and returned to scanning the docks.

"Shut the feck up," Rubo said with such anger that it caused both Alyiar and Bolyiacov to glance around at their leader. The comms unit was projecting an image of the Ankh, one of the local dealers they used to move or acquire goods both in and out the networks. He was good at his job but drove a hard bargain. Then again, so did Rubo.

"I'm sorry but that's the way it is," the Ankh replied. Dressed in a beautifully hand tailored suit, the Ankh had a thin build with somewhat knobbly joints, high cheekbones and a long face. His pock marked skin suggested some childhood disease, but since his suit was more expensive than the surgery to correct his face would have been, Alyiar suspected that it was some cultural thing.

"You don't feckin' tell me what's what you little shite. You're just one little fixer, who can easily be replaced… or discarded."

"I mean neither you nor the Dalang any disrespect," the Ankh smiled smoothly, "but things have changed. Some of my other clients, including many of your fellow Federalists, have objected to our arrangement. Added to that, the Ministry of Justice has increased it's presence in Lai-Jung. Last year they brought in a new unit of Cybernetically Enhanced Infantry…"

"I don't give a feck who they brought in!" Rubo shouted. Across the docks, the cyberjunkie looked up from his game. Bolyiacov and Alyiar exchanged a look. He nodded, and she walked calmly off the platform.

"...from DuZhod," the Ankh continued, "Their colonel is a hierarch... a DuZhodian Hierarch."

That silenced Rubo. He sat looking at the screen. Across the docks, the kid's head had gone back to bobbing and his jaw was slack. He was either fully enthralled with his game again, or simply pretending to be. Bolyiacov was no where to be seen.

"That's in addition to information just supplied to me from the Dalang about new initiatives by Ripper's Raiders..." the Ankh left the idea hanging.

"I'll see if I can set up a meeting." Rubo pulled the cable from the comms box and the monitor went blank.

Across the docks, Bolyiacov stepped out from the shadows and knelt by the side of the game pariah. The boy didn't look up.

"You think our comrades have sold us out?" Alyiar asked without looking at Rubo. He split his attention between Bolyiacov, the boy and other possible threats.

"No." Rubo was packing up his comms equipment.

Still kneeling, Bolyiacov slowly moved her hand, raising it to the level of the boys throat and forming a circle between her middle finger and thumb, as if she were about to flick his ear. Alyiar looked for signs of a back up unit or rescue squad. He saw none.

"We've been ignoring directives from the Council," Alyiar said, "They might be afraid we're going to splinter, or some of the other cells who resent that we've taken over their operations..."

"Are scared to death of us. And the Central Council doesn't come down on units that are effective," Rubo said locking the case and standing up, "We've been growing and grabbing the headlines and this is the price of success. It's what we wanted. It's part of the plan."

Alyiar met Rubo's eyes. The leader stared at him for a long moment before smiling and putting a hand on his shoulder. Alyiar knew Rubo meant what he said. He smiled and nodded in return. Rubo stepped away, chuckling softly as he made his way down the dock.

Alyiar focused his attention back to Bolyiacov, still sitting all but motionless in front of the boy. She flicked her finger at the junkie's adam's apple and the kid jerked once, then went into convulsions. No sirens sounded, no armed guards suddenly appeared. Bolyiacov remained staring at the boy for some minutes after his body stopped thrashing.

As per regulations, after having followed a heading away from the fleet for one week and while they were between systems in the deepest interstellar space, Alex opened his orders. They were heading to the Alterande sector to follow up on the recent increase in terror attacks and insurgency. It was nothing he hadn't already known for some time. Still, it was nice to have it officially confirmed.

After announcing their destination to the crew, he turned on the do not disturb light outside his cabin and leaned back in his chair. He ignored the text that was streaming across his desktop, and paid no mind to the slowly revolving holographic starcharts of the sector to which they were heading. Instead he watched recording after recording of the terrorist whose image was projected into the center of the room. He studied the man's the extreme ectomorphic build, the long deformed skull, the curving arabesques of his tattoos. This was the Dalang, the spokesmen and alleged leader of the Wayang Terror Cell whose brutal attacks Alex intended to put to an end.

"People of Sophyan space unite! Stand up and take heed!" the recording ranted, "The time for revolution is now! Even as I speak the Imperialist Overlords are ripe for the taking…."

The Dalang's rhetoric was nothing more than an amalgamation of catch phrases derived from others. He demanded equality for the people, claimed totalitarian domination by the hierarchs, spoke of the threat caused by allowing sophants equal status, and shouted the need for social reform. There was nothing at all imaginative in what he said, only in the way he had branded it with this bizarre caricature of a talking head. Alex was certain beyond a shadow of a doubt that he had never seen such an iconoclastic man-thing before. Still, there was something familiar in the way he spoke, his gestures and inflections; something Alex could not quite place.

He launched a comparison program looking for similarities in physical motions between the Dalang's speeches and those he had on file from his time in the Archon sector. Clenching his teeth Alex stared at the images a moment longer. Only after his jaw began to ache did Alex close the recordings.

At last he could begin what he had joined the Raider's to do. He opened the countless intelligence files on terrorist actions and insurgency in the Alterande sector and began to attack them in a slow, methodical manner. The files were the key to finding the link, and the Linking Agent. Before he would finish his analysis, however, he would need to ready his crew for what they would be facing.

CHAPTER 12

"Holy Shit!" Chrom shouted, suddenly toggling back into Tactical and staring at her line officer. D'Ascoine was wholly focused on remote piloting the two missiles he'd just snap-shot launched; an action that had given away their location to the enemy. Throughout the ship warning signals blared as the enemy's active arrays began searching the area where the Hunter had previously been lurking undetected. D'Ascoine seemed unconcerned.

"Bloody hell," Fotheringday's voice could be heard through the hatch up to the bridge. Chrom felt herself sink into her gee-couch as the CO gunned the reaction drive engines and rolled the ship. He didn't light up the fusion rockets, however, at least not yet.

"Red-Jack! Red-Jack!" Smith shouted over the ship's comm system, "I have four new contacts bearing two-nine-two by fifteen and two-nine-three by one-six-three. Incoming at rate of seven naught four… Damn! I have active radar, there are two hawks in the air!"

"All turrets to point defense!" Fotheringday commanded.

Chrom had already switched her commands over to automatic radar targeting, causing the turret to 'hose down' the area of active radar contact with all lasers firing. One missile vanished, but Bowman fired another shot at the ship he had been targeting. She guessed he hadn't realized what had happened, nor heard the command that had been given. The other three missiles continued and enemy laser began hosing the area they were in.

"Bowman!" Chrom shouted, spinning her turret towards another missile, "Anti-Missile-Defense! Now!"

The Marine Corporal responded at once. She didn't blame him. D'Ascoine hadn't parroted the commands the way he was supposed to.

"Gunnery Command! Chamber and launch a decoy!" the CO ordered, "Engineering, prepare for a series of quick burns of the fusion rockets."

"Engineering, aye, sir," it was Fran's voice that answered. She sounded remarkably calm for a newbie.

As Chrom viewed the world from her laser's point-of-view, she noted that D'Ascoine didn't respond to the command to drop the decoy. She opened a window into his point-of-view. D'Ascoine remained focused on piloting his missile towards its target, softly cursing the erratic flying that was causing him to lose LOS comms contact with his weapon. Furious, she was about to take over control and follow the skipper's order when the Army officer finally rotated the missile cylinder and launched the decoy. The action took merely a second, but it seemed an eternity. He didn't follow protocol and note what he had done.

"Stand by for evasive maneuvers! Chamber another decoy."

The ship leapt forward as the fusion engines let loose maximum thrust. The ship spun, twisted and turned into a series of sharp, zigzagging maneuvers as they tried to lose the incoming targets. Whatever else he was, Chrom decided that Fotheringday was a good pilot. Not the best she had flown with, but better than most.

Toggling back to her turret's viewpoint, she focused fully on trying to clear the different missiles homing in on them. Vector lines drawn across the starfield helped her mark her next target, spinning icons told her distance and speed. She began to hose down the new area with laser fire.

With the fusion engines at full blast, they had completely lost the Hunter's principal weapon, stealth, but with so much firepower bearing down on them, she didn't see that the Captain had another choice. Chrom's twin beam lasers struck and the missile exploded before the single rapid pulse laser activated. She moved to the next target, but two new incoming missiles' appeared.

"NavCom! Chaff and ECM! Gunnery Fire Decoy," Fotheringday shouted.

Smith released a cloud of metallic and radioactive dust. She honed in the impressive jamming devices of the stealth ship, targeting the incoming missiles. D'Ascoine fired off another decoy, this time when he was ordered to. One of the incoming missile erupted from the electronic counter-measures. Bowman scored a double hit, killing two with one sweep of his lasers. Chrom missed a third which was coming dangerously close.

As the decoy launched, Fotheringday cut the direct fusion drive. He made two quick course changes with the mass reactors, then let the Hunter drift through space. They went silent once more, trying to use stealth to their advantage. One of the remaining missiles fell for it, and streaked off after the decoy. The other began to perform a classic circular search pattern, broadcasting loud-active radar and other sensor signals as it sought out its missing target.

Far in the distance, a sudden bright light with a slow receding glow indicated the detonation of a nuclear missile. It was the one that D'Ascoine had snap-shot launched, the one that had given away their position. Though a mixture of electromagnetic noise filled the area, Chrom noted that two of the enemy ships seemed to disappear. D'Ascoine cheered, but the Gunnery Sergeant knew the kill would make almost no difference.

Smith engaged the electronic counter-measures, broadcasting an array of confusing and penetrating commands at the incoming weapons. Another missile exploded in response. Bowman destroyed yet another and Chrom a sixth, but it was too late.

A bright light filled the optics portside, and less than a second later Gunnery Control's bulkhead erupted. Bowman was instantly torn to shreds by the scattering shrapnel, his screams filled Chrom's ears as she saw her own legs ripped away from her body. Sharp pain gave way to horrible ache. Darkness followed.

"Well… that could have gone better," Chrom's voice sounded rough, even over the ships comms.

Alex could not help but agree with the Gunnery Sergeant's assessment. To his side, Alex could hear Smith groan and saw her wincing at the residual pains of her phantom death. The simulation did not last long after the first enemy strike; the damage done by that point was too great. Alex rubbed the shoulder where his implants had been told a bulkhead support ripped through his body. It would take quite a few minutes before the tingling memory of his agonizing sim-death dissipated.

"Well, ladies and gentlemen," Alex said, aware that his normally plumy tones and calm demeanor sounded slightly stilted, "We are all dead. I will, of course, still need to review the records and the auto-analysis, but does anyone have an idea as to why we were killed?"

"Yeah." Bowman's voice sounded irritated, "We gave a solid targeting solution to our enemies with the launch of that last nuke."

"That is exactly the case," Alex said, "One of the problems with ships like our own is that we are not afforded the luxury that larger ships are given. We are small and do not have enough point defenses to counter significant numbers of enemy missiles. What is more, unlike our larger brethren, the enemy can hopefully not see our engines. We can only take on larger warships such as frigates, or squadrons of corsairs like the one we faced, if our position remains covert."

To his side, Samantha slowly turned her head to look at him. Her mouth was open, her eyes narrowed, and a frown grew on her brow.

"Now, admittedly," Alex continued, "the odds of us coming up against a situation like the one we just faced are remote, but it could happen, especially against aggressive insurgents like the Dalang. Even against single ships, we should always keep in mind that silence is our best weapon. There are many larger merchant vessels, not to mention Federalist corsairs, which are as well or better armed as we are. Remember what we learned here today. Mr. D'Ascoine, thank you in your help in illustrating the point."

"My pleasure, sir," D'Ascoine responded in a self-satisfied tone.

"Very well," Alex said, "We will have a debriefing at fourteen-hundred hours."

"Ms. Smith, would you take the Conn while I…." Alex stopped short as he noted the anger and disbelief in his XO's eyes.

"You're covering for him?" Smith asked.

"Not precisely, no," Alex answered with mild irritation, "We can't have the crew think he is quite so inexperienced."

"Why? Because he is a hierarch?" She leaned forward, her voice on the edge of insubordination.

"No. Because it will undermine their confidence and make them worry needlessly."

"Needlessly?"

"I understand your concern, Lieutenant," Alex responded as he unstrapped himself from his gee-couch. "But I assure you, Leftenant D'Ascoine will be up to snuff by the time our mission begins."

"How can you be so sure?"

"Because this is not my first command," Alex said as he stood and switched to an open channel, "All hands this is the Captain. The Executive Officer has the Conn."

"All hands this is the XO," Smith said in a professional tone, even as her glare met Alex's dismissal of the topic with an unprofessional distain, "I have the Conn."

"Leftenant D'Ascoine," He said over a personal comm channel as he climbed down the gangway from the bridge to the TOC, "Please join me in my quarters."

CHAPTER 13

Sinner had a smug smile as he climbed up into the bridge. It grew wider when Samantha turned in her seat and shot him an angry look. As soon as she saw it was him, however, her features softened but retained an irritable edge. It didn't take a sophontologist to figure out what was bothering her.

"Happy with the drill?" He asked stepping into the cockpit. Her expression hardened once more. This time he thought it looked comical.

"What the hell has you in such a good mood?" she asked, turning her attention back to the NavComm station. She flipped a switch on the command console and a new holograph appeared on the display. Bars jumped up and down on a glowing plane showing the background noise from their sensor readouts.

"Mission accomplished," Sinner said as he perched on the edge of the empty pilot's station.

"When?" Samantha looked up at him once more, a small smile appearing on her lips.

"During the sim," he responded. It gave him just the slightest thrill to have surprised her. It wasn't often he got one by without her noticing, "While our TOMO was in the process of getting us blown to hell."

"And you already altered the logs?"

"Barely needed to. The captain's quarters are next to Gunnery Control, where else am I going to send a repair drone if we take a hit mid-sections."

"You took a hell of a chance, what if the attack had been real?" She turned back to the console, pressing the attitude control, subtly adjusting their position to better pick up a signal.

"You think he could run a sim on this ship without me knowing it? Besides, if it had been real his quarters would have been torn apart, but, everything was just where it should be, including his personal computer."

"You don't think he'll notice?"

"Oh, now you start getting all cautious?" Sinner reached over and adjusted one of her controls. She slapped his hand and turned it back.

"When have you known me to leave any signs?" he continued, "No ma'am, we're well and plugged into his personal system, downloaded the first set of backups already. He'll never know."

A text window opened to Samantha's side and a hovering series of numbers scrolled across its field. She gave it a quick glance and frowned before turning back to the dancing bars. "What about the files from Personnel? Have you broken those?"

"Give a man a chance, would'cha? I've got a grade four working on it and the stuff you lifted off central INI."

Samantha manipulated her controls with a quick series of hand gestures and sat back. The numbers stopped scrolling and the dancing bars settled into a regular pattern.

"Did I ever tell you you're the best?"

"Probably not often enough," Sinner said.

"Alright Harpur," Chrom said with the hard edge of a Marine Sergeant that made Fran's colon clench, "Let's get this started. Do you know why you are more dangerous to me and mine than a complete and utter imbecile?"

"Because I am a natural, Gunnery Sergeant?" They were standing in the armory with the target range behind them and row after row of weapons and suit lockers in front of them. Despite the fact that she had not been ordered to, Fran found herself standing at attention as if the Gunnery Sergeant was dressing her down.

"No!" Chrom shouted, making Fran jump, "I couldn't give rat's ass if you're jackless or not. Hell, half the time I need to train reliance on implants out of people. No you stupid Navy Pussy, you are a threat to me and mine because you believe you know anything at all."

Fran closed her eyes and winced. Believing she knew something was about as far from what Fran felt as she could imagine.

"You just proved that by trying to guess what I was thinking! How the hell are you supposed to know that? My first and most important job is to stop you from knowing and start you to thinking! Got it?"

"Aye, aye Gunnery Sergeant!" Fran said. Trying to sound gung-ho, her response sounded like a kid playing soldier. She tried to stifle a belch.

"Take an antacid already." Chrom paced around Fran, eyeing her up and down like some piece of substandard livestock. "I know you received small arms training during basic, but all that means is you know enough to be dangerous, and not to the enemy. So Bowman and I are going to train you over again, starting at square one: Francis Harpur, you are not a Marine. Do you understand that?"

"Yes, Gunnery Sergeant." *No duh.*

"Good, that's a start. Means you've got promise. Now, let's get you familiar with the Marines' best friend, the OS-745 Combat Extra Vehicular Activity suit!"

Gunny Chrom stepped up to one of the equipment lockers and opened it to reveal a large armored space suit, the kind Fran had seen Marines wearing in combat drills. It was built of a heavy cloth-like material, and had solid plates that covered the chest and limbs. The helmet was similarly armored, with a solid visor that could slide over the reinforced clear viewplate and lenses that dotted its surface like the eyes of a spider. Over the upper arms and shoulders were a series of articulated plates that overlapped like the hide of an armadillo. Here and there Fran noted sealable jack-ports where the wearer could plug in weapons to allow for direct feeds, assuming the wearer had implants, otherwise it would just display in the suit's HUD.

"The OS-745 CEVA," Gunny Chrom said, eyeing the armor like a convict looking at a stripper, "is a state of the art multi-purpose non-powered man-portable piece of extra-vehicular activity equipment that is combat ready, thus C.E.V.A: *see-va*, get it?"

"Yes, Gunny," Fran said. Of course she knew the acronym, but a fear filled sense of incompetence grew inside her just the same.

"It is capable of operating in anything from a complete vacuum to ten atmospheres of pressure." The Gunnery Sergeant spoke in the precise you-are-an-idiot tone that seemed to be issued to non-coms across all services. As she did, she pointed to each element of the suit, as if to illustrate to a person of substandard intelligence, "Its exterior is covered with a layer of "chamelo-mesh" programmable camouflage, capable of remembering over 1500 different configurations. It has integrated injectors that are capable of delivering appropriate medical or combat supplement treatments subdermally, and a built-in CPU with twice the computational capacity of your top of the line compad. It can be plugged into shipboard and personal weapons and all sorts of your pansy ass NavCom equipment."

Fran swallowed back another belch as she looked at it. *How am I supposed to learn to use this while I'm learning so many other things at the same time?*

As Chrom droned on and Fran tried to memorize each function of the suit, a growing sense of unease filled her. She tried to suppress it, but it turned to fear as she realized what her needing such protection meant about their upcoming mission. Fran knew she was not a Marine. What was more, as she looked at the armor she knew she didn't want to be one.

"...In short, it is one hell of a space suit and the best friend you will ever have!" Chrom said, smiling at the suit before turning back to Fran, "There is in fact only one problem with OS-745 and that is you will not be wearing one!"

It took a second for the words to hit Fran. When they did they struck like an electric shock and she turned to look at the Gunny with wide eyes. "What?"

"You heard me," Chrom said with a warm and softening smile, "But don't worry too much, I don't wear one either. Come with me."

CHAPTER 14

"To the crew of the *HMS Hunter*," Alex said with a forced smile.

"Here, here!" D'Ascoine raised his glass with a flourish and drank half of it in a single draught. Samantha smiled politely and nodded before raising her glass, as if she needed to consider the toast before drinking to it.

Alex did not truly wish to be spending the evening socializing with his officers; he wanted to be studying the files, learning more about the Delang and his terrorist network. If nothing else, however, Alex's time in limbo as a Morale Officer had taught him the value of bonding with his subordinates. As a result, he had gathered his officers in his cabin for a formal meal together at the earliest possible opportunity.

"The Alterande patrol is a very sought after duty," Samantha said. Alex watched her sipping her drink, and walking about the room eyeing his décor. As ever, he had decorated his quarters in a traditional Hammonrie style: even setting the holounit walls to simulate wooden paneling with brass and copper detail. It made him feel a bit more at home, as did the objects d'art and personal décor he had placed around the room. They were handmade and dominated by organics and natural stones: again a traditional, if expensive, element of his people.

Smith picked up a bronze stature and turned it over, no doubt looking for a maker's mark. "You must have friends in high places."

"Nonsense," D'Ascoine said, throwing himself into one of the occasional chairs and draping his leg over one of the arms, "The Ripper just knows a good captain when he sees him."

"Actually, I suspect that we received this assignment because of the crew, not the commander," Alex said, taking a seat in the work chair. He had moved it out from behind the desk before his officers arrived.

"Perhaps," D'Ascoine said smiling, "After all I do have a bit of a reputation."

"I think he meant the enlisted men," Samantha said over her shoulder.

Alex watched her move onto examining a crystal sailing ship. It had been made by a Billanobian artist a century before re-contact with the ancient Terran Federation and was worth five times his annual salary.

"I meant all of you," he said, ignoring the cavalier way she handled the priceless object, "Alterande is an important patrol, sitting on the Fringe with the start of the Corridor Stellar Archipelago in its heart. It serves as the transport and communications link to the Billanobian Hegemony, and is a constant target of insurgent actions. If Van Trappini did not have faith in the crew and its ability, we would not be here."

"You served in the region before, haven't you sir?" Samantha asked as she gazed at the hologram of a painting of his ancestral home.

"No, I was posted in the neighboring sector, Achron," Alex replied matter-of-factly, then spoke to the air, "Mergatroid? Would you put on the string quartet mix number three?"

"Certainly sir," the bored intonations of his personal house management program sounded.

"You loaded a valet program on to the ship's systems?" Samantha asked, turning around with a look of surprise, "Isn't that against regulations?"

"Pish-posh regulations," D'Ascoine said over the rim of his glass.

"It is and I did not. I am afraid it is nothing out of the ordinary Lieutenant. I brought my own personal computer along and networked it to the room control. It is the image holder on the desk, the one with the picture of Sally on it."

"I didn't mean to imply that you were doing anything wrong sir," Samantha turned to face him, an apology on her face, "Captain's privileges after all and…."

"No need to explain, Ms. Smith." Alex gestured to the free chair and smiled. "You want to know what kind of a man your new CO is, just as I would like to know more about each of you. To that end, I would like to invite the both of you to join me in a weekly dinner, just the three of us. Give us a chance to relax a little."

"Juan Hiro," Samantha said as she finally sat down, "that is Lieutenant Commander Zea, used to have a weekly dinner session with the whole crew."

"It is a good idea," Fotheringday said, "but traditionally I should be invited by the crew to dine with them, not just force myself on them like an invading conqueror."

Samantha gave a half nod. Glass in hand, D'Ascoine stood up and walked to the desk where the decanter sat.

"After all," Alex said, watching his TOMO help himself with a cocked eyebrow, "the crew needs time to themselves, a chance to let their hair down and complain about me… and the two of you for that matter."

"You want to encourage dissention in the ranks?" D'Ascoine asked, stopping in mid-pour.

"There is a great difference between dissention and simple complaining Leftenant," Alex said with another honest smile, "Our job is to tell them to do things they may not want to; running into the line-of-fire and such. There will be a certain amount of understandable resentment caused by that. If the three of us are cloistered in here at a regular time on a regular basis, that will give them a chance to let off some steam. These are professionals Razza, the non-coms at least know when and where to draw the line."

"Weekly meals it is then," Samantha said looking at her captain. Meeting her eyes with a smile, Alex felt like some new species she was observing for a report.

Sinner and Samantha sat cross-legged around a campfire in Samantha's personal interface room. Behind them, the huge manta like form of her mother's survey ship stood with its landing ramp down. Off in the distance they could hear the cheerful song-calls of Meridothites, the indigenous sentients of her homeworld. Occasionally a splash would sound as one or more of the aquatic avioforms jumped into the fjords and played with its mates. When she felt wistful, she would sometimes come to the sim and play with them. Tonight was not one of those nights.

In front of her, Sinner had taken up his favorite avatar, that of a small polar bear. About him were spread a number of digital windows and elements of floating text. Sometimes he would appear to fumble with one or another of them as if trying to fish out some object, but mostly he just sat and stared. Samantha occasionally contented herself with counting the blinks in his ursine eyes, trying to determine when he was present and when his avatar was just on automatic.

"How long?" she asked.

"Not long," the bear responded, "I got the Captain's personal machine to link over to our subsystems. Now all I gotta do is to make it think we're him while we access the data. Meanwhile why ain't you looking into the files we took from personnel or the one's he uploaded onto the ship?"

"Because I'm still waiting for our programs to hack into them. You might have found it easy to link into his personal machine, but he's not a complete fool. Most of the files on the ship's systems are pretty well guarded, and funny enough, so are those from central INI."

"Fair 'nuff." Sinner replied. He stopped for a moment, crinkled his snout, then pushed the window he was working on out of the way and pulled over another with his paw. He began picking away at it furiously.

From out of the bushes one of the Meridothites appeared. It was the simulation of Noctuchk, her childhood best-friend. It waddled up to the edge of the fire, tilted its head and blinked five times expectantly. Samantha gave a soft smile as she looked at its stout blue-grey form; a body that looked so sleek in the water, and so comical on land. She shook her head a little sadly and the sim-Noctuchk sighed and wadded off, de-rezzing as it returned to the background of the sim.

"Can't you hurry it up?" Samantha looked back at Sinner, who was now surrounded by glowing vector based icons of some program he had opened.

"Not if we ain't gonna be detected. What's the rush?"

"I'd like to know who we're dealing with before we get to Alterande."

"That's weeks off."

"At the rate you're working...."

"Patience Lieutenant. Now, see if… you just…. keep your voose-suit on… you will see a master at…. Fuck. Never mind."

Samantha looked away. She considered going down to play with the simulated Meridothites after all, she hadn't done that in some time. Like the sim-Noctuchk, some of them could have AI-sims turned on so that they acted like some of her childhood friends. Alternately, she could always read some of the latest sophontological reports from the IAS.

"A-ha!" Sinner cried out.

Pixels fell like rain, then trickles of color and streams of reality washed away the scene of Meridothia and replaced it with the image of a study. Tall darkened bookshelves lined the walls with antiquated leather bound volumes. Great French doors looked over a manicured park, and overstuffed chairs sat by a fire. Samantha found herself sitting on the floor, while Sinner lounged on a chesterfield, his ursine bulk making the leather sofa bend under his weight.

"How... predictable," Samantha said looking around. If she would have drawn the archetype of a hierarch's interface room, this would have been it.

"I don't know. It don't seem too bad if you ask me," the polar bear said.

Samantha stood up looking around. This sim was only a backup of the system he would keep on his implants, but what they were searching for was years old anyway. She just hoped it was here. Looking at the manufactured interface room, it was clear the books were icons of files on different topics. Some were work related, others personal, many were on historical topics. There were thousands of them; she hoped they would not have to troll through them all. Behind her she heard Sinner launch an AI powered query. She turned to see a non-descript, ghost like figure assisting the Chief as they each started to touch the volumes on his side of the room. Smiling, she turned to the desk.

It was leather topped and wooden, delicately engraved with a handful of geometric patterns in the Billanobian noblesque style. On it stood a letter opener, the picture of a slim young redhead in a tennis skirt, and a few objects d'art. She reached first to the picture and touched it ever so gently with her forefingers.

"Hello, darling," the image at the center of the room said. It was the woman in the picture, wearing a floral patterned sundress and smiling quite brightly. She was striking with a lithe athletic build and bright blue eyes. Her hair was a mélange of auburns and gingers, her smile was bright and lively.

"I went to the Bilisph'untoro party the other night, Gahd how I wish you were there," she tilted her head and pushed her hip to one side, "It was simply dreadful, and poor

Sashi… he was the only non-human present and they didn't even have anything he could eat. He simply stood there dripping and trying not to leave a trail when he slid along the floor. Needless to say Buttons and I saved him. We managed to slip out and go Silverbies, which was seuper. Buttons was soon taken with a bright young man and vanished, so Sashi and I…." Samantha touched the picture again and the woman vanished.

What a waste of breath she is, Samantha thought as she turned to the other objects on the desk. *A ball of obsidian, a model of an ancient interplanetary ship, a glass shoe, a quill, a….* She stopped and looked once more.

"Sinner?" She asked and the polar bear turned around, "What was that name we came up with?"

"Hammond?"

"No, the ship that went missing in Archon?"

"*Silver Slipper*," he responded, then followed her eyes to the glass shoe on the table.

She looked at him and back at the crystal shoe before reaching and touching it. The room melted away and was replaced with the hard cold surfaces of a ship's cargo bay in ruins. Twisted metal erupted from the side where a bulkhead had been torn apart by some other ship's weapons. Plasma arced in one corner, giving nightmarish strobes of light to illuminate the room. Littered through the room were a hundred or so hyberchambers, the kind used to transport the poorer members of society.

Around them walked eight figures dressed in the distinctive OS-745 armor of Imperial Marines. Another strode about more heavily in an OST-1000, its powered limbs sending vibrations through the deck as it stomped among the remnants of the cargo hold. The Marines were fighting a force of gravity that she and Sinner did not feel. Their guns cautiously targeted the hyberchambers, but even from a cursory glance Samantha could tell the occupants were already dead. Low class hyberchambers like these required constant power. Once power was cut, you only had a matter of minutes to revive the poor bastards stored inside. These people had been dead for a least an hour.

"What the fuck?" the polar bear Sinner asked from across the room.

Samantha merely shook her head in response. She looked in one of the chambers. It contained a young boy looking like he was sleeping. She was grateful that at least he wouldn't have felt it when his unit failed. Next to him lay a K'thanga, with only its three buglike eye-clusters showing in the viewport. It was just as dead as the child.

"Hey Sammy… take a look at this."

Samantha walked over to the Chief and noted the figure on the floor. He was dressed in a simple uniform worn over a voose suit. Over his left breast he had a green cross and a name tag marked with a smile and the words "Chuck Nakisura: Ship's Purser." His face and hands were bloated and black, his eyes bloody messes. He had decompressed when enemy fire had torn open the ship's hull.

"Look," Sinner said, "He didn't even try to put on his bubble helmet."

"Nope," Samantha said, "he's tethered up right by the life-support controls though. He died trying to keep power to the hyberchambers."

"Lyndeswurl Lines." Sinner read the patch on his uniform, "Ain't they Imperial?"

"They sure are Sin," Samantha said.

"So why the fuck are Marines walking through this like a combat zone? Did they stop a terrorist attack?"

"Apparently not," Samantha said.

"And why the fuck does the Skipper have this saved on his desktop?"

"Good question."

"From what I can tell the sim ends right outside this chamber," Sinner said, "You asks me? This is one fucked up piece of shit to keep in your Interface room."

The Marines suddenly froze and looked up seeming to receive a message. Then Fotheringday's voice sounded loudly over comms system, "Cease Fire! Cease Fire!"

The scene dissolved, and then started over again. The sim was on a loop.

CHAPTER 15

Sinner strained to show no reaction as he watched Fran work through the integrated interface waldos in her flightsuit. It was painfully slow. In the cybernetic version of the ship's refueling skimmers, her simple avatar moved in jerky, spasmodic motions. She appeared as nothing more than a simplistic, cartoonesque version of herself wearing an unedited set of prefab clothing; she hadn't even added realistic texturing to her skin. She stepped forward, stepped back, turned and stepped forward again as she moved her sim-self into position. Once in a while she would suddenly jerk into motion or stumble, probably as she tried to adjust some camera angle. It took all of Sinner's self control to stop himself from taking over and doing the work himself.

When she finished her task, her avatar simply stood there motionless staring ahead. Sinner had to open a window into the real world before he realized that she was looking at him expectantly, a small hopeful smile on her face. Minimizing the VR window and maximizing his view into the real world, he shook his head.

"How the hell do you expect to operate drones if you have that kind of delay?" He asked. The crestfallen look on her face made him feel like he just kicked a puppy.

"Well, I... uh... don't normally use that kind of..."

"Whatever. We'll figure out some kind of work-around," he said, "but it's going to take twice as long for us to get used to working as a team."

"I know," she said, her head dropping, a small frown creasing her youthful brow, "Sorry."

"Still, you did a good job on the filter," he said, his avatar putting a hand on her avatar's shoulder, "Your program is okay, and the way you wired the purifier was inspired. You'll get there, it'll just take a little longer."

Fran returned to work, still dejected. It was only later that he realized that she was probably never aware of his avatar's reassuring touch. He wondered if he had even said the comforting words aloud, or only in the virtual world which she had already logged out of.

Bolyiacov leaned against the building wearing her bored-in-black look. She sported short blond hair and pale skin, her height set at exactly two meters. Her eyes were tuned to black with flames dancing in their center like tiny bonfires. Haute-culture number four. She was the visible muscle.

Alyiar was wearing a street-urchin skin: tiny pale body with knotted red hair kicking a ball against the wall in endless repetition. Preadolescent of indeterminate sex; he was the stealth protection. Not that there looked like there was much to guard against at the moment.

Rubo had been nervous recently, a bit more on edge. They were avoiding easy marks and used more security even when dealing with their fellow Federalists. Wylde bitched about it, but Alyiar guessed it was tied to the increased Imperial interest in their cell. He kept his eyes and ears open as he pretended to play in the trash strewn gutter.

Overhead, buildings rose above the street, leaning in as they ascended until all that could be seen of the sky was a thin line of grey. Here and there walkways cut across the urban canyon, some of solid construction, others little more than wires and pipes thrown across the breaks in buildings. No sign of any enemy, only his fellow revolutionaries.

"I'm tellin' ya, man," one of the local-yokel insurgents said as he tried his best to impress Bolyiacov, "Once the Empire grows to a certain point, the Emperor plans to introduce a Billanobian hierarchy across the boards. Remove the last vestiges of the Confederation. After that, you can kiss your civil liberties goodbye."

"You don't say," Bolyiacov said in dry tones. She was far from impressed. Her head moved back and forth like a security camera. Alyiar wondered if she had turned on an Eliza and let the pre-programmed response generator come up with her side of the dialogue.

"I do say," the yokel said, "it's the Emperor's plan, always was: first turn the Sophyan Confederal Republic into the hegemony that is the Sophyan Empire, then turn that oligarchy into a hereditary aristocracy with his family at the top!"

"You could be on to something there," Bolyiacov said. Her scan reached one limit and returned along its path. She paused briefly at the street vender who was hocking stolen watches. It was Wylde doing the same kind of undercover stint as Alyiar. Her gaze moved on.

Alyiar didn't bother to hide his amusement at the yokel's efforts. Dressed as a child, people would only notice if he didn't laugh. He clutched his ball and scanned for other threats, knowing it was time to do a test. Human-powered taxis pressed by, one of the drivers madly cycling to move her pair of overweight customers from the Imperial Core. He didn't have the heart to add to her woes, so he chose another target. Alyiar let his implants do a quick calculation and kicked the ball at an angle that hit a passing peddler's cart. A shower of fruit and trinkets fell and the woman who pushed it began screaming in a dialect Alyiar couldn't understand. It didn't matter, he cursed her in response and started throwing loose trash from the street.

Sitting in the middle of a blanket covered with fake designer watches across the street, Wylde noted who reacted to the scene and who didn't. The woman picked up her things and Alyiar reclaimed his ball then threw it at her. More trinkets fell. The woman moved to chase Alyiar. He ran around the corner and waited for her to leave. When he returned Wylde flashed a series of street signs noting that there were two extra goons since the last count. That made Alyiar nervous. Inside, something must have changed.

"So how 'bout you?" the yokel was still trying. "How long you been with the resistance? I've been in the fight for three…."

A plain black fire door burst open onto the street, smashing against the concrete wall with a resounding crash. Rubo stormed out of it trailing three of the other Wayangs. None of them were in Stalker form, but behind them the head of the local insurgents followed.

"…and I'm telling you," the woman was shouting, "We don't take kindly to threats, and we don't take orders from the Delang!"

Rubo stopped short, spinning on his heels and facing the woman with cybernetic speed. She stepped back two paces in surprise.

"You owe money," Rubo said, "It's as simple as that."

"This isn't a business," the woman said, her voice not quite living up to her words, "it's a revolution. You and the Delang should try to remember that once in a while."

"And you and your amateur hour here should try to remember that you're just one little piece in a much bigger struggle. Keeping that struggle going takes money."

"So does keeping yourself in thousand credit suits," she said, looking Rubo up and down.

Rubo didn't move a muscle, he just telescoped out his forearm. The fist jack-hammered into her face, her nose erupting with blood. The Wayang Stalkers by his side were through the door in a flash, grabbing whatever bodyguards were lurking in there. Behind him, Alyiar heard the distinctive cracking of bone as Bolyiacov took out the yokel who had been hitting on her.

Alyiar wondered if the guy finally got the hint. He didn't move, however, he was still in stealth mode; ball in hands, waiting for other threats to reveal themselves. They didn't. Not even the lurking goons.

Rubo, Bolyiacov and the guys on security backed out of the street. Wylde gathered up his goods like a fence afraid of becoming a crime of opportunity. Alyiar continued to play the urchin, staring on with a mixture of fear and adrenaline intoxication.

The public Wayang made it to their car and took off. Wylde ran down the street. Alyiar went back to kicking his ball against the wall: watching the local insurgents gather themselves and scamper back into their holes. He waited another hour to make sure they weren't launching a revenge strike before heading out and making the long circuitous route back to their own safe house.

The Captain's cabin sounded with the ever present rush of air from life support and hum of the *Hunter*'s engines, but Alex didn't notice it. He sat looking at the star chart of the Alterande sector that filled the room and beyond, spilling into the darkened walls to project those areas beyond the focus of his attention. It was a very good map with a great deal of detail that could be gleaned at a single glance. He smiled briefly when he noted its author: Lieutenant S. Smith, INI 12th Fleet. The smile didn't last long as he strained to see a pattern in the data before him.

Rotating around an unseen axis, the stars moved around his room providing him with a 360 degree view of the region of space to which they were headed. Some stellar bodies stood alone, but most lay in clusters and long chains: the archipelagoes, many of whose paths were matched by glowing indigo lines. The lines marked the primary routes of trade and communication that followed them: the Mains.

There were scores of them, but in Alterand, one stood out from the others. The Corridor: the great bridge of stars that linked the Sophyan Empire with its greatest alley and economic partner, the Billanobian Hegemony. Billanobia lay across an immense gap in the stars, a void that channeled communications along the Corridor and the web of Mains that lead to it. It was this particular trade route that kept merchant vessels coming to Alterande, despite the fact that it remained a hot bed of insurgency.

Alex sighed and began his work. As he opened the reports, the stars where each incident occurred twinkled with a red aura, demonstrating its location and that of any associated episode. Some were simple cases of smuggling and black marketeering thought to be associated with the insurgency. He put those aside for the time being, and as he did, the twinkling red halos around the associated stars vanished from the star map.

Next he identified the more run-of-the-mill Federalist assaults. There were standard guerrilla attacks on Imperial Army Guardian patrols, bombs going off in Embassies or Imperial Administrative centers, attacks on ancillary targets and infrastructure. He marked these with a silver halo before turning to those that remained.

Those that were left were different. Though the nature of their crimes ranged the gamut of terror crimes, they all had one thing in common: their brutality. Scanning through the reports, the ruthless methods stood out from the others. Attacks on schools, assaults on nightclubs, kidnappings, mutilations, hate crimes and acts of piracy were not uncommon to the Federalist cause, but the degree of violence and the manner by which it was delivered were all too familiar to Alex. They matched the style of those he had investigated previously: the ones that had led up to the *Silver Slipper* incident.

He marked these suspicious cases in gold, and then leaned back in his chair, tented fingers poised before his clenched mouth. There was something odd about what he was seeing, a pattern of some sorts, but Alex couldn't quite put his finger on what it was. Working on a hunch, he opened up another file. Immediately, the scale of star charts reduced to allow the new map to be fit within the room.

Next to the map of Alterand, the image of the neighboring Archon sector appeared. The map was not as good as that produced by Samantha, but he knew it well enough that it didn't need to be. It was the map that his former subordinate Kyle Hammond had compiled some years prior, the map that Alex and his one-time commander, Sir Richard Al Escobar had used in their hunt of the Federalists.

Looking at them side by side, Alex struggled to see a pattern, but nothing presented itself. Saving the image, Alex closed out the maps and decided to take a new tact. Opening the archives of the ARAG's files, he began reading through the summary reports of Federalist activities in the region starting with the very first attack on record.

CHAPTER 16

Wearing the skin of his Polar bear self, Sinner hovered in space and watched Samantha work. Normally, it was a pleasure to behold her floating at the center of her navigational program, commanding the universe like a sorcerer's apprentice. This time, however, she stood with arms crossed and her head tilted to one side as she studied the CO's star charts with a furrowed brow.

"I just don't get it," she said, "What is he trying to see?"

"Don't ask me, it's all a bunch of red, gold and silver spheres." Sinner flew over to one of them and sniffed. A text window opened in his mind's eye and he watched as a series of extreme ectomorphs with swirling tattoos massacring people in a bank, "Filled with a gooey inside."

"He's compiled two sector maps; one of which is the mission map I made for Ripper. The other a decent version of Archon that's pretty out of date. Still, it's been updated with some more recent data on attacks, probably from the Raider's central archive."

Sinner humphed as his eyes narrowed. With twitching snout, he flew over to an otherwise insignificant region of space where a single gold aura stood out alone. Flicking the image with single claw, the sphere chimed in resonance like a crystal glass and a title appeared over its head: the *Silver Slipper.*

"I'll bet that file doesn't appear in the *Raider's* records," he said, a cartoonesque smile growing across his muzzle.

"You'd win that bet," Samantha said, her brow furrowing, "Any more details in it?"

"Nope… just a placemarker as far as I can tell. Funny though, I would have thought it would be noted in silver, huh?"

Samantha's avatar closed her eyes for a moment. "There are a few other records in here that don't come from the 12th either: a couple from the Ministry of Justice, a few from the Imperial Guardians, quite a number from the Office of Statistical Analysis, even one or two from the Billanobian consulate."

"Not normal, but he's well connected. What's biting you?"

"It's something about the overlay," Samantha drifted towards Sinner, pointing to this star or that, "In the Archon sector, both the gold and the silver attacks follow typical haphazard patterns of the Federalists. They launch attacks that occurred where the opportunity presents itself, so there are very few along the well patrolled routes of the Mains."

"Makes sense, more patrols, less opportunity."

"But over here, in the Alterande sector there's a big difference between the two sets, see?"

"You mean besides there being more gold attacks than in Archon?"

"The silver marked attacks follow the same sporadic patterns in Alterande as in Archon, but look here, in Alterande there's a higher frequency of attacks along Mains and other well guarded avenues of commerce. All of them are gold."

Waving his paws before him briefly, Sinner created a query. A series of captions materialized above the gold records, they noted the dates of the attacks compared to the dates that the 253rd Fleet patrolled each system.

"Those are some ballsy mother fuckers," he said peering at the results, "Look how deep they are into the patrol zones, and they cut it pretty damn close in some instances. There's one over there where a normal patrol of the 253rd arrived no less than a day after the assault. They got a big haul too."

"Uh-huh," Samantha responded absently. Sinner turned to see her surrounded by a cloud of open files – some texts, others sim recordings. Her polychrome eyes narrowed and her avatar picked its cuticles.

"What you got?" He asked flying over to her as if he were bearing down on a seal.

"Nothing." Samantha's voice sounded surprised and irritated. "Absolutely nothing. I can't for the life of me figure out what he's looking at here. In Alterand, all of the incidents marked in gold are tied up with the Wayang Cell, but in Archon all of the gold marked reports predate the earliest known Wayang incident by a couple of years. So, what's he up to?"

Fran stood in the simple black standard Naval issue OS-500 armor clutching a 0-G shotgun that the Gunny had given her. Next to Bowman, dressed in his OS-745 and carrying the AAR Mark 5 Combat rifle, she felt naked and unarmed. Chrom had said that Fran was still too erratic with her fire control to be trusted with a weapon that could penetrate the Marine's CEVAs, so she was stuck using the "no-skill" gun that would probably also fail to even slow any insurgents they came up against.

Across from her she saw Lieutenant Smith smile at her and nod in encouragement. Fran gave a pathetic smile back, noting that even the XO was more heavily armored, and she wasn't even supposed to be entering the enemy vessel in this drill. Armed with a high-output laser, a pistol and a drusus style short sword at her hip, Smith leaned against the bulkhead like a seasoned pro. Her black armor was equipped with armadillos and enough extra armored plates that at least she didn't look comical next to the heavily clad D'Ascoine and Bowman. By comparison, Fran looked like a victim waiting to happen. At least she knew that the Gunny wouldn't be dressed in anything more protective. She wondered where Chrom was.

"You ready for this, kid?" Sinner's voice came from the pod-shaped combat drone on the floor. With its large, bird-like legs collapsed underneath it, and its twin weapons arms folded over its top, the drone looked more like a remote controlled car than an attack robot, but Fran knew it was a very deadly machine, more heavily armed than anyone present.

"No," she responded.

"Don't worry, Fran," Bowman said, his faceplate was still up and she could see his smile through his visor, "You'll be great."

"Just remember to duck," D'Ascoine said with a chuckle, "and avoid shooting me."

"I'll try."

"Adjust your shots for medium range and you'll be fine," Lieutenant Smith said, putting a reassuring hand on Fran's shoulder. Looking into the mandellan's eyes, Fran felt comforted.

A loud clumping noise sounded down the hall, somewhat reminiscent of the combat drone in walker mode. Looking up, Fran saw a set of heavy powered combat armor larger than any she had seen before. It looked like a headless giant with rocket and grenade launchers mounted across its shoulders. A large Rapid-Fire Rail Gun was swivel mounted on its waist.

"What the heck is that?" Fran asked, her jaw dropped.

"This," Chrom's voice sounded from a loudspeaker in the headless behemoth, "is an OST-1012, the very latest and greatest form of powered heavy combat extra-vehicular activity suit."

"Like it?" Bowman asked the Gunny.

"Won't be able to tell until after a few runs, but so far the interface is worlds better than the One-K."

"An OST ten…?" Fran asked staring at the walking tank that contained the Gunnery Sergeant, "You said you were going to be wearing the same half-assed armor I was!"

"No, Able Technician, I did not," Chrom replied, emphasizing every syllable as she loomed over Fran, "I said that I didn't wear an OS-745. You went off knowing instead of thinking again."

Sinner laughed. Fran belched.

"That's just mean, Gunny," Bowman said, chuckling as he shook his head.

"Nice NCO's end up with dead Marines," Chrom answered.

D'Ascoine laughed and moved into position. Lieutenant Smith shouldered her weight off of the bulkhead and came to a ready-for-combat stance.

"Tell me again how the guy who served in my post before me died?" Fran asked.

"See? There you go! Now you're thinking!" Chrom cheerfully answered. Bowman didn't look amused.

"Right, everyone into positions!" D'Ascoine ordered. Smith gave him a look that he seemed to ignore. When she sealed the faceplate of her armor, Fran followed her lead.

"Ready when you are, sir," she said, looking into the air.

"We are beginning our drills against a known hostile, maximum force is permitted." The Skipper's voice sounded over their comms. "The Exec and A.T. Harpur will hold the airlock against counter boarding while Leftenent D'Ascoine will lead the others into the other ship. Get ready. Simulation will begin on my mark…. four, three, two, one…. Mark!"

"Ready to blow the hatch on my command," Samantha said, and after a nod from D'Ascoine she gave the word, "Blow the hatch. Open fire."

Fran jumped at the loud explosion, but even before the smoke had cleared she was pulling her trigger with the others. She could feel the hum as the accelerator hurled its rounds down the length of her gun's barrel. Once they had passed her team members the rounds fired again. Inside the gaping hole that had once been an airlock, the small casings of her bullets sent flechettes down the gangway. Blasts from Bowman's and D'Ascoine's grenades rocked the corridor, while beams of light told her that Smith was opening fire with her laser. Electric blue plasma discharges leapt from the arms of Sinner's combat drone and a stream of explosive rounds from Chrom's RFRG tore up the other side of the airlock. The noise was deafening and Fran doubted anything could have lived in that mess.

"Leftenant," Smith said, remaining in shooters position, but no longer firing.

"Cease fire!" D'Ascoine shouted in a sing-song voice of command, "By numbers people! Ready? Charge!"

He disappeared into the smoking hole, followed closely by Bowman, Chrom and finally Sinner. Gunfire and explosions followed immediately. Fran spared a quick glance to the Exec and was met with a comforting nod.

"Ma'am?" Fran asked, "Is it really like this?"

"No Fran," Samantha said in a calm voice, "Sometimes it's worse. Sometimes the enemy is well armed. Sometimes there are hostages."

Alyiar watched as Rubo tied the transponder beacon around the Meridothite. The small blue-grey bird thing looked frightened. It tried to approximate a human smile using its beak, but that only made Rubo sneer all the more. The only thing that had kept it alive thus far was its comical look was less repulsive than the rest of the crew's had been. They had not been so lucky.

All around Alyiar were the carcasses of a different species, Rendethi, whose stump like bodies were topped with delicate antennae they used for smelling. Around those fernlike organs were three long, flexible noses they used as manipulative organs, like the trunks of an elephant. Similarly placed around their base were larger versions by which they pulled themselves along the ground. As far as Alyiar could tell, they had no eyes what-so-ever. Even as they surrendered, he was revolted by the slimy aliens, and knew that meant his leader would be even more disgusted. Rubo had opened fire and shot them all when one had slipped a long tongue out of one of its 'foot' trunks. Now all that were left was the equally non-human navigator and the thousand or so Rendethi passengers, all of which were in hyberchambers. They, at least, had a monetary value. The bird-like sophant did not.

"Now, my feckin' horrible little friend," Rubo said to the Meridothite as he turned on the transponder, "You're gonna deliver a message for us."

"Yesh?" it said, again trying to smile. Big mistake.

"You're gonna let them know that the Wayang Cell can strike anywhere it likes, even along the Mains."

"Yesh yesh! I vill!" it said, a desperate hope appearing on his face. Rubo started moving it towards the end of the corridor. It waddled as quickly as it could, thinking it was being shown mercy. Alyiar felt sorry for it.

It was only when they stopped in front of the airlock that it began to understand. Before it could do more than let loose a single squawk of panic, Rubo pushed it inside. It scrabbled at the glass for almost a minute before he vented it into space. Alyiar turned away in disgust, but still checked the comm channels. Taped to the bloated and frozen corpse, the transponder was playing the latest of the Dalang's messages.

CHAPTER 17

Alex took a sip of his port and listened carefully to his officer's bickering. It was late after one of the officer's meals together. After dinner, port and cheese had led to harder spirits, which in turn led Alex to spark the debate to which he now listened with care.

"So, you're saying that you honestly believe you're inherently better suited to govern than others in society?" Samantha asked D'Ascoine with incredulity.

"Yes. Are you honestly saying that you believe that you're not?" Razza said with a cocked eyebrow.

Alex held back from the fray, at least for the moment, but was certain to remain the good host by providing brandy to Razza, gin-and-tonic to Samantha. He slowly nursed a nice tawny port for himself. The alcohol further fuelled the debate, adding both to his enjoyment and his knowledge of his officers, not to mention the unit in which he now served.

"Yes!" Samantha said, gesticulating with her drink, "and you are saying you honestly believe that you're genetically and culturally more fit to rule than anyone else?"

"Yes. Of course. Look at it. I come from a long line of individuals who have ruled, who earned their place at the top of society and kept it. Generation after generation,

D'Ascoines have excelled at the accumulation of wealth and power, and have had enough respect from those who live under our rule to have maintained our position. Yes, that more or less demonstrates my lineage's right to rule."

"So, you have a right to rule because you are descended from great men and women?"

"In part yes, but it's not exactly as if I haven't accomplished great things on my own. I'm well decorated with many accolades."

"Has it ever occurred to you that part of the reason you have those accolades is because you are who you are?" Samantha leaned forward, "That you excelled because you were brought up in an environment where you had access to the resources that made it easier for you to get such awards?"

"Of course I did," D'Ascoine said with a shrug of his shoulder, "and of course that gives me an advantage. But then again I was raised to rule, I have the personal experience and background that has trained me since birth to lead. Does that give me an advantage? Yes! However, when it comes to the welfare of society, I whole heartedly believe that we should be ruled by those best suited to do so. If part of the reason for that is tied to the social facts of their birth, so be it."

"And you don't think that is inherently unfair?"

"No."

"Unbelievable."

"When it comes to the good of society as a whole there are often injustices that we must accept." D'Ascoine put forward his empty glass; Alex obliged him.

"I think it is easier for you to accept because you are not the one facing the injustice," Samantha said, shaking her head before taking a sip of her gin-and-tonic.

"That is a good point," Alex said, finally deciding to add to the conversation, "but unlike its predecessor, Imperial Society is not simply a hereditary elite is it? It is in fact a meritocracy; those who prove their own abilities can in fact raise their social position and influence."

"Yes, in theory," Samantha said, turning an irritated eye to Alex, "but the fact is that it's easier to do so if you already have access to wealth and power. It was easier for Razza here to receive honors for his actions because he was more likely to be noticed in the first place. Just like it's easier to cover up one's failures with power as well."

"Actually," Razza said before Alex could react, "I would say I was more likely to have performed those actions in the first place because I was a hierarch."

"You are unbelievable."

"Thank you."

"Alright," Samantha said, leaning back as she tried a different tack, "let's say for one moment that you are more likely to perform such acts than a lay person… isn't it possible that's true because you have more invested in society? And that you have more to gain from ensuring that the society survives?"

"No, but even if that were true, don't you think that society should reward that fact regardless?"

"Not if it perpetuates an inherently unfair system." Samantha's gesticulation slopped some of her drink onto the floor. Alex pretended not to notice.

"Is it not society's role to ensure its own self-perpetuation?"

"And to improve its own nature," Samantha said. She was now perching on her seat, her face flushed. "We could make it a better society."

"Better by whose definition?" D'Ascoine asked.

"By many peoples."

"Whose?"

"Well obviously mine for one."

"And you still deny that you think you are better suited to govern than others?" Alex asked with a small smirk.

"Yes."

"But you are valuing your own views higher than those of D'Ascoine here?"

"Well yes, but that is because I am better educated in sophontology."

"Better educated by whose standard?" Alex asked, allowing a small half-smile form on his face.

"Well I do have a doctorate in the topic."

"Indeed you do," Alex continued, "a doctorate that you received because you came from a genetic background that made you physically and mentally capable of getting such a degree …."

"It wasn't just genetics!" Samantha clenched her fists. Alex thought she might actually stand up. "I received the degree because I worked for it! I earned it! As an individual."

"True." Alex's forced his smile to become less mocking and refilled her drink. "But what made you able to do so? What gave you the edge over those who did not complete their doctorate, or indeed didn't start one in the first place?"

"Well, my background I admit." Sipping her gin, Samantha leaned back in her chair. "I came from a family that encouraged such pursuits."

"Indeed you did, and that led you to pursue such a profession, and as a combination of both your own inherited traits and your social experiences, you received your doctorate."

"Yes. I was in fact lucky enough to have such a background, there were many who were not so lucky, but that doesn't make them inherently less worthy?"

"No it does not," Alex said, "But what it does do is make you an expert in sophontology where they are not. It makes you better suited to discuss and philosophize about such things than they are."

"Yes, but..." Her ears were beginning to redden.

"And you have this due to a combination of both your natural inheritance and your nurtural one. You are a better sophontologist than D'Ascoine here because you were raised with the values and the access to resources that allowed you to become so. Similarly, those raised to be rulers are better suited to rule because they have been given the access to those resources that allow them to become so."

"But that does not mean that there are not those outside the class, or in my case my profession, that do not have valuable insights or contributions to make."

"And our society allows them to make them!" Alex said, "They can move up the social ranks, and be recognized for doing so by performing well and having those attributes be recognized by society."

"But there are many who will continue to have no voice."

"That's true of any system," D'Ascoine said, helping himself to more brandy.

"You assume that the only way to have one's contributions to society recognized is to rule that society," Alex said quickly before she could respond. He didn't want her side tracked, not yet. It worked.

"Of course I am not saying that!"

"But you are saying you are right whereas the majority of the people in the Empire, indeed of Meridothia, disagree with you," Alex said, "You are in effect saying that people should agree with you because you know better than they do, but isn't that by its very nature anti-democratic?"

"No, I'm merely saying that one's ability to influence society should not be determined merely by birth." Samantha's gesturing once more spilled a small amount of her drink. She looked first to her hand, then at the droplets on the floor.

"But in Imperial society it is not." Alex watched as she used a napkin to wipe it up. "There are the meritocrats. Is it not simply possible that your denial of the intrinsic nature of social ranking is a denial of your own responsibility to society?"

"Oh, I would like to understand that comment," Samantha said. Sitting back up she looked for a place to put her wet napkin.

"Right-oh Skipper! You've got her there!" Razza spoke up suddenly as leaned forward and returned to his attack,

"Smith you are a mandellan, but you deny that you should take up the role of rulership. You're really just ducking your own responsibility!"

"I would say that by serving the state in the ways that I have, I'm not ducking my responsibilities, but rather use my skills where they are best suited."

"Well then so am I!" Razza said with a smirk of superiority, "I am serving in the military, where I have shown my skills and talents, and when I am done I will serve in the Senate – having gained a solid understanding of how combat is performed."

"But you won't have a solid understanding of how the everyday people of the Empire live their lives!"

"My dear girl," Razza said in his best condescending tones, "One does not have to be a pig in order to farm them."

"Give me patience," Samantha muttered as she rolled her eyes, "Nor does being born in a manor give one an ability to rule."

"True," Razza said, "there are servants, I suppose."

"Samantha," Alex interrupted before the argument degenerated even further, "Do you ever find your Egalitist sympathies at contrast with our mission?"

"How so?" she asked, arms crossed once more.

"Well, before the Empire, the Egalitists used to be solid allies with the Federalists, both speaking for a more egalitarian form of government."

"Well you could say the same about the Hegemonists, but I doubt very much that anyone would doubt the Ripper's animosity towards the terrorists."

"True, but the Hegemonist faction was never truly in favor of the kind of democratic elections that both the Federalists and the Egalitists' sought."

"No, but then again the Federalists opposed sentient rights, the corner stone of the Egalitists' views."

"It seems a relatively minor difference if you ask me," D'Ascoine added.

"Minor?" Samantha straightening in her chair, "It's absolutely fundamental to the difference between the two schools of thought! Federalists represent those who believe in democracy for human beings alone! All other races were to be subjugated to them…."

"Us technically," Razza said, trying, it seemed to Alex, to stir up the storm.

"Fine, us," Samantha answered, not quite rising to the bait, "Egalitists believe whole heartedly in democracy yes, but also in the equal rights of all sentient beings. In the end, you might even say that was the reason why the Egalitists stayed within the Imperial system and the Federalists went outside it… the most fundamental right of any sentient being is to live. The Egalitists do not believe that they have any right to force others to live the way we choose, while the Federalists seem to believe that humans, and their own political branch of humanity in particular, do have the right to tell others how to live their lives. If you ask me, they've missed the point completely.

"The point of democracy is that you can't force it on other people," Samantha continued, "and that it sees all people as equal with an equal say. So any terrorist is, by definition, betraying democracy. It's one thing to voice a political opinion, another to go so far as performing acts of civil disobedience or even warfare against the state, but terrorism and piracy are nothing more than cold blooded murder. Putting a political name to it is nothing more than an attempt to justify their crime-rings and make themselves feel better about their atrocities."

"Yes," Alex agreed as he leaned back. His chair reclined slightly in response. "But what about the peaceful wings of the Federalists? Any sympathy towards them?"

"Of course," Samantha said, "and perhaps such peaceful elements can be brought back into society. Even the guerrillas, well those who engage only military targets, even they have a chance."

"Isn't that argument somewhat semantic?" Alex asked, "How does it go? I am freedom fighter, you are a rebel, he is a terrorist?"

"There is a far cry from attacking military targets to attacking civilian ones captain," Samantha said. Her eyes were now narrowed, her voice rigidly calm, "Failure to recognize that is a crime more common in totalitarian states than in democratic ones!"

"I completely agree with you," Alex said and realizing he was striking too close to the mark, tried to turn the topic, "but if we are to catch our quarry, don't you think we should try to think like them a little? Find out what changes a person from being a peaceful demonstrator to fighter for freedom or a terrorist?"

"What motivates them?" Samantha said in openly angry and intoxicated tones, "What motivates them are the unequal chances across society! The lack of ability to rise above one's position and a feeling of desperation!"

"Thus you will never find any hierarch pirates," D'Ascoine added unhelpfully.

CHAPTER 18

"Gah, I can't believe how much I ache," Fran said, collapsing into her berth.

"Gunny's got you running the course, huh?" Bowman asked with a smile. He was laying down in his unit, reading with his feet up. "I swear between the training she's got you doing and the drills she and the ol' Razza Dazza run, I can't get any time on the practice range."

"So you've gotta lie in bed?" Fran said rolling her left shoulder to try and loosen the muscles, "Poor you. Tomorrow I'm supposed to be able to break down an AAR-5 in three minutes."

"Standard Marine practice," Bowman said, "Breakdown and build up your combat rifle. Only difference is we've got to do it blindfolded and a fuck of a lot faster."

"Yeah, but I'm not a Marine."

"Your in the ARAG now, Fran." Bowman put down his PAD and swung his legs over the edge of his berth. "If you're gonna stay alive you gotta know this stuff."

"I know, but I had no idea what I was getting into when I agreed to the transfer. I thought I would be… I don't know, fixing sensors and things."

"From what I can see you have been."

"You know what I mean."

"I do," Bowman said, "It's hard I know, but you're doing great."

"I don't feel like it. There's so much to learn."

"No one expects miracles, and maybe you should stop trying to do it all on your own."

"What do you mean?" She stopped rubbing her shoulder and frowned at him.

"I mean: I sleep about a meter away from you. You want help with the Mark Five, ask."

"But you've got your own shit to deal with, Ed."

"Did it ever occur to you that you are part of my shit? Do you really think I want you guarding my back with that pop-gun of yours? I mean a 0-G shotgun is all fine and good for crowd control and all, but it won't do much against even light body armor. Besides, in an ARAG we all watch each others' asses. It's what Special Ops is all about. Now come over here and let's look at that gun, huh?"

The *Hunter* lay silently at the edge of a star system that sat on a minor trade route deep inside the Alterande sector. With the dorsal hatch open and a web of antennae spread out for half-a-kilometer, the ship quietly listened to the wide range of the electromagnetic spectrum searching for the hidden and unseen. Lenses, dish receivers and myriad other sensor equipment stuck out from the uncovered modular bay, ruining the symmetry of the ship, but allowing the *Hunter* to fulfil her primary mission: spying.

It was the second week since they had begun their mission in earnest, seventh since they left the fleet, and so far they'd found nothing new. That, however, was hardly a surprise – surveillance took time and patience.

Samantha tuned the sensor array carefully before piloting one of the probes into a better position to cover a blind spot. Turning back to the analysis monitors, she saw nothing more than random noise. That too was expected. She logged it and began the system survey all over again.

"This is the XO," Samantha reported into the ship's log, "Oh-two-twenty hours, day One-Seven-Four Imperial. Completed third scheduled manual scan: no contacts. Engaging third AI scan… now."

Noting that the ship had initiated its auto-examination, Samantha eyed the status meters and decided to return to her investigation of Alex's past. Just before the two missing years of his record, Fotheringday had been investigating a local insurgency cell with connections to the Federalist movement. Then came the two year gap in his record followed by two years as a morale officer and one in customs duty. There was nothing out of the ordinary noted in either assignment.

That left the two missing years, and for details of that she had to wait for Sinner to crack the INI files. Sometimes, however, one could find as many answers by looking at a question obliquely as one could by seeking them straight from the source. As a result, Samantha turned to information from outside the services. She started with her only lead: the *Silver Slipper.*

"*Open query:* Silver_Slipper *in INI-db41174\Insurance Records\Attallic_Main,*" she gave the mental command, "*Show results.*"

She smiled as seven different files were returned to her. One was the initial listing of the ship, its description, categorization as a star liner, and the different coverage taken out on it and its crew. Two others were listings that involved minor accidents which occurred long before Fotheringday had even been assigned to the sector. The other four records, however, were dated to the end of the blackout period and appeared much more promising: Claim Report AttSec1471-A: Damages SS Silver Slipper, Claim Report AttSec1471-A.ec1: Errata and Corrections, Claim Report AttSec1471-A.InvRep01: Investigator Report of Damages SS Silver Slipper, and Payment Scheduling to File 1471/A: SS Silver Slipper.

Samantha took a quick review of the sensors, ensuring that nothing had changed around them, and then returned to the files. They read with the kind of language one could expect from insurance reports, perfunctory and to the point with numerous acronyms and focusing on monetary reports. Even so, they did contain extremely useful information. Whatever happened to the *Silver Slipper*, the ship was a complete write off for the company that owned it. A skim through showed that the damage was severe, the loss of life high, and that many of those who had survived required major surgery, organ regrowth and cybernetic replacements.

"*Sinner?*" she called, opening a private channel over the comms system, "*Could you take a look at something for me?*"

"*Actually, I was just shutting down for the night,*" the response came. He sounded groggy.

"*I'd just like you to take a look at this file, it shouldn't take long. It's an insurance investigator's report on the damage to that ship we were discussing.*"

"*Oh. Right. Send me the link.*"

Once she had set the engineer on reviewing the technical report, she focused on the remaining three reports in the order they were filed. The first showed that the ship had been mistaken for an insurgent's vessel in the Alhoro system and subsequently attacked by the *HMS Renfield.* The second report, the one noted *Errata and Corrections*, rescinded that information and instead suggested that the *Slipper* had been under attack by hijackers when the *Renfield* intervened. The final report listed the final payout to the company, including the coverage for the loss of life and personal items by the passengers and crew.

Samantha narrowed her eyes and called up the list Sinner had made of the trust funds that the Captain had set up out of his own personal accounts. Slowly and meticulously, she compared the list of payments by the insurance company to the list of recipients of Fotheringday's generosity. It wasn't an exact match, there were more individuals who received money from the Captain than those who had been paid by the insurance company, but the similarities were astounding. A quick examination of the recorded ship's manifest from the initial insurance report further confirmed the correlation. The then Lieutenant Alex Fotheringday had set up trust funds for the survivors and families of the victims of the *Silver Slipper* incident.

"*Sammy*?" Sinner said, "*Far as I can tell, all the damage to this ship happened as a result of some pretty heavy weapons fire. There's no indication of anything else… no on board hijacking attempt, nothing. External fusion and pulse laser fire, serious missile damage and the like.*"

"*All the kind of damage that you would expect to be caused by a Rapid Assault Corvette*?" she asked.

"*That would do it. Only exception is that according to the investigator's report, the ship's control systems might already have been down before the damage was done.*"

"*Interesting*," Samantha said, "*Thanks, Sin. Now get some sleep.*"

She leaned back and thought about what she had found. There was little doubt that there had been a cover up. Clearly the *Silver Slipper* had been attacked by the *Renfield*, an attack later blamed on piracy. However, the questions remained: why, and was it on purpose? Had Alex been on mission, intercepting a terrorist ship with hostages, had it been some kind of seriously black op, or had her new Captain been murderously negligent?

CHAPTER 19

"Chief? Are we supposed to be..." Fran started, but as she noticed the glazed eyes and trail of drool on his chin, she stopped. "Never mind."

She suppressed a shudder at the thought of his 'oneness' with whatever machine he was working with, and suppressed another when she thought of the web of wires linked to his nerves that allowed him to do it. *The whole thing is just gross, even if it does make him a better engineer.*

Looking back at the master engineering panel, Fran noted the readouts suggested that the system recharge would be complete in an hour and twenty-two minutes. After a day's powering up the HO drive the ship would be able to jump again, but there were still a thousand things left to do before that anyway. Their next transit would take them into a star system instead of the empty space they had been traveling through for the better part of a week. Being in system meant they would once more engage in their stealthy observations. They would deploy the sensor arrays, launch their satellites and then simply wait and watch the ships move around the system. Before they could do any of that, however, the Skipper had ordered them to realign the optical array...

again. After the past few weeks the process had become routine.

I can do this, Fran thought, *I am so totally checked out on this system. I know I can do this. Besides, the Chief is obviously doing something for the XO. Take some initiative Harpur! Do it yourself.*

She looked over the varying data in front of her, tuned the holodynamic displays to give readouts on the sensors, and then slipped on the display visor she wore whenever she wasn't wearing her helmet. Flicking a button on her belt, she activated the integrated gloves and plucked at the projected controls. She watched the series of drones and microbots activate and crawl their way to the optical array. She muttered commands into her microphone, typed others into her keyboard and tried to manually control one of the service drone manipulators using the holodynamic interface.

Damn it! She said as she over compensated and brought one of the telescopic lenses out of alignment. Taking a deep breath, she calmed herself and did it again.

Sinner makes it look so easy. Why the hell can't they make the holocontrols as sensitive as the ones that respond to implants? But she knew the answer, the implants responded to signals that were sent directly from the brain, cutting out the middle man of the i/o device. Still, she kept at it and eventually managed to get the optics with a 0.2 percent variance.

"Up to Astrographics standards," she said to herself, "Just the way the XO likes it."

Fran smiled to herself and let her visor clear just in time to find Sinner staring at her. *Was I supposed to get approval first*? She wondered as she blushed and began to stammer.

"Good work, kid," Sinner said before she could explain, "and you did it without even being asked. You got promise."

"Thank you, Chief," Fran responded, still embarrassed, "I wasn't sure if you wanted me to…."

"Normally no," Sinner said, "But I've been working overtime to settle some problems and, to be honest, I appreciate you taking initiative."

"Is that the project you're working on with the XO?"

"How'd you know about that?" Sinner asked cheerfully.

"I got my ways," Fran said mischievously, but noting the Chief seemed ever so slightly stressed by it, she added, "I noticed some stray signals while I was trying to figure out why we lost contact with that drone during the combat exercise. I tracked them down to a scrambled comms link between you and the XO."

"Really?" Sinner said, his eyes narrowing for a moment before he broadened his smile. "The Lieutenant and I have been working some bugs out of the predictive software she came up with, but we didn't want anyone to know about it until it was further along. You know, in case it's a complete flop."

"Would you like my help?" Fran asked, "I'm pretty good when it comes to programming, maybe I could lend a hand?"

"It's a nice thought," Sinner replied, "but I think you got your hands full enough for the time being. New ship systems, ship boarding drills, combat drills and, of course, the histories you've been reading on the side."

"How'd you know about that?"

"I got my ways too, kid. I appreciate the offer, but you should just focus on what you've already taken on, yeah?"

"Sure," Fran responded in a cheerful manner she didn't feel. She returned to her awkward manipulation of the ships systems.

Alex rubbed his eyes, trying to drive out the images of the *Silver Slipper* and focus on the present. It had been over a month since they'd entered the Alterande sector, yet he still hadn't found the correlations in the record that he was seeking. There was little doubt in his mind that the present pattern of activities in Alterande matched those of Achron three years prior. They had the same methods, same type of bombings and very similar guerrilla activity, only… only they were different, better.

Alex was missing something and he knew it. There was some connection between timing of the guerrilla attacks, the terrorist attacks and the piracy, but something was absent from his analysis. Some of that was no doubt due to the intentional lack of detail provided to him by the 253rd fleet, a fleet that was known to resent the glory and funding that went to Ripper's Raiders. Still, he felt that he was overlooking something else, something obvious.

He tried to compensate by searching through the ship's library, reading older and older reports from the archives of the 12th Fleet. Some were superb, like those written by Lt. Warren McGovern: ten years old and still seemingly appropriate. Others, however, seemed more superficial. Indeed, in many ways the more recent files seemed less apropos to his examination than the older ones.

Is that due to some return to older patterns? Some inadequacy in recent commanders? Alex wondered, *Or is it simply due to an increasing reluctance to share information between the fleets? I never found this kind of substandard reporting coming from the 253rd when I was in the 117th. Sir Richard would be disgusted, so would Hammond for that matter.*

Alex pulled his fingers through his hair and sighed. Looking at the image of Sally that sat on his desk, he thought of his duty, clenched his teeth, and returned to the files.

"Belay…!" Kyle Hammond woke to find himself sitting bolt upright in bed, drenched in a cold sweat. Next to him he felt the woman whose name he couldn't quite remember roll over. Light reflected off the chromed jackports implanted in her temples. Hammond thought he heard the distinctive snick of razor implants extending from her fingers.

"You alright?" her voice was calm, but not quite soothing. It had the heavy accent of a native of Lai-Jung Prime.

"Yeah. Dream," he said as he sat up on the edge of the bed. The woman grunted and rolled back over. He didn't hear the razors retract.

Hammond stood up and padded his way across the small cramped cabin to the head. Closing the door behind him, he sat on the edge of the sink/vanity without bothering to turn on the lights. He counted his breaths in rhythmic sets of twelve as he waited for his heart to stop racing, but he knew he wouldn't be able to fall back to sleep.

He opened the starcharts he kept on his implants and examined the different navigational data he kept there. Work might at least alleviate some of the aftershocks of having revisited the *Slipper* again. It had never worked before, but hope springs eternal. Besides, the recurring nightmare often fuelled him to greater successes than he accomplished when he was merely cold and calculating.

Closing his eyes, he looked at the maps, comparing the flight plans of Cameron-Inglesie ships related to different elements of the Federalist Insurgency. He noted how some of Sir Richard's freighters skirted the fringes of those areas where the Wayang Terror Cells were active, and how dangerously close they came to areas where Hectoro's Molly McGuires were known to operate. He decided he would need to alter some of the regular runs, just to be sure.

The decision would take fewer chances, and Hammond knew Sir Richard wouldn't like it. The hierarch preferred bold action, but as he himself had put it: they were underdogs in a hostile market. Sometimes bold action was needed to win, but sometimes a gram of caution was called for. With that thought, he closed the maps, opened his eyes and returned to his place next to the woman whose name he couldn't remember.

CHAPTER 20

"So tell me, Samantha, where did you learn to play tabula?" Alex asked. Smith was hunched over the race track of a game board, her eyes flitting between the pieces. Her arms were crossed, her lips tightly pursed and still this was the most relaxed he had seen her in his presence.

"I'm a sophontologist," she said without looking up from the board, "ancient games, and indeed any form of social reproduction is interesting to me. Besides, the mathematical nature of tabula, its descendent games like batgammon, or even like chess have always intrigued me."

She moved two of her polished emerald pieces so that they ended up in the same square, protecting each other from a "bump." Leaning back, she looked at her captain with a forced smile. Alex smiled back, took up the dice and rolled them: a four and a three.

She plays the odds, Alex thought, *and keeps a very close and defensive game.*

"And yourself?" Smith asked, "How did you come across a game from prestellar Earth?"

"Love of history, I suppose," Alex responded. He chose to move a single piece twice. It left the piece exposed but closer to the end of the track, "I've always enjoyed the study of the past, not just the knowledge of events, but the process of discovering them, if you know what I mean."

"I do," Smith said with a smile. It was perhaps the first honest smile he had seen on his XO's face.

"Do you ever regret it?" Alex asked, "Leaving the Astrographic Service?"

"Now and again." Her tone was once more clipped, defensive. She took up the dice and rolled a two and a five. "But there is a duty to perform here, and I can't spend my life hiding in the shelter of academia."

"Academia has its importance to society as well. Sometimes I wonder if I would have been better off pursuing a career as a historian."

"Really?" Smith replied, looking up from the board and meeting his eye.

The two of them sat silently for a moment, staring at one another. She was pretty, even for a Mandellan, and the intelligence that he saw working behind the prismatic eyes made her more so. He found it hard to believe that an intellect so powerful could be motivated by revenge alone. With views of democracy so close to the Federalists and views on Sentients in line with the Imperialists, he could not believe that even her parents' murder would drive her to the Hegemonists. Yet here she was; talented, intriguing and beautiful. From the edge of his vision he noted the strength in her long limbs, thought of the grace in her movements, and his mind went to Sally.

"It's your move," Alex said, clenching his jaw. Samantha leaned forward with a small smile and once more placed her pieces together in a defensive position.

"Oh my gah, Gunny!" Fran said, "Did you see how the Leftenant kicked the ass of that guy who shot you?"

"No, I was too busy rolling around the ground in pain," Chrom responded with an attitude.

"What?" Sinner said, "You got a grudge 'cause you took one in the sim?"

"It fuck'n hurt! Besides, the TOMO was taking unnecessary risks."

"I don't know," Bowman said, "you ask me, he's showing a fuck of a lot more guts than I would've suspected from a privileged army officer."

"Yeah," Chrom added "With other people's lives."

"He's real kick ass in a Simulation," Sinner said as he tossed beer packs to the others in order of rank.

"Oh you're one to talk," Bowman said, "I've never seen you go on a boarding mission at all."

"Hey! I was there today!"

"Riding a combat drone," Fran said, "Meanwhile here I am, just a little natural standing side by side with the Corps."

"She's got you there, Sin," Bowman said.

"There's danger in being a goa too." Sinner objected, "I could get hacked, get feedback..."

"Get shot?" Chrom said, "Face it there, Sinner old boy, the little girl's got you down."

"What can I say? I ain't stupid enough to put my body in harms way."

"Good point." Chrom chuckled.

"So you don't think Razza's any good as a TOMO?" Fran asked Chrom.

"Nah, he's okay," the Gunnery Sergeant said, "I was just sore 'cuz I got shot."

Fran looked at her for a moment. Something ever so slight in the Gunny's tone made her wonder if Chrom was being honest in her response. Chrom smiled in return and passed a beer.

"No matter what you think of his boarding actions," Bowman said, "One thing I gotta hand to the Leftenant, over the past few weeks he's gotten a fuck of a lot better on the guns."

"Just 'cause he hasn't killed us in a while don't make him an Ace there Corporal," Sinner answered.

"Hey, I'm just saying he's better."

"Do you think the Skipper has had something to do with that?" Fran asked.

"How you mean?" Sinner asked.

"The two of them have been spending a lot of time together," she said, "Do you think maybe he's been training him?"

"Could be," Bowman agreed, "that'd explain why his tactics have increased."

"Maybe," Sinner said, "Assuming the Skipper's any good himself."

"He seems that way in the sims," Fran said looking back at Chrom. For a woman who loudly disrespected anyone who wasn't a Marine, the Gunny was remaining very quiet on the topic of the CO.

"Who do you think's writing the sims, kid?" Sinner said.

CHAPTER 21

Alyiar tracked the incoming missiles as they broke formation, each a dozen meters above the ground, rocketing its course through the city. He targeted in on one, the fiber optic sensor leads grown into his retina picking it up, his implants taking over his eye muscles allowing him to follow the missile's supersonic speed. Aiming ever so slightly in front of its course, he pulled the trigger and felt the kick of the plasma rifle: had he not been enhanced, it would have thrown him to the ground. The missile exploded, sending a cascade of debris down into the already smoldering area of the city.

"Hundred thousand each," Rubo said from behind him. Alyiar kept watching the urban disaster of a battle field.

"What?" the local militia commander asked, disbelief raging in her voice, "I could buy them retail for..."

The ground trembled, then shook. A heartbeat later the detonation of the other missiles drowned out the rest of the woman's indignation. Had there been any glass left in the windows of the building around them, it would have shattered. Grey dust settled from the cracked concrete. In one corner of the city, a tall building collapsed in on itself. It had been one of the rebel's last observation posts.

"I don't see a feck load of retailers here talkin' to ye,'" Rubo said. Alyiar could hear the smile in his voice. There was some untold history between his leader and the head of the local freedom fighters, maybe from back in Archon. Whatever it had been, she was with Hectoro's people now; except that for the moment, neither Hectoro nor any other rival Federalist groups were here. Only the Wayang network had managed to run the Imperial blockade.

"We can't afford them, Rube." The woman's voice was almost pleading. It was the first time Alyiar had ever heard someone outside the Stalkers refer to Rubo by name.

Strands of the woman's dirty blonde hair escaped her ponytail and hung across her face. With a beseeching expression, she seemed desperate, pitiful, and out of place. Despite the weapons she wore, she looked more like an accountant than a guerrilla leader.

A distant boom sounded. Far out beyond the edge of the city, Alyiar saw the clouds of dust rise up on the edge of the plain. Even with his implants, he strained to see that far. Small arms fire sounded from some distant corner of the city. The sound of an RPG followed. Waves of mortars arced over them and a new series of detonations shook the ground.

"Looks ta' me that ya' can't afford not to have them," Rubo replied as the dust began to settle. He was obviously enjoying himself.

On the edge of the plain, Alyiar could see trees crumble as black dots moved out from the stand of sticks that had once been a forest. He raised his Mono-optic and saw the details of the latest threat. Each vehicle was the size of a house and covered with weapons: three super-howitzers, missile turrets, heavy plasma cannons and who knows how many RFPG's and other anti-personnel weapons. Imperial Armor was taking the field.

"Tanks," he said over his shoulder, "Imperial Rakasasha Class Heavy Armor."

Around each of the behemoths he saw an array of subcraft; flying, rolling, no doubt swimming and tunneling.

Mobile AI driven drones, each supporting their own parent vehicle with an array of combat accessories. These people were fucked.

"Goddammit Rubo!" the militia commander said, "You can see what we're up against!"

"Payback's a bitch ain't it?" Rubo said, "And this is just the Guardians… what'd ya think happen if they send in the Rangers like they're talking?"

"There are children out there…. Refugees who have nothing to do with this fight!"

"Yeah. Ninty-thousand."

Alyiar saw the tanks shake and a wall of smoke form. The bright tails of launching missiles shown through it.

"We still can't…."

"Incoming!" Alyiar yelled. The rolling thunder of the artillery sounded even as they began to run. A moment later wave after wave of shells began to detonate, marching forward towards their position. The ground buckled as the impacts occurred. They raced from the building.

Concrete was hurled into the sky and rained down across the city. Alyiar saw men and women scream, but the sound of it was drowned out by deafening blasts. Soon they vanished in clouds of smoke, or falling shells.

Leaping down the stairs to the metro, Alyiar took five steps at a time. Parts of the arching tunnels collapsed as they ran down to deeper levels. He tuned his eyes to infrared when he could no longer make out the passage ways. He no longer even cared if Rubo was behind him. He was running far too fast. He only stopped to check on his leader's welfare when they had gotten three levels down. He saw that Rubo was two steps behind him, carrying the rebel leader in one hand. She was coughing madly; Alyiar and Rubo's implanted filters saved them from that fate.

The dust settled and the ground stopped shaking by the time the woman managed to stop coughing up the debris that had filled her lungs. She was half sitting, half sprawled on the ground, looking up with daggers at Rubo and himself.

Her eyes were red with burst blood vessels. From the PAD on her belt, the desperate reports of panicked resistance fighters were coming in. Rubo bent down to her, the look of kindness on his face was betrayed by the malicious mischief in his eyes.

"We've got an installment plan if that'll help."

Sinner watched his Commanding Officer sit behind his desk, reading file after file. With the bulk of the INI files cracked, Sinner now spent most of his time spying on his "so-called-captain," figuring out what he was up to. Some of what Fotheringday looked at were modern reports of the Wayang, other files were those that he had brought along with him from Archon, and still others were archaic Intelligence; reports dating back thirty years. It was this last group that confused Sinner the most, for they went back to the point where the Ripper first took over the 12th Fleet, and some touched on neither Archon nor Alterand. Instead, they seemed to examine wider patterns of terrorism, and occasionally elements of fleet deployment. Still, none of them were directly about the Ripper; nor Samantha for that matter.

"It's his background as a historian," Samantha had said, "He's trying to get a fuller picture of what's going on."

"If you say so," Sinner had responded, but something seemed out of place about it. Still, he had never known Samantha to be wrong about such things. Besides, it was the more modern files that the CO seemed obsessed with.

Fotheringday spent most of his off-duty waking hours looking for some form of pattern shared between the two sectors. In one sense, he could see why. Technically speaking, there was a definite similarity in the kinds of devices that each used in their bombings. In fact, the new reports they had downloaded from a merchant ship they'd observed and hacked, showed the detonators used to take out a social club. They were identical to the type outlined in a report that Fotheringday had filed three years prior. The same could be said of the black-nano-tech the Wayang were using. That was particularly damning, as that the sources for those blackest of black weapons were extremely limited.

Even so, there were lots of differences too. A greater focus on money and a tendency to avoid direct confrontation with Imperial Forces were trade marks of the Wayang: not so with anything that had happened in Archon. Not to mention the clear and central leadership of Dalang and his creepy Wayang Stalkers. There wasn't any such obvious leadership in the Archon sector: at least not during the periods that the Captain kept revisiting. The Wayang also seemed better funded right from the beginning, with a fuck of a lot more smuggling ops. Why the CO was so convinced…

Fotheringday suddenly sat up in his chair and snapped Sinner's attention back to what he was looking at: a third rate recording of a kidnapping from some months back. After staring at the array of recordings in front of him, Fotheringday waved his hand and one of the numerous camera angles filled the room. Wayang Stalkers pulled out guns and moved around a nightclub, shooting body guards and manhandling hierarchs. Sinner switched his view to a different security camera to get a better look at the images.

"Stop," Fotheringday said, "Rewind one fifth speed."

Looking from a better perspective, Sinner watched the scene rewind. Men and women stood up as blood flew back into their heads, the strange tattooed ectomorphs strode backwards into the shadows. The images froze once more, and Fotheringday switched angles again, focusing in on one scene. Sinner peered closer, into the shadows where a well dressed woman seemed to be lurking. The recording ran forward and he watched as the figure slowly began to change shape. Her long bones stretched, her skull elongated. When she stepped once more into the light, curving tattoos marked her skin. The image began to run backwards once more, this time tracking the woman before she entered the shadows.

Sinner created a new file and fed the data stream into it, logging the filepaths and ensuring it recorded everything the CO did. For a moment he was impressed with the Commander, then he saw Fotheringday launch a pattern recognition program that looked for individuals with similar features appearing in other videos. His admiration for the man died at that point: it was a waste of time. After all, someone who had metamorphosing implants that could let them change the shape of their skull could no doubt change their appearance more subtly as well.

Bonehead, he said to himself.

Noting the time, he realized he had duties to perform. He toggled back to his body. Around him, the Captains Quarter's vanished and the comfortable clutter of Engineering took its place. He blinked water back into his eyes as he looked around. Across from him Fran sat at her station staring at him. As his eyes met hers she looked away as if she was embarrassed.

"What's up, Jackless?"

"Nothing, Chief," she said, blushing, "Just wondering if I should… er.. well wipe your chin before it chapped."

Sinner laughed and rubbed his mouth against his sleeve.

CHAPTER 22

Samantha walked around the bridge of the *HMS Renfield*, taking in the details. Thus far the sim-record had showed nothing out of the usual, and certainly nothing that would have justified the level of security systems set around it. Sinner had said that it was the hardest file he had ever hacked. Even given the Chief's propensity for exaggeration, that was still saying something. Had it not been for the excessive security placed around it, Samantha might never have examined the record, and certainly wouldn't have bothered watching as far as she had. Thus far it had shown little more than a change of command and a series of jumps. The virtual fortress that had been built around it, however, suggested that she view it in its entirety, no matter how mundane it seemed.

The image that hovered at the center of the *Renfield*'s bridge showed a slowly tumbling ship. A series of changing bar charts, text based readouts and twisting vector targeting resolutions were projected around it, noting every nuance of the star liner's slow spin. Reading them, Samantha saw the targeted vessel had an extremely low power output, but sensors suggested that the ship still had some working systems. That was suspicious.

Below the mass of holographic icons, in the Control Pit, the bridge crew of the *HMS Renfield* toiled in their sunken workstations. Some were plugged straight into the ship through their implants, others gestured to their holodynamic interfaces. Among the latter was a single sentient alien, a petty officer whose long armored flight suit vaguely resembled a giant arthropod. Some of its crew mates gave the sophont a wide berth; others seemed to pay it no mind at all.

As for herself, Samantha placed her avatar on the Quarter Deck, a raised platform that spanned the bridge and separated Command and Control from Tactical Command. Next to her was Alex, standing tall in his black armored flight suit trimmed with gold, legs shoulder width apart, arms held behind his back. Young, handsome and confident, he looked the model of both a Naval officer and an Imperial hierarch.

Samantha found herself staring at him, not quite able to overcome how young he seemed. It was as if he had aged far more than the four years that had passed from this recording. What ever had happened, had certainly taken its toll.

"Lock targets and charge weapons," Alex said, his refined, aristocratic voice had not changed. The commands were repeated in chorus by the men and women in the Gunnery Control pit behind him. "Has there been any response to our hail?"

"None so far, Skipper," the man next to him replied. Samantha knew him from the other files, Sublieutenant Hammond, a junior line officer who had worked with Alex before. According to what she had gathered, Hammond would have been in charge of this mission, but Alex and his line commander, Sir Richard Al Escobar, had used their influence to convince the powers that be that Fotheringday was the better man for the job.

If Hammond held any resentment, he didn't show it. He stood to Alex's side, hands gripping the command rail before him, loyally carrying out Fotheringday's commands. Hammond's own black and silver flight suit was not quite a striking as that of his new found CO, but he looked every centimeter the professional as his eyes darted over the varying displays. Occasional navigational icons popped into the air around him, reducing from hologram to the rail monitors once acknowledged. Samantha admired his abilities with both Navigation and sensors.

"They just keep playing the same message," he reported, "continuing their distress call and noting the ship's ID as the *Silver Slipper* out of Antillis."

The name caused Samantha's head to snap around. She felt the blood suddenly drain from her as the ramifications of what she was watching sunk in. She swallowed hard and her avatar's finger rubbed its thumb.

This is it. She thought of contacting Sinner, but she knew he was asleep. Between cracking the files, spying on Alex, and training Fran, not to mention doing his duties, he needed his bunk time more than anything. For a second, she considered waiting to watch it until he was awake, but only for a second. She had searched for too long to discover her CO's secret. Her eyes widened and she began to note every detail.

"Very good, Mr. Hammond," Alex said, "Helm, maintain course. Gunnery, prepare to engage."

It was a dangerous situation; Samantha had been in similar one's herself. This ship, the *Silver Slipper*, was broadcasting a wide band distress call, and it could well be exactly what it claimed. Then again it could also have been an insurgent vessel playing dead, trying to lure an unsuspecting merchantman in before opening fire or engaging in a boarding action. The fact that Alex, an Intelligence Officer, was here in command of a Rapid Assault Corvette showed that he and Al Escobar suspected the latter. How he had known to be here, at these precise coordinates? That was another question.

"Sensors, are there any new contacts in the system?" Alex asked.

"No new contacts detected, sir," the sentient answered. Samantha noted that Alex seemed to call on the Sophant more that he did the others. In contrast, Hammond seemed to avoid looking at it, a reaction that Samantha saw frequently among the Raiders.

"Mr Hammond, would you please begin a verbal RVD?"

"72053 meters… 72048…. 72036 meters… 72024… speed differential 200 kmh… distance 72012… 72000-"

"Mr. Hammond?" Alex interrupted, "I don't suppose you could use a base ten system instead of base twelve could you?"

"Sorry sir," Hammond said, blushing with some embarrassment, "my people use…"

"It's quite alright," Alex said, "just continue with the Imperial norm."

"71910… 71900… sir we'll be at optimal fire range on my mark. Four, three, two one….Mark!"

"Very well. Tactical, open fire. All weapons."

Samantha's response mirrored that of Hammond, both turned to stare at Alex. As the command was parroted behind them, Samantha saw Hammond open his mouth. He stammered out an objection, but it was too late. The *HMS Renfield* opened fire on the small drifting vessel.

"You son of bitch," Samantha said, staring at the younger version of Alex, "Do you know what you've just done?"

Explosions wracked the ship as the pulses from fusion cannons hit home and the lasers sliced across its hull. Fires erupted all around it as missiles exploded close enough to damage, but not so close as to destroy. Text appeared around the image, noting the changes in the ship's tumbling speed and trajectory.

Alex had completely ignored regulations. He had opened fire on a civilian vessel without clear provocation. Even if he did suspect it was an insurgent trap, rules of engagement specified that he could not fire on it until it had fired on them.

"What could have possessed you?" she asked the recording. Alex's image stood tall and proud in response.

The outcome of the combat was never in doubt; the battle was never going to last long. The *HMS Renfield* was a Rapid Strike Corvette designed for precisely this kind of mission. She was essentially an engine with four fusion cannons, six missile batteries and twenty rapid pulse lasers. She was not stealthy, she was not subtle, and she did not have a very great range, but the *Renfield* was extremely fast, extremely maneuverable and exceptionally deadly. Even if the *Slipper* had been a Federalist Corsair, she would never had stood a chance, but *Silver Slipper* had not even been that.

Samantha watched the rest of the sim confirming what she had feared for months. She filled with disgust as Alex called for the *Renfield* to quiet her guns, then authorized the boarding party. What followed then only made the situation worse. Expecting insurgents at any turn, the Marines stalked through the ship expecting an ambush. As one squad made a familiar path through the destroyed hyber chambers, Samantha watched the horrible realisation of his mistake pass over Alex's face. Again, too late. Trusting the intelligence of their highly decorated mandellan hierarch of a leader, the second squad simply opened fire when came across a small group of survivors. Alex shouted out the desperate order to cease fire, but by then the damage was long past done.

Still the recording did not end and Samantha watched Alex as he stood on the bridge trying to hide the trembling of his hands. His eyes darted back and forth, as if he were desperately trying to see where he had gone wrong. He called up the navigational charts authored by Hammond and compared their position to the coordinates he projected from another file. Samantha checked them as well. They matched exactly. He checked another file, and again she saw that they matched exactly. He stood dumb for a moment, then left the files open and walked over to his XO. Hammond had been throwing up in the corner.

"Mr. Hammond," he said, standing straight and proud as if nothing had happened.

What now? Samantha asked.

"I am relieving myself of command," Alex said in a matter of fact tone, "The *HMS Renfield* is yours."

Samantha turned off the simulation in disgust and stared with fury at the walls of her berth. It seemed fairly clear now that they were dealing with an incompetent after all; one whose power allowed him to dodge the bullet he so rightly deserved. The records showed that his colleagues and crew were not so lucky; his fellow officers had been mothballed. They were given dead end jobs or drummed out of the service. Al Escobar was assigned to some innocuous post in the 253rd that was significantly below his grade. As for Hammond, he was signed on as Navigational Officer on a transport vessel for the 117th and mustered out of the service not long after. The Marine Officer, Leftenant Ch'teng also retired and went into private security; each of their careers had been ruined.

And Fotheringday? After killing a ship filled with innocent civilians, he had been shoved off to some minor duties for three or so years while the records and memories of his crime were buried and forgotten. Waiting an appropriate period in hiding, he returned to Naval Intelligence, and even managed to convince the Ripper that he should serve in the Raiders.

But that doesn't make sense, Smith thought as she stared at the roof of her bunk, *Why the hell would the Ripper help the son of his rival? And why would Van Trappini let an incompetent into the ARAG of all things? The ARAG is his best of the best… and neither Van Trappini or the Ripper would endanger it, not to mention hobble my ability to run my network. Not without good cause. Clearly, I'm missing something.*

"This is excellent work, Harpur," Lieutenant Commander Fotheringday said with a broad smile, "Excellent work."

"Thank you sir," Fran responded, barely able to keep from beaming with pride.

"And you are certain they haven't detected your surveillance?"

"Certain?" Fran said with a sudden frown, "No sir, I'm not certain. They could be leading me blind... I mean, like, I don't think they have any idea that I've been phreaking their stream or listening into their conversations, but… well… the Chief is pretty amazing, and the Exec… well you know…"

"I do know," Fotheringday said with a warm smile, "They are considerable opponents, but sometimes that very superiority creates a bit of vulnerability. So as far as you are aware, they do not know of your observation?"

"Not as far as I'm aware."

"Excellent, Harpur. Keep up the good work."

"Yes sir," Fran said, but inside she felt a twinge of guilt.

"Something bothering you Fran?" the Skipper spoke with a kindness in his voice that reminded her of her father.

"Not really, sir, it's just…. well I feel kinda bad about it sir."

"About what? The exercise?" the Captain said with a smile, "No need. This is designed to keep everyone on their toes. By spying on your shipmates, you are helping to identify their weaknesses, and the same is true of their attempts to hide what they are doing. It's just like the combat drills only in intelligence gathering, we constantly work to improve."

"But they don't even know that I'm watching them."

"Just as would be the case if an enemy was watching them. Keep feeding me their communications and you will be helping make them and the rest of us safer. You've identified one vulnerability already… they do not suspect you are a threat because you are a natural, but what they see as a disadvantage is exactly what you are using as a strength. If you could be both, you would be the perfect spy. As it stands, I think you make a very good operative just as you are. Now, you are dismissed, I suggest you get some rest. You probably need it."

"Thank you, sir," Fran said, "I will."

When she walked back into her quarters, Bowman was shadow boxing a holograph. She shook her head and began to hum as she opened her bunk. Plopping down, she saw Bowman stop his exercise and stare at her.

"What?" She asked, still beaming.

"Why are you so happy?" he asked, "The way you've been working, I would have thought a long bitch session was in order."

"Oh I don't know," Fran replied, "I guess things are finally starting to make sense."

"Really? Now that's something to worry about."

CHAPTER 23

Outside, a brightly plumed bird flew across the sunny bay as picturesque waves crashed onto the private beach belonging to Cameron-Inglesie Distributors. Inside, Sir Richard Al Escobar, CEO of said company, sat at the oversized boardroom table listening to the local Vice President of Cargo Development drone his excuses about the downturn in revenue. Following the flight of the bird, Sir Richard wished he were outside. He didn't really need to hear the excuses, eleven years as a well decorated Naval Intelligence Officer and a lifetime of training made him more than capable of knowing what was going on with his business. He stifled a yawn and turned his attention from the window to the vast array of holographic maps and graphs orbiting the room.

Why do people seem to think that boring reports can be made less so with pretty pictures? Across from him, an attractive woman whose name escaped him looked equally bored. She was the local Head of Security, and had requested a private audience with Sir Richard later in the day. He wondered if it was for personal or professional reasons.

Like many individuals living on the Imperial Fringe, she wore her implants as a bold statement rather than a subtle tool. The jack ports at her temples were polished chrome and an otherwise realistic prosthetic hand gleamed with copper. It did little to improve her looks to Sir Richard, and he wondered if it was her actual preference or if she did it to be less conspicuous in the region. According to Hammond she was quite competent at her job.

"As you are no doubt aware," the VP said, pointing to the web of routes that crossed the mains, "The company's traditional focus has been on marginal routes that extend off of the mains, while under your adept leadership, we have actually opened new routes along the mains that directly compete with the megacorporations and have broadened our interest into non-shipping related interests as well."

He noted the map of terrorist and pirate activity in the Alterande sector and in his mind's eye, opened up the map that Hammond had provided him. *Do these people really think they can get better information than I can?*

"These new initiatives have proven extremely successful," The Vice President said, "Far more so than the old routes. To that end, it may well be time to reduce our more rural routes and focus wholly on the Mains."

A small frown lighted upon the brow of Sir Richard, and he uploaded one of the Cameron-Inglesie route maps directly onto his implants. Overlaying the company map and Hammond's, his frown increased. He added a third map, provided by his former INI colleagues in the 253rd.

"While building our manufacturing capacity and continuing to broaden our interests." Though his boring tones never showed the slightest waiver of emotion, a tiny tick appeared below the VP's eye shortly after Sir Richard's first frown.

The hierarch barely noticed, instead examining how the buffers around different Federalist cells overlapped. The paths of his company's ships passed in and out of these regions in a carefully orchestrated manner intended to avoid any unexpected surprises. Yet Hammond's map showed that some of the ships under the former Naval officer's control had been rerouted away from the areas where the core Federalist cells were active.

"By using ships capable of greater jumps we can travel more quickly along the mains than the standard vessels," the Vice President said, now visibly sweating, "Up until now we've kept these ships for long hauls to remote systems, but by redirecting them to the mains we will be able to compete directly with the larger companies. This will also avoid the less patrolled routes and thus increase convoy security during this period of increased terrorism. In fact, I feel that…."

"Haven't the Federalists recently refocused their attentions onto the mains?" Sir Richard said, keeping the maps open in his mind's-eye. Multi-tasking was another skill he'd learned while serving with INI.

"Not… not that I'm aware, sir," the VP was now looking at his Head of Security.

"I'm certain I saw a recent release by that horrible tattooed ectomorph stating that the mains were their new targets." Sir Richard turned his attention on the woman with the highlighted implants.

"I haven't seen any reports to that effect," she said, turning to him with a calm, professional aloofness, and perhaps the slightest hint of a knowing smile, "Though…"

Her exception was never finished. An explosion ripped through the room, and splinters of wood flew through the air. Sir Richard instinctually covered his face; slivers drove into his hands. He was blown backwards, falling head over heels, and rolling as he hit the ground. The bomb wasn't large, not by the standards he had seen in Archon, but the explosion was enough to drive a plank of the shattered boardroom table through the torso of the man next to him.

Sir Richard looked about the room, his ears ringing from the blast. He saw a spider web of cracks spread across the windows separating the bay from the meeting room. Dust began to billow through the room, far more than he would have expected.

Coughing heavily, Sir Richard shook his head and tried to stand, but a spike of agony shot through his skull. He stumbled back to his knees. Pressing his hands against his eyes, he inhaled sharply as the pain spread. That caused him to cough even more.

Across the room he heard the high pitch scream of a woman rise above the other cries and moans. Forcing himself to look up, he saw the local Head of Security on her hands and knees, keening loudly. Her face was contorted with pain. At first he could see no more damage to her than anyone else, cuts, scrapes, a peppering of splinters imbedded in her skin. He almost told her to shut up.

Then he saw it happen, blood began to drip from her nose. Her eyes began to redden, forming red tears. A scarlet foamy mass began to bubble from the edges of her jackports. Her body began to tremble.

"*Black-nanotech.*" Her message was broadcast across the Cameron-Inglesie Emergency Network, just before she collapsed. That she managed to send it astounded Sir Richard, his own agony was too great to even think. The pain behind his eyes kept growing as windows randomly opened and closed across his vision. Slowly, everything faded to white.

"I'll be honest with you, sir," Chrom said, standing at-ease in front of Fotheringday's desk. At first, she had found the leather bound books projected on the wall comically ornate, but over the past few weeks she had begun to find them almost soothing. "Getting the Leftenant to listen to suggestions has not been the easiest assignment I've ever had."

"I recognize that, Gunnery Sergeant," Alex said, nodding towards the occasional chair with a smile, "but it does seem to be working. His recent approach to ship's tactics are far better suited to our mission."

"I think that may have more to do with your sessions with him than mine sir." Chrom sat down, but even reclining, she kept her professional demeanor.

"Nonsense. It is a two pronged attack, and it is working well. What is your view of his handling of troops?"

"The Leftenant is still a bit reckless, sir, but sometimes that's what's needed."

"I will be keeping an eye on that."

"Thank you, sir. I'm sure we'll be fine."

"I am lucky to have you, Gunnery Sergeant. You have not only managed to help with the Leftenant, but to keep the process hidden from your colleagues."

"It isn't good for troops to doubt their officers, sir."

"Indeed. What about the others? You think we are ready for the real thing?"

"No one's ever ready for the real thing sir, but they're about as ready as they're gonna get. In the end, who can tell what's gonna happen in a real firefight?"

"Certainly not me," Alex replied. Chrom noted the muscles in his jaw slowly working.

Whatever else she thought about her CO, Samantha had come to realize that Alex Fotheringday was prolific. The number of summaries, reports and analyses coming out of his team seemed to increase geometrically during his tenure as second in command of intelligence for the *HMS Stoker*'s Cruiser group. Yet, despite her initial irritation by this fastidious documentation, Samantha gradually found herself intrigued by their content.

His two hundred page history of insurgency and conflict within the Achron Sector initially seemed nothing more than an indulgence in his love of academia. As she read, however, she saw how he traced the change in ground tactics and terrorist targets and demonstrated an increase in outside influences in the regional insurgency. He showed how local causes that had nothing to do with the Federalists had been co-opted, and how that had flavored the Archon movement with a virulent form of xenophobia.

Twenty reports summarized different shipping records, helping create a model for assessing likely targets. The prediction of the attack on the *Silver Slipper* was included in that model, and while events apparently proved that hypothesis wrong, Samantha could find no mathematical fault in the process. Indeed, three other attacks had been successfully stopped using that model.

"So why did you decide to command this particular mission and not the others?" she said, closing those cases. Stretching in both her bunk and her interface room, Samantha looked out at the sunrise across the fjords of her homeland and smiled at the distant call of the merodothites and the closer bellow of a sealshark. A cool breeze blew in across the ocean, and the smell of bacon drifted to her from inside the simulation of her mother's exploration craft; a reminder alarm that she should not forget to eat.

A lesser investigator might have stopped after finding the record of the massacre, others merely skimmed the rest of the files, but knowing what had happened didn't tell Samantha why. Why Alex had made the tragic mistake? More to the point, why had the Ripper assigned him to the *Hunter*?

Yawning, she ignored her stomach and pressed on to the next report. Sinner was cracking the last of the files, and she was getting near the end. Soon she'd be focusing on the investigation reports and recordings preceding the *Slipper* incident. Those would be the telling elements, but the other data, summaries and analyses were giving her a significant insight into her skipper. They showed that his analytical abilities were strong, despite having made such a heinous error. She opened the next file.

It began like many of his others, noting the long history of insurgency in the region, and how it changed with the influence of the Federalists. It paid particular attention to the increase in the use of black nano-tech and the financial emphasis of some of the insurgent activities, patterns that matched what they were now seeing in Alterand. Then she found what she was after:

…It is therefore suggested that an operation to capture a Federalist ship engaging in pirate activities within a two system sweep could readily supply us with linking agencies between local insurgency and the Federalist operations within the Alterande Sector. There is no need to emphasize the value of obtaining a Linking Agent, and the increase of activities within the Attallic Main clearly suggests the presence of such an operative….

Samantha sat up in both the real and virtual worlds. Her eyes narrowed to the sun that hung low on the horizon.

"A Linking Agent, Alex? If you had captured one, or just their ship's information systems, you would have carried off quite a coup."

Intel like that could have tied together whole networks, and perhaps even broken the back of the insurgency in that sector. It was typically arrogant of Fotheringday to think that he could apprehend a Linking Agent, but also explained why he had wanted to command the mission himself, and why he had been so aggressive. A Linking Agent might well have suicided rather than been taken captive, and a nuke or properly rigged overload of the engines could have taken out the *Renfield* as well. A fear of losing both the intel and his crew might almost have been enough to have explained his recklessness, but not quite. To act on hypotheticals without solid proof, was there anything that might justify such a grievous disregard of caution?

Samantha closed the files and thought of her own choices after the death of her parents.

CHAPTER 24

"There you go," Alyiar said, putting down the last of the crates. He wore the form of a large black man with a scar down his cheek. A new look for a new planet; a new front for the revolution.

"That's enough antibiotics, bandages and food-bars to last three months," the woman said, "I can't thank you enough."

He thought her name was Pip, but he wasn't sure. Her hair was brown, her eyes the same. She was wholly unremarkable, but the kindness and gratitude in her eyes made her more attractive than any woman Alyiar had seen in a year.

"It's why we do what we do," he said.

Behind them the blue plastic tarp that served as a door flapped as the driving rain drummed steadily on the plastic roof. The walls were cinderblock, the floor mud. A hand full of men and women moved the supplies into a tin-lined hole in the middle of the room. Below them were a series of tunnels where the goods would be stored. This time there were few weapons in the shipment, though the goods were still stolen.

"It's what keeps these people alive." She smiled and he could not help but smile back.

Outside, countless refugees struggled on the edge of a city of five million. Once, before the Sophyans arrived, the city had been wealthy and growing, now it was crippled by the influx of those escaping the violence. Even so, there were still nightclubs and restaurants where the wealthy sat in luxury while the displaced were forced to settle on the unstable slopes of mud.

The tarp was suddenly pulled back and Rubo strode in. He was soaking wet, and it made the bulge of his side arm plainly visible through his jacket. Fortunately, few if any of the local gendarme ever came to the slum on the hill.

"We set here?" Rubo asked. He had to shout to be heard over the rain.

"More or less," Alyiar responded, more to the woman than to Rubo, "but there's a good chance this whole place could slide into the valley."

"*Not our problem, mate*," Rubo broadcast, but said, "It's feckin' terrible I know."

"I've been trying to get them to move for a year," the woman said, "but there isn't really anyplace to go. The fighting in the highlands keeps driving people off their lands and…"

"I wish we could help," Rubo said, "but we've just got our marching orders."

"Where to?" Alyiar asked.

"Back inside. There've been developments."

It was code. Rubo had been summoned by the Dalang, Alyiar would take the other Stalkers to Lai-Jung. Orders would follow.

Alyiar nodded and turned to say goodbye to the woman. He found himself in a sudden embrace. He had to stop his reflex to snap her spine.

"Thank you," she whispered into his ear. Her body was soft, gentle and warm. A subtle waft of spice came from her hair. He closed his eyes and felt a long forgotten ache inside, but Freedom's Struggle would not wait.

"Frankly, Sir Richard, the doctors say the only reason you weren't killed is that your implants were Imperial military grade. Even so, if you had anymore of them, not even Imperial safeguards would have saved you."

Sir Richard looked at his aide and nodded. The green décor of the company med-bay seemed odd without a doctor, but Sir Richard had sent away the medical staff for the moment. He turned his still aching head to the local Vice President, whose face was heavily bandaged.

"Did your Head of Security make it?" he asked.

"Never had a chance," the VP said.

Sir Richard nodded, his eyes narrowing. There was an awkward pause before he stood on shaky feet.

"Either that bomb was intended as a message," he said, steadying himself, "or she was the intended target. I suspect the former."

"Why would…?" the VP asked.

"The price of success," Sir Richard said, pointing towards his torn jacket. His aide grabbed it at once and brought it to him. "There are a series of ships out of Lai-Jung that were rerouted by one Mr. Hammond. I'd like them returned to their previous courses, understood?"

"Yes, sir," the VP said; his face said otherwise. It didn't matter, as long as it was done.

"I want my ship ready," Sir Richard said to his aide, "have them plot a course to Lai-Jung."

CHAPTER 25

Samantha opened one of the last recorded sims documenting Alex's investigation prior to the *Slipper*. Thus far, nothing she had seen justified his reckless choice to fire on a civilian ship, nor the Ripper's blatant disregard of it. Pretending she was reading a Sophontological report, she dropped into the recording and let the pixels fall. As a scene materialized in front of Samantha, the simulation drove out the confined space of her berthing unit.

She was in a cool and quiet park with small patches of snow still clinging in the shadows of the trees. Muddy grass clung to the shoes of those few mid-morning strollers who frequented the banks of the swollen river. It was too early in the season for any but the most dedicated of joggers, and too early in the morning for care-giving parents to push their prams along the pathways. Still, the turbulent waters made for very picturesque viewing from the calm safety of the park for those souls who cared to venture out. White caps churned on the water and, as the river threatened to spill its banks, the sound of large rocks thundering down the channel bed punctuated the deafening roar. It was all safe, of course, all predicted, and all exactly as it should be according to the science of terraforming. Even so, the mesmerizing power of the water and the empty promise of it breaking its restraints still drew a handful to its banks, to watch and witness – and dream.

Samantha saw few such dreamers on the morning that the recording was made. A young couple stood by the rivers' edge and talked furtively between themselves, a sentient non-human who fumbled with an image recorder made for human hands standing some distance down the bank, and a shabbily dressed man lay huddled on a sheltered bench under the tatters of what might once have been a blanket. Occasionally another man or a woman would stroll by with a pet or a child, but that was rare.

Looking at the angles, Samantha quickly calculated that there must have been seven recording devices, but she could only account for five of them. Clearly somewhere in the scene there were other observation points that were being manned. The team doing the surveillance must have been very good, deserving of the reputation that the *Stoker*'s Cruiser Group had once mustered. She unconsciously nodded with technical respect and returned her attention to the focus of the recording.

The sentient alien, a Miltrhope, occasionally drew her attention as it burbled to itself and used its traction bladders to move its long thin carapace into a better position to capture its desired image. As it did, the vaguely bug-like creature nearly dropped the three lensed recorder. It managed to grab it last minute with the small sucker covered bladders it used in place of hands, and issued a series of clicks that she recognized as a mild form of swearing. Its burbling noise returned as it raised the device to its twelve eyespots and focused on whatever it was the creature was trying to record. She felt a touch of empathy towards its struggle to live in a world made for a different species.

Yet the Miltrhope was not the focal point of the recording: that was the young couple, who also appeared to have noticed the creature. They seemed to feel anything but sympathy for its dilemma, however, and shot the occasional disapproving glance towards it. She heard the occasional pejorative term wafting from the couple before they inevitably turned their attentions back onto themselves. After a period of impatient glances and meaningful glares, the couple stole an uncomfortable kiss while the creature continued chirping to itself and fiddling with the recorder. Before long they returned to their intense conversation.

The man on the bench appeared oblivious to all of it as he muttered incoherently, scratched obscenely, and shifted his tattered blanket. Samantha noted that the woman occasionally looked at him as she spoke in hushed tones to her companion, but did not seem overly concerned with the ragged man. This came as no surprise to Samantha, according to the ancillary files on the Attallic capital, the number of homeless in the city had increased after the rise in guerrilla and terror attacks in provinces. Many refugees had been sent across the world and the Imperial Relocation effort had been fairly good about finding them housing. The subsequent partisan actions, however, had put additional stress on the system and refugees had become more common. As was frequently the case, it seemed that here too those who were least able to look after themselves were those most likely to fall through the cracks.

The Miltrhope let loose a high pitched squeal, drawing both Samantha and the couple's attention back to it. With a bubbling glee, the sophant looked at the image that it had somehow managed to take, and with what passed for a smile, made its way further down river to attempt to master its art in a different location. The couple looked up once it left and began speaking a bit more freely. Samantha moved closer to hear what they had to say.

"You're sure this is the right data?" the woman asked, pushing a long strand of dirty blond hair behind her ear.

The man grunted in response, and then looked back in the direction that the alien had wandered off.

"If the information isn't right, then it's of no use," she said, a fierce look in her eyes.

"Feckin' bug eyes," he muttered, "there was a time when a thing like that wouldn't have been allowed out in this city, not to mention been able to afford a top notch…."

"Look," the woman said in sharp but hushed tones, "if these coordinates are not right…."

"They're feckin' right!" the man replied, "That's the course they'll take. You hit 'em there, you'll get what you're after. We just better get the guns in return for the info. My people've got the bloody Guardians coming down on us in Pro'torin province. Not the local militia, I mean feckin' Imperial Guardians! If we don't get some feckin'…"

"Keep your voice down," the woman said, "I know you… we… need the weapons. I know. But we can't give you the shelbies until we get them from the Federalist Central Council, and they won't give them to us until we get our dues."

"Sometimes I think you Feddies are more interested in your dues than the fight."

"Your business is only a tiny bit of our industry," she said glancing around as if worried that her companion might already have drawn undue attention, "You'll get the shelbies when we do, and we'll get them after we do our business. Got it?"

"I'm not a feckin' idiot."

"Sometimes I wonder."

"Oh thank you very much."

"That last bomb…."

"Got 'em scared," the man said, "It got 'em worried."

"It made a mess," she said looking back at the river, "It was children, Rube. That doesn't make for good publicity."

"It was mostly bug-eyes, slymmies and slithers. They don't have children, they have spawn."

"There were humans there too. Little limbs don't make for good viewing no matter what the species, but any humans…."

"They were loyalists! Thing-lovers! Imperialist-running-drones who…"

"I know what they were," the woman said, "but right now the shipment is more important than a statement. No bombs, no sniper attacks, not even any raids on military sites. Not one."

They stood quietly for a short time longer, looking at the roiling river. Samantha thought their cover as lovers was strained by the hostility they felt towards each other, but might have held for the casual observer. Each continued to shoot the occasional glance over their shoulder, the man more frequently in the direction of the alien, the woman towards the homeless man. They kissed again, though no more comfortably this time than the last, and trading small packages, separated and left the park individually as if they had never met.

A text screen opened noting a scrambled, randomized and encrypted signal was being broadcast, one that matched INI standards. It ordered a surveillance team to follow the movements of the couple as they made their independent ways back home, but the simulation remained focused on the park. Samantha speeded up the recording, waiting for something to happen. She slowed it down when the ragged man clenched his tattered blanket tightly around himself and stood up. He was a big man, far bigger than he had appeared when huddled on the bench. His movements were slow, shuffling and deliberate, as if each action was painful. He rubbed his eyes and coughed before mumbling obscenities to himself once more.

After brushing the odd bits of rubbish off of himself, he shuffled with a slight limp over to the river's edge and bent down close to the muddy earth. He began to gently prod the ground where the couple had been standing, as if looking to see what treasures they might have left behind. If she hadn't been looking for it, Samantha might not have noticed the sudden movement as a snake-like drone slithered through the muddy grass and ducked into the rags that served as his clothing. The man didn't react to it immediately. He stayed crouched by the bank and continued to fiddle with the sodden earth.

Finally, he awkwardly raised himself up to stand on unsteady feet, coughed out a wad of phlegm, and shuffled towards the garbage containers. He rummaged through them for a few moments before weaving his way out of the park. Samantha froze the image and approached the man. Only then did she recognize him. Alex and his observation drone had been the last two points of reference, the ones she couldn't calculate.

It was a good disguise, and a good surveillance op. Had she not been watching this as a recording, she never would have identified any of the different surveillance stations. The man and the woman, the Federalist and the local insurgent, seemed to have no idea they were being recorded. She knew from the records that Alex had let them go. There was no indication, none what so ever, that they had known they were being observed. His conclusions seemed solid: these people were planning an assault on a merchant ship, and doing it at the time and coordinates that the *Silver Slipper* was intercepted. The dead man's roll, the corollary data, everything suggested a pirate-style ambush that had never happened.

"No wonder you fired so freely," she said to the image of the captain dressed as a tramp, "You were set up."

"I'm so very glad you think so." Alex said, but his voice did not come from the recording. Toggling out of the simulation, Samantha looked up to see her CO looming in the door of her berthing unit, the door that she had locked shut.

CHAPTER 26

"How long have you known?" Samantha asked.

"Pretty much since the Chief broke into my computer," Alex said, "But I had my suspicions long before that."

Alex leaned over her, his arms spread wide holding his weight on the top of the hatch. He completely blocked the exit of her berth, trapping her within. She looked up at him and met his polychrome stare with her own. He wore an interrogator's face, impenetrable to even her skills.

"Sinner was…." she began.

"Just following orders?" Alex interrupted, "Please, Lieutenant, I think you both know that would not qualify as an excuse even if it were true."

Samantha swallowed hard as she drew up her knees and moved backwards on her bed. It was, of course, a court martial offense. They could face dishonorable discharge, jail time, possibly even correctional therapy. Rippavitch would never let it come to that, but with a Fotheringday on the other side of the case, a full investigation would be launched. Stories would leak to the press, hearings would be held in the Imperial Senate; the political fall out would be devastating for the Ripper. At the very least her networks would be ruined. A cold dread filled her as she realized that she had just handed the Imperialists the very political tool they wanted; she had set up the Ripper and in so doing, destroyed everything she had worked for.

"What do we do now?" She asked, feeling her fingernail dig into the soft flesh of thumb's cuticle. She didn't try to hide it.

"To start with, you will stop going through my things," Alex said, a small smile on his lips softening the harsh contrast of his clenched jaw. He exhaled a quiet chuckle before stepping back from the berthing unit and giving her room to breathe. The holowalls of her and D'Ascoine's cabin were off, leaving the room sterile and impersonal. A quick glance at her comms signal confirmed what she already guessed: the room was locked by Captain's Order, sealed off from outside observers.

"Why didn't you say anything?" She asked after a long silence.

"At first I wanted to give you enough rope to hang yourself with," Alex responded. He leaned against D'Ascoine's berth, his armed crossed before him. "Later, as I got to know you, I wanted you to see the evidence for yourself. See if you came to the same conclusions I did."

"Why?" she asked. Crouched in the back of her bunk, her eyes traveled across his face, trying to read him with no success.

"I would hope that was obvious," Alex said with a crooked smile, "I have come to respect your analytical abilities. I wanted to compare them to my own; as dispassionate as I can be, I am still biased. If a woman who so clearly resents me came to the same ones however, that would add significance to my hypothesis."

Samantha stiffened. "I don't resent you."

Alex stared in silent response.

"I don't," she said. Moving to sit on the edge of her berth, she swung her feet to the ground and studied her captain for tells. "I simply don't trust you."

"Because I made a mistake or because my political views are different to yours?"

"Because I can't figure out why you're here," Samantha said, "I can't figure out why the Ripper and Van Trappini allowed you into the Raiders, not to mention the ARAG."

"You don't like being kept in the dark is that it?" Alex asked. The muscles in his jaw began to slowly pulse.

"Not when it comes to the lives of my crew."

"Your crew?" Alex chuckled. "Is that it? You distrust me because I was given this command over you?"

"That has nothing to do with it," Samantha said, and slowly came to her feet, "These people are my friends. We've risked our lives together and I sure as hell didn't want to trust them to a CO who from all indications was either an incompetent or a mole."

"And now? Which do you think I am now?"

"I don't know. Probably neither, but I'm not sure that having a captain hell bent on revenge is any better than other options."

"Revenge?" Alex all but shouted, causing her to jump. He took a single step towards her and came to his full height. "You think this is about vengeance? This is about bringing the people responsible for that massacre to justice!"

She had never seen him angry, and suddenly realized exactly how powerfully built her fellow mandellan was. It took all her training to stop herself from flinching as he loomed closer. She readied herself for action as he raved on.

"This is about making certain that they cannot do it again! Did you see how those people died? Not just the one's in the *Silver Slipper*, but the victims of the other bombings? Have you seen the handiwork of this Dalang and his Wayang Stalkers? They use nanobot-devourers in their bombs, neuron-targeters that cause insatiable itching, agony and madness as they work their way through the victims' nervous systems. That kind of technology has to have come from the darkest elements of the Federalists. You know that as well as

I. Hell you might even know who would have supplied the black-tech!"

"I don't," she said calmly, "If I did, they wouldn't be around anymore."

They stood toe to toe, his polychrome eyes furiously searching hers. She heard the sound of his grinding teeth.

"You know what makes it worse?" Alex said, his voice softer, more controlled. He took a step back. "They do it for money. The Federalist politics are just an excuse. These people are about profits."

"The Wayang and those like them, perhaps. Others do it because they believe that violence is the only path open that will bring democracy."

"And you think that justifies their actions?"

"No. Anything but," Samantha said, shaking her head to hide her sudden irritation, "That's why I serve here, to stop such people from destroying the ideals that my father spent his life trying to promote."

"Really? That is all?" Alex said with venom behind his sarcastic smile, "You were an award winning Sophontologist; an explorer whose career was just beginning to take off. Rising star of the Imperial Astrographic Service from what I understand. Then three months after your parents' death you transferred to the 12th Fleet and became a very special counter-terrorist operative. Are you telling me that had nothing to do with vengeance?"

"The Wayang and those like them claim to be fighting for democracy," Samantha said, her finger returning to her ragged cuticle, "But by using terrorism to promote their cause, they betray everything that they say they stand for."

"And you betray them right back." His voice was calm and damning.

"You have no idea what you're talking about!" Samantha said with more force than she had wanted. She found herself glaring at her CO, her feet shoulder width apart, her hands free, open and to her sides. A sharp pain grew in her right thumb. Samantha tried to calm herself, her skin still prickling with anger. He'd struck too close to the mark and she searched his face to see if he realized it.

"Maybe," Alex said, his arms once more crossing as he leaned against D'Ascoine's berth, "I have been wrong before."

"My role is to stop the pointless bloodshed. That is all," she said. Calmer, Samantha measured her breath, and regained composure. Her eyes traveled over his face, searching his expression for signs of a cunning ploy. What she found was desperation.

"I know that," Alex said, arms open and his eyes almost pleading, "I have no doubt that you are here to bring an end to their reign of terror. So am I. You may not believe it, but I am trying to stop the killing the same way you are, regardless to the cost."

"And what was that cost, Commander?" Cold calculation replaced her angry reactions.

"What does it matter?" He looked away. She knew she had him.

"What price did you pay to get the Ripper and Van Trappini to let you into the ARAG? How did the washouted son of the Author of the Empire get to lead the most coveted position in the Naval Intelligence?"

"I put forward my case to the Ripp-"

"Don't even try, Alex. You want me to trust you? You want me to put the lives of my friends unquestioningly in your hands? Give me a reason to believe you!"

Alex stared at Samantha for some time, his eyes darting over her face as he clearly contemplated his next words. Yet it was not distrust that was slowly growing across his expression. It was shame.

She let the silence extend uncomfortably. Out of the corner of her eye she saw drops of blood from her thumb on the floor. She ignored it.

"You want my help?" she asked, her voice perfectly measured with calm and befriending tones, "Tell me what it was that you gave him?"

"I proxied him my votes," he said abruptly, looking away so as not to meet her eyes.

"What?" Samantha stepped back as if struck, certain she couldn't have heard him correctly.

"I took my votes in the Imperial Senate," Alex said, his face draining of color, "the ones I normally let my father cast for me, and I proxied them to Admiral Rippavitch for the duration of my service. I betrayed my father, undermined his position in the Senate, broke long standing political alliances and alienated the Emperor by giving the Imperial Opposition my votes."

Samantha sat back on her bed, her mouth open. *No wonder the Ripper wasn't concerned with being in the Senate for the vote. Alex probably cost his father his position as the Emperor's Privy Councilor.*

Alex stood silently, looking at the floor as she stared at him. After a moment, he turned his gaze back towards her. He looked vulnerable, alone and lost.

"I traded my family, my friends and my position in order to ensure that these people, these terrorists, were stopped. What did you trade for your cause, Ms. Smith?"

PART III

Engaging the Enemy

CHAPTER 27

Samantha saw the mass of feelers, beaks, antennae and eye-spots raced down the gangway, scrambling its way on great tentacles that ended in claw covered maws. A horrible screeching noise sounded from it as it made the airlock. Fran screamed and opened fire, holding the trigger until the AAR-5 was empty. An eruption of fluids filled the chamber.

"Cease Fire! End simulation!" Alex's shout was filled with anger. The holograph and direct feeds to their suits and implants stopped, though the image of the gory mass of the dead alien remained.

"What the bloody hell was that?" he said bearing down on Fran.

Samantha stepped forward to Fran's side. Alex's voice was filled with anger. He had been losing his temper with increasing frequency over the past two months, but usually at himself, and never in front of the crew. The Able Tech was shaking.

"I… I don't know, sir," Fran responded, "I've never seen one of …."

"Not the Blaharin!" Alex gesticulated towards the bullet ridden corpse on the floor. "I mean your action! Why did you open fire?"

"It was charging, sir, I thought…"

"Harpur! We are boarding a Federalist gun boat, one that we intercepted in the act of piracy! Did you understand that about our simulation scenario?"

"Yes, sir."

"And so why in the name of God did you choose to shoot the Blaharin?"

"Sir, I think she was taken off…" Bowman started, but a furious glare from the captain silenced him.

"I thought it was attacking us, sir," Fran said, her voice trembling, "I thought it was starting a counter-boarding action and…"

"You have been reading all about the history of the insurgency movement haven't you? In all of that reading, have you come across one incident of a non-human sentient being involved in an act of insurgency?"

"No, sir."

"And do you know why that is?"

"Because the Federalists target sophants."

"That is right," Alex said more calmly, "and so that individual running towards us?"

"Was probably a hostage, sir." Fran looked at the ground.

"Very good. You just shot a citizen of the Empire running to you for help."

"Sorry, sir."

"Sorry doesn't cut it. Gunnery Sergeant!" Alex said to Chrom, "I thought you said this crew was ready to assault the enemy."

"I did, sir." Chrom responded. She stood tall, at attention and did not flinch.

"Do you call shooting civilians ready?"

Samantha was about to interfere. Fran's mistake would have been terrible in the real world, but this was a sim and Alex's reprimand was going over the top. Samantha had little doubt as to why. She'd already opened a private channel when help came from an unexpected source.

"It wasn't the Gunnery Sergeant fault, sir," D'Ascoine said, stepping forward, "Nor that of Able Technician Harpur. It was mine, sir."

They all stared at the Army Officer-cum-TOMO. The only sound was the rush of air through the *Hunter's* lifesupport.

"I was in command of the boarding party, and I should have prepared young Harpur here for the possibility of finding captives. I will ensure that the scenarios I run in the future better prepare her, and the rest of us, for survivors."

Alex glared at him for a moment, and then Samantha caught his eye. At first she thought he was going to tear into her as well, but then he looked away and seemed to take a deep breath.

"Very well, Leftenant," Alex said, his voice more calm, "Let's carry on with the drills. Ms. Harpur? You will be more careful in future, yes?"

"Aye, sir," she responded, but her voice was still shaky.

"Then let us take it from the top," Alex's voice was almost gentle as he gave the command to restart the program. Behind him, Samantha noticed Fran stifle a burp.

Kyle Hammond looked at the news report and shook his head. As the footage of Federalist guerrillas raining mortars down on a military base played, it showed many of the rounds going astray, landing in the shanty town nearby. The image made him sick.

"Just who do these idiots think they're helping?" he said to no one in particular. He turned his eyes out of the shuttle's viewport, where the blue and white horizon of Lai-Jung Prime was slowly filling the window. It was a grimy little world at the nexus of the Corridor main, a client state of the Empire and a frequent stop on his business runs for Sir Richard.

"Themselves," a woman's voice sounded from next to him, "Just like everybody else."

Hammond found himself looking into the mirrored implants of one of the locals. She was a striking woman, with fair skin, high cheekbones, and shoulder length dark hair that fell across her brow in a shaggy fringe. He wondered what her eyes were like behind the reflective surface of her built-in wrap around lenses, assuming of course that she still had eyes. *Typical Fringe world technophile.*

"They say they're out to help the disenfranchised," Hammond said, deciding to play devils' advocate, "Haven't you heard the Voice? He says it's all about the little guy."

"Yeah, right." The woman took a sip of her beer. A small vibration began to rattle the bottles behind the bar. The ship was decelerating.

A local tough, he thought to himself, noting how she scanned the rest of the velour covered lounge. She held herself like some kind of street muscle, her accent heavy with local flavor. *Or hooker maybe.* The news story changed to something on exploration.

"Mind if I change the channel?" she asked. There were only three other people, each wrapped up in their own little worlds.

"Not in the least."

The image of a newly recontacted species of sentient aliens was replaced with a heavily armed ground vehicle racing through the maze of an arena. Guns and explosions went off all around it. More local color.

Tuning out both the violence and the attractive woman, he decided to look at the corporate returns. Word had arrived that Sir Richard was coming to Lai-Jung; apparently there had been some trouble he wanted to discuss with Hammond, but what that might have been wasn't outlined in the message. Even so, Kyle had a pretty good idea of the range of possibilities: Sir Richard was not the only one with intelligence sources.

He opened a map of Alterande in his mind's eye, noted the route of different ships, and began calculating how and when each shipment would arrive. If he was going to be debating Sir Richard again, he best be prepared. He only wished that Sir Richard had let him use the Cameron-Inglesie yacht for this trip: it had a much greater jump capacity and he could already have access to the full set of files available at the local office. It seemed, however, that the hierarch felt he needed it himself.

Pretending to be a ship-watcher, Alyiar wore the skin of a teenage boy. He pressed his nose to the glass, as if enthralled by the arrival of the shuttle. Around him the people of Lai-Jung Prime walked down the concourse, queued at security points, and generally just milled about. The only difference between them and passengers anywhere else was that the inhabitants of Lai-Jung Prime were technophiles, and that irritated Alyiar.

Down on the tarmac Wylde was dressed as a cargo handler, pointlessly moving crates around while keeping his eyes open and preparing to strike. On the shuttle Bolyiacov had a close eye on their target. She wore her haute-culture-number-four again, having argued it was the form most likely to seduce. That hadn't seemed to matter to their target, however, he had not even made a pass. Still, at least she had eyes-on the target.

"*... and so I logged into the tech-six level and holy crap...*"

"*... I got the latest interface upgrade for my implants....*"

Snippets of broadcast conversation floated by Alyiar as he watched the bright orange and white shuttle make its way to the disembarkation area. He tried not to listen, tried not to feel the desire to return to the virtual hell that his heart and mind longed for, tried not to be revolted by the local population's love of technology. It was so much like his own, so much like what he had been before Rubo had saved him. He hated them almost as much as he hated his desire to return to being like them.

The shuttle rolled to a stop on the bright green crosses and static discharge arced to the ground. Across the side of the large delta winged vessel was the orange logo of Cameron-Inglesie Distributors, a small local company that had thus far escaped the attentions of the Wayang Network. Alyiar suspected that this latest assignment marked a change to that. It was the only reason he could think of that explained why they were watching this otherwise unextraordinary middle manager. What he couldn't figure, however, was why Rubo had ordered them to ensure this guy was kept safe, for now anyway.

High in orbit around Lai-Jung Prime a standard broadcast was received at the Imperial Orbital Consulate. It had been launched by a pattern recognition spybot running as virus in the Broluv starport's security system. The program had noted a mathematical analogy in the facial features of one of the passengers in a recently arrived shuttle and so uploaded the image and scans to its central hub at the local office of the Sophyan Imperial Ministry of Justice.

Upon receiving the data, one of the subroutines of the DuZhod Interactive began an immediate analysis. The results were passed up to the local hub of the interactive, which in turn decided to immediately download them to Colonel Lord Ursus DuZhod. At that moment, the Colonel was in the process of a very different investigation, but when he received the news, a cold, thin smile appeared on his face. He closed the files on the recent changes in personnel within the 12th Imperial Fleet and refocused his attention on the activities of the Wayang Terror Cell. Slowly, he raised a long thin finger to one of the chrome nodules on his bald head and absently polished it.

CHAPTER 28

"I don't know, he seems jumpy if you ask me," Sinner said. He and Samantha had stopped hiding their private meetings and instead had taken to meeting up for coffee or a quick meal between shifts. It wasn't difficult to arrange; as XO, Samantha was in charge of setting up the rota. Still, it seemed to Sinner that she was also making sure she and the Skipper spent private time together too. He told himself that it was in order for her to better observe the CO. He also insisted that it in no way bothered him.

"If I'd killed a ship load of people I might be a little nervous too," Samantha answered. Elbows on the table, she cradled a spiced coffee in her hands.

"I got no problem with post-traumatic stress, but I don't want someone with it commanding my ship."

"I don't know, with a TOMO that's as gung-ho as D'Ascoine, maybe someone who's a little gun-shy isn't so bad."

"Bullshit. What if he fails to attack a viable target because he's too cautious? We could end up deader than a dead thing 'cause he's afraid of killing civvies?"

"I don't think he'd make that kind of mistake." Samantha passed him a tube of dinner.

"I guess history show's he tends to go the other way."

"God, Sinner, give the man a break," Samantha said, scowling at him over her coffee, "he's trying to make amends."

"You're defending him now?"

"I'm not defending anyone, but he was set up. We both agree on that."

"He also failed to follow SOP," Sinner said, gesturing at her with the tube of Protein Bourgogne, "Last time that got a bunch of civvies killed, this time it might be us. Besides, he's still the kind a guy who let all the officers around him take the fall."

"I don't think he even knows about that. I watched the footage of his tribunal. He tried to take the blame. He was out of the loop with what happened afterwards."

"Either way, the result was the same. Hammond, Al Escobar and Ch'teng were left out to dry."

"I'm not saying that the man's a hero, but I'm happy to know he isn't a fool."

"You ask me? The jury's still out on that." He gave his dinner tube a hard suck, remembering the days when Samantha would have been sure to schedule enough time for them to cook a meal together.

"Sinner, would you just give him the benefit of the doubt for a while?" She gestured with her coffee, slopping some over the edge. "His approach to analysis seems solid. The Dalang uses the same methods as the group he was hunting in the Archon sector. The Wayang Cell looks like an evolutionary step. So we keep an eye on Alex, of course, but who knows? We might even be able to turn him to our side."

"What side would that be?"

"The side that puts an end to this violence." She slapped the table with her hand.

"Is it? 'Cause my side is the one that doesn't get me killed."

Bowman was clearly exhausted as he walked into the cabin. With his helmet under his arm and armor half undone, he barely glanced at Fran as he headed towards his berth, but that was enough. Fran blew her nose and tried to hide the fact she was crying, but it was way too late. Bowman had already stopped, concern written on his face.

"What's up?"

"Nothing. I'm just being stupid."

"Yeah, right," Bowman replied, "'Cause you're a real dumbo. What's bothering you Fran?"

"Homesick I guess."

"Bullshit," Bowman answered, "I've seen you homesick. This ain't homesick."

"Great, now you're telling me how to feel?" she snapped.

"What? Fuck no! Sometimes it helps to talk you know? But if you don't want…"

"Oh god, Ed, I'm sorry," Fran said, tears welling up in her eyes once more, "I… I just… how could you tell I was… well…."

"Lying?" Bowman sat on the edge of her bunk, "Shit girl, I'm Marine Recon on Intelligence duty in a Counter-Insurgency unit. Ever think that close-observation work might just be part of my deal? Now tell me what's up. Or not."

"I'm sorry Ed, I just…"

"Stop apologizing Fran," Bowman said. His big, heart warming grin didn't quite win out over the weariness in his eyes. "You're not doing anything wrong."

"I do everything wrong! It's like I can't keep up. Everybody's got implants and does everything better and faster than I do!"

"You could always get implants yourself you know? The Navy will pay for it."

Fran shuddered as she felt a cold wave of disgust run down her spine.

"But you don't have to either," Bowman quickly continued, "Look, Fran, we've all been at this for years.

You've been at it for a few months. Nobody expects you to do more than you're doing, and you're doing great by the way."

"Tell that to the Blaharin I blew away," Fran muttered, looking away.

"Oh fuck, Fran, it was a sim! You made a mistake? Huh? Who hasn't?"

"The Skipper didn't seem to see it that way?"

"Sometimes skippers can be dicks, even the good ones. It goes with the job. No one is disappointed that you are part of the crew."

Fran smiled a thank you, but didn't really feel any better. Bowman was a great guy, and meant well, but she doubted that the others felt the same way. Maybe in the Highfield Arcology she was normal, maybe even better than normal, but here she was a cripple that slowed down the crew.

Alex sat at his desk, his head feeling like it was going to explode. The brightly colored sector map floated in the center of his cabin with various text windows hovering around it. A picture of the Dalang was projected on the wall across from him. Alex stared at the bizarre face that seemed to mock him.

"Two analgesics please, Mergatroid."

"Begging your pardon, sir," the AI's bored voice sounded, "but that would exceed the recommended dosage at this time."

"I know. And a black coffee please."

"That, sir, is also not recommended."

"Just do it."

"Very good, sir."

Two tablets and a cup emerged from his desk. He washed one down with the other and ignored the queasy feeling that followed. Waiting for the pills to take effect, he looked at the image of Sally on his desk.

"Why did I listen to you?" he asked her picture. Bright, cheerful, smiling: she was the opposite of the creature on the wall.

The chime on his door sounded. It was an irritating noise at the best of times. He reduced his files as he gave permission to enter.

"Hello, sir," Samantha said as she strode through the door. Her eye sparkled and she wore a warm smile that froze the moment she looked at him. "I'm sorry sir. I could come back later."

"Do I look that bad, Lieutenant?" he said with an attempt to seem welcoming. He was glad to see his XO warming up to him, and wanted to encourage it. He had even begun to enjoy their interchanges. Unfortunately at the moment any form of social graces was proving to be an effort, "What can I do for you?"

"It's… um… it's our game night, but if you're busy…."

"No… no come in," Alex said shaking his head and toggling the walls of the room back to their wood paneled projection, "I completely lost track of the time. Besides, I could use the break."

"Thanks. I need it too," she said as she sat down opposite him. Spreading out the game pieces, she smiled and spoke lightly of events on the ship. Despite himself, after ten minutes of the game, his headache faded as he lost himself in the jovial conversation of his Executive Officer.

Sally finally stopped worrying about Alex as she watched the Billanobian dancers move in slow graceful circles about the ancient forum. There were hundreds of them, dressed in the wide variety of formal robes, scarves, gowns, suits, and other forms of traditional dress; each representing one of the myriad castes within the ancient culture. Three main themes existed in the dancer's costume and moves, however: the flowing robes of the intelligencia castes, the sleek smoothness of the warrior castes, and the simple utilitarianism of the worker castes. The steps of each dancer also matched their roles in society, and each turn of the dance saw them touch one another, at just the right time and in just the right order: a symbol of the interconnected nature and balance that was Billanobia. A simple wind-flute was played in the background, and punctuated by the small bells, cymbals and chimes worn by the dancers and sounded at each contact.

The result was a beautiful, calming symphony of simplicity, hidden in the most remarkably complex performance. This was, of course, only one of the Minor Dances. The Great Dance was performed only on Billanobia itself, and it was a performance that never ended, but merely had dancers step out for a time and be replaced by others; a performance that had been going on un-interrupted for nearly a thousand years.

Sally loved the Great Dance, and indeed the many small off-shoot Minor Dances it produced such as this one. When she was a child of ten, her father had taken her and Rudy to the Great Dance during her first tour of the old Empire of the Sophyan's greatest ally and she had been transfixed. Long after her older brother had grown bored, she had remained watching the dancers, studying their movements, noting the repeating patterns, hypnotized by their gravity and complexity – seeking to understand the hidden meanings of the great symbol of Billanobian culture. Years later she still struggled to understand all the nuances of the dance, but then again, that was the point. Ever changing, but always the same, the Dance was the great icon of Billanobia.

Out of the corner of her eye, Sally saw Jonathan pass through the forum, and make his way towards the café where she was supposed to meet him. She sighed, disappointed that he was on-time, punctual even, for their rendezvous. Making the proper ritual gestures, she left the crowd observing the dancers and made her way out of the forum, across the galleries and to the small unobtrusive café where many dealers in antiques and fine arts gathered to trade with each other and their clients. She found Jonathan waiting there for her.

"Lady Symbletyne," he rose as he greeted her, smiling as he softly kissed her cheek. He was a good looking man, thin with light brown hair. He was well groomed, but with slight wrinkles to his clothing, like an academic who could not be bothered with properly pressing his clothing. His reputation, which Sally had briefly sampled some years back, was that of a ladies man, not overtly womanizing, but certainly with more than his fair share of girlfriends and one night stands. Most, if not all of these had been broken off without hard feelings, and indeed with promises of continued friendship, but contact inevitably broke down, and communication failed.

His profession, that of a dealer in fine arts and artifacts, only served to enhance his romantic endeavors, or at least his reputation in that department. It brought him into constant contact with the kinds of men and women who would appreciate his autotellistic knowledge of antiquities and high culture, the very sorts of people who were charmed by such knowledge. Yet if he found that his knowledge assisted with his ability to flirt, he also found that his flirtations added to his ability to sell his art, and so his reputation as both a lover and as an art dealer grew hand in hand. Of course, such skills and background also made Jonathan perfect for other sorts of things. There was always some reason why art dealers could be seen in different corners of known space.

"Jonathan," she greeted him with her stunning smile, and accepted the chair that he offered her, "How are you darling?"

"Wonderful. Couldn't be better? And yourself? Keeping well?"

"Seuper darling."

"So I hear. Rumor has it you've been seen about the circuit with a certain young naval officer." He spoke with a touch of envy in his voice, and just loud enough to be overheard.

"Indeed, Alex and I are beginning to get a little serious."

"You break my heart, m' lady." He sat opposite her.

"Don't tease… no one breaks your heart, Jonathan."

"But they do! All the time!"

"I'm sure…."

A small pot of tea arrived, and he poured it. They sat and chatted idly for almost an hour until at last they felt certain no one was listening. Still they continued to discuss art for a requisite amount of time there after before they got down to business.

They made no secret about the passing of the data crystal. He handed it to her in clear sight of everyone, and she held it up and looked at it plain for everyone to see. Afterwards they kept on the topic of the acquisitions that Jonathan might make for her. When they were done, Sally kissed him on the cheek, and made her way back to her hotel, not even glancing at the dancers as she passed. After she examined the crystal, Sally booked the first express passage to Lai-Jung.

CHAPTER 29

It was oh-four-hundred in the morning and Samantha needed coffee. She had been working ever since her watch ended and longed to clear her head of maps and figures. She wanted a new perspective, but unfortunately Sinner was asleep. Besides he had been a bit irritable recently. She would just have to work through the problem on her own.

She headed towards the lounge, noting the do-not-disturb light above Fotheringday's door was still off. She paused for a moment before dismissing the idea of bothering him. It was too early to bring her analysis to the CO, besides he might just have forgotten to turn on the light. She continued on to the mess-lounge, eyes half open she walked into the dimly lit room.

"Good morning, Lieutenant."

Samantha jumped in surprise, hand going to the sidearm that wasn't there. Alex leaned against the counter, coffee in one hand, the other outstretched towards her. "Sorry, I didn't mean to startle you."

"No, sir, it's alright, I… didn't expect to find you here," she said, "You don't normally come into the mess-lounge."

"I needed to clear my head," he said with a smile, "Coffee?"

"Please."

"Hot spiced coffee, dark roast, sweet," he said to the dispenser. It began to hiss and whir in response. There were dark circles under his eyes that had been growing steadily since he had taken command. "What have you been working on?"

"I've been making a series of maps based on our results and surveys," she said, moving across from him and staring expectantly at the dispenser. She smiled when she realized he had ordered her coffee as she liked it.

"Any luck?"

"Not really. I've noticed a couple of patterns but I can't quite figure them out."

"Show me what you have." He handed her the coffee. "I can use the distraction."

Samantha gave the mental commands that called up an astrographic workspace in mess-lounge. A multicolored star map of Archon and Alterande appeared in the center of the room. Gold halos hovered in some areas, other colors also hovered around certain stars. Some overlapped the gold, others overlapped each other. A blinking green icon with a green line tracing its path noted the *Hunter* and the course it had been following.

"This looks familiar," Alex said.

"I thought your maps were a good place to start," She said in an unapologetic tone, "This is the survey data as it presently stands. I overlaid it on top of the information you brought from Archon and put it into a temporal framework. Three years ago there were ten groups working in Alterande, last year five and now only three."

"The Voice, the People's Front, and the Wayang."

"On this map, the yellow markers are bombings, kidnappings and other general terror attacks. The green and the blue markers note piracy and hijackings. Green are the systems where reports suggest interstellar craft were used, blue are those reports where non-jump capable system boats are suggested."

"The gold ones represent those apparently linked to the Wayang network." Alex added.

"As you can see," she said, watching him rather than the map, "there is no spatial or temporal relationship shown to link any of these things."

"Completely random."

"Haphazard actually," she corrected in a calmly patronizing tone, "Random is…"

"Quite right of course," Alex said, "Please continue."

Samantha swallowed hard and nodded apologetically. Still cringing inwardly she stood and walked into the map.

"This is where it gets conjectural," she said, adding new series of highlights to the map, "If you run the results through a canonical correlation analysis you find that several clusters form, indicating certain levels of similarity..."

"Pardon me, Lieutenant, but what did you just say?"

"Canonical correlation analysis? You know, old school exploratory multivariate statistics?"

"Actually, I must admit that I don't know," he said with a relaxed smile, "but I am happy to take your word for it. You did some number crunching and what did you find?"

"After a few runs and some data cleansing, I found some similarities between certain attacks. I went back to the data and, well you can see what I mean. There is almost something here, but what it is, I don't know. It's like there's something missing."

"Good lord," Alex said, his eyes slowly narrowing as a smile grew across his face, "how could we have missed it?"

CHAPTER 30

The stars suddenly leapt their positions, and the crew of the *Hunter* immediately scanned the system in front of them for threats. Once they determined they were safe from immediate attack, they activated their full sensor array. As antennae, optics, and other such sensors bloomed out from their alcoves, the dorsal hatches opened and launched the satellites like pollen released from a flower. The *Hunter* was no longer sleek; she looked like some form of beautiful and deadly deep-sea life.

Inside, Alex smiled as he watched Samantha perform her rigorous search. Her eyes dashed from monitor to monitor, and from holographic projection to unseen VR projection as she manipulated the cybernetic and holodynamic controls like a woman engaged in some ancient kata. Below them, the gunnery crew followed Samantha's commands precisely, targeting areas of space with their own sensor equipment, avoiding the use of active sensors; keeping the *Hunter* silent and hidden.

As hours passed, Samantha and the gunnery crew took brief breaks to rest their eyes, grab a coffee, or report to the Captain on their progress. Alex kept abreast of their situation as he double checked the analysis he and Samantha had performed. The pattern that had emerged was obvious, once they knew it was there. The terrorist attacks tended to occur just before or after Imperial forces patrolled an area, suggesting among other things that the Wayang had access to some very sensitive data.

Regardless, once Alex and Samantha had added that missing piece, they could see the routes and schedules of pirate activity, and occasionally even interpolate the actions of individual ships. They searched for acts that were either grossly violent or tied heavily to profit, and soon identified systems and dates where the Wayang Terror Cells were likely to strike. One had been within their reach.

"Commander," Samantha said, blinking awake after an extended period of jacked-in drooling, "I think we have something here."

"Indeed?" Alex looked at the holographic image that Samantha projected between them.

"If you look here, on the surface of the gas giant, you can see a disturbance of one of the lower layers of clouds breaking through the upper atmospheric layers. The same thing again appears over here, and over here." Samantha pointed to the image hovering between them. A sporadic series of brown lines and curlicues appeared in the broad tan-and-brown twenty-second band of the swirling gases of the giant planet.

"A con-trail?" Alex asked. Despite his familiarity with such observation, he was fairly certain he would not have noted the detail.

"Bowman caught it. I'm pretty certain it can't be natural. This sort of pattern is indicative of ships at depth coming up, either to return contact with observation satellites or in some other way get better readings of the outer system."

"Rather like a ship on lurker duty."

"Or a terrorist preparing for an act of piracy. Whoever is down there doesn't want anyone to know it."

"By itself, that does not mean they are insurgents," Alex said.

"I suppose," Samantha replied, "They could be simple criminals."

"Or they could be completely innocent," Alex said, "Merchants having some difficulty or another, corporate security ships ensuring safe passage for a convoy to come, or even members of the 253rd on patrol."

"What do you want to do, sir?" Samantha asked, eyeing Alex suspiciously.

"Assuming they are periodically breaking the surface to check in with surveillance satellites, when are they next due?"

"They're due to surface in the next two hours."

"Excellent, we will hold position and keep an eye out for them. Well done, Lieutenant."

Samantha saw the next con-trail appear less than an hour later. It was scattered and difficult to track, but present all the same. A moment later she realized that it was not alone. There were, it seemed, multiple vessels flying in formation.

"Either we missed the other entry points or the additional trails are sub-craft of a larger ship," she said, "Either way, they're lurking like pirates."

"Let's not jump to conclusions," Alex said, and Samantha thought that she detected just a hint of nervousness in his voice.

"Of course they're pirates," Samantha said, cocking her head in disbelief, "and probably insurgents. They're sitting in a gas giant without their transponders on. What else would they be doing?"

"They could be merchants having difficulty with a skimming scoop."

"If they're merchants, then why no transponders?"

"I don't know about you, Lieutenant," Alex said, adjusting a holographic control, "but if I were a lightly armed merchant ship in an unpatrolled system like this, I wouldn't want to broadcast my position to any ship that happened to jump into system."

"With all due respect, sir," Samantha said, "I know it's possible that these are innocents, or even colleagues, but it's pretty unlikely. Especially considering that we expect the Wayang will be..."

"That approach did not work out so well for me the last time I tried it," Alex responded in a dry tone, "Now, if you would be so kind, withdraw our satellites and start to broadcast the transponder signal of a Type III merchant carrier."

The *Hunter*'s fusion rockets engaged creating a new star in the system; a great sword of nuclear fusion burning like a shining beacon to any who cared to look. Accelerating at a little over two-gees, it slowly gained momentum as it entered into the star system proper. Each moment the engines' fired the ship increased its speed, though at less than half of its maximum and with a greater inefficiency in its burn than any Imperial warship would have. Alex's plan was not to arouse suspicion by rocketing at velocity through the star system like a warship. Instead they approached with the velocity of a plump, well-funded, and poorly piloted inter-stellar trader. They made a very attractive target.

Three days later, at the mid-point of their journey, they cut the engines, turned the ship around and re-launched the satellites. One after another they fell from the ship, each following their pre-programmed course. They would use their own engines and the gravity well of the planet to slow themselves into a stable orbiting constellation. When the satellites were on their way, Alex fired the main engines again and began their deceleration. For two more days they continued to slow their momentum until they entered a far orbit of the gas giant where they used the planet's gravity to make their final braking maneuvers.

As Alex turned the ship towards the planet, the giant sphere slowly filled the viewport. Vibrant stripes of red, gold and amber gases, churning with touches of white, brown and crimson filled Alex's vision. It was both beautiful and monstrous in its scale. Any of those storms could tear the *Hunter* apart if they were not careful, and the pressures at depth could crush even a heavy warship's armored hull. Then, of course, there was the danger of attack.

"Constellation in final position, sir," Samantha said, her finger rubbing over her gloved thumb, "and comms-link locked in. We will be ready by the time we hit orbit sir."

"Thank you, Lieutenant," Alex said with a nod, "Pull in external sensors. All stations report and make ready for re-entry."

CHAPTER 31

Alex raised the *Hunter*'s nose and brought the ship down into the gas-giant's upper atmosphere. They came in fast and hot, giving the impression that they were more interested in refueling quickly than in whatever dangers might lurk beneath the clouds. The ship began to vibrate, then to shake. Flames flickered by the windows of the cockpit as they took a steeper than ideal descent. Here and there Alex jostled the controls, causing the ship to shimmy slightly back and forth, increasing the ship's trail and creating the impression she was larger than she really was.

For a time, Samantha lost contact with the satellites, as their re-entry interfered with the tight-beam radio reception they had been using. As the blackout started, she kept her eyes on the optics, looking for threats that might hit them at their most vulnerable moments. It was unlikely for an enemy to attack now unless they were out to destroy them outright. Attacking in re-entry would merely annihilate the ship, and there would be no profit to be gained by such an action. If Alex and Samantha were right about the Wayang, these people would go for the money. If they cared only about instilling terror, however, they might try to simply blow the

Hunter out of the sky. Alex remained impassive while Samantha's gloved finger ran over her inaccessible cuticle.

Once they had stopped their re-entry burn, Samantha regained contact with the satellites and Alex decreased their speed through friction with the near liquid atmosphere. He extended the air-brakes and slightly opened the landing gear, enhancing their contrail and the subsequent illusion that they were a larger ship. The bumps and vibrations shook the crew to their teeth, but the effect was perfect. Far below them the other vessel moved in to attack.

"Sir," Samantha said, her eyes locked on her readouts, "I've detected a change in the dynamics of the anomaly's course and MagRes notes a solid contact at bearing 261 by 273 degrees. Target has a heading of fifteen degrees, with a planer ascent of… twenty-five. We have a confirmed bogey."

"Understood. All hands, we have a bogey at 261 by 273 degrees, mark it as Alpha contact two."

"Contact marked as Alpha-two aye, sir," Samantha responded. At once the sensor suites in the gunnery control tagged the small glowing object with the name Alpha-two.

"Gunnery, Conn." Alex said, making a fine course adjustment.

"Gunnery, aye," D'Ascoine responded.

"Open missile ports and prepare to launch decoy, if you would be so kind Leftenant."

"Aye, aye and Tally Ho Eorl!" D'Ascoine said, adding the jovial battle cry used by the people of Hammonrie in the War of Extinction.

"Tally Ho, Hussar," Alex replied with a smile, waiving away Samantha's inquiring look.

"Missile ports… open," D'Ascoine said, "Decoy ready."

"Launch decoy!"

"Decoy away!"

The decoy missile dropped from its rack and fired its rockets at once. It sped away from the ship, wings springing out from its sides and small panels arising from its casing. At a distance of twenty meters sections of it began to rotate in alternate directions, causing disturbances in the atmosphere that matched the contrail of the *Hunter*. When he saw it activate, Alex cut engines, drawing in the airbrakes and landing gear while Samantha killed the transponder. The *Hunter* became silent; the missile broadcast loud radar signals, heat signatures and took up the transponder signal. It mimicked the merchant ship that they claimed to be in every way.

Once they stopped creating turbulence, their ride was much smoother. It allowed the crew to concentrate more keenly, and keep their eyes peeled for incoming targets. Gliding through atmosphere, they subtly changed their course, gaining distance from the decoy. The crew maintained a focused silence broken only by the constant roar of the gas-giant's atmosphere outside.

Riding the planet's currents, Alex allowed the ship to drop suddenly. He followed the contours of a great cloud head and dove into a noxious orange gas-bank. Turning on the turjet engines, they silently cruised in closer: lurking to catch the lurker. Samantha let loose a sigh while Alex clenched his jaw. Now they were the hunters, and the pirates, if they were pirates, were the prey.

"Sir, I have two more contacts," Samantha said, "They are flanking our primary bogey on either side."

"Very well, mark them Beta and Gamma."

"Beta and Gamma, aye, sir."

"Gunnery, Conn." Alex checked the readouts as he spoke, ensuring they were making no trails through the gases.

"Gunnery, aye,"

"Leftenant, we have two more bogies, I'm sure you see them. Please have turrets one and two mark them respectively, and keep your attention on the primary target."

"Understood, sir," D'Ascoine responded.

Alex's telemetry told him that the TOMO was flying the decoy like a fighter, using feedback along the LOS comms to see the world as if he were sitting in the non-existent cockpit of the missile drone. He could, of course, have let the decoy fly itself, but Alex was pleased that the Army Officer was not doing so. Human control increased the unpredictability, supplementing the believability of the decoy.

As the distances closed between their three targets and the decoy, Alex noted Samantha fine tuning the varying sensors. Glimpses from the high-optics on the orbiting satellites, and the different passive sensor readings gave better insights to the nature of the vessels they targeted. Their targeting solutions also became more solid.

"Sir," Samantha said, glancing over from her controls, "Considering their speed and trajectory, I am fairly certain that we're looking at two fairly small close orbit or hypersonic fighters. Their contrails suggest that they displace less than ten tons, and their mag readings indicate much of that is metal."

"Robot fighters?"

"That's my guess. The primary target is displacing considerably more volume, and mag readings confirm it's fairly large, at least five-hundred tons, but probably more than a thousand."

"These are professionals," Alex said.

"Very much so. I hope that… Sir! The fighters are making a move!"

Moving in for the kill, the Beta and Gamma contacts revealed themselves fully. They had needle noses and delta wings: the classic design of hypersonic robot fighters. When they hit the hyperbola of their assault arcs, the mother ship behind them also picked up speed. Swirls of hydrogen bloomed behind it as its turjet engines spun into action. It burst out of the cloud cover in which it had been hiding. Shaped like a great teardrop, contact Alpha passed by the *Hunter* close enough that Alex could see it with his own eyes. The high quality optics on the spectre-class vessel, however, picked out the details.

"The mother vessel is a 1150 ton *Pyrma* class cargo ship," Samantha reported, "She's been modified to have two more turrets… has drone launch pods and looks like she has no idea we are here."

"Very well, Lieutenant," Alex said, "If you could…"

All at once, they attacked. The fighter-drones opened fire on the *Hunter*'s decoy with beam weapons that passed through the cloud of hydrogen that the decoy was carving around itself. The shots, clearly intended to hit the supposed source of the contrail, caused no damage to the missile, but would have seared a starship.

"Refueling vessel! You are out-gunned and outnumbered! Stand-by to be boarded!" The pirates' announcement was accompanied by the exploding of a missile above and in front of the decoy. No one on the *Hunter* had detected its launch.

Alex pressed a button. Before them the armored viewport closed, and a photoreal image was projected over its form. He signaled Samantha to begin a broadcast.

"Attacking vessel," Alex said, his message traveling along a laser link to the decoy and maintaining the illusion that it as the source of the signal, "This is the Sophyan Imperial Warship, HMS *Hunter*. You are in violation of Imperial Law, surrender or be destroyed!"

A volley of shots came from all three contacts. The decoy exploded into a thousand fiery pieces that plummeted into the depths of the gas-giant.

"Gunnery Control, Conn." Alex switched to internal channels and spoke in a calm voice. "Fire fire fire."

In instant synchronicity, Chrom and Bowman opened up on their pre-selected drones. Each of the turrets fired two solid beams of amplified light invisible to the eye. The beam lasers struck home on the respective fighter-drones, searing damage across the fighters but also added an increasing accuracy and range. Each turret's third weapon, a rapid pulse laser, opened fire at once. Explosions ripped through the fighters' fuselages. A plume of smoke trailed from the engines of Chrom's target, Beta; Bowman's target Gamma lost part of its wing.

Meanwhile, a missile fell away from the *Hunter*'s launch port, dropping several hundred meters before D'Ascoine took control. To everyone's relief, the missile flew on a stealthy slow burn mode until it closed in on the enemy. Only then did D'Ascoine turn the bird active. As its rockets flared to full burn, radar and thermal signals blared from the missile. It leapt immediately to life, driving itself home towards his target.

On the bridge, Samantha engaged in electronic counter-measures, jamming the enemy ship's sensors and navigational arrays. She added static and confusion to the enemy ship, making it more difficult for them to detect and target the already hard-to-see *Hunter*, and disrupting the enemy's control of their robot fighters. The results were an immediate irregularity in the enemy flight patterns.

Alex pulled them into a steep right side rolling dive, dropping deep into the underlying cloudbanks. His maneuver kept their small ship hidden as lasers swept the area where the missile had become active. D'Ascoine's missile exploded beneath the pirate ship. Debris fell from its hull.

"Alpha contact showing signs of damage," Samantha reported as she toggled between real and virtual displays, "The two fighters remain in a search pattern, using active arrays… there's thermal blooming around our previous position… Alpha is sweeping the area with lasers… I've got a solid lock."

"Gunnery, Conn," Alex said, leaning this way and that as he piloted the ship, "On my mark launch two missiles at Alpha contact and have the turrets take down the fighters."

"Gunnery, standing by," D'Ascoine responded.

"Gunnery, open fire."

Once again the turrets cut a deadly swath. Chrom's lasers immediately hit the Beta fighter; it exploded at once. Bowman's shots sliced off the second drone's engines. It dropped like a stone into the depths of the gas-giant. Only

Samantha was aware of its death thralls as the sensors picked up the sounds of it being crushed under the tremendous pressures of the planet's atmosphere.

D'Ascoine dropped his two missiles from the *Hunter*. Each fell for a full two seconds before their rockets turned on to a slow burn. One missile moved towards the Alpha target; the second curved a meandering course. Five seconds later his first missile went active and burned a clear contrail towards the *Pyrma* class ship.

The pirates returned fire at once, launching four missiles and letting loose the blue fiery pulses of plasma cannon. The volley surprised Alex in its firepower, they were even more heavily armed than the *Hunter*. He changed their course again, leaving the enemy missiles to circle in the wrong location.

The pirates' lasers destroyed D'Ascoine's first missile long before it reached its target. He lit the second up at once, and the swift rocket flew in behind the enemy, exploding meters below its tail. The detonation shook the enemy vessel. Samantha reported more metallic debris falling from the ship.

D'Ascoine launched another volley while Chrom and Bowman targeted the only remaining enemy craft. Gases leaked from its hull.

The pirate ship launched missiles and fired their lasers and plasma cannon in random search patterns. They had no idea where the *Hunter* was, but Alex eyed their cannon all the same. It could easily take out the small stealth ship if it hit them at close range. Boarding the enemy required very close range indeed.

The enemy suddenly changed course and speed. Alex lost sight of it, though the marines kept their weapons on target.

"Contact Alpha has begun rapid ascent," Samantha announced, "They're trying to cut-and-run."

"Excellent," Alex said with a smile, "Gunnery, Conn. Target the missile racks and the fusion turret, but allow her to make orbit. We want her in one piece."

Contact Alpha escaped from the gas giant's atmosphere at a full three-gees of acceleration, faster than Alex had anticipated. He cursed himself; the *Hunter* had greater speed, but he would need to light his own rockets to catch them. That would give away their position and abandon their best weapon: stealth.

"Lieutenant," he said turning to Smith, "how long until that ship is out of range?"

"If we don't engage the fusion rockets, one hour twenty-two minutes seven seconds before they escape our max range, but they'll be outside effective range in only forty-six minutes."

"Mr. D'Ascoine," Alex said with a smile, "I would appreciate it if you would ensure that our friend has to alter his course. A lot."

"Perhaps a nice nuclear flower in his path?" D'Ascoine asked.

"Two," Alex said, "low-yield warheads, with the second missile on delay. Not too close now. We do want to have something left when we get there."

"Aye, aye, Skipper."

Inside the ship's bowels, the missile loading cylinder turned, and the weapons launched. Both missiles cut a slow winding burn until they were a safe distance from the *Hunter*. By the time the first went to active burn, the marine gunners had caused still more damage to their target. The enemy lasers leapt towards the first missile as it lit, but Samantha's electronic warfare had its effects and the *Pyrma* class ship's point defenses failed.

The warhead detonated a little more than a kilometer in front of the fleeing vessel. A brilliant light flashed, followed by a carnation of glowing gas that quickly faded as it dispersed. The enemy ship briefly glowed as incandescent dust with speckles of debris erupted from its surface.

As the pirates returned fire and adjusted their course, the second missile lit up and rocketed farther in front of the Alpha contact. The pirates fired their engines full thrust to avoid the anticipated blast, and the second explosion caused no damage. Yet the forced maneuver slowed their escape and allowed the *Hunter* to close.

More fire erupted from the enemy ship's pitted hull as Chrom and Bowman's lasers finally took out its engines and weapons. The pirates were dead in space. Alex lit the fusion rockets and closed in for the kill.

Next to him, Samantha read off their relative distance and angles with a mantric rhythm. It reminded Alex of another Executive Officer whose base-twelve countdown still haunted him, but this enemy had fired first.

CHAPTER 32

The Marines stood around the inner hatch of the ventral boarding airlock, readying for action. Bowman and D'Ascoine were clad in plate-style armor of their OS-745, their beloved AAR-5's pointed at the floor. Breast plates, greaves, and armadillos were supplemented by back mounted thruster packs for zero-G maneuvering. Bowman kept his visor open, while D'Ascoine relied wholly on the VR of his sensors.

Meanwhile, Gunnery Sergeant Chrom stripped down to her voose suit, opened the hatch on the back of her huge OST-1012, and gripped the bar handles on either side. In one fluid motion, she hoisted herself up and slid into it with a comfortable ease. Her legs slipped into the cavities within the heavily powered and armored carapace's leg units. Shock-gel cushions inflated to hold her weight as she wiggled herself into place. Plugging in her i/o cords, she opened her implants to the suit, and sealed up the hatch with a mental command. Then she ran through the suit systems to ensure that the waist mounted Rapid Fire Rail Gun, shoulder mounted mini-missiles, and Rocket Propelled Grenades were ready for use. By the time she was done, the ship had docked to the enemy vessel, with control of the *Hunter*'s weapons given over to the bridge crew and the gunnery AIs.

A moment later, the huge and weapon covered combat drone rolled into the room followed by a very nervous looking Fran Harpur. Clad in her OS-500, Fran was clearly nervous. The lightly armored greaves and cuirass looked awkward upon her thin frame, her 0-G shotgun hung clumsily by her side, and an AAR-5 was gripped tightly in her hands. Bowman gave a reassuring nod and a quick thumbs-up.

The last to join the boarding party at the ventral airlock was Alex. He was clad in an OS-585, a full Navy CEVA that was lighter than that of the Marines but still had a heavier cuirass and armadillos than Fran was afforded. With his AAR-5 in hand, pistol on one hip, officer's single crystal steel drusus on the other, and the cammo patterns set to Naval Black, he cut a striking image.

"Begin boarding at your leisure, Leftenant," Alex said, "Tally ho."

"Capital!" D'Ascoine said, "Well girls and boys… ready when you are."

They circled around the inner airlock, each in a well choreographed position with their weapons pointed at the hatch in the floor. When they had all taken their places, the combat drone raised up to a menacing height on its retractable legs. It had a large and pod-like body, with heavily enweaponed arms that stood out to each side. They were equipped with portable plasma-cannons, RFRG or rapid fire rail guns like Chrom's, and variable yield lasers capable of serving either as a targeting device or a death dealing weapon. The rack of light anti-tank weapons mounted along the drone's back was loaded with bazooka rounds.

"Mr. D'Ascoine, you have command of the troop," Alex said when the drone was in place, "On your order."

"Troops, ready your weapons!" D'Ascoine barked, "Harpur! Open the primary airlock!"

Stay calm, stay calm, stay calm, Fran chanted to herself as she pressed a button and opened the inner airlock door. Her hands were sweating and shaking ever so slightly, her mind fully aware that this was not a drill.

The Marines shouted "clear" and filtered into the large extendable airlock. Fran followed, closing the first door behind them and activating the comm relay box that connected through to the *Hunter*. Stifling a burp, Fran moved to the front once more, and taking a deep breath, opened the outer airlock door. Beyond it stood the exterior hatch of the pirate ship to which they were attached.

D'Ascoine, the Marines and the combat drone all stood poised, their weapons aimed at the sealed door. Fran felt her heart in her throat. She swallowed hard and began to work on hotwiring the airlock of the enemy ship.

It took a long time. She had to burn through the outer control panels and try to wire and crosswire the enemy's airlock. Sinner advised as he could, but that only made her more nervous. On her sixth attempt, she dropped her pliers.

"Bowman," D'Ascoine ordered with impatience, "Shaped charge."

"Belay that order." Alex's command came through the comms. "That will risk hull integrity and endanger any prisoners they might have."

"But sir, I…" D'Ascoine said in a peevish voice.

"Continue, Able Technician," Alex said.

Fran tried twice more and the door slid open. Inside was an empty airlock.

"Carry on, Leftenant."

D'Ascoine nodded, Corporal Bowman immediately moved forward, and Fran stepped back. She was both relieved and upset; fully aware that D'Ascoine's use of explosives was a comment on her own ability to hotwire the door. It took Bowman less than thirty-seconds to place, set and detonate the charge.

As the smoke cleared, the boarding party flooded through the enemy airlock, guns at the ready. Riding the combat drone as only goa could, Sinner took point, quickly striding into the corridor with his heavily beweaponed arms pointing at possible dangers. Radar, sonar and a range of other sensors that reached far beyond his own perception flooded the corridor, lighting the passage across the electromagnetic and audio spectrums. He knew the exact distances and primary composition of every surface. He could read the reflection of heat sources off of every wall. His high-range gamma wave and EMR sensors revealed the working of electronics behind the walls. His heightened and parabolic hearing could detect the variations in the footfalls behind him, filter out the echoes, determine exactly how much noise each of them was making, and estimate how far that noise was carried down the hall.

He stopped on his mark and the others moved into position. Behind "him," Bowman took the left-flank, with D'Ascoine on the more vulnerable right. Sinner gave the hierarch credit for that: whatever faults the Leftenant had, cowardice wasn't one of them. Behind them Chrom followed up in the headless giant that was her OST-1012, creating a classic diamond attack formation. Looking through the "eyes" of the drone, Sinner could see the various active sensors Chrom used as she panned the surfaces around them searching for traps.

Once they were sure it was clear, Sinner retracted the limbs of the drone. Its legs folded below its pod like body, allowing it to rest on its treads. Its arms drew in onto its top creating a single massive combination of firepower. Within two seconds, it became a far more compact, tank-like device, allowing others the ability to easily shoot over its top.

Rolling forward on point, Sinner's consciousness glided along the corridor. He stayed alert and fed his information to those behind him. Coming to a T-junction, he paused, first scanning with his cone of penetrating radiation, then extending one of the robot's microfilament sensor pods around the corners. To the left, Sinner saw three figures in environmental suits, two armed with combat rifles, the third had what looked like a laser. On the right was a team of two gunmen, one of which had a large weapon that Sinner did not recognize.

"Alright people," D'Ascoine said, "Attack plan Tango-Juliet One.... Ready? Go!"

Fran stood guard in the extendible airlock, hands sweating profusely as she tried to ensure no counter-boarding action could rush the *Hunter*. Using a heads-up projection, she tried to keep track of the progress of the boarding party without letting her attention leave the long threatening hallway before her. She strove to keep a steady aim as she watched the video feed from the others as they moved forward. She felt like she would puke.

She jumped as the *Hunter*'s inner airlock opened behind her. The Skipper moved up to her side, patted her shoulder and nodded in his armored helmet. She felt a wave of reassurance fill her. The airlock door sealed behind them.

"Keep your visor-shield open and clear of projections for the moment, Able Tech," Fotheringday said, and she could almost hear his smile, "You real-eye the gangway while I look with suit-enhanced vision. That way, even if I am fooled, you won't be."

"Aye, aye, Sir," she said, and found to her surprise that she was smiling. A series of gunshots and blasts sounded from down the hall. Continued small arms fire followed. She caught her breath, but her hands were no longer shaking.

Sinner rolled forward, pivoted his arm-mounted weapons platforms in each direction and opened fire. Laser light, plasma energy and armor piercing bullets filled both corridors. Behind him, Bowman and D'Ascoine knelt at the corners and unloaded the rocket assisted grenades from their own guns. He heard synthesized ping noises as the enemy bullets bounced harmlessly off the drone's armored surface. Blasts from both the grenades and the plasma bolts shook the ship. The combat was over before it began; blood, gore and smoke filled the corridors.

"First junction secured," D'Ascoine reported with a smile.

"Very good," Fotheringday said, "advance to the bridge with caution. Those troops were well armed."

"Aye, aye, sir," D'Ascoine responded, "Corporal, drop a spybot and shaped charge here. Chief, take point. Gunny, rearguard."

"Aye, aye sir," the two non-coms responded in unison as they implemented the order. Sinner rolled forward, Chrom stood facing the left hand corridor and Bowman placed a small camera at the intersection and wired an explosive charge across the corridor. When they were done, they re-formed into a diamond and moved down the hall. His rear camera showed that true to form, Chrom walked backward for a few meters every ten or so paces.

Scanning ahead as they moved, Sinner noted that thus far, the ship's configuration matched the standardized plan of a *Pyrma* class cargo ship that they had downloaded from the library. Exactly. That made him suspicious. This vessel was thirty years old if it were a day and had been augmented with extra weapons and bays for fighter drones.

"What is it, Chief?" Chrom asked.

"There's something not…."

The bulkhead at the far end of the corridor dropped down: a false wall moving with blinding speed to reveal an array of anti-boarding defenses. Two anti-tank rockets launched from sockets in the wall and raw plasma energy erupted from other emplacements. Sinner flooded the hall at once with high yield lasers scanning at rapid motion, detonating the rockets before they'd traveled a meter. The corridor filled with a rolling cloud of fire, but as the bolts of plasma tore into him, white hot fragments of the drone flew as the near fusion level energy detonated its armor. Bowman and D'Ascoine were thrown back two meters, the Leftenant crashing into Chrom before crumbling to the ground.

Damaged, but not down, Sinner opened up with all of his weapons, targeting the hardened points in the ship bulkhead. The defenses at the end of the corridor exploded as his guns hit true, but not before responding in kind. Behind them another hidden door opened and a well armored squad of figures fired on the drone. Explosions rocked the hallway. Pieces of bulkhead tore through the ship, and feedback caused Sinner to scream as the combat drone was knocked flat by another plasma bolt.

Chrom watched the combat drone drop to the deck and shook her head.

"Fucking robot Navy pussy," she said as she saw the enemy filing into the corridor through the smoke and flames. She didn't hesitate. Even through the powered armor she felt the silent vibrations of her RFRG. A stream of high explosive armor piercing rounds shredded all that they came in touch with. Designed to penetrate the armor of an OST-1000, or even a tank if it was lucky, the ammunition left little of the pirates at the end of the hall. Inside her combat gear, Chrom briefly heard the thud of bullets hitting her, but the standard rounds did no damage.

As the smoke cleared she was glad to see that Sinner had managed to take out the anti-boarding weapons before going down. She fired a shoulder mounted missile at it all the same. After a second, there was no-one at the far end of the corridor to fire upon. She spun around quickly to check her rear, then returned to a defensive stance facing the charred gangway in front of her.

"Sound out!" Alex ordered. On his display he could see that Bowman's biometric signs were slightly erratic, and D'Ascoine's through the roof.

"Tango One!" came D'Ascoine's voice, filled with fury.

"Tango Two," Chrom said, calm and collected. Her feed scanned corridor and her two downed comrades.

"Tango Three," Bowman's call came out as he came to his feet. He sounded dazed.

Looking through D'Ascoine's feed, Alex saw that Bowman's right shoulder guard had been torn apart and seared by the molten pieces of the drone. Feedback sensors from his CEVA told Alex that nothing had penetrated the deeper layers of his armor, but sensors could be wrong.

"Frickin' four… gaddammit." Sinner's voice sounded more like the victim of a hangover than a combat.

"Damage D'Ascoine. Is anyone wounded?" Alex asked.

"Fine, sir… we're fine," D'Ascoine reported as Alex watched him check out his troopers, "A bit shaken, and the drone is down for the count, but we're still good to go."

"Your feed shows…."

"Suit damage, nothing more," D'Ascoine said, "We can bloody well take this ship."

"Proceed with caution."

The three marines moved forward with even greater awareness. At the end of the corridor they encountered the remains of what had once been between six to eight personnel. Doing a quick head count, Chrom doubted there could be many more left on board. Advancing with caution, they opened doors they passed and tossed in flash-bang grenades to stun any inhabitants. They found none. Either there was another trap or they'd killed most of the crew already.

Before long they came to the double sealed doors of the bridge. Bowman placed a breaching charge on the airlock and they blew it open. D'Ascoine immediately tossed in two flash-bangs. Screams sounded and inside Chrom saw two crewmen in old fashioned vacuum suits grasping at their eyes and rolling on the deck. Bowman and D'Ascoine rushed in, thrusting the two crewmen against the ship's controls, subduing them in moments. Chrom held the door. Nothing came forward.

After twenty more minutes of searching, the ship was declared secure. Three prisoners were taken, one of whom had been unconscious in engineering. The rest of the crew had been killed. Most importantly, the primary target of the mission, the ship's computer, was recovered intact.

As Lieutenant Commander Fotheringday strode into the cargo hold where the prisoners were being kept, the room fell quiet. Watching their faces it was clear to Chrom that the pirates hadn't expected a mandellan lord, with his tall strong build and imposing Imperial Naval black. He walked into the bay area, helmet under his arm, casting a cool gaze around the room. He turned his prismatic eyes on the captives.

Chrom watched her CO with a mixture of admiration and trepidation. He was well armed and armored, but his helmet was off and his weapons away. She knew that the first impression would be as important as any number of later threats or coercion; the image he presented was one of confidence and control.

"You really should have surrendered, you know," he said in his calm, deep and educated voice, "it would have made all of our lives far easier. Now, tell me, which of you is in command?"

The pirates looked at each other for a moment, but did not answer.

"Despite your failure to comply when I first ordered you to, I am still in the position to offer clemency should any of you assist. All you have to do…"

Chrom was taken off guard. They had taken ample time to secure the prisoners, but somehow one of them had managed to free himself. The figure leapt up and was on the captain before she or other marines could react.

"Dalang!" he shouted. Chrom watched with horror as the villain reached her CO with a single-crystal steel blade in his hand and a murderous look in his eyes.

Fotheringday reacted with smooth, easy – almost lazy motions, as if completely unperturbed by the assault. He blocked and deflected the knife with the gentle sweep of one arm, and casually stepped aside. Grasping the assailant's hand and exerting pressure on his wrist, he used the pirate's own strength and aggression against him. The blade fell to the ground as Fotheringday slammed the man against the wall, holding his wrist at a painful angle and pressing his own body against that of the terrorist. There was the slight crunching sound of tearing ligaments. The fight was over before Chrom had the chance to take two steps.

"That was not exactly what I had in mind," Fotheringday said in a bemused and almost kindly voice, "Sergeant, would you please ensure that the other prisoners are properly bound?"

"Aye, sir," she responded by doubling the bindings on the other two prisoners and resecuring the one that attacked the Skipper. They searched all three terrorists again, but found no additional weapons.

"Well then, I suppose we need to give these men a little time to think. Leftenant, escort these gentlemen to the brig units."

Chrom watched as the Captain walked calmly out of the hold with an air of amusement on his features.

"Not bad," Bowman said on a private line.

"For Navy," she replied.

Back in his quarters, with the door to his cabin sealed shut behind him, Alex leaned heavily on the bulkhead and dropped his helmet. Images of drifting toys and bloodied bodies flashed through his mind. His breath was ragged and he was covered in a cold sweat. His hands trembled out of control. Slowly his knees buckled out from under him and he slid to the floor.

CHAPTER 33

"I am fairly certain that that's all we'll get from them," Samantha reported while Alex nodded in response. His eyes had not moved from hers since she started speaking, and for the first time in her life she realized how disconcerting the shifting color wheels of a mandellan's irises could be.

She was perched on the edge of one of the comfortable armchairs in Alex's quarters, D'Ascoine lounged in the other. As ever, Alex was behind his desk. He seemed more calm and collected than he had since he took over. She felt anything but and couldn't figure out why.

"Unfortunately," Samantha continued, "none of our prisoners knew very much. The command and boarding crews of the *Van Deer Lieuw* were killed in the assault. But, what we have found is interesting. Unless these pirates took a ship intact, they normally received payment for their stolen cargos from a contact they called "Ankh" in Binghouse, a city on Lai-Jung Prime. I know it. It's a small time place."

"And if they did manage to take a whole vessel?" Alex asked. His eyes sparkled, and a very small smile touched his lips. Samantha smiled in response.

"Then the first mate would take the ship to some other location, but our prisoners have no idea where that might have been."

"What about this Rubo fellow?" Alex asked. For the first time in the meeting, his jaw tensed ever so slightly.

Samantha shrugged and drew a breath through her teeth. "Nothing more than a name mentioned once or twice by the command crew, I'm afraid. He was obviously a Federalist, and likely Wayang, but our captives didn't know anything else about him."

"That's all you've gotten out of them?" D'Ascoine asked, putting his feet up on Alex's desk, "Time to put them back into the tank if you ask me."

Alex's face remained impassive as his eyes went first to the TOMO's feet, then to his face. He didn't say a word.

"The prisoners were forty-eight hours in total sensory deprivation," Samantha said, turning to look at D'Ascoine for the first time since the debriefing began, "Any more is a violation of Imperial Regulations."

"Fine," D'Ascoine said, rolling his eyes, "Use other techniques."

Alex cocked an eyebrow and turned his attention back to Samantha.

"If I thought it would do any good I'd keep pressing," she said to the CO.

"I know that," Alex said with a nod and a smile, "and I respect your expertise in this, Lieutenant. These are low level criminals who use the insurgency as an excuse. That is exactly what we expected to find. Indeed, we obtained two names and not only a world, but a city for making contact. We now have a great deal more than anyone has had on these people before. Thank you, Lieutenant, a very thorough report."

"Thank you, sir."

"Your report, Leftenant?" Alex said, swiveling his chair towards the TOMO.

"Not much that we didn't already know, old bean," D'Ascoine said with a smirk.

Alex met the smile with an expectant stare. After the briefest of pauses, D'Ascoine pulled his feet from the desk and sat up properly in his chair.

"The *Van Deer Lieuw* was armed with weapons that come from outside Imperial space," D'Ascoine said, his manner now stiff and professional. A slowly spinning holographic schematic of the ship they had taken appeared over Alex's desk. "But they're based on Imperial design. The lasers are standard mid-yield things, but the targeting systems and plasma cannon look Federalist. The kind they sell to rebel groups here and there."

"What about the fighter drone control systems?" Alex asked.

"Those are definitely Federalist in origin," D'Ascoine said, and as he spoke, the corresponding systems on the holograph shown brightly, "but according to Chief Sinclair, they've a few really new innovations. So do the tracker satellites they had in orbit. Doesn't match anything that's on the books and no makers' marks or serial numbers. Not even filed off; never had 'em. Maybe a new faction supplying the goods?"

Alex looked meaningfully at Samantha. "That would support our working hypothesis."

"They might still have bought them legitimately from a small company," Samantha said, "There are a few Fringe and Interface corporations who don't bother with tagging their inventory. Out beyond the periphery tracking stolen goods is almost impossible."

"Indeed," Alex said leaning back in his chair, "Well done, Leftenant, but do keep looking. As for my own investigations, most of the pirate's logs seem to correlate with what you say. They were obviously careful to avoid discussing any illegal actions directly, but even so, it is clear that they moved stolen cargos through Lai-Jung. When they managed to get a ship intact, however, they would move it through another, unspecified location. Unfortunately, their captain wasn't a fool and the logs are no better at indicating where that might be than the prisoners are. Still, they had enough recordings of the Dalang to show they were part of the Wayang network."

"That's something," Samantha said.

"It is at that," Alex said with a warm smile. He leaned forward and softly slapped his palms against his desk. "Now, I suppose we have been lingering around this system long enough. It is time to move on I think, but with a bit of a change in plan. We are going to bypass the base at Listun Ferrigus and take the prize ship and the prisoners directly to Lai-Jung."

"You have a plan, sir?" Smith asked.

"I think it is time to try to find out a bit more about the re-sale of our items."

"Con, Engineering. No residual spiking from the ER drive, ma'am. We're clear."

"Very well, Chief," Samantha's voice sounded from the comm, "Begin the recharging process."

"Engineering, aye." Sinner typed in a series of commands for the ER field generator as he mentally instructed its power plant. He and Fran had been working on their prize ship, the *Van Deer Lieuw*, for two days and most of the damage was fixed. It was taking a lot of jury rigging and reprogramming, but they almost had it licked. In a day or two it would be just him and Sammy alone on the ship, and truth be told, Sinner was looking forward to it. He hadn't spent much time with her recently, what with her working so closely with the CO. It would be good to be alone with her for a while.

"Chief," Fran said, "The fusion rockets are performing at eighty-seven percent, and the HO is running at full value."

"That's good, Fran. Are you still getting feedback from the rockets?"

"Nope, I think I got it down." Fran sounded more than a little tired. There were dark circles under her eyes. "Yep, it's stable."

"Goddamn kid, you've come a long way."

"Thank you, Chief," Fran said. She gave a smile about as wide as he'd ever seen.

"No, I mean it. You're damned good for a natural, I'm impre–" two bells sounded in the Engineering chamber, broadening his smile, "Woo hoo! It's Oh-Beer-Hundred! An' I'm buyin'!"

"I'll be along in a minute," Fran replied, turning back to her console, "I just want to get the robots onto insulating that feedback."

"Bullshit," Sinner replied, "That could take hours."

"I know that's why I want to get started on it now so that I can…"

"It can wait," Sinner interrupted

"Okay. Maybe I'll just…."

"Maybe you'll just come with me to the lounge, meet the friggin' jar-heads and have a few brewskies! That's an order."

"Okay… okay… but can I have some alchopop instead?"

"You're just too much, kid," Sinner said as he shook his head and smiled. Putting his arm around her shoulders like a proud father, he led Fran back to the mess-lounge of the *Hunter* where they celebrated a job well done.

Hammond read the report of the attack on Sir Richard and paused. Sitting in a bland office of the Lai-Jung Headquarters of Cameron-Inglesie, he stared at the holowalls, not seeing the market reports projected there. He blinked repeatedly before launching a query for other bombings in the sector. He cross-indexed the results with reports of sectarian violence between elements of the Federalists, and compared it with assaults on Imperial Hierarchs. He opened his reports on the new anti-insurgency efforts: particularly those involving the 12th Fleet and the

Ministry of Justice. He compared the INI reports Sir Richard gave him to the information he had received from his own sources. He cross checked it against the Cameron-Inglesie routes, and frowned when he noted that the one's he had changed had been re-routed back to their original courses. Then he compared them against his records for attacks committed by insurgent groups.

"Twelve, twenty-four, thirty-six," he said, his eyes scanning the images, examining the charts, and counting up incidents that seemed to cross-check. "Damn it all, what the hell do you think your doing?"

CHAPTER 34

"*Why are we watching this guy*?" Bolyiacov asked. She stood at a copper kiosk that sold porn and coffee. Neither looked very good.

Electric cars ran through the streets, but they did little to reduce the fumes of the decaying industrial city. Fringe worlds were often bad, but Lai-Jung was worse. Huge empty stretches of dangerous wilderness broken up by urban sprawls like this one: a walled city whose defining characteristic was disparity between the rich and the poor. Dark crumbling architecture filled this part of the megalopolis, while in the distance towering buildings glistened at the city's heart. The Imperial revitalization had not yet reached this portion of its client state's redevelopment.

"*Because Rubo told us to*," Alyiar responded as he followed their mark into the bus station. It stood near the outer wall. Until he had headed towards it, Alyiar couldn't figure out what a man like this one would be doing in such a crummy part of the city.

"*Look at him*," Bolyiacov said, putting down her magazine and picking up another, "*He's a mid-level corporate drone. Who the hell is going to pay us for him?*"

Inside, the station was a status symbol of a bygone era. Huge, with marbled floors and arching ceilings, there were cracks along the surfaces and scaffolds that held up portions of the walls. At one end of the entrance hall, Imperial drones crawled over the surfaces, repairing the crumbling surfaces. Alyiar absently noted them as a good target for a bomb.

"*Who knows? Who cares?*" he said. The man changed directions and headed to the toilets. Alyiar signaled Wylde to be ready. "*We're good soldiers. We do what we're told.*"

The target suddenly turned from his course again, veering from the bathrooms, Alyiar did not. The smell of stale urine soon filled his senses as he wondered if the man suspected he was being watched or just uncertain where he was going.

"*Speak for yourself,*" Wylde said, heading out of the bathrooms and passing Alyiar without a glance. Alyiar opened a mental window to follow Wylde's progress. He was now on the target's tail, heading towards the ticket booths.

"*I just don't see what profit we might make from this guy,*" Bolyiacov said. She picked up yet another magazine, this one about the local gladiatorial car combats.

Alyiar reduced her window and focused on Wylde. He was in line three places behind their target.

Activating his bladder, Alyiar let loose a stream into the graying porcelain basin. His attention on the operation, he missed and nearly hit his shoes. The man next to him gave him a disgusted look.

"*We watch and keep him safe. At least until we're ordered to do otherwise.*" Alyiar said. He smiled apologetically at the man to his side. Wylde focused his parabolic hearing on their mark.

"This ain't a library, lady," the man at the kiosk said to Bolyiacov, "Buy something or move on."

"Fuck you," she said, but put down the magazine and walked inside. It was getting close to her activation point anyway.

"I'd like a ticket to Binghouse," the voice came from Wylde's feed. It was their target.

Alyiar zipped up, not bothering to wash his hands. The man who had been next to him gave another disgusted look. Alyiar couldn't care less. Back in the large echoing hall, he headed to the departure hall.

"Round trip?" the teller asked.

"One way."

Binghouse was hardly the kind of place that a respectable business man would head. It had a starport, but was separate from the sprawls; it was more the kind of city that the Wayang would frequent. It was also the home of the Ankh. That sent up signals.

"Name?" the teller asked their target. A thick layer of bullet and bomb proof glass separated them.

"Hammond, Kyle," the target responded.

Alyiar reached the security checkpoint and passed through unchallenged. He walked down the ramp to the long corridor with gates and windows into the bus garage. He could see the ranks of buses that lay behind the reinforced glass gates. Huge armored behemoths with mini-gun turrets, flame throwers and rocket launchers mounted along their sides. A cavernous gun-port beneath the driver's viewport suggested a front mounted tank gun. Outside the urban zones, Lai-Jung was a violent world, especially the roads.

Alyiar passed the gate marked as the Binghouse Express and stopped three gates up. He sat on the floor, and waited. He wished he had slipped into a stall and changed his form in the bathroom, but it was too late now; their target was walking through security. Alyiar stared at the ground, hoping to hide his face. He checked in on his companions.

Wylde had the ticket and was walking past Bolyiacov. It was a smooth handoff, and unless someone knew to look, no one would have noticed him pass her the ticket. Two minutes later she was standing beside Hammond in the line, waiting to get onto the giant armored bus. She tried flirting with him, but he politely brushed her off. He pretended to read some data from a PAD, but in fact kept an eye on Alyiar.

"*Who the fuck is this guy?*" Alyiar asked.

"*Who knows? Who cares?*" Bolyiacov said in a snarky voice, "*We're good soldiers. We do what we're told, right?*"

Looking around the bridge of the *Van der Lieuw*, Samantha sighed. Designed for at least four people, it was considerably larger than that of the *Hunter*, and built for the kinds of operations performed by a cargo vessel. Yet it had been modified, first by the pirates who put extra weapons controls systems in, and then by Sinner, who had jury-rigged the controls so a single person could fly the ship. Here and there she could also see the places where he had repaired damage done in the attack. As ever, Sinner had done a great deal in a short time.

Once this was a legitimate cargo ship, she thought, *what happened to change that?*

A chime sounded in her mind and a text message scrolled across the bottom edge of her peripheral vision. She opened a window into her interface room and saw her own avatar in a third-person stance standing on the fjords of her home world. Samantha maximized the text that was floating around her VR self and read the more detailed accounts that told her that the ship's command, control and communications systems were ready. She nodded to herself and her avatar mimicked the motion.

"How's it going, Sin?" she asked, opening a ship-wide comm channel. Through the visual window that appeared in her mind's eye she saw his feet sticking out of a corroded access hatch. Tubes and wires crisscrossed everywhere around him.

"We're all set, Sammy," Sinner said, without bothering to change camera angles or project an avatar, "It looks more like an experiment in plumbing than an engine room, but it checks out."

"Are you sure that you have that fluctuation accounted for Sin?" Samantha asked.

"Yes, yes, and the irregularities in the Essar-Rosenthal field. The HO generator is running as good as she'll get, and well inside of what we need."

Samantha paused expectantly, but no joke, tease or jibe followed the comment. A small frown touched her brow and she sighed.

"Alright then," she said and paused a moment more before pressing a button to open the ship-to-ship comms, "*Hunter* this is the *Van Deer Lieuw*."

"*Van Deer Lieuw* this is the *Hunter*, go ahead," Alex's voice sounded over the ship-to-ship comm.

"I'm ready to begin navigational synchronization," Samantha said.

"Very well," he said, "Calculate away. I'll be waiting to adjust values here when you've finished."

Samantha had to hand it to Alex, he didn't have any problems either accepting or delegating responsibilities. Many – no most of her previous COs had felt some strange sense of competition with her, even the ones who she got along with. Alex didn't, even though her investigation into his past had given him every reason to resent her. In fact, she doubted there were many ship's captains who would allow their Executive Officers to plot the course of tandem jumps, but Alex seemed to recognize that she was a better navigator and wasn't threatened by the fact.

She plugged into the portable interface defense buffer system she and Sinner had hardwired into the *Van der Lieuw*, turned it on, and maximized her interface room. Her view of the ship's bridge vanished, and she quickly dropped from the virtual Meridothian setting to the floating star field of her navigation interface.

She opened the *Van der Lieuw*'s navigational records and groaned. Even without comparing light cones and the like, she could tell that some of the data was far out. Sloppy navigational processes were not very common among private merchant captains, but at least one of the navigators on this ship had been very lazy.

"Sinner?" she said in the real world, though she had not dropped out of the navigation interface, "this is going to take a while."

"Oh big shock there," Sinner said, "You're normally so quick about it all…Sloppy even."

"Just letting you know." She smiled. That was the Sinner she knew and loved.

Slowly but surely she scrutinized the data, comparing errors, comparing corrections, going through the whole process step by step. As she did, she began to see the hand of different navigators in the records. Some were good, some good enough, and some just plain bad. It was going to take hours.

She scanned through the data, noting her regular points to check accuracy, then suddenly stopped. Buried in among all the data was one piece of precision recording. She had to double check it to be sure.

There was a correction in Inglesie system that adjusted for a 0.044 percent variance from the projected values that was always observed when measurements were from the side of the system facing the galactic-core. It was an extremely minor variance caused by an unknown anomaly. It was probably created by some object in deep space that was nevertheless near enough to the system for it's gravity to create a light bend. It was, in fact, so minor it would not cause any real navigational difficulties. Even Samantha had never bothered to explore its causes, but someone even more anal than her had corrected for it while leaving all the other data rough and inaccurate. Somewhere in the back of her mind, that rang a bell.

Looking at the core records, Samantha noted that the information had been downloaded from another ship, and smiled to herself. *That explains it, probably someone they hijacked. Bastards.*

She continued on, but something about the correction still bothered her. She kept on working, but her mind returned time and again to the data. It wasn't until she created the Bradley projection that it dawned on her where she had seen the corrections before. She suddenly stopped, looked at her personal navigational records, and opened a channel to the *Hunter*.

"Alex, we have to talk. Now."

CHAPTER 35

The forward saloon of Sir Richard's corporate yacht was large and luxurious. A red curving sofa wrapped around the forward arc of the ship, and the viewports behind it provided a marvelous panorama of the vastness of space. Plush curvilinear loungers and chairs were precisely placed in small groupings throughout the room to provide intimate conversation areas. A variety of stylishly amorphous sculptures decorated the tables and the occasional blank spaces on the walls were fitted with abstract art of the Jacundi period.

In the aftward section, three steps led up to a sliding glass panel, behind which lay Sir Richard's office. At the moment, the panel was open, and Sir Richard leaned back in his desk chair with tented fingers watching a mass of recordings. Some were simple two-dimensional windows that hovered in the air, others were proper holograms that moved around the room.

The central media was a recording of Admiral Lord Rippavitch that had been played at a Senate meeting on education reform. As ever, it was stirring and more than a bit aggrandizing. He made occasional reference to the work of his gallant anti-insurgency fleet, and spoke frequently of the superiority of education provided by the Empire's predecessor, the Sophyan Confederal Republic. Sir Richard only paid it the most peripheral of attention. After all, it was bill that everyone knew would pass.

Instead he focused on the hovering images showing news reports of the increase of piracy and guerilla activity along the Alterande and Archon sectors. Such reports seemed somewhat contradictory to the claims of success by the heroic Admiral. From Sir Richard's perspective, the insurgency appeared to be growing, perhaps not in size, but certainly in professionalism.

When the image of the bizarrely tattooed ectomorph with an elongated skull appeared, he muted all of the other recordings and listened specifically to its proclamation. When it didn't say anything he hadn't expected, Sir Richard returned to comparing the location of the insurgent attacks to the areas where his own ships were headed. He was deep in that analysis when his attention was suddenly drawn back to the recording of the Ripper. He immediately froze all the other recordings, rewound the former Head of the Hegemonist's statement and listened to it replay.

"...is why I am pleased to cast my vote in favor of this bill," the Ripper said, "along with those who proxied their votes to me, the Archduke D'Ascoine, the Primate of Ramanith, the Eorl of Hammonrie, the Senator of Xiang-chi, the Speaker of...."

Sir Richard rewound the recording twice more, making certain he heard the title correctly. He checked the Senatorial Records just to be certain of what he knew full well already. The Eorl of Hammonrie was Lieutenant Commander Lord Raiden Alexander Parviz Fothingday: Alex. He leaned back in his chair with a furrowed brown.

"So that's how you managed to get posted to the Raiders," he said. His eyes dashed between the image of the Ripper, that of the Dalang and the maps that compared insurgent activities to his own shipping routes. His frown deepened.

Alex looked at his Executive Officer with curiosity as they hurried through the *Hunter.* To say she seemed anxious was an extreme understatement. They had been minutes away from making a jump when Samantha had insisted on meeting face to face in his quarters. Now she was striding from the airlock to his quarters with frantic purpose, but her head looked to the ground as if she were in deep thought.

"It's in the data log, sir," Samantha said as they entered his cabin, "I was going through the navigational data, when I noticed something. It was obvious really, I should have caught it when I first reviewed the records, I suppose I had only done an initial scan but still…."

"What, exactly, are you talking about, Lieutenant?" Alex asked, sealing the door to his quarters behind him. She stood in the center of the room, eyes glimmering and a deadly serious look on her face.

"Well sir," she said, taking a quick breath as if to calm herself, "I was reviewing the *Van Deer Lieuw*'s navigational data and noticed that the data from the Inglesie system, which is always about 0.044 off the projected values, had been corrected. Now, that is a tiny variance and even I never bothered to track it down, but the otherwise sloppy records from the *Van Deer Lieuw* had removed it."

"Unusual I agree, but they could have downloaded it from one of their victims," Alex said. He still couldn't see the need to interrupt their transit.

"At first, that's what I thought," Samantha said, gesticulating with a closed fist and punctuating her points with her thumb. It was the exact same technique her father used to use in his debates against the Emperor, "The more I thought about it, the more it reminded me of something. I thought I'd seen that data corrected once before."

She turned from Alex and began to pace up and down the small room like a caged animal.

"It turns out I did," she said, looking at the deck as she made her short circuits up and down his cabin, "after we had downloaded the NavCom records from the fleet… the 12th Fleet…. Another ship had also already noted the variance, an Imperial Naval vessel: the *HMS Reichmann*."

Alex leaned against the door and folded his arms. He was beginning to see why she had wanted the secrecy.

"Now sir, 0.044 is really only a minor variance, one that wouldn't cause any navigational difficulties. Most navigators don't even bother looking for data like this, but well, I guess my Astrographic background makes me a little… well..."

"Precise?" Alex offered with a smile.

"Anal," Samantha said, pausing her stride long enough to smile, "but I always check this sort of thing and keep it to try and improve my accuracy. It's a compulsion I guess. I checked the data against that of over a thousand ships that have passed through Inglesie, and none of them have ever corrected that variance, but these two ships did, and they are the only two ships that have."

"A rather unusual coincidence."

"More than unusual, the corrections in both readings are identical," Samantha said, stopping immediately in front of him, "There's no way that two different navigators could have come up with these corrections independently. They'd to have made the same observations using the same equipment at the exact same location and the exact same time. The data was shared."

"The two ships could have encountered each other before, or indeed, they might have uploaded the information from a third ship that had made the correction themselves."

"No, I thought of that," Samantha replied, then started pacing again.

It struck Alex that she was very attractive when impassioned, then he drove the thought from his head.

"The corrections on the pirate vessel weren't uploaded," She said, staring at the ground as she walked back and forth, "they were entered manually. The ones I found from the

Naval vessels had been exchanged only twice since they were recorded by the *Reichmann*: once to the *HMS Aramus* which is part of Ripper's Raiders, once to the *HMS Résolut*. We got it from the flagship directly."

"Is it possible that the data taken from the *Reichmann* had been gathered from another vessel? Perhaps a pirate vessel that it had encountered?"

"Very unlikely," she said and stopped at the far end of the room. Her eyes looked down in the manner of a person checking data through their implants. "The *Reichmann* is a System-boat tender: a repair, refueling and supply vessel. It's unlikely she would have been directly involved in an anti-pirate action."

"Do we have the name of the recording officer?"

"No… no." Samantha half sat on his desk, still clearly accessing the archives, "It's a third hand download with shorthand metadata: all we have is the officer's rank and initials, but unfortunately no serial number. A Sub-lieutenant KH, recorded on day 157 year 30 on the Imperial calendar."

"A year and a half ago," Alex said, "Do we know which fleet they were with?"

"The *Reichmann* was assigned to the… 117th but also seemed to work closely with the 253rd out of Alterande, and seems to have done at least one mission in conjunction with elements of the 12th…"

"What did you say?" Alex asked, and he felt his stomach drop. He was no longer noticing his anxious XO. The mental exercise had suddenly taken a very real and personal turn. "Did you say the 117th?"

"Yes and the 253rd. They tended to…" Samantha stopped, her kinetic frenzy freezing as her eyes met his. "You were serving in the 117th when you were set up for the *Silver Slipper*."

"Indeed I was."

CHAPTER 36

After coming out of jump and ensuring the *Van der Lieuw* was still with them, Alex looked at the command displays. The Lai-Jung system lay spread out before them, cartographically illustrated in the holograph projected between the pilot and navigation posts, displayed as a vector map on the monitors, and seen in part as glimmering star-like points of light through the viewport in front of him. Sitting at the tail end of the Corridor Main, the system was a remarkably busy port. The central star was a middle-sized dim yellow star surrounded by fifteen orbiting planets of varying magnitudes and types. Each had some form of habitation on it, though many were nothing more than a handful of scientists, miners or military personnel. Only three of the worlds had any sizable population, and the principal of these was the fourth planet from the local star: the planet known to most people as Lai-Jung Prime, though its inhabitants called it Broome.

The majority of interstellar traffic centered on this world, a major trading post that stood as a client state of the Sophyan Empire, independent but protected by the Imperial forces. The *Hunter*, however, set course to a different planet: Al Derone, the system's largest gas giant. The Empire's principal bases in the Sector orbited that world. Elements of the defense forces of Imperial Army Guardians and the assault troops of the Imperial Army Rangers had command posts there. So did the Imperial Astrographic Service.

Yet beyond a doubt, the largest presence in Lai-Jung was the Sophyan Imperial Navy's 253rd Fleet whose central hub of operations was their facility at Alterande High Command. Warships of every denomination orbited, docked or slowly moved around the array of spacedocks and command centers that made up the Naval base. Alex slowly maneuvered the ship through the orbital traffic, past the half-million ton battleships and five thousand ton destroyers, by the five hundred ton cargo vessels and troop movers, to the slowly spinning disc of the Central Command and Communications Hub – the true headquarters of the 253rd.

Sensors told Alex that Samantha was piloting their prize ship on a perfectly parallel course behind him. Gradually the two of them moved to their pre-assigned docking positions. As he allowed the great space station to seal its docking clamps on his ship, he noted the flexible airlock extending to the damaged hull of the *Van der Lieuw*. In a moment, their prize and prisoners would no longer be Alex's concern, though the data that he and Samantha had removed from its logs would be.

Alyiar lurked in the alley, his fingers shortening, his skin changing from pale to black. Bladders beneath the skin of his chest squeezed liquids out while gel became solid, turning mammaries into pectorals. He reached into his pack, pulling out a new jacket as other changes occurred throughout his body.

His eyes were focused on the decaying bricks and concrete at the end of the alley, beyond the green dumpster that hid him from sight. People occasionally walked back and forth, but not many. Binghouse was not a big city, fluctuating somewhere between a hundred and thirty to two hundred thousand; census figures in Lai-Jung were hardly accurate. There was a local police presence, of course, but it was not something to worry about.

Alyiar was more concerned with the local gangs than the cops. The criminal elements of the wild zones of Lai-Jung were volatile, with shifting loyalties. Still, the Dalang had managed to recruit at least one of the local set of roadraiders who ranged the highways outside the urban zones. The Wayang provided them with weapons to defeat their rivals and in return they provided the Wayang with a percentage of their take. But Alyiar didn't trust them. They were not in it for the revolution; they were in it for themselves.

"*I'm coming up to your spot,*" Bolyiacov said.

"*Acknowledged,*" Alyiar said, opening up a window from her perspective. She was following too closely, wearing her Haute-number-four again which was directly against what he had told her. The subject, Hammond, seemed unaware, but it was hard to say. He had been wandering without purpose all day long and that by itself sent warning signals to Alyiar.

Looking through Bolyiacov's eyes, he watched the man closely. He was either unaware of their presence or very good at faking it. He stopped in the occasional junk store, looked at some of the gun shops, bought the Sophyan Financial Times, did nothing of any consequence. The only problem was that it begged the question of why a corporate drone would come to a hole like Binghouse in the first place.

Hammond suddenly changed course just after he walked out of Wylde's cover zone and two blocks before he entered Alyiar's. It was the only blind spot in their coverage, a necessary risk they had been forced to take. He crossed the street and quickly headed the other direction. The odds of him having done so by accident were astronomical.

"*Fuck,*" Bolyiacov and Wylde cursed in unison.

"*Keep walking,*" Alyiar ordered as he stood up, "*Don't let him…*"

A sudden whooshing noise filled the air, immediately recognizable to all three of the Wayang Stalkers. Looking through Bolyiacov's eyes, Alyiar barely had time to see the rocket propelled grenade before it smashed into the building next to her. Her feed faded immediately to static as the explosion rocked the ground where Alyiar stood.

"Bolyiacov! Bolyiacov!" he shouted as he raced down the alley with cybernetic strength. A cloud of smoke and dust billowed at the far end, filling the street. There were no signals coming from her feed at all. His feet pounded into the ground as screams started sounding from ahead of him. None of them were hers.

"*What the fuck is going on?*" Wylde asked.

Alyiar ignored him, he just kept running. He was two steps from the end of the alley when a short fat woman appeared from out of the dust. Her hand grabbed Alyiar's chest, and slammed him against the wall. As his back hit the bricks, the air was crushed out of him, but his body was ready. Razors shot from his nails, his arms pistoned back and readied to slam his hands into the skull of the fat middle aged woman who held him off the ground.

"Calm the feck down," Rubo's voice came from the fat woman, "and call off the feckin' troops."

Alyiar paused, his body weaponry still ready to spring. He began to cough on the dust, he'd forgotten to activate his lung filters.

"Now Al!" Rubo dropped him, his stubby hands suddenly caressing Alyiar's chest.

"*Stand down,*" Alyiar broadcast, "*and standby.*"

Rubo crushed his lips into Alyiar's just as a troop of soldiers appeared out of the smoke and raced into the alley. They were not local cops responding to an attack, they wore the dove-grey uniforms of Imperial Guardians, and were led by a woman in the grey and blue uniform of the Ministry of Justice. Six of them ran down the alley, two others kept running down the street. Above them Alyiar heard the sound of hoverdrones circling. He pretended to enjoy the small fat woman's kiss as Rubo groped him. The soldiers kept running, passing into the next street.

"What the fuck was that?" Alyiar asked, staring in the direction the Imperial soldiers had run.

"A close call," Rubo said, his hand still pressing Alyiar against the wall. His eyes went in the direction of Bolyiacov.

"She's dead," Rubo said, "The RPG went off right next to her, she never had a chance."

"How the hell…?"

"The Dalang's been keeping an eye on you since you arrived," Rubo said, finally stepping back and brushing the dust off Alyiar, "and so it seems have those bastards."

"We've got to hit the fucking Imperials back for…."

"The Guardians would've interrogated her, not killed her."

"Then who the fuck…?"

"No time to worry about that crap now," Rubo said, "Call back the troops to your rendezvous, we're being sent back to the base; moved out of the line of fire."

"What about Bolyiacov? What about the target?"

"Bolyiacov is dead, there ain't nothing we can do about it. As for the target, don't you worry about him mate," Rubo said, "just make sure that the Stalkers shake whatever tails they might have picked up."

CHAPTER 37

Once protocols were complete and re-supplies were ordered, Alex turned command of the watch over to D'Ascoine; he and Samantha had other work to do. They made their way to the 253rd's Special Intelligence Liaison Officer or SILO. The SILO was a post created specifically to coordinate information between the much toted counter-insurgency forces of Ripper's Raiders and the Alterande Sector's own, more mundane home-fleet. Taking the transport to the fifth level, Alex and Samantha followed the light indicators that led them along the floor until they came to the Intelligence Section. There they were given coffees, and asked to wait.

It did not take long for them to be greeted by an individual whose ID signals identified it as Ensign Throom Popolopolis. 'He' was the first non-human intelligence officer that Alex had seen since being assigned to Ripper's Raiders. Despite Naval Regulations, there were no sophonts in the 12th fleet and he suspected the assignment of Ensign Popolopolis was an intentional slight.

Like all t'K!room, Popolopolis was a radially symmetrical quasi-vertebrate, whose flexible central body was kept within the confines of a large spherical environmental suit.

Openings in the suit's shell permitted the Ensign's fourteen more-or-less evenly spaced tentacle-like limbs to emerge. Each limb was a highly flexible stalk that ended in a flower-like sensory-manipulative organ. Eight leaf shaped appendages, seven eyestalks, and a series of fourteen crab-like pincers radiated around a central ingestive orifice. All of the long, neck/limbs were covered in a ballistic cloth fabric which ended where the colorful orchid-like head/hands started. There, by the head/hand, each sleeve-collar was noted with the stripes and laurels of rank similar to the sleeves or collars of the human Naval officer's counterpart.

"Greetings!" Ensign Popolopolis boomed, clicked and squeaked as it greeted them through the translator device. "It is my pleasure to welcome you to Alterande High Command! I am the Assistant to Lieutenant Corduroy, the Special Intelligence Liaison Officer."

"How do you do, Ensign?" Alex stood as he greeted the envoy, "I am Lieutenant Commander Fotheringday of the 12th Fleet's Advanced Reconnaissance and Attack Group, and this is my Executive Officer, Lieutenant Smith. It is a pleasure to be here."

"I do well and yourselves? If you would be so kind as to follow me, I would be happy to guide you to Lieutenant Corduroy," Popolopolis said, and soon turned to guide them down the hall. Like many of his species that worked with humans, Popolopolis seemed to address Alex and Samantha with only one of his limbs – treating it as if it were its only, or at least primary sensory facility. Using a private comm channel, Samantha noted to Alex that this was done solely for the benefit of the humans. Each of the t'K!room's sensory manipulative organs was fully functional, capable of seeing, hearing and dexterous handling. Like human handedness, they did tend to develop a primacy in one limb, but among themselves, did not rely on it as much as the young Ensign was doing. He chatted cheerfully as he wheeled himself through the halls, stopping at last at the office of his superior, Lieutenant Corduroy.

Inside was a generic naval office with generic art depicting generic ships of the fleet. Behind a desk sat the SILO himself, a man in his late twenties who smiled in a professional, but somewhat reserved manner. As Ensign Popolopolis showed them in, Lieutenant Corduroy stood and gave a forced smile.

"Lieutenant Commander Fotheringday, Lieutenant Smith, welcome to Alterande High Command," the Lieutenant said, giving a brief nod that dismissed the alien Ensign, "I understand you have some prisoners to turn over to us."

Samantha nodded and smiled a thank you at Popolopolis as it scurried from the room. Alex kept his attention on Corduroy. The three of them remained standing around his desk.

"We do indeed," Alex said, giving a glance at the chairs that were not being offered, "Due to Lieutenant Smith's cunning we were able to predict the location of an attack and intercept a pirate ship before it had trapped a commercial vessel."

"I saw the report you las-commed in," Corduroy said, "Good work that. We would, of course, appreciate a copy of any records you managed to download. Did you note anything interesting in them?"

"Nothing significant," Alex lied, "Although it does seem like they traded a great deal of their booty here at Lai-Jung."

"I'm afraid that doesn't surprise me," Corduroy said, finally gesturing for them to sit, "One drawback of Lai-Jung being a client state is that it is independent. While we of the 253rd are given some overall broad powers, we're in no way empowered to police the marketing activities that occur here. The Ministry of Justice has a bit broader power, but even they are limited here. Lai-Jung may benefit from our protection, but doesn't have to obey our laws."

"Charming."

"I suppose we should set up a meeting between yourself and Captain Helsinki, the head of INI for the 253rd. He'll want to debrief you and all."

"At his leisure," Alex said, "Indeed, as long as we are on the topic, when might I have access to the Intelligence files for the sector?"

"I took the liberty of creating a summary file for you on all our active counter-insurgency operations, and gave you a priority clearance to our database for such research."

"Thank you, Lieutenant, I greatly appreciate that. Does that also give us access to other, non-insurgency data as well?"

"Uh, not at present," Cordoroy looked back and forth between Alex and Samantha, "I thought you'd only really be interested in the piracy and terrorism reports. Isn't that the remit of the 12th Fleet?"

"Yes, absolutely," Alex responded, "but I have often found that getting a clearer idea of the overall activity within a region can help me to establish patterns that I might have otherwise missed."

"I suppose," Lieutenant Corduroy said, looking a bit put-out, "well, I'll have to bring this up with Commander Zimmer. I'm afraid I've never been asked for access beyond the counter-insurgency files before. He may be a little reluctant to give you too much clearance. Some of that information is need-to-know only."

"I only want to form an overall picture of what your fleet has to address on a daily basis, nothing particularly sensitive," Alex lied.

The DuZhod watched again as the blonde woman with the stylishly lithe body was torn open by the explosion. Part of the DuZhod's identity was frustrated by the untimely death of the Wayang Stalker, part cursed the primitive surveillance systems of Lai-Jung, and part was highly amused by the entire situation. They launched a wide range of analyses and set several AI's and biogenic avatars to attempt to identify those with whom she had been working.

They were creating additional analytic algorithms when they were interrupted by a summons from Commissar Pushkin. The timing was irritating of course, but when the Head of the Special Flying Squad on Anti-Imperial Activity called, the DuZhod knew it was easiest to answer. The Ursus identity did not like to be severed from the rest of the DuZhod Interactive, but duty called and the He began to separate from the We.

The direct feed i/o jacks withdrew, and with them so did the fast-line connection to the Interactive. As the fiber-optic connections were severed, the biogenic avatar known as Colonel Lord Ursus DuZhod was forced to interface with the other local members of the Interactive by wireless connections alone. He was removed from the hyper-cognitive state of the collective processing and returned to the semi-autonomous state that was his lot. To most humans it would have felt like wakening from a dream, but to Ursus it seemed more like dropping into a deep unconsciousness; a slow world confined by the limits of isolated biological minds.

He opened his eyes as the gee-gel separated from his face, showing his inner eyelid. He sat up before that protective membrane slid open vertically and revealed the mirrored surface of his own visual sensors. He looked around the Ministry of Justice office space that contained his tank and blinked once. Drawing his long, thin arm from the viscous liquid, he ran his thin fingers over his bald skull before stopping to polish one of the chromed metal studs that stuck from his scalp – receivers for a variety of transmitted signals.

Releasing the flaps that sealed his nose against liquids and vacuums, the Colonel took a deep breath, the first for some time, before letting it loose in a heavy sigh. It was not that he hated his time in semi-connectedness; quite the contrary. The central DuZhod truly enjoyed these sojourns into the so called 'real' world, but this particular DuZhod avatar frequently found the companionship of the unconnected to be dull. The speed of verbal communication was sloth-like, and the lack of central order was disgraceful. Even so, the information that this avatar uploaded was crucial. What was more, if his central-self was to be happy, the avatar could endure the more boring periods between his experiential communicative linkings to other biological units.

As he fully unfolded his long thin, ectomorphic body from the grey-green liquid of the gee-gel, he felt the varying inserted tubes and wires of the life support systems extracting from his body. It occurred again to DuZhod that if the rest of the Empire were to actually understand the true nature of the DuZhod Interactive of Zarquin, they would have found it abhorrent. For them, it would have been far worse than any aspect of alien culture that they had encountered since the wars with the Graast. Indeed, he suspected that should humanity and the rest of the known sophants ever come to understand the DuZhodian view of the universe, they would most likely have immediately declared war against the Interactive. As it stood, however, only a handful of individuals outside the DuZhod understood it, and they found the Zarquin far too useful to condemn. Even so, those few individuals would no doubt have felt more comfortable if the Interactive merely collapsed, disappeared, or better yet, had never developed at all.

The history of the DuZhod Interactive dated back to the chaotic period following the fall of the Second Empire: the Strife of the Made. At that point, the DuZhod had represented a single research vessel of exceptional size that had been manned by a series of brilliant minds. When it had become clear that the civil wars that were haunting humanity were spreading, the *USS DuZhod* had jumped into the vast wilderness in order to avoid the chaos that was destroying their society. They had traveled for the better part of a generation from place to place when it slowly dawned on them that the Strife was not going to end anytime soon, and that chaos would reign the stars for centuries.

Those intrepid men and women considered their options and decided that they wished to keep some element of science and society alive for the future. They did not have a large enough population to maintain genetic diversity among themselves, and needed the knowledge and understanding of their experts to survive. So they decided to start self-recorded cloning: a process where the memories of a donor were downloaded into a developing clone of that individual. The process had been invented centuries before, but the spiritual in the society of that time had said that it was a violation of life and free will to enforce one set of memories upon the body of another. For the proto-DuZhod, however, such issues of morality were academic. The need to save the knowledge of humanity for future generations outweighed such philosophical nuances.

That by itself would have been enough to condemn the DuZhod in the eyes of many cultures, but in fact it was only the start. The crew had started to become more and more integrated into the ship. They used cybernetic implants to communicate with both each other and the ship's systems. They found greater and greater relief from the boredom of their long isolation through interacting in a virtual reality environment. They created sophisticated artificial intelligence programs with whom they shared thoughts and responsibilities. In time, many spent so much time interacting through an electronic medium that they lost the sense of where their own thought processes ended and other peoples began. It did not take long for the crew to begin running AIs loaded with their memories, thus allowing them to live, as it were, as machines.

The DuZhod produced multiple clones, downloading the same individual's memories into them for the good of the community. In time, these individuals differentiated from one another based upon their own experiences, but they continued to log-into the computer version of themselves to back up their thoughts. Thus, the computer-selves became aware of all of their cloned selves, but the clones only tended to know what they had experienced. Before long the clones were not considered the 'real individuals' whose memories were being backed up on machines. Rather it was the machines who were the 'real individuals' and occasionally become embodied in the biological form of a clone.

When memory files were shared between the AI-selves, there was a blending of individuals into a collective super-self. The crew lost their individuality and became the DuZhod: a collective We of cyborgs and computers that sought to experience more, to add to its knowledge and experience. Yet, the nature of their limited experiences and repetitive realities resulted in boredom, so clones were thrown into dangerous and mortal games, linked to the central beings the entire time of course. They became a society of computers that played person games.

When they came across the Zarquin system, a human society dying from a lack of the technologies necessary to keep its atmosphere processors working, the DuZhod saw a better way to fight ennui. They stopped their searching and created a new home. The people of Zarquin were dying and desperate to survive, and so they readily agreed to join the Interactive without truly understanding what it meant. The result was the addition of a billion new minds to the interactive, all with a strict access protocol that allowed the DuZhod to have greater control and access than the Zarquin. It took only a few generations for them to become truly integrated into the DuZhodian interactive mind.

A few generations later when the expanding Sophyan Confederal Republic encountered the DuZhod, the technocracy was already fully in place. Recognizing the military and economic superiority of the SCR, the DuZhod happily joined the confederation sharing their technology and entering into full relations. In order to more fully interact with the biologics, they even grew their own Hierarch Avatars. The Baron Ursus DuZhod was one of these, a biogenetic avatar who was ever present in the military. Each of these clones would die from time to time, and be replaced with another which the SCR saw as a separate legal entity, but which the DuZhod Central being saw as a mere subroutine of itself.

To this end, the Baron Ursus DuZhod was presently seen by those about him as a Colonel in the Imperial Army's Guardian forces. He had, however, the memories of two generals, three admirals, and dozens of other officers, not to mention the overall collective identity of a culture that numbered in the billions. As a result, he often grew tired of enduring the attitudes of those who outranked him yet failed to recognize that he had the experience of having outranked them on more than one occasion. It made him long for a full return to the Interactive.

This desire was somewhat helped by the fact that he had brought a part of the Interactive with him in the form of his ship, a unit of Cybernetically Enhanced Infantry, and a hundred other systems with which he was in constant communication. It also helped that he had co-opted elements of Lai-Jung's native systems by hacking, cracking and otherwise absorbing them. He was, in some senses, omnipresent in the High Consul starport, and quasi-present throughout the rest of the system.

Right now, however, his biologic avatar was reducing its omni-presence so that it might focus its attentions on interacting with his immediate superior, Commissar Sir Iolo Pushkin of the Ministry of Justice. The Commissar was better than most, he supposed, but evidently did not understand the nature of the Interactive, nor Ursus' own position within it. Pushkin treated the Baron with respect, and listened intently to his opinions, yet he clearly did not understand his own natural place in comparison to avatar of the millennia old DuZhod. Still, serving as Guardian Attaché to the Ministry of Justice had, thus far, proven a relatively enjoyable incarnation. Even if Ursus and the rest of the DuZhod viewed the task in the way that most humans would view a computer game, it had never given the Commissar reason to complain; the DuZhod took their games very seriously.

Ursus had conscientiously performed both the military actions and the Sig-Int tasks that the Commissar had requested – and had shown to his so called CO the rather useful forms of information extraction that the DuZhod had created over the past few years – skills that Pushkin had requested be used on more than one occasion. As a result, Ursus was somewhat confused at having been summoned to his commander's office. Still, as ever, he maintained this pleasant if condescending smile as he dressed in the hard greys of the Army Guardian uniform, and made his way through the corridors of the Ministry of Justice to the office of the Commissar.

"Ah, Ursus, come in," Pushkin's warm tones filled the hall, "I am glad you came."

"Yes," the Baron responded in the bemused tones of his feeble voice, "I am – heh – sorry for ze delay, but – heh – I am afraid I was - eh - somewhat indisposed. How can I be of help Commissar?"

"I need to pick your brain, Baron," Pushkin responded, gesturing to Ursus to take a seat. As was appropriate, Commissar Pushkin wore the charcoal grey uniform of a ranking official for the Imperial Ministry of Justice, touched with the dark blue markings denoting him as part of the small Imperial police force. What the uniform did not note was that as Sector Head of the Special Commission on Anti-Imperial Activity, the Commissar bore the rights and writs of an Imperial Warrant that granted him wide and frightening powers to impose the will of the Emperor.

"We have received a report from Imperial Naval Intelligence that one of their ships has managed to capture a pirate vessel in the act," Pushkin responded, "and they managed to obtain some prisoners which they will be bringing to us in due course. I would like you to perform the interrogations, when they arrive."

"But of course, Commissar."

"There is more," Pushkin continued, reading Ursus's unspoken question, "Related to one of your investigations, in fact. These people are not part of the local fleet, they're from the 12th Fleet under the command of Admiral Rippavitch."

"I see…." Ursus responded, and unconsciously began to finger one of the chrome blisters on his skull, "Zhat is very interesting."

"I thought you might find it so."

"What are zheir names?"

"The ship is commanded by a Lieutenant Commander Fotheringday, his first mate, or whatever the Navy calls it, is Lieutenant Samantha Smith, of Meridothia…."

"I see… very interesting indeed."

"I would like to know as much as you can obtain for me about them before they arrive. Once they are here, I would like you to extend that knowledge."

"What – em – what means am I – heh - heh – am I allowed to use?"

"Fotheringday is the son of the March Warden of the same name, and if my sources are correct, there is also one of the sons of Lord D'Ascoine on board. It would not do to antagonize them too much. I understand that neither one of them is particularly in their respective fathers' good books right now, but by the same token I doubt that either the March Warden or the Duke would take kindly to members of their house being too closely inconvenienced."

"Ah… I see…. Perhaps… perhaps a little infiltration."

"Whatever you think is appropriate Baron," Pushkin responded, "but be careful."

"But of course."

CHAPTER 38

"I'm sorry, Lieutenant, but there will be another delay in getting you access to the other files," Ensign Popolopolis said. His flower-faced appendage looked Samantha directly in the eyes, but the crab like pincers at the orifice clicked in a manner she knew indicated the t'K!room was uncomfortable.

"What's the problem this time?" Samantha asked with a smile. She wondered if Alex was having any greater luck with the bureaucracy than she was. His last account suggested that he wasn't. Three days had passed and they had been given only the most casual access to the Alterande Fleet's records.

"Between you and I," Popolopolis said as his skin changed to grey and black zebra stripes, a sign communicating secretiveness or conspiracy, "I think it is really just politics."

Unlike most of the members of the 253rd that she and Alex had met, the Ensign took a quick liking to both Fotheringday and herself for the simple reason that they shared meals with it. Most other personnel frequently found the t'K!room's tendency to tear apart its food with its pincer-like shredders to be unappetizing, but Samantha was a sophontologist who had spent her whole life interacting with alien cultures, and Alex had grown up in the cosmopolitan court of an Emperor who favored sophonts. As a result, the Ensign's flesh tearing pincers that shoved meat into its sphincter-like orifice did not really affect either one. Since dining was an important aspect of social bonding among the t'K!room, the two mandellans had already become closer friends in a few days than it had made since joining the Navy.

"Politics?" Samantha asked.

"It is simple really," Ensign Popolopolis said as its 'prime' head hovered close to her. Another of the flower ended limbs wrapped its petal like fingers around a large hunk of meat and shredded it. "There is an overall sense of indignity felt by the members of the 253rd towards the 12th fleet."

"Why? We're all on the same side, aren't we?"

"Against the Federalists yes, but you must remember that from the Alterande Fleet's perspective, Ripper's Raiders come in and grab the glory, while the members of the 253rd must face this everyday. Did you know that less than one third the number of decorations are given to the 253rd than the 12th?"

"That has to do with the nature of our missions. The Raiders target hotspots, tracking down the most dangerous cells and destroying them, while your job is to patrol."

"True," Popolopolis responded as he extended another of his limbs and examined Samantha from the side as well as the front, "but then again that is because you are given the wherewithal to identify where such hot-spots might be. I have always wondered where the concept of the phrase hot-spot came from."

"I believe it comes from a description of increased heat, indicating volcanic activity," Samantha answered. The t'K!room were known for their multitasking abilities, a function of their multiple sensory capacity. It was frequently difficult to keep up with them, but she tried. "There's only so much funding available, and surely our ability to focus on terrorists only reduces the number of insurgent and pirate attacks as a whole."

"In the short term, but it does not take long for new insurgency cells to appear and new terrorist acts to be performed, often as reprisals for the last of your raids. How did the term evolve into its common usage? Why would an area of volcanic activity have anything to do with the location of pirate bases, for example?"

"I think it relates to the concept of searching for volcanic activity, or perhaps I was wrong and it originates from house fires… either way it eventually became part of common usage there after. So, you're suggesting that the Raiders' sweeps don't actually reduce terrorism?"

"So you don't know for certain if the origin is volcanic or fire-fighting? I do not suggest it, but there are others in the fleet that do. Some even think that the sweeps have increased pirate and guerrilla activity, though that could be professional jealousy."

"You don't feel such jealousy?"

"My kind is not jealous by nature. Our culture is based around performance and merit alone, not socio-cultural manipulation for alpha dominance. It is a trick of evolution. So you don't know for certain if the origin is volcanic or fire-fighting?"

"Oh, sorry, no, not for certain." Samantha took another bite of her meal, Popolopolis continued to shred his.

Fran stepped into the armory area to the sound of gunshots. In front of her Leftenant D'Ascoine and Corporal Bowman stood facing the far wall with about one meter of space between them. Each had their side-arms drawn and stood in standard shooter pose: legs shoulder width apart, one hand supporting the other to give maximum accuracy. Bowman was shooting the small standard shipboard issue PPL-110, while Leftenant D'Ascoine was using the large handgun that he normally kept holstered at his side. Unlike the compact PPL-110, the Army officer's gun was about 25 cm long, with two ammo clips, one in front of the grip and the other within it, providing twice as much ammo and the capacity to more readily vary the rounds one carried.

Damn! Fran thought looking at her watch, *I could have sworn Ed said that practice started at oh-two-thirty.*

"Leftenant, I am so totally sorry," she said when the shooters came to a stop, "I could have sworn you said practice began at oh-two-thirty. I just… I just don't know what happened. I mean I was working on the system, but I could have stopped at any time and…"

"Don't worry, Fran," Bowman interrupted her, "We're just having some fun, getting in a little pistol practice before we get started, eh?"

"Really?" Fran asked, hope suddenly appearing in her eyes.

"Yes AT Harpur," D'Ascoine responded, "Really. Though in future, Corporal, I suggest we let her suffer a tad bit longer. The look on her face was well and worth it."

Fran blushed and looked down, embarrassed while Bowman chuckled. She walked over to the weapons locker and entered her password, trying very hard to become invisible. The act seemed to work; the two began talking about their guns.

"As you can see, Corporal," D'Ascoine began as he handed his handgun to the trooper, "the FAP-17 not only holds a great deal more ammo, but allows you to mix and match rounds from the different clips using your implants if you jack in."

"I can see the advantage, sir," Bowman responded, "But I must admit that the higher caliber rounds give it a bit too much kick for my liking."

"Too much kick? What kind of a soldier are you boy?" D'Ascoine said with one eyebrow cocked and a condescending smirk on his face.

"I'm a *Marine*, sir," Bowman said with pride, "and us Marines need to be ready to work in zero-gravity at any given time. With all due respect Sir, you fire that monster in zero-gee and you'll find yourself spinning out of control in the other direction. And if you have it set on fully automatic, you might as well be holding onto a rocket that spits bullets at your squad."

"If that was respect, Corporal, I wouldn't want to see Marine insolence," D'Ascoine replied. He wore a broad smile when he said it, but Fran noted the slight edge to his words, "But I do see your point. I think I'll keep it set to single shot while we're in space. Harpur? Grab our rifles, would you? I think its time we get started."

"Aye, sir," Fran responded, selecting three Automatic Accelerator Rifles from the locker, as well as a zero-G shotgun that she was still keeping as back up.

"Good girl," D'Ascoine said taking his gun, "Now… let's get started with target practice, eh?"

At once the holographic projector units in the far wall and armored lockers flickered and shifted to create a long distance target range with varying bull's-eyes set at varying distances. The three shooters loaded the stock and grip clips with standard targeting blanks, and the fore-mounted grenade accelerator with thud-rounds, the kind of ammo that used kinetic energy to knock you on your ass while delivering a stun-worthy electric charge. Checking each other's positions, they adjusted their line, took up their stances, and opened fire with the AAR-5s.

After unloading her clip, Fran smiled. She had made her personal best. Turning to inform the others, she noted D'Ascoine staring at her, his eyes traveling up and down her body. Fran found her heart racing in response, uncertain if she was uncomfortable or excited by the intensity of his look.

"Spread your legs," he ordered.

"Excuse me?" Fran asked, her eyes widening as she all but dropped her combat rifle.

"Spread your legs," D'Ascoine repeated with a crooked smile, "Your shooting stance is wrong, your feet need to be further apart."

"Oh," Fran said, turning crimson as she followed the order. *Please let me just die now.*

"Lieutenant Corduroy," Alex said as he stormed into the office, "this is beginning to become a bit farcical, don't you think? If you are going to obfuscate, the least you could do is to be a bit more subtle about it."

"I'm not sure I know what you mean," the Lieutenant responded, trying to appear innocent. He did not stand up.

"What I mean," Alex said, glaring down, "is that both Lieutenant Smith and I already have INI security clearances that supersede those necessary to obtain access to the level of information that we require, and that the ability to gain access to that information should merely be a matter of protocol."

"I appreciate that sir, but those protocols have to be followed." Lieutenant Corduroy turned his attention back to the files hovering over his desk, shifting them about.

"And I appreciate that, Mr. Corduroy, but your people are making administrative mistakes. So many of them that I am beginning to wonder if I will be forced to discuss this with the General Accounting Office, I believe there is a branch in orbit about Lai-Jung Prime."

"You think that will threaten me?" Corduroy asked. The files vanished with a flourish of his hands, his eyes narrowed and his lips tightened. "No offence, *sir*, but I doubt that a Lieutenant Commander making a complaint in an Imperial Administrative Office will really get much result."

"You're right of course," Alex said in a quite tone as he leaned over the desk, "but then again a hint from an Imperial hierarch, and voting member of the Senate will start a full investigation, one in which you are specifically named. They might be interested to discover that you have been interfering with an Imperial investigation. They might even find reasons to have the Ministry of Justice investigate you, personally. I understand they have a branch office here as well."

The INI Lieutenant paled and stood up. Apparently, he had forgotten the color of Fotheringday's laurels.

"Sir… your lordship, honestly, it's not that I am trying to create problems…."

"And it's not that I don't sympathize with your situation," Fotheringday said, softening his tone, "I know that the forces of the 253rd are doing the bulk of the work against the Federalist insurgents, and I have begun to realize exactly what you are up against: a network far more extensive than just the range of headline grabbing attacks that the Raiders deal with. I can see that while the 12th gains the glory, the 253rd is left to clean up the mess."

"It's more than that, your lordship."

"How so?"

"Well, sir, to be honest, sometimes the best information we have comes from trying to follow leads that get wiped out when you guys come in and go for glory every two or so years. Once that happens, some of the best intelligence trails suddenly go dead."

"I can see that, and I can see that there is a larger picture here than the Raiders are presently addressing."

"Well I must say that your predecessor didn't seem to understand that. He would come in and demand whatever he wanted of me or my predecessor, and never return any information in response. Traditionally, intelligence seems to flow from the 253rd to the 12th and never return. Your people get a great chance to find bases and such, and we are left to do the dirty work. It used to drive Sir Richard crazy."

"I can understand that, but believe me, I am all for cooperation and reciprocity."

"I would like to believe that your lordship."

"Give me a chance," Alex said, and smiling added, "And please, while in this uniform, I am a Lieutenant Commander first, and a Hierarch second."

"If you say so, sir."

"By the way, Lieutenant, who is Sir Richard?"

"Oh, sorry. Lieutenant Commander Sir Richard Al-Escobar, my predecessor. He retired about a year and a half ago."

It was unusual for Alex to lose his composure, but for a moment, his face froze and his color drained. Suddenly, the pieces began to fall into place, and he had to admit that he did not like the look of what he saw.

CHAPTER 39

Without explanation, Alex decided to change tack on the focus of his own investigation, leaving Samantha to keep following through on the Naval records. She was surprised to find that her first reaction was not resentment, but concern. She wondered what she had done to disrupt the growing camaraderie between herself and the Skipper. Her concern grew to curiosity when Alex stopped using the facilities provided for them on Alterande High Command, choosing to work from his cabin instead. He hadn't come out for two days.

"I wouldn't worry," Sinner told her as they breakfasted together in the *Hunter*, "He's completely ignoring the Naval Intelligence data. He downloaded a copy of the Civilian Port-Authority's arrivals and departure records for the Lai-Jung system and is spending all of his time looking at that."

"You're still spying on him?" Samantha asked. She cradled her sweet spiced coffee in her hands.

"Of course," Sinner said with a scoffing shrug, "Aren't you?"

"He knows we were doing it, Sin," Samantha said. She put the coffee down suddenly, spilling some over the edge.

"Yeah and he didn't order me to stop did he?" Sinner took a bite of a croissant that had been delivered complements of Lt. Corduroy. The SILO had been very helpful since Alex's last visit.

"I thought maybe you'd have better things to do with your time," Samantha said, shaking her head. She wiped the coffee from her hand with a napkin before cleaning the spill on the table.

"Do you want to know what he's been up to or not?"

Samantha gave Sinner a bored stare.

"The CO has been utilizing some pretty hot-shit search engines to compare arrivals and departures, but he's also performing a manual review of the data, reading through each entry on his own."

"Alex is nothing if not thorough," Samantha said.

Sinner did not look impressed. "He's been focusing on three specific vessels that have arrived in the past three weeks, all registered to Cameron-Inglesie Distributors LTD. Two of them are still in-system. One is a luxury yacht."

"He hasn't been looking at the new Intel from the 253rd?" Samantha asked. Her fingernail picked deeply into her thumb, but she barely noticed.

"No. None of it. Still upset that I've been watching the CO?"

"I think I need to press the Skipper for some more information." Samantha put down her coffee and stood up.

"About time," Sinner mumbled, but Samantha was already walking out of the lounge. In a few steps she was standing in front of Alex's door pressing the buzzer. She had to do it again before she received the invitation in.

"More cleared material came today," Samantha said with a cheerful smile as she entered, "Still not what we're looking for, but I will be able to begin looking for… Alex? Is everything alright?"

"Mmm? Oh… yes," Alex responded. The room was a mess of hovering files, reports and charts. Even the holowalls were nothing more than a surface filled with diagrams and news reports. Alex looked up from his chair, the circles under his eyes were magenta.

"I'm glad you came," he said after blinking then rubbing his eyes, "I'm afraid there is going to be a change of plans… I think your attentions will be better spent elsewhere than in searching through the INI records."

"Found something?" Samantha frowned as she sat across from him.

"Perhaps. Regardless I will need you to help me follow it through."

"But what about our mysterious navigator?"

"To be honest, Samantha, I think we might be chasing the wrong man. Tell me Lieutenant, have you downloaded the navigational records from the 253rd yet?"

"I just finished the up-dates and comparative corrections, and before you ask, there's nothing showing the *Reichmann*'s correction of the Inglesie anomaly being shared with anyone in the 253rd. So far the only records from those vessels that have shown that update came from the 12th Fleet."

"That seems a bit unusual." Alex was grinding his teeth loudly. He looked a wreck, "What about the ship?"

"The *Reichmann* is a tender and supply ship," Samantha said, moving even further forward on her perch, "Her role in the 117th means it works closely with 253rd. Corrections noted by its navigator should be flooding the entire fleet by now."

"And there is no record of them outside of those from our own fleet." Alex's eyes focused elsewhere, beyond the confines of the cabin.

"Not one."

"Right," Alex said, still staring into the distance.

"Alex?" Samantha asked, putting her hand on his desk.

Suddenly standing, Alex took on the decisive tones of a CO giving orders. "Download the new records into the *Hunter*'s Intel Library. I am going to need help on this one. I think Harpur will do."

"What are we looking for?" Samantha felt an irritation that he did not want to use her. The fact of that feeling only served to irritate her more.

"Deleted files," Alex said as he started to pace across his small cabin, his hands behind his back, "Somebody seems to have erased all records of the Inglesie correction from the records of the 253rd and perhaps from the 117th. The only reason we came across them ourselves is that the *Reichmann* was on a joint operation with the 12th. Whoever erased the files had access to records in the other two fleets, but not the Raiders."

"Only someone with a level seven security clearance could have deleted those files."

"Indeed, Samantha, and that kind of clearance is a good deal higher than a Nav-Com officer on a supply ship would have." Alex spoke with an animation that showed no signs of his earlier exhaustion, though the reddish-purple rings remained beneath his eyes. "In fact, it could only readily be done by someone who is Argon-Blue approved."

"Someone in intelligence," Samantha said, "You know who."

"I have my suspicions, but I hope they are wrong."

Fran squirmed in her seat. For the first time the mess-lounge seemed uncomfortable. The whole crew had gathered together and was awaiting the Skipper. No one said a thing, though Bowman gave her the occasional smile. She had never seen the crew so pensive and yet, from what she could tell, none of them had any idea as to why they were gathered.

"Thank you all for coming," Fotheringday said as he strolled into the room. Fran could not help but think that the thanks seemed a bit silly since none of them had any option but to attend the meeting.

"Recent events have created a bit of a change in our plans," he said as he stopped in the middle of the room, "It would seem that there could be a mole inside or in some way associated with Naval Intelligence here in Alterande."

Fran felt her jaw drop and leaned forward. To her side she heard Bowman gasp.

"Since we have no idea how far the treason goes," the CO continued with less concern than he showed while commenting on a tactical drill, "we will be investigating this on our own. There is to be no discussion of this phase of the operation with anyone outside this room. Is that perfectly understood?"

"Aye, aye, sir," Fran responded. Around her the others did the same, but she noted quick glances shared between the NCOs. D'Ascoine's eyes narrowed and his neck grew flush.

"We are going to Lai-Jung Prime where we will divide into three groups," Alex said, "The first group will consist of Able Technician Harpur and myself. We will be working in the Imperial Consular Complex orbiting Lai-Jung Prime and serve as the central contact point for the other two groups. The second group will be led by Leftenant D'Ascoine and consist of Chief Sinclair and Sergeant Chrom. You will be following up on the leads provided to us by the *Van Deer Lieuw*, and particularly focus on the individual they identified as the Ankh. Chief? I believe that you have some contacts with the underworld on Lai-Jung?"

"What gave you that idea, sir?" Sinner asked. He was lounging nonchalantly on the sofa. Even Fran could tell he was lying.

"Please do not waste my time, Chief," Alex's voice became cold as he spoke, his polychrome eyes focused on Sinner, "After dealing with our colleagues in the 253rd, my patience is already thin. You were not assigned to Intelligence merely because of your engineering skills, were you?"

"No, sir," Sinner looked over to Samantha. When she nodded, he continued. "Over the past few years Lieutenant Smith and I have managed to make contact with a number of underground and black market groups. Some of them are on Lai-Jung."

"Any reason you haven't shared this information with the rest of us?" D'Ascoine asked in a petulant tone. The reddening of his skin had moved up to his face.

"It's not standard procedure within Naval Intelligence to discuss the details of previous missions, Leftenant," Samantha responded in calm, matter of fact voice. D'Ascoine scowled at her, but remained silent.

"How extensive is your network on Lai-Jung?" Alex asked, turning to Samantha.

"It's reasonable sir," she said with a calm smile, "Sinner and I could investigate a number of possible sources, one or two in particular come to mind."

"Do you feel you could be recognized if you went down under a different cover?"

"No, sir, but I think that the legends Sinner and I already worked up would serve us better. If we…."

"You won't be going with the Chief, Lieutenant," Alex countered, "I am afraid that I have other plans for you."

PART IV

Lai-Jung

CHAPTER 40

Sir Richard Al-Escobar took a handful of nuts and tried to listen politely to the inane banter of the pretty twenty-four year old daughter of one of his colleagues. He nodded sympathetically as he took another sip of his vodka martini, and discretely cast his glance around the rest of the party, looking for a way out of the conversation. None immediately presented themselves.

"So, it only makes sense to bid for entry into the Empire, don't you agree?" she asked, clearly trying so hard to make a good impression, to say all the things she thought would appeal to an Imperial Hierarch.

"Perhaps," Sir Richard replied, "but then again the Lai-Jung system does benefit from many of those advantages as a protectorate already, yet it is not subject to Imperial law, or Imperial tax for that matter. In some ways you might be best off staying exactly how you are."

"Really?" the girl was obviously surprised, and the unexpected comment obviously caused her social panic, bless her. As a native of Lai-Jung, she had so clearly expected that any Imperial, not to mention a hierarch, would express the opinion that everyone should join the Empire, it never occurred to her that perhaps the portrayal of Imperial attitudes was also a stereotype. *Ah…youth.*

"Absolutely," Sir Richard continued, "For one thing, you couldn't be certain how the law would view the dueling arenas…"

A familiar look of relieved realization crossed her face. She was plainly assigning him another Imperial stereotype: culturally sensitivity. Sir Richard disguised his smirk with the airs of a man amused by the wit of his companions.

What is it about twenty-four year old women? he wondered as he politely listened to her attempt to say the right thing in response to what she viewed as his politically-correct critiques of Imperialisation, *Teenage girls seemed so much more sophisticated than boys of that age, when do they lose that advantage? Twenty? Younger? They don't seem to realize it, though, and their attempts at condescending sophistication just fall flat. Twenty-four year old men, however….*

The sudden loud laugh and boisterous opinions of a young male project director nearby him grounded Sir Richard's thoughts. *Then again, maybe it's not that she's so juvenile but that I'm forty-two.*

The girl laughed at one of his off hand comments in a contrived manner and bumped her hip into his. Casting her eyes invitingly over her glass, she toyed with the swizzle stick in a provocative manner. *My god,* he thought, *is she flirting with me? I'm old enough to be her father!* Then he considered the calculations. As the eligible head of Cameron-Inglesie Distributors, Sir Richard made a very good catch, especially for the upwardly mobile daughter of local manufacturing magnet. He gave the girl a more appraising glance.

She was pretty, but then again anyone in Lai-Jung who had the money could be pretty. Noting the stylishly modeled shape of her ears, and cut of her waist, Sir Richard decided that her looks were the result of facial surgery and body sculpting. The trendy nature of it removed the attraction. Compared to women like Lady Sally Symbletyne, the girl was boring. Sir Richard's mind lingered on the memory of the redhead.

It was not for the first time that the image of Alex Fotheringday's girlfriend had haunted Sir Richard. Sally was an extremely attractive woman: light, witty, naturally attractive. But how was a mere second generation business Baronet supposed to compete with a mandellan lord? He couldn't, even if the disgrace of the *Silver Slipper* was publicly known, he had no chance. Fotheringday remained an ancient, influential and wealthy family; Sir Richard was a comparative upstart.

What is one to do? Sir Richard popped another nut into his mouth and once more cast his glance around the room to find some hope of escape from the woman's droning.

It was then that he noticed Her. She was tall, tanned, blond, and moved with a catlike grace. Not the gentle tentativeness of a domestic feline, but the sliding power of a jungle predator, each step filled with confidence and strength. Her smile lit up the room and to Sir Richard's mind at least, her figure was perfect. She did not have the slightly plump look so common across the Alterande sector these days, nor was it the thin waif-like look that was so popular in the Imperial Core. She was both well toned and voluptuous – very voluptuous – a fact that was highlighted by the cut of her neckline. Tantalizing glimpses of long shapely legs were seen as she walked. The plunging backline of her dress suggested the swell of firm buttocks.

She must be a model or actress, Sir Richard thought as she laughed in an easy, comfortable manner. She glanced around the room, catching Sir Richard's eye before he could look away. He smiled and turned, before becoming vaguely aware that his colleague's daughter had asked him a question.

"Oh… her," the girl said as she looked over her shoulder to see what had distracted her quarry.

"I don't think I've seen her before. Who is she?"

"Some socialite from the Imperial Core. Upper middle class I think. I saw her at the Bargos party about two days ago. Gods know what she's doing here."

"Social climbing like the rest of us I suppose."

"Sir Richard! I swear you are so frank," the girl laughed, placing her hand predatorily upon his lapel.

Oh joy, he thought, and found himself involuntarily re-engaged into the conversation. When he next dared look around the room, She was gone.

"I must admit, sir, I don't quite get it," Fran said as they crossed the airlock into the Imperial Orbital Consulate.

"Don't get what, Able Technician?" Fotheringday responded. He looked up and down the concourse, attempting to orient himself in the great revolving cylinder.

"We're going to a police station?" Fran asked, pulling out her PAD and looking for directions through the orbital station's broadcast network. Four different forms of security were called up.

The Lieutenant Commander turned to the left and strode up the gradually curving floor of the orbital. Fran followed, walking clumsily for the first few steps. It was an aspect of life in space that Fran had not yet gotten used to, the curvature of revolving space station floors. Despite her knowledge of centrifugal force, her eyes told her body that the arc of the station floor was an incline, so each step felt like she had missed the bottom step on a flight of stairs. She tried to cover it as best she could, looking forward to each time they walked along the station's axis.

"In a sense it is a police station, yes," her CO responded, "But not a local or even system-wide constabulary or security force. We are going to the Imperial Ministry of Justice's Police Barracks."

"But I thought the Army Guardians served as the Imperial Police. Isn't that what makes them different from the Assault forces like the Rangers?"

"Yes and no. You come from a corporate arcology don't you?"

"Yes, sir," Fran responded, feeling ignorant.

"Then it is not surprising you haven't come across the Imperial Police before. You see, the Guardians are both an occupation and defense force. They stand guard at the borders, provide emergency relief and occupy worlds that have natural disasters, been conquered or show signs of unrest, but they are not actually police.

"Imperial Police officers are quite different. There are only very few of them, only a million or so across the whole Empire. Most Imperial laws restrict the actions of governments, and the like; they do not really apply directly to individuals, so for the most part the Empire leaves the governance of the population to the local authorities and constituent states. As a result, there's not really much of a need for a Police force."

Fotheringday turned down a corridor and stepped into a transport tube. As the door closed behind them he continued his monologue. "Most Ministry of Justice personnel are magistrates, lawyers or ambassadors of a sorts. They review the laws and governance of individual member states, planets and star systems. If governments are breaking Imperial law, or if one of their sets of laws are deemed to be in violation of the Empire's codes of civil rights, the situation is addressed through the Imperial Bureaucracy and court system."

Fran looked into the Skipper's polychrome eyes and wondered if she would ever stop feeling like an idiot. Every time she got halfway decent at something, she discovered ten new things she needed to know; things that having an implant would allow her to download quickly. *Why did I ever join the friggin' Navy?*

"In contrast," the Skipper said as if he were blithely giving a lecture, "the MoJ Police investigates and enforces the few laws that the Empire has which do affect individuals. So while the Navy addresses hijackings and piracy and the Guardians address planetary acts of insurrection, there are a number of laws, such as say… tax evasion, that wouldn't be appropriate to use the military to enforce."

"Right… okay," Fran replied, nodding, then shaking her head once more, "No, I still don't get it. Why are we going to a police station, sir? Has someone evaded their taxes?"

The Skipper replied with a laugh. "I'm sorry, Fran, I'm babbling. You see, in addition to its team of lawyers, judges and petty crime investigators, the MoJ Police Force has Special Commissions, or Flying-Squads, led by specially assigned magistrates, or commissars, who investigate anti-Imperial activities."

"And you're hoping that we'll have more luck getting information out of them than we have out of the INI office at Alterande High Command."

"We're looking for a different sort of information, really, but effectively yes. Ah! Here we are."

The doors of the transport tube opened to reveal a large concourse that appeared to run the length of the orbital station. The great hall-like avenue was decorated with plants and fountains, and a mixture of shops and services were peppered between government offices. Directly across from Fran and her Skipper was a large marble façade, decorated with doric pillars in a style reminiscent of the First Federation: a common design for MoJ structures.

They entered through the large central doorway, passing through the security check point armed by grey clad Imperial Army Guardians. From there, they made their way to the large reception desk where there was a man dressed in a blue and grey uniform of classic Imperial design, but with a silver badge upon his breast. The Skipper greeted him formally and said that they had an appointment with Commissar Pushkin. A brief check was made and they were quickly guided into the facility.

As they walked through the halls, Fran was reminded of the corporate security stations she had seen in school trips. There was a certain mixed air of busy behavior and relaxed attitude as men, women and aliens in blue and grey uniforms talked, joked or otherwise went about their business. Yet there were other elements that were missing from what experience and the media had told her was a police station. For one thing there were no criminals, or even individuals looking like criminals. For another, there were a larger number of people in normal business suits who looked more like lawyers than cops. There were also more than a few Guardians about, some carrying side-arms and looking like soldiers, others that were unarmed and walked with an air that reminded her of the INI spooks. Mostly, it seemed more like a part of the Imperial Civil Service than the cops of the broadcast media.

They passed through two more security checks before they entered the office of the Special Commissioner. It was spectacular, with wood trim, real paintings, and what appeared to be original sculptures placed about the room. A large conference table stood at one end, a comfortable lounge-like set of sofas and chairs in the center. At the far end was an enormous desk with two large chairs in front of it. A single, even larger chair was behind the desk. Presently it was turned to look out the window that ran the entire length of the far wall.

Beyond that glass, assuming it was glass and not a monitor, lay the remarkable scene of the central axis of the orbital station. A huge garden parkland wrapped around the inner cylinder of the great revolving tube that was the Imperial Embassy complex. Woods and grasslands, rivers and lakes curved their way along the 'open air' axis of the station. A tall, bald and impossibly thin figure in the uniform of an Imperial Guardian stood next to the chair looking down as if speaking to someone within it.

"Ah! Commander Lord Fotheringday! Welcome!" came a voice from the chair. It spun around to face them as its inhabitant came quickly to his feet. Striding across the large office with extended arms was a tall man with a chest like a barrel. He had sharp good looking features and light brown hair. He wore a charcoal grey uniform, far darker and less military than the Guardian who stood next to him. On his chest he bore combat ribbons, including a Trinary Cluster for Heroism. A double row of golden laurel leaves were on his close cut collar, but his shoulders had no epaulets of rank. The laurels were the equivalent to a Commodore or Brigadier. He moved with strength and vigor, while behind him the tall thin Imperial Guardian followed like a tardy shadow that drifted at its own pace.

"I am most pleased that you could see me, Commissar," her skipper was saying as he took the offered hand.

Ignored for a moment, Fran made a quick scan of the desk. She noted one picture of the Commissar in the rich greens of the Imperial Army Assault forces, another with him in the greys of the Imperial Guardians, and yet another of him surrounded by somewhat younger friends taking what seemed to be a law degree.

"It is a pleasure to welcome one of my esteemed colleagues from the Imperial Naval Intelligence Service," the Commissar said with a broad and honest smile, "Please, let me introduce one of my most trusted lieutenants, Colonel Lord Ursus DuZhod, commander of the Imperial Army Guardians assigned to our commission."

"I am… heh... most pleased to meet you," the greeting came from the tall grey shadow of a man. Coming into her view for the first time, the man's appearance sent shivers down Fran's spine. Dressed in the pale grey of the Guardians, he was an extreme ectomorph: skeletal in his build. His bald head was studded with small chrome nodules and sockets; his eyes were perfect silver mirrors set in the gaunt hollows of a skull-like face. His complexion was a pasty-grey pale, as if he had never seen sunlight. He gave a tight smile and nod to the Skipper, before his blank mirrored gaze fell on Fran. He seemed to hold her in his sights for longer than she felt comfortable with. The lack of pupils, however, made her uncertain whether he was staring at her or looking somewhere else completely. Regardless, she smiled and nodded her head, noting that her own reflection in the man's eyes seemed small and insignificant.

"Most honored, Lord Colonel," Fotheringday responded, "Please allow me to introduce my junior yeoman and research assistant, Able Technician Frances Harpur. She is assisting me in my investigations."

"Delighted to meet you, Ms. Harpur," Pushkin greeted her informally, without rank and with an extended hand. She uncertainly returned the firm handshake.

"So, you would like to review the Ministry's archives?" Pushkin said, returning his attention to the Skipper. Fran noted that Colonel DuZhod seemed to continue to stare at her. He didn't blink.

"If it would be alright," Fotheringday responded, "I thought it only diligent to examine your somewhat extensive records."

"It seems logical to me," the Commissar said, "though I cannot remember the last time an Intelligence Liaison from the 12th fleet examined our records."

"Zhat would have been Sub-Lieutenant Warren McGovern, eighteen years ago, in the year Sixteen by Imperial Calendar," the Colonel responded, his eyes mercifully having drifted to the Skipper. They still hadn't blinked.

"See? Before my time," the Commissar added.

"We have summaries of your reports on file," Fotheringday said, "both at Alterande High Command and back at the Raider's Headquarters. They are very thorough, but there are often pieces of information that one can only gain by examining the initial documents. I have found one obtains a more complete picture of activities by examining a range of records from across the services."

"I cannot agree with you more, Commander," Pushkin said, "And the Ministry of Justice will of course be delighted to assist you in your investigations. I assume that you will also share your information?"

"I would be all too happy to pass on any relevant data," the Skipper said with a smile. Fran wondered if she would be able to tell if he was lying.

"In that case, Colonel, if you could be so kind as to see that Commander Fotheringday and Ms. Harpur are set up with an appropriate level of access to our records. You understand of course that there will be certain security matters and on-going investigations that you will not have full access to."

"Of course," the Skipper responded with a smile.

"Then, Ursus, give them any assistance they might require, and set them up with some office spaces to examine both the digital and analogue datasets."

"With pleasure Commissar," the Colonel responded, bringing his heels together and nodding his head.

"Now, if you don't mind I have some additional matters to attend to," and with that, they were dismissed from the Commissar's office and followed the disturbingly smooth gate of the cyborg colonel to the offices that had been prepared for them.

CHAPTER 41

Monique knew that in some ways, Lai-Jung was supposed to be the model of a Free-Trader system. At least, that was what they had taught her in the crèche. What she knew for certain was that other than the dirt side of Broome, the Lai-Jung system was a melting pot of technologies, companies, alien races and different cultures thrown together under the mantel of totally unbridled bartering and commerce. She also knew that life on her home world stood in stark contrast to that.

Broome, or Lai-Jung Prime as the Imperials called it, was not a place of wealth. It was a mixture of corporate arcologies, megalopolan sprawls, balkanized mini-states, walled city-states, and the total anarchy of the Wildlands. Wealth flowed in the arcologies, but seldom left those self-contained fortresses. Urban sprawls had areas of high tech luxury, but also corners of decay where the gangs fought over urban wastes. Then there were the Wildlands, ruled by roving bands of motor-tribes who drove their armed and armored ground vehicles; raiding the roads of commerce and barely held in check by the supposed governments of the abandoned hinterlands.

The Free-City of Binghouse fit right in the middle. A walled city-state in the Wilds set at the intersection of three major roadways and dropped right next to a large corporate arcology. It was the kind of place where high-fliers and lowlifes uncomfortably shared a haven of sorts. Monique had no question which side of the border she fell on.

Raised in a government run orphan's crèche, she had fallen in with the gangs by the age of eleven, been beaten and raped by the age of twelve, and committed murder within two weeks of her subsequent release from the hospital unit. In time she fled the crèche and turned her talents to stealth, theft and petty burglary. She became affiliated with street bikers and road raiders, watched the arena duels and gradually made a name for herself in the city as a cat-burglar and general criminal menace. Now she ran a loose alliance of free-lance thieves and mercenaries on the darker edges of the local underworld. A few well placed friends whose connections ran much farther a field made that a profitable niche to hold.

Tonight, however, she doubted she would see any of those more influential contacts. She cast her steady mirrored gaze across the crowded Ravenskeller bar, toggling between the UV, IR, nightvision and the natural optics of her solid-mirrored shade implants. She unconsciously flicked her razor-edged slasher fingernails in and out of their fighting positions.

"So I lined that fucker, Kraumps, up in my sights and let him have it!" Beccs' words were slurred as she sucked down another beer. Monique knew that Beccs had good reason to be celebrating tonight. Her minor gang of road-raiders had just taken on elements of the Danes, one of the major players among the gangs of motor tribes in the region. It had been in the arena, and shouldn't have called for reprisals like a road fight would have, but Monique doubted that mattered much to the Danes. Being beaten by a small time gang wasn't going to sit well with them, not while they were in the middle of a long standing cold war between the tribes.

But tonight Beccs was oblivious. She was three sheets to the wind, and doped up on a hallucinogenic cocktail of who-knows-what, celebrating a remarkable victory. As a result, Monique stayed alert, watching her now-friend and one-time lover's back while she celebrated. What was more, Monique had called on the friendship of a few of her nastier colleagues to back her up in case of trouble.

She caught the glance of one of them, a man who went by the work name of Blade, but who his friends called 'Chippy' due to his large number of cybernetic enhancements. He couldn't afford the Imperial stuff, so the Chip-meister always seemed a little on edge, and a little prone to going berserk in combat. Still, he was one tough son-of-a-bitch, and tonight Monique was glad to have him on her side.

As their gazes met, each nodded and returned to scanning the room. Monique noted that the other members of Beccs' gang were a bit more subdued than their leader. Roxie, the blond bombshell and the gang's media favorite, was talking up a tall dark and very handsome arena-duelist, while Sydney was keeping her distance and playing it cool as only Sydney could. Dotty and Jane were no where to be seen, but Monique assumed that they had each hooked up with some guy or another that had caught their fancy. All of them were having a good time, as they should. Only Beccs was really out of control. So, Monique stayed close to her friend and hoped that Beccs pulled soon so that she and Chippy could relax a little.

She looked at Beccs, almost amused as the road-raider chatted up the leather clad trucker by her side. She noted how the man's eyes occasionally strayed in her own direction, as if to invite Monique into a threesome.

Oh wouldn't that be just something to brag about, Monique thought, *a threesome with a blond and a brunette. If you could just get a red-head you'd have a hat trick.*

She smirked at the man and focused her attention back to the crowd, noticing that Blade was discretely trying to get her attention. Her razor nails flicked out instinctively as she readied herself for trouble. Blade nodded towards the door, and following his gaze, Monique's eyes did not fall upon a threat, but rather upon an old business acquaintance. A middle-aged man with a broad build and close cropped salt-and-pepper hair gave her a subtle smile from the door.

His name was Wishbone; a fixer who dealt in high-end high-tech Imperial stuff of the best quality. What he asked for in return varied – sometimes it was a job, sometimes it was information, sometimes it was just money – but regardless of what he wanted, his deals were normally good trade. Monique had never quite figured out who he was, or what he was after, but at the moment he was making a B-line straight for her.

"Ms. Sable," he said with a smile, nodding to Becc's then glancing to his right and left before meeting Monique's eyes directly, "I'm so glad to find you here."

"Good to see you too, Wishbone," Monique responded, and noting the strong and striking black woman to his side asked, "Who's this?"

"This here's Annie," Wishbone replied, "A business partner of mine."

"What happened to your last partner? Sammy wasn't it?"

"Oh, she's around. Off on other business at the mo'."

"Too bad. I kinda liked her."

"No kiddin'? I never woulda' guessed."

"So, what brings you into town?"

"Lookin' for the Tinman, hopin' you might know where to find him."

"The Tinner's around. Why you want him?"

"Business."

"Anything I can do for you?"

"'Fraid not this time. It's more the kinda thing you get a fixer for than a slink."

"Fair 'nuff. He's got some kind of deal going down off at Djangos. You might find him there."

"Any way of making certain I will find him somewhere?"

"Maybe."

"What might that be?"

"Things have been getting a little tense around here these days. I was thinking maybe you could score me some firepower, the kind that could give us a bit of an edge."

"That'll cost you more than lettin' me know where to find the Tinman."

"I was thinking a discount. Say twenty-percent on some AR-302s?"

"You gotta be kiddin' me? You want twenty off on combat rifles? Leave the fixin' to the Tinman girl, I got better things to waste my time on."

"What kinda deal would you be…?"

Monique was interrupted by a sudden burst of action. Two men with knives had emerged out of the thronging mass of the crowded bar and made a lunge at Beccs. Before she could react, Annie, Wishbone's new female friend, had delivered a knife-hand blow that disarmed one of the assailants, and followed it with an open-palmed uppercut to the man's nose. Blood sprayed across the room as the man flew off his feet and landed crumpled on the bar-room floor. Monique turned to face the second attacker, but found the man standing straight and frozen, Wishbone's right hand clutching his face, blood streaming out from where his fingers had dug into the man's skull.

Fucking hell, Wishbone's a serious cyborg! Monique realized, noting how he double twitched his left hand and a small plastic automatic pistol popped from under his sleeve into his grasp. Across the room there was more commotion. She turned to see that Sydney was wounded, but Blade stood over her beheaded attacker, his implanted arm-scythe dripping with blood. Elsewhere, another hitman was dead after Roxie had fended for herself.

Shit, Monique thought as she stood razor-claws out in a defensive posture before Beccs, *I barely had time to react.*

"I can see what you mean about things heating up here," Wishbone said, withdrawing his fingers from the man's skull, "Annie ol' girl, I thinks its times we beats feets."

"Wishbone!" Monique said grabbing his arm, then more quietly continued, "You watched my back. You didn't have to."

"What was I gonna do? Watch you guys get whacked?"

"You coulda," she said, paused in thought, then added, "Clinton Street Bridge, seven-PM tomorrow night. I'll make sure he's there."

"I'll see what I can do about your equipment."

Monique watched as the black-marketeer and his companion walked out of the bar. She felt as if she was seeing him for the first time.

"*I hope that you are not seriously expecting to trade military grade combat rifles to those people?*" D'Ascoine's voice sounded over Sinner's and Chrom's implant comms as they made their ways through back alleys.

"*Maybe,*" Sinner responded mentally while trying to shake the brain and gore off of his fingers, "*Depends on what I can get.*"

"*Somehow I don't think that would be such a good idea, eh? Supplying a criminal element with Imperial Military hardware?*"

Chrom and Sinner looked at each other with a knowing glance. The Sergeant shook her head and wiped the spattered blood off her otherwise pristine leather jacket.

"*They'll get the stuff one way or the other,*" Sinner sent, "*Better from us than from the Feddies.*"

"*I don't think so.*"

"*Listen, Leftenant, with all due respect, you really don't have that much of a background in this kinda thing. That's why the Skipper more of less said this was my ballgame, you know what I mean?*"

"*Actually, I doubt very much that our illustrious CO had this kind of thing in mind. Even if he did, I do believe that last time I checked, I still outranked you.*"

"Excuse me for a minute," Sinner said to Chrom, then switching to a private channel to address the Tactical Officer, "*You know, sir, somehow I don't think the CO had a lot things in mind did he? I mean, he certainly didn't have it in mind that his Tactical Operations and Marine Officer would use his position of ship security to make recordings and porno-sims of the female members of the crew did he? But so far, he's not found out about that... and neither have they.*"

"*I'm sure I don't know what you are referring to.*"

"*You know, Leftenant, I'm a hacker, a cracker, a goa and the Chief Engineer; there ain't much that goes on shipside that I don't know about. And I'm tellin' you, right now, that I'm pretty damn sure you know exactly what I'm talkin' about. So either you shut up, don't say nothin' and get a cut of the action, or suddenly the Skipper, the XO and the Sergeant over here find out exactly what you're up to. Your choice. Somehow I think that if even you're lucky enough to avoid a disciplinary hearing, you still won't miss having the girls kick the living shit out of you.*"

There was a long pause in the comms line before Leftenant D'Ascoine gave the command to continue as planned with the mission.

CHAPTER 42

Alex sat slumped in the undecorated cubicle he had been assigned at the MoJ, an optic cable inserted into one of his uniform's i/o ports. In his mind's-eye, however, Alex was in a great Second Empire oval chamber filled with ranks of desks, rows of books and the avatars of a hundred or more civil servants, police officers and other researchers. He had chosen one of the more traditional interfaces to work within, which for Alex made the research more comfortable. Now he anxiously awaited the arrival of a research assistant to help him acclimatize to the MoJ's archival protocols.

Here and there throughout the great library chamber there were avatars wrapped in slightly glowing green translucent spheres, either sitting alone or more often in small groups; classic examples of individuals working on secret materials, or classified conversations being held between researchers. Over all, however, the atmosphere was one of a calm determined busy-ness. He was in his own element and delighted.

"*Lieutenant Commander Fotheringday*?" a soft female voice sounded from behind him. Alex turned to see a remarkably attractive woman standing by his side. She was dark, with mocha skin, long loosely curled hair and large, expressive brown eyes. Her lips were full, her smile bright, and her figure, dressed in a professional looking pants-suit, was naturally lithe and athletic while still maintaining its curves.

"*Welcome to the User Interface Library of the Ministry of Justice Archives, Lai-Jung. I am Ms. Tara Miller,*" she said, placing her hands behind her back and standing 'at-ease', "*I have been assigned as your personal assistant and help interface during your stay here.*"

"*Excuse the question Ms. Miller, but may I ask who you are and if you are... how should I put it? Real?*"

"*I am Ms. Tara Miller: TH1198,*" she responded, and moved a stray lock of hair behind her ear, the same sweet smile on her face, "*a Semi-Autonomous User Assistant and Help Interface Program equipped with a Grade Three Artificial Intelligence. I have been designed with a range of functions based around assisting biologics with digital research and analysis. These include a full access memory storage, a secretarial interface program, an extended series of help files, relaxation and recreational programs, fetch and investigate subroutines, an automatically updated librarian subroutine, and a variety of other user designed functions. A full list is available upon request. I am release seventy-four of the program, a product of the DuZhod Software Group (PLC). Full release notes are available if you would like.*"

"*Not at this time thank you,*" Alex said with a smile, "*Does everyone get such an assistant?*"

"*No,*" Ms. Miller said, tilting her head, "*I was assigned to assist you by Colonel Baron Ursus DuZhod, who sends his greetings and a message. Would you care to review the message at this time?*"

"*Yes please.*"

Ms. Miller turned to the side, gesturing like an assistant game-show hostess. The air next to her sparkled, filling with pixels that shaped themselves into the form of a man. He vaguely resembled the Colonel Alex had met the day before. In the virtual world, however, DuZhod's avatar was broad and muscular, he glowed with a golden luminous presence and streams of data seemed to flow in and out of him, some approaching and moving away like casually swimming fish, others like rays of light that stretched out around him. His form was almost divine in the cyber reality of the research library. Alex wondered if this façade was merely created to impress or if this angelic incarnation was how the man truly viewed himself.

"*Welcome, Lieutenant Commander Lord Fotheringday,*" the image said. His voice a full, sonorous and lightly accented form of that he had witnessed the other day. "*I wish you luck in your research. In order to best facilitate your work, I have provided you with Ms. Miller, a cyber-thrall research assistant. I think you will find her most useful. If you have any requests or are in need of any assistance that Ms. Miller cannot provide, it will be possible to reach me directly through the cyber-thrall's communications links. If you find that you have need to access materials that are beyond your security clearance, please communicate this to Ms. Miller, and I will see what I can arrange. Some of this may come to you censored of course, but I think that you will find the overall access will serve your purposes. Good luck.*"

The image faded, and Ms. Miller, who had stood motionless during the presentation, turned back to smile at Alex, her hands held in front of her.

"*Please, thank the good Colonel for me would you?*"

"*Of course. I will send a message immediately,*" she responded, casually flipping a strand of hair behind her ear. She shifted her weight from one leg to the other.

"*Well, I suppose we should begin then,*" Alex said, "*if you would be so kind as to start by gathering the Ministry's annual summary reports for the last ten years on anti-Imperial activities within the sector?*"

"*Of course. Which Ministry?*" she placed her hands behind her back and stood 'at-ease.'

"*The Imperial Ministry of Justice,*" Alex said, realizing that he was in the Archive for the Empire's entire civil service for Alterande and the surrounding sectors.

"*Of course. Which sector?*" She asked, shifting her weight.

"*Alterande,*" Alex said, and recognized his mistake, "*In fact, let us assume that unless otherwise specified, all requests will be for records from the Imperial Ministry of Justice, and for the Alterande Sector.*"

"*Of course,*" she responded, tilting her head.

"*If you could gather the summary reports for the Special Commission for Anti-Imperial Activities over the past ten years, that would also be extremely useful.*"

"*Of course,*" she said, her hands held in front of her, "*That may take some additional time due to security levels.*"

"*Understood,*" Alex nodded, "*If you could just have the records placed at my desk space as they become available. Could you also please deliver copies of the annual summaries from the Imperial Army Intelligence service for the last ten years.*"

"*Of course,*" she said, shifting her weight, "*That may take some additional time due to security levels.*"

"*Indeed. Do you have copies of corporate security records here as well?*"

"*That depends upon the corporations and the activities they are reporting,*" she responded, casually flipping a strand of hair behind her ear.

"*If you could provide a full list of the companies whose security reports have been available over the past ten years in addition to the other files, I will start by browsing through the archives.*"

"*Of course,*" she responded, and walked towards the central library desk as leather bound volumes began materializing on Alex's assigned workstation. He strolled over to the general data shelves, casually perusing them. He wanted to explore the kinds of records they had. Though there were very specific patterns he wanted to investigate, there were several reasons he didn't wish to seek those elements out directly.

At the moment, his theory was both hypothetical and distasteful, and his evidence circumstantial. Sir Richard had been his CO in Archon and the Liaison between the 12th and 253rd Fleets; he also had business interests that could easily serve as a conduit for smuggling. He was perfectly placed to pass intelligence, money and weapons to the Federalists, but there was no actual evidence of wrongdoing. What was more, Alex knew from personal experience that the Dalang was a master of misdirection. Alex would need to perform a meticulous and methodical investigation before he was willing to admit that Sir Richard was anything other than a victim.

Adding to the complexity were Alex's suspicions that the MoJ was closely monitoring which records he was reading. If he looked too long or too directly at Sir Richard, it could easily launch a MoJ investigation. Alex had tainted his friend once by leaping to conclusions, he did not wish to risk doing so again. At least, not unless he knew for certain Sir Richard was guilty.

Alyiar walked down the street, flanking Rubo on the right while Wylde took the left. Dressed in badly fitting business suits, they took the form of local heavies, the kind of toughs for hire that frequented the free city of Binghouse. Elsewhere around the city other members of the Wayang Network provided hidden cover or acted as eyes. None of them, however, were Stalkers. The rest of the elite shapeshifting unit was spread out elsewhere: many having been sent back to the base.

At the moment, Alyiar didn't see any significant threats, but then again he hadn't seen any when Bolyiacov got whacked either. The image of the scattered remains of her torn up body being devoured by their own nano-devices raced through his mind. He suppressed the thought, and looked again for possible assailants; another pointless endeavor.

"What the fuck are we doin' here Rube?" Wylde asked, voicing Alyiar's own thoughts, "We're grouped up like fish in tank. If they hit us like they did Bolyiacov…."

"Who do ya' thinks' gonna try to hit us Wylde?" Rubo asked. He didn't turn around, didn't look nervous, he just strolled down the street looking like a man making a point.

"The Imperials, obviously."

Alyiar noted some movement on a building top. A quick telescopic focus showed that it was one of their own men. He moved his eyes on elsewhere.

"What the feck makes you think it was the Imperials who attacked us?" Rubo asked. They turned a corner. In the distance the roar of motors was punctuated by the sound of heavy weapons fire. The cheers of a crowd drowned it out: the sounds of a matinee combat.

"The Guardians came around the corner…" Wylde said. Something in the tenor of his voice made Alyiar look at him. He was sweating.

"Do you really think that the feckin' Imperial Guardians would blow one of us up if they had us in their sights boyo? Especially a unit commanded by the DuZhod? No kid, they had you down and were planning to wait for contact before sweeping us up for interrogation."

They turned a corner again and the street took on a new air. The roads were swept, the rubbish was gone, a tall white building glimmered ahead of them. Around its front were a series of well manicured shrubs. Rubo set a course straight towards it.

"You think that was another Federalist group?" Wylde asked as they trotted up the steps of the hotel.

"I don't know who it was," Rubo said. Opening the door, he turned to Wylde and looked him dead in the eye. "What makes you think it was one of our comrades?"

"I don't," Wylde answered, a bit too quickly, "It's just the only other set of people I could think of."

Rubo held his eye for a heartbeat longer, then entered the hotel lobby. Wylde followed, and Alyiar took up the rear. He was no longer watching for threats from outside, his eyes were wholly focused on Wylde.

"You two stick to the lobby," Rubo said as soon as they had stepped inside, "I'm going up for a meeting. You know the drill."

Wylde nodded, Alyiar stared at Wylde. Rubo nodded and headed to the elevator.

"What?" Wylde said once Rubo was gone.

Alyiar stared for a moment longer before beginning to casually scan the room. Ten minutes later one of their local contacts, the Ankh, arrived.

It took less than a week for Sir Richard to come across the Woman again. For several days he had been unable to get her out of his thoughts. It had even distracted him from his work. He had attended the kinds of clubs and restaurants that he thought a smart debutante from the Empire would frequent, even used some of his security resources to look for her. In the end he assumed with some regret that she had just been passing through and had already left the system. Then one day, out of the blue, she came upon him unexpectedly.

Sir Richard was sitting in the Business Class bar of the luxury slow boat from the Argris Orbital Habitat to the planet surface on his way to a meeting. He generally preferred the slow boats since they tended to be more comfortable than the fast boats. They made up for the longer ride by providing a much greater degree of service and decorum. Since his business contacts had not yet given sign of having arrived in system, he thought he might as well enjoy his trip down to Lai-Jung Prime. He absently cracked open the fruitnuts at the bar, popping them in his mouth as he kept his attention fixed on the broadcast duel being played on the 3DV set in the corner. He was slightly anxious about the delays in his business transactions and the combat on the viewer helped to alleviate that.

He winced as one auto-gladiator dived out of the way to avoid the heavy-trike that slammed into the razor edged arena wall behind him. Rolling to his feet, the man shot twice into the holes that had been torn into the side of the three-wheeled vehicle's armor before running around the next corner. The trike driver gunned his engines in pursuit, but ripped off most of the remaining armor on his right side as he pulled away from the wall mounted razors. Sir Richard wondered briefly if the pedestrian might actually make it out alive.

"I must admit I don't get it," said the alto tones of the woman who sat down next to him.

"Don't get what?" he responded, casting a quick sideways glance to his unwanted companion, only to make a sudden double take. It was Her.

"I don't get this sport, if you can call it that," she said with a nonchalant smile. Sir Richard smiled in return and looked into her sparkling green eyes. Today, she was wearing a standard charcoal business suit, her golden hair pulled behind her ears. He felt his heart skip.

"Autoduelling?" he responded, "It is a bit on the brutal side, but the people here like it."

"But it's a blood sport, doesn't the Empire have rules against deep political relations with cultures that have slavery and such?"

"Yes, but the people who enter the arena do so voluntarily."

"What? This guy here, the one who is running around that maze with a pistol while people in armed and armored cars are shooting at him, he's doing that voluntarily? What does he have a death wish?"

"Not at all. Well, not necessarily anyway," Sir Richard responded, noting how the cut of her business suit tastefully accentuated the fullness of her figure, "He's a convict, a lifer, and he's given a choice. He can spend the rest of his life in a prison, or he can enter the arena. If he gets out alive, he's a free man."

"The odds don't seem to favor him," the woman responded noting the tracer bullets from a passing car miss the man's head by centimeters. The convict fired two shots that bounced off the vehicle's armor and ran for cover once more.

"Well it wouldn't serve the criminal justice service very well if they did. I think less than one in a hundred or so people actually make it."

"Why attempt it then? A gin and tonic please," the woman said to the bartender as he approached. Her skin was perfect.

"Because if they do, they not only get out of the rather dark corporate prisons, but also become celebrities. Lots of lucrative media and advertising deals."

"Ouch!" the woman said as the pedestrian managed to fire a lethal bullet into a hole in the trike's armor, "What about that guy? He's a convict too?"

"No. Professional gladiator I suspect," Sir Richard responded, noting the delicate arch of her upper lip, the full, almost pouting nature of the lower one, "I take it you're not from around here?"

The pedestrian ran to the side of the trike and pulled the bloodied remains of the rider out of it.

"Grab the grenade launcher! Grab the grenade launcher!" the bartender chanted as he watched the screen.

"Is that allowed?" the woman asked as the pedestrian jumped into the now empty trike and began driving off.

"You can take what you can salvage, but he would have gotten a better reputation if he had stayed on foot and just… oh…"

The match ended abruptly when a car rammed straight into side of the trike. It let loose with twin machine guns as it pinned the smaller vehicle against the wall and crushed it. It was hard to tell if the criminal was killed by the stream of bullets or the razor edged arena wall, either way he was quickly liquidated. The slow motion replays of the kill did nothing to reduce its gruesome nature.

"Barbaric, but a bit of local color," Sir Richard said, "You didn't answer my question."

"I'm sorry, I was… uh… distracted by the... why do they keep showing that?"

"There's big money on the bets, and it's one of the things that fans like to know. I am Richard Al-Escobar, by the way," Sir Richard said offering his hand.

"Ainsley Dumachelle," the woman responded, turning her bright green eyes from the horrors of the screen to the friendly smile of the Hierarch, "What was your question?"

"I had asked where you were from."

"Oh, the Imperial Core sectors."

"Obviously, I mean what system? What planet?"

"I'm from Delgota'ar in the Illianite sector."

"Ah, they specialize in plant-fibers for food stock don't they?"

"Among other things," she responded with warmth, "I'm sorry, I didn't mean to assume that… well I guess I've just found that most people out on the Fringe don't know much about the Core. Not the smaller systems there anyway."

"Well technically, this is the Periphery, not the Fringe," Sir Richard replied, "but you're generally right. I'm fairly well traveled."

"You're an Imperial aren't you?"

"Yes, I come from the Cameron subsector, part of the Alterande sector but still within the Empire proper."

"Sorry again."

"No worries."

"It's just that most of the Imperial citizens I've met since arriving in Lai-Jung have been diplomats, part of a trade delegation or in uniform."

"What makes you think that I am not?"

"Well you're not in uniform."

"Retired."

"Really? What service?"

"Imperial Navy. I mustered out a couple of years back to go into the family business. Commerce, mostly merchant trading and distribution, a few other sidelines though. What about yourself?"

"I'm an actuary."

"For who?" Richard asked, *An actuary? You mean this gorgeous creature has a brain as well?*

"For Dalicoriate, it's a division of the Zhuddardha Group."

"You work for a mega-corporation? Very impressive."

"Not really. Billions do."

"So, what brings you to Lai-Jung?"

The conversation was cool and easy. Sir Richard could not believe his luck. This woman, this gorgeous woman, seemed to take a liking to him, and made him laugh in a way that few others did. He barely noticed that the ten hour flight had ended by the time the ship landed, and found himself rushed to get her details once disembarkation had begun.

"I'm staying at the Hotel Therese in the old quarter of Rehan," she said, tilting her head and blushing slightly.

"Rehan is a lovely city," Sir Richard said, his stomach was flipping as he steeled his nerves, "A seaside resort with some old colonial remains. Perhaps I could take you out to see the sights?"

"I would love to."

CHAPTER 43

Sinner scanned the networks for likely candidates. Passing mostly un-noticed, he flitted through the chat-rooms, think-halls, sensoromas, and gamespaces of Lai-Jung. He focused mainly on the different nets of the Prime world, since the time-lags of those would be the smallest – but kept his eyes open on the orbitals and even far-system channels since one could never be certain what electronic back-alleys might come in useful. In many ways Lai-Jung's cyber-space was no different than any standard Imperial world; it had the same general blend of interest groups and threads, but in general the network was fairly slow, and in places almost primitive. He could find himself surfing in a completely state-of-the-art cyber-community at one minute, and suddenly dumped into a slow wire-lined system the next. For business it must be a nightmare, but for those who dealt in the black-arts like himself, it was a playground filled with a thousand electronic shadows and bolt-holes.

He scanned channels and watched the comms as they filled the ether, checking both the real world and virtual world location of different players as he jumped from room to room and network to network. There was a team of murmuring workers on the old railbridge that overlooked the

Clinton Street bridge. They shuffled around the construction like zombies, working with their cyberized bodies as they interacted on the virtual planes. He tuned-in to their comms channels to check out their viability as an observation station.

"...*But if one examines the Peponian view points in light of a more experiential concept such as....*"

"...*Of course one can see the influence of CcO in humans, but to see the same chemical processes occurring in non-human species....*"

"...*Where as if you examine the transition in burial rites in the Upper Seine Basin (Terra) between the tech-nine and tech-ten periods, you can note a change in the role of implied reciprocity in the social structure....*"

It was typical Prole-sav stuff. A never ending dialectic of ideas, theories and obscure intellectual pursuits being streamed in written, mind-spoken and image based formats across the networks while their bodies, or what was left of them, performed mindless labor. They moved crates, fixed equipment, and did the sorts of things that mostly required a robot drone, but occasionally needed some intelligent input. It was a lifestyle that Sinner couldn't associate with: high-flying intellectuals who effectively sold their services doing manual labor. They let their bodies perform rote actions under the control of their implants until a sentient decision needed to be made, all in order to get enough money to let them spend the rest of the time in a cybertech virtual reality of arcane discussions and philosophical investigations.

Still, it took all types, and Sinner supposed that at least the Prole-sav added to society in both physical labor and the production of ideas, even if those ideas were beyond what Sinner could understand, or even care about. He decided not to try hacking or negotiating into one of the prole-savs, however. Hacking could piss them off, which could bring an awful lot of attention, and as for striking a deal with one of them, the Prole-sav tended to drop such agreements if a really interesting article, thread or thoughtline was posted. He looked elsewhere in the group.

He found one or two Playerjunkies, wasting their lives in VR gameworlds, but then discovered exactly what he was looking for, not in the work force, but on the riverbank between the bridges. He hadn't noticed the broadcast signal while first looking; it was weak and sporadic, but as he observed the Playerjunkies, he caught the presence and focused in on the signal immediately.

It was a Gamepariah, laying twitching by the river wall of the city. His body was deteriorating, starving and dying of thirst, while his mind still strove to continue playing whatever VR world he was logged into. His ability to play was decreasing as his brain gradually deteriorated through the neglect of his body. Gamepariahs could be found everywhere, but were especially common on worlds where the cybertech had only recently been reintroduced. They were usually young wireheads, more often than not human males, who became so involved with some game or another that they literally forgot to eat, bath, drink, anything. Unlike the prole-savs or the smarter Playerjunkies, they became so wrapped up so quickly that they never bothered investing in the implants that would allow them to ignore such basic functions. Instead, they simply disappeared into the nothing of the cyberworld, thinking they could control it until finally one day they died a quivering mass. The academics of the Prole-savs community also fell prey to such situations, but the prole-savs looked after their own. Playerjunkies tended at best to be too wrapped up in their game to notice the disappearance of a player; at worst they saw such disappearances as favorable to their own game scores.

To Sinner, the gamepariah represented something quite different. He could hack in to the young man's implants, and set him up as an observation post for D'Ascoine or Chrom to use while observing the rendezvous with the Tinman. Another set of eyes, one that would go unnoticed by his underworld contact.

It was not that Sinner distrusted the Tinman, quite the contrary. He rather liked him, but the Tinman was a fixer like himself, so Sinner liked to be careful. He would have felt happier if Sammy was backing him up, or even working as the faceman. Samantha was a real pro, great on the comms gear, quick on her feet, and able to sweet-talk millions out of a miser. Unfortunately, she had been assigned elsewhere. What bothered him was that she hadn't argued the fact; she had just up and did what Fotheringday wanted.

That left Sinner out in the cold, having to rely on two jarheads to back him up. Worse than that, one of the jarheads wasn't even a jarhead, he was a ground-pounder and a poncy one at that. Still, Chrom had proven herself more than once, especially in a street situation, and D'Ascoine could be controlled. Sinner had gone into worse situations with worse backup.

After a few minutes, he established the link into the nineteen year-old gamepariah's implants and began his work as a goa: riding the boy's systems the way he remotely controlled robots. The feeling was sickening, the feedback he received told him just how ill this kid was. It made Sinner regurgitate on himself before he could block it out. The feeble mind of the boy, weakened by starvation and dehydration, struggled against Sinner's possession of his implants, but he was too ill to perform any counter-hacking procedures, if he even knew them. Sinner turned the boy's head and had him stare at the Clinton Street Bridge where the meet was going to happen. In return, he managed to provide a feedback surge that activated the pleasure centre of the kid's brain. Once established, he linked the feed from the kid into the observation systems that D'Ascoine would be running, and left the link live.

He set a note in his Reminder Software to inform the medical services about the kid when the meeting was done, and went on to find more points. He only had two more hours until the meeting, and wanted to make sure his back was covered.

REF: LJ-CMRN149-87642-340-99670 B3: COM I Pushkin (KoE3)

Re: Cameron Sub-sector – Analysis of Counter-Terrorist Measures between 002/032 and 001/033.

At this point in time, there has been a clear reduction in the amount of both Anti-Imperial activity and general criminal activity within the Cameron Stellar Archipelago. Considering the marked increase in violent crimes in the area that had been recorded in the preceding six months (See Report REF: LJ-CMRN149-64757-340-99670 CIC3), it seems clear that the military actions carried out by elements of the Imperial Navy's 12th Fleet were more successful than the covert actions previously utilized by the MoJ. The decrease in crime rates suggests that many of the crimes were sponsored, if not conducted, by the Federalist rebels. It goes to show that in this instance, the recommendations of LTCDR R. Al-Escobar (INI-FLT253) were in fact superior to that the position held by myself and other elements of the MoJ....

Alex rubbed his eyes, an action mimicked both in the real world and in the virtual reality archives. He then turned his attention to the more recent summary statistics on general terrorist activities. The amount of organized criminal activity that occurred in territories that Sir Richard governed had significantly reduced to almost zero. Pulling up a list of ships that had been attacked in Alterande since the Raider's crackdown in the region, Alex noted that none were in fact registered to his former commander's trading company, Cameron-Inglesie. He looked for incidents of attacks against facilities owned by the Cameron-Inglesie Corporation; again, he found none.

"*Ms. Miller?*" he asked, and the AI avatar came to him at once.

"*Yes sir, how can I be of help?*" she asked, tilting her head.

"*Could you please give me the Ministry of Justice Report, reference: LJ-CMRN149-64757-340-99670 CIC3, and the Imperial Revenue Service's list of corporate profits held by the Cameron-Inglesie company over the past five years?*"

"*Of course,*" she responded, her hands held in front of her, "*That may take some additional time due to security levels.*"

It was an answer Alex had grown used to. He continued to scan through other documents to bide his time. The odds of coincidence had slowly been decreasing. Apparently there was something between Sir Richard's company and the Federalists, but what, exactly, he could not determine. Ritchie's company was miraculously free of attacks from pirates or insurgents. That would normally suggest collusion, but the recent attempt on Sir Richard's life, and the fact that he had been a strong proponent of the attacks on terrorist bases tended to counter that argument. Alex remained perplexed, and was becoming increasingly frustrated.

"*Lieutenant Commander?*" the Ms. Miller avatar asked as she stepped forward, "*Colonel DuZhod has requested that he meet with you at your convenience in regards to your queries involving the Wayang Terror Cell and the Federalist leader known as the Dalang.*"

Alex blinked at the avatar as the request sunk in. Had the Ministry noted his focus on Sir Richard?

"*Of course, anytime he wishes.*"

"You know, sir," Fran said as she sipped the acidic coffee they had gotten from the gazebo in the center of the central axis park, "I'd like to thank you supporting me so much."

"Pardon?" Fotheringday asked, blinking as his mind was pulled from whatever wanderings it was involved in, "Supporting you how?"

"Well, sir, what with my being a natural and everything…."

"Ms. Harpur, you are a remarkable young woman who shows a lot of potential, natural or not. I would be being lapse in my duties if I didn't encourage you."

"Thank you, sir," Fran said, turning beet red and stammering, "but I… I mean you even interrupt your work to sit and talk to me, and... and…"

"Nonsense," the Skipper interrupted with a smile, "I need a break now and then too, you know. Besides, I have rather come to enjoy our little chit-chats."

"Me too, sir."

Fran was truly enjoying getting to know the Skipper one-on-one. A part of Fran wanted to say so, but she knew it would be inappropriate. She blushed even more deeply as she fell into an embarrassed silence.

"I was hoping I might find you here!" a bright and cheerful voice interrupted the awkward quiet. Fran turned to see a striking woman with warm auburn and ginger hair, bright blue eyes and a flashing smile walking towards them across the concourse. She was small and lithely built, with long white legs showing beneath a floral sundress. Focused wholly on the Skipper, the woman didn't even seem to notice Fran.

"Sally!" the CO said as he stood to greet the newcomer, "What are you doing here?"

"Looking for you of course," the woman responded as they briefly brushed lips. Fran found herself deeply irritated. After the two pulled back, the redhead seemed to suddenly note Fran's presence.

"Sally Symbletyne," she said, offering Fran a soft white hand.

"Where are my manners?" Alex said, "Please, Sally this is Able Technician Francis Harpur. She is a very promising member of my crew assisting me in my work. AT Harpur, this is Lady Charlotte Sally Symbletyne of Khyber-Puq… a very dear friend of mine."

A girlfriend, Fran thought to herself. "I am honored to meet you Lady Symbletyne."

"Oh gods! Don't call me that! It sounds like I'm forty! Please, I'm just Sally."

"How did you know where I was?" Fotheringday asked, mirroring Fran's own thoughts. It didn't seem like the Commander to give away their location. What was more, he shouldn't even have known that they were heading to Alterande until they had made two jumps.

"My dearest Alex, I simply looked. After all, I knew you were assigned to Ripper's Raiders, and I knew you had shipped out to do whatever mission it was that you do. I knew that the Raiders hunt terrorist and pirates and such. In the end, I figured I'd go to where the largest numbers of Feddies were, and that there'd be a good chance of finding you."

"The wiles of the Symbletyne mind," the Skipper said smiling, "How long were you going to wait?"

"Until I got bored I suppose." She batted her big blue eyes and looked up to the side.

"Not long then," Fotheringday said.

"Quite the contrary," Sally said, pouting and sticking out her hip, "This is such a seuper place, so charmingly barbaric, I could spend ages here."

As the woman began to babble, Fran suddenly felt very awkward. Despite herself, she felt a twinge in her chest, a pinch of nausea in her stomach, and a feeling of embarrassed disappointment filling her soul. *Of course he's involved with someone*, she thought as she noted the interaction of the two, *and even if he weren't he never would have noticed me*. But the close environment in which the two had been working had allowed her to fantasize. No matter how much she knew they were fantasies, there was still a disappointment when faced with the reality that her CO was in fact involved with a strikingly beautiful red-headed hierarch.

"…Well then, dinner tomorrow night," the commander was saying.

"Delightful. You sure you can't make it tonight?"

"No, my dear, duty calls."

"It's always duty with you navy types."

"Indeed," the Skipper responded, "Speaking of which, I think it's probably time we get back to work."

"Kill joy… can't you just sneak out and have some fun?"

"I am afraid not. I do look forward to tomorrow night though."

"I'll make certain you're not disappointed," Sally said, and kissing him on the cheek, walked away hips swaying and allowing herself a glance back over her shoulder as she disappeared into the parklands.

"Shall we, Ms. Harpur?"

"Certainly sir," Fran responded. As the two made their way back towards the MoJ archives, she glanced over her shoulder.

"She seems very nice," Fran lied.

Sir Richard leaned over and kissed her. It was a soft gentle kiss, with the hint of a deeper passion on both sides, but he held back. He wanted things to go right with this woman. Ainsley was no quick conquest, he liked her, he actually liked her, and he wanted things to go perfectly. She was so… lovely… and smart to boot.

Ainsley looked up at him with her big green eyes, smiled sweetly and opened her mouth as if to speak. Then closed her mouth and fidgeted with her fingers. Smiling broadly, she opened the door and got out of the car.

"That was a lovely evening," she said, and looked as if she were about to invite him in.

"I would like to do it again sometime," he replied, "soon."

"Just give me a call," she replied and closing the door, she walked with a slinking confidence to her hotel. Sir Richard watched her as she entered the doors, smiled, and then told the driver to take him home.

CHAPTER 44

Alex watched as the blast torn body of the blonde woman decayed in fast-motion. Her high fashion features bubbled and disappeared as if fast-motion eaten by invisible maggots. It was a typical nano-tech self-destruct option used by interstellar agents, but its price tag made it very rare among terrorist groups: even the Federalists.

"*Zhey have access to some very sophisticated equipment*," Colonel DuZhod said. He wore the same quasi-divine avatar he had previously appeared in, a tall well built man with slightly luminous skin. This time, however, data streams did not flow in and out of him. In the real world, the two of them were in a sealed room deep in the MoJ building. It had no external links and no internal cameras. Alex suspected he was being made privy to very sensitive materials by being allowed to watch this Sim-Record.

"*Was there anything left to analyze?*" Alex asked, watching as the flesh vanished from the woman, revealing a series of metallic cords laced through a steel and ceramic skeleton.

"*No*," Colonel DuZhod answered.

A grey clad Imperial Army Guardian ran into the scene. The man leaned forward to grab the remains, but was pulled back by one of his comrades. A moment later the robot-like skeleton erupted, imbedding shrapnel into the wall. Within a second even that began to boil.

"*She was my best lead,*" Alex lied. He had all but forgotten about the query he had launched to identify her. "*Anything on the shooter?*

"*We had additional surveillance,*" the Colonel said as the sim rewound to the point the woman was hit by the rocket propelled grenade, "*But whoever did zhis was very professional.*"

When the RPG flew, the Colonel gestured and a trail of glowing lights streamed from his hand across the simulated street. The bricks of the building became translucent and a short fat shadow appeared standing over an object marked with an infrared heat signature. The object faded from white to yellow, then yellow to red. The shadow seemed to spray it with an aerosol and as the corpse in the street deteriorated, so did the object. The shadow disappeared into the building. A moment later a short fat woman emerged and dashed down a blind alley.

"*Zhat is all.*"

"*Any sign of the rest of her team?*" Alex asked, turning to his colleague.

"*We have been unable to identify patterns in zhe other Wayang Stalkers,*" the Colonel said, as the recording continued in the background. Screams of bystanders sounded once more as the body rotted away.

"*Really?*" Alex said, and a slow smile crossed his face, "*I might be able to be of some help with that. I managed to isolate some elements of one of the others. He has no clear pattern in his shape shifting, but has a heavy accent from the Archon sector. Uses specific phrases like 'feck' that suggest he is from the Attillic Main. I would be more than happy to give you my files on it if you think it would help.*"

"*Zhe Commissar and I would greatly appreciate zhat Lieutenant Commander.*"

"*I will get them right now, if you'd like?*" Alex said, suppressing a smile. He unplugged from the virtual world and made his way back to the *Hunter*. Sharing the data could lead to more information on the Wayang Stalkers, but it would also help distract the MoJ from following his research into Sir Richard.

Sitting at her cubicle in the MoJ Headquarters, Fran's hands shifted and twitched through the air as if she were at a control consul. With her VR headset in place, she was blind to the real world before her, seeing only the computer generated one and hearing only the sounds that the earphones fed her. She spoke commands into a microphone as her begloved hands occasionally darted to and from the invisible typing plane. From time to time she plucked a virtual object from the air and dropped it in front of her like a cook adding a spice to a pot. She was completely unaware that her every action was being watched.

Within the cyberspace of the Imperial Archives, Fran concentrated on her work. Words, numbers, icons and codes hovered before her, and she slowly wove them into a complex query to be fed into the massive databases of the Imperial bureaucracy. From time to time she would call up a pre-constructed bit of search parameters. It would hover in the air to her side where she would grab it and add it into the appropriate location of the query she was constructing. Sometimes she would halt her typing to insert her hands into the code and separate it, entering new commands or dropping preconstructed lines into the algorithm, weaving a question to run through the system and extract the data that she needed.

"*Simon*," she said, "*I need file forty-seven slash A one.*"

"*Of course*," the avatar responded, shifting his weight.

An icon shimmered into existence in his hands and he offered it to Fran as one might offer a drink on a platter. The Semi-Autonomous User Assistant and Help Interface Program, Mr. Simon Miller, took the form of a tall handsome man in his mid-thirties dressed in a business suit. Fran was oblivious, perhaps intentionally so, to any resemblance that he had to a blond version of Lieutenant Commander Lord

Fotheringday. She had selected the avatar's configuration from a wide range of options, and would have died of embarrassment had she realized the similarity.

"*Now pull up file slash slash Cameron query thirty-eight from the current folder in the reserved programs four list.*"

"*Of course,*" the avatar responded. Once she took the code from him, he tilted his head, then held his hands in front of him.

A dull thick headache was forming behind Fran's eyes, and her brain began to feel as if it were wrapped in wool. She ignored it and ran the query. It returned with a syntax error. Biting her lip and shaking her fists before her, Fran growled in frustration. She moved to rub her eyes with the palms of her hands, but instead hit her visor and drove it into the bridge of her nose.

"Ow!" she said, hanging her head she sighed with more frustration before raising the VR goggles and repeating the gesture. Goggles on her forehead, hands still over her eyes she leaned back in her chair and blew out another sigh. Then, picking the sleep from her tear ducts, she let her hands fall to her sides, keeping her eyes closed in the blissful dark.

"*Save file,*" she gave the command, took a deep breath, opened her eyes and looked at the room she sat in for the first time in three hours. The murmuring quiet of the archives research room was broken by the half-scream half-shout of surprise she let out.

Standing directly before her, staring at her with his mirrored eyes, was the unmoving, unblinking and totally silent form of Colonel Lord Ursus DuZhod. The chrome studs on his head glimmered, but his pale sunken features showed no sign of emotion. He looked all the world like the depiction of the undead that haunted the horror media of her teenage years. Even after her scream he stood unmoving. Fran stared back in open mouthed shock and revulsion before her rational mind returned.

"Colonel sir!" she said, coming to her feet. He continued to stare in silence at her for a moment.

"At ease, Able Technician Harpur." His voice was soft, accented and slightly effeminate. He blinked and slowly moved his right hand up to his temple, where his long skeletal index finger slowly rubbed the chromed i/o jack that was implanted there. "I see… heh heh… I see zhat you are quite busy here."

"Yes, sir," Fran responded, suppressing a shudder at the appearance of the creature-officer before her. *He is like the cyborg monsters of the holos.*

Working with Sinner for so long, Fran had begun to forget that the Chief was a wirehead, but here she saw the very in-human embodiment of that which she most feared.

"I must admit," the Colonel said as a tight thin smile spread across his face, "zhat I find you most… interesting."

Following her training, Fran did not respond, but inside she was anything but comforted by this revelation.

"Yes… heh heh… indeed, you see… in my… time… heh… I have met very few individuals who have voluntarily remained incapacitated such as yourself… but even fewer who have yet also chosen to work with technology, and I was quite curious as to how you managed to get by."

"I'm sorry sir, I don't follow you. Incapacitated?" She knew exactly what he meant.

"Ah…yes… sorry… you have no implants. In my somewhat… heh… extended experience, I have found zhis a significant handicap. Most individuals have accepted cybernetic implants or similar devices as soon as zhey could unless zhey were… heh… what I would describe as technophobes… and yet you are not afraid of technology. So, I find myself asking why you choose to live in such a limited way?"

"Permission to speak freely, sir?"

"But of course."

"Well, sir, I don't see it as a limitation, and to be honest, there are a fairly large percentage of naturals throughout the Empire."

"Yes… perhaps say… nineteen point two percent… heh… but most of zhem do not have zhe opportunity to have such implants. Only zhree point two seven zhree eight percent of the population are voluntary naturals such as yourself and zhat… heh heh… zhat is hardly a large percentage… heh. So my point remains: most naturals do not zhen zhrow zhemselves into a career so dominated by technology and in which one would face such restrictions from being without such implants. Surely you must note how more restricted your access to zhe different systems of our everyday life are?"

"These… uh… these issues are fairly… well they're kinda like…personal sir," Fran said, afraid of appearing rude.

"Personal?" He said, the hint of an expression on his face appeared, almost as if he did not understand the word. Then he smiled, "Personal… heh… yes… I suppose zhey are. Please… continue."

Fran hesitated, uncertain as to how to react, uncertain as to the protocol for her actions. She saw her own, frightened image in the colonel's mirrored eyes. Her stomach started to gurgle.

"I… uh…it's like...." She struggled to gain her balance. "Well I guess it's like I don't really want anyone else getting into my head, if you know what I mean."

"No. Explain."

"I mean, I can see the value of the direct interface with computers, but I don't want to have other people, you know, able to access my thoughts."

"Why?"

"Because they're personal," she replied. She was beginning to feel trapped in her cubicle.

"Ah … heh… personal. Zhat word again. Zhere are many misconceptions about being linked you know. It is of course completely possible to put up walls to limit external access, and of course, one could choose not to link into zhe network. No link… no outside access."

"I suppose, but I know people who were totally absorbed by having the wirehead implants. I mean, there was this one guy at school, Bill Sonnerbie, and he became one of the murmuring millions you know? Last time I heard, he was walking around as a street cleaner, talking to himself and linked into the network all the time. He used all his money to improve his implants so he'd have a better connection."

"And was he unhappy in zhis way?"

Fran stared at him, blinking. It had never occurred to her that Bill might enjoy walking around like a zombie.

"Zhere are many individuals who become so altered," He said, tilting his head and smiling in an almost human way, "become absorbed by games or intellectual pursuits… zhere are even a few who include a deeper and deeper access to zheir minds, until at last zhey cannot distinguish zheir own zhoughts from zhose of others. But zhey do zhis zhrough choice. Zhey are not invaded by some outside force. In so becoming totally part of an interactive, zhese people experience a personal wholeness zhat one who is not so linked can never experience."

The Colonel looked almost whimsical while speaking, as if he were describing some vision of paradise. Then his gaze returned to Fran and his smile regained its tight control, "But most individuals do not become so joined. Zhey simply live zhere lives with a high capacity to access zheir files, and interact with both each other and zhere machines."

"Yeah I know," *does he think I'm an idiot?* "but then there's the implanting process. I don't really want nanobots crawling about my head spinning little network connections and maybe going all Grey Plague on me."

"I have heard of such concerns before. Strange fears. Would you be interested if zhere was a way to directly interface without having implants?"

"I guess," Fran said, "But how could you without an implant? I mean, you like, need to have some kind of interface."

"Ah… yes you do, but… heh… you see zhere are other ways of creating a direct user interface. Zhere are races who are incapable of receiving implants you see, and we of zhe DuZhod Interactive can only view such a zhing as a terrible handicap. As a result, we have developed a field inducer technology zhat allows us to create a helmet zhat one wears. It uses vast series of highly sensitive metabolic scanning devices to read and send different neurological impulses in zhe brain. By stimulating electrical and chemical responses, it creates zhe same effects as a direct implant. Zhe result takes some time and training to learn to utilize, and is not as effective as implants, but it permits a greater interaction with zhe computers."

"And this work on humans?"

"We have altered zhe signals in such a way zhat it has been used on humans… heh… yes. It has helped many to see zhe truth behind cybernetic society."

"And there are no long term effects?"

"None. You must first get a total metabolic scan so zhat the system can be calibrated to you, but… heh… zhis is only an in-depth version of what you do when you log into your workstation."

"And there are no implants?"

"Zhat is what I said, yes. Simply a helmet," the Colonel said with the first truly gentle smile she had seen on his face, "One you need never put on again if you do not like the experience."

"And you have this equipment here?" Fran asked, her eyes narrowing. She was unaware that she leaned ever so subtly towards the Colonel.

"But of course…" DuZhod smiled.

Samantha walked into the elegant room of the Hotel Therese, closed the door, and performed an electronic sweep of the room to detect for bugs. She walked around the room, running the handheld device over the soft dark furniture, but saw no hint of surveillance equipment. Regardless, she ran the sweep twice more before she downloaded her report onto her PAD and plugged it in the more sophisticated communications equipment she had brought with her.

"*Nest, this is Osprey,*" she sent the mental comms.

"*Osprey, this is Nest, I copy,*" Bowman's voice sounded in her head.

"*Nest, I'm ready to upload the information to date. Nothing startling so far I'm afraid, but we're making progress.*"

As she transmitted the information, she made her way to the bathroom and removed the left grey-green contact lens that was bothering her so much. Using standard cleansing solution, she washed it. She looked momentarily in the mirror and noted her odd appearance: one green eye, one colored with prismatic spokes. She had seen herself with odder appearances, tanned to black with her hair in an afro, vampirically pale with long straight red hair, even painted blue with green tattoos. She did not particularly care for undercover work, but her background in ethnography and her skin's natural ability to change from pale white to dark brown based on natural amounts of sunlight did give her an advantage. All the same, she would rather sit behind the chair of the Nav-Com position than lie to strangers. Then again, she would rather study people than spy on them. Nevertheless, she would do what ever it took to do her duty.

"*Information received, ma'am,*" Bowman noted, "*How are you doing?*"

"*Well enough, Corporal,*" she responded, "*Any update from the others?*"

"*All systems are go, but no new developments.*"

"*Keep me informed. Also, see if you can arrange a meet between myself and the Skipper.*"

"*Will do, ma'am. Take care of yourself.*"

"*Thanks.*"

Samantha thought for a moment about her parents, and the death they had faced. She thought about serving with the Ripper, using her skills to help him defeat the forces that brought about their death. She thought about vengeance, and doing what was right, and whether these things all added up. She thought about these things almost every night.

Tonight, however, she forced herself to drive such thoughts from her head. She was on mission, and expected to go out on another date with Sir Richard within a few hours. She had yet to see anything that linked Sir Richard with the acts of piracy or terrorism, but Alex had seemed convinced that such a contact might be present. She decided to trust him, at least for the time being. Besides, the truth could clear Sir Richard just as easily as condemn him.

She replaced the contact lens, blinking as it positioned itself and locked into place. Returning to the bedroom, she laid out her outfit for the evening. Once ready, she looked at the clock, decided she had the time, and changed to go to the pool for a stress relieving swim.

"Well, if you think it might help you, I don't see any reason why not," Alex said, noting that it was perhaps not the answer that Ms. Harpur wanted to hear, "Of course the choice is entirely yours."

"Thank you sir," Fran responded, a slight frown on her face, "I'll certainly think about it. I must admit, it would be useful to be able to interact more fully with the computers, it's just that… well, may I speak freely sir?"

"Please do," Alex responded, but Fran still seemed to pause a moment.

Alex waited, looked out across the axis parkland of the orbital, and took another bite of his couscous. He thought of Sally, out there somewhere in the orbital doing what ever it was Sally did while he was on mission. It didn't make him at all comfortable to have her around. Still, what was he to do? He put thoughts of his girlfriend out of his mind.

It had been another long morning in the archives, though he was more than satisfied with their progress so far. They had gathered a large amount of data that was beginning to form a pattern, one that he didn't like. One that suggested that parts of Sir Richard's company might be involved in smuggling, or worse. They had found nothing that tied Richie directly to the crimes, but nothing that cleared him of them either. The personal nature of it made it all the more necessary to step away from the VR library and sterile MoJ offices.

In the garden that filled the central axis of the station, he was able to catch his breath and gain perspective. Yet even beyond that, he enjoyed these sojourns with Fran. His conversations with her were revitalizing. They allowed him to clear his mind and think of other topics. They refreshed his ability to continue scanning and reading the interminable reports. Sitting with Fran and looking out across the park, he noted that his jaw clenched just a little less tightly.

"Well, sir," Fran said at last, "It's just that… to be honest, I'm not all that comfortable around the Colonel, if you know what I mean?"

He looked back at her as she leaned heavily on the iron table. She had developed greatly over the past few months. She was proving to be a fast learner. She was quite bright and had an analytical mind. Indeed, he began to wonder if he should be recommending her for OCS.

"The DuZhod are a very different type of people," he said with a smile as he put down his food and focused his attention on the young rating, "and I would agree that it is important to remain cautious regarding the sharing of too much, too quickly. Indeed, some of the methods used by his particular brand of Guardian are a bit… shall we say draconian? Even so, the Colonel does appear to be a loyal officer and member of the hierarchy. I would not be too concerned about him."

"I know, sir, I know it's just silly… but… it's just that he like reminds me of one of those… well…"

"Villains from a holo-movie? That is because such movies are based upon stereotypes, Ms Harpur."

"I suppose so sir…"

"I cannot say for certain, but I suspect that he does it on purpose."

"Sir?" Fran tilted her head quizzically, her cup halting midway to her mouth.

"The good Colonel is a specialist in counter-insurgency… has it ever occurred to you that there might be times where it would work to one's advantage to seem, how to put it? Disconcerting?"

"Not really, sir," Fran said, a small line appeared on her brow, "at least, not enough that I would want to spend my whole life that way."

CHAPTER 45

"How's it goin', Nick?"

The Tinman looked over at Sinner and put out his hand in sign of welcome. A cool breeze flowed over the concrete bridge, ruffling the Tinman's hair. Below them Sinner could see the rocks in the bottom of the wide shallow river.

"Wishbone," the Tinman said with a smile, clapping Sinner's returned hand with his own, "good to see you. I heard you helped out a couple of friends of mine the other night. Thanks."

"I like the girl too… and I'd hate to see a good customer get whacked."

"All the same, thanks. What brings you back in system?"

"Business," Sinner replied.

Nicholas "Tinman" Tinnoush was an A-class fixer in a C-class town. Sinner could never figure why he didn't relocate to one of the starports. That's where all the real action was, but then again, maybe the man knew what he was talking about. After all, there did appear to be at least one major interstellar black-market contact in Binghouse, possibly even a Federalist.

"Business with who?" the Tinman asked.

"With you, for one."

"So I hear… so I hear. What ya' lookin' for?"

"I'm lookin' to make contact with someone who deals in hardshit hardware. You know real blacklist stuff, someone known as the Ankh."

"Ankhenatun?" Tinman asked, stepping back and shaking his head, "You're looking for Ankhenatun? Fuck man, I keep my ass clear of his shit."

"Why? What's so bad-ass about the Ankh?"

"He's more than just a badass, he's political. I mean real political. He's got contacts from on-high that keep an eye out for him, clear the way when it needs clearing."

"What kinda contacts?"

"I don't know," Tinman said, then leaned on the concrete rail and looked out over the river, "Someone with money and sway. On top of that, the Ankh is backed by pros. Not local ass boys mind you, or even semi-pros out of the megacities. I mean real pros, off-worlders. The kinda people that are chipped with ultratech and would kill you as soon as look at you. So, like I said, I keep my distance."

"What else can you tell me about him?"

"Not a lot. I've met him once or twice, done some peripheral business with some of his peripheral partners… but nothing real serious. I know he deals in hot items, will trade or barter with high-tech weapons and pays top value for good merchandise."

"How about ships?" Sinner asked, leaning closer to the Tinman as he rested on the rail of the bridge, "Does he deal in ships?"

"Not that I know of, though I wouldn't be surprised to find out he moved pirated vehicles. He comes in and out of system on a fairly regular basis. Uses Binghouse as a kind of stopping point, never goes to the Sprawl."

Sinner nodded and looked down river, noting how the water churned as it passed through the gated arches of the city wall.

"You got a pirated vehicle or something?" the Tinman asked, looking at the same spot.

"I got some clients who want to know a bit more about the man, that's all. Can you point him out to me?"

"Fingering the Ankh isn't exactly a safe thing to do."

"What's your price?"

"There's gonna be a turf war soon," the Tinman said, turning to face Sinner, "between the Danes and Highlanders."

"What's that got to do with you?" Sinner faced his contact and smiled. "You always stayed out of that kinda shit."

"Yeah, well, normally. But this kinda thing is bad for business. It escalates and next thing you know, I can't arrange anything for anyone. Now what the hell kinda fixer can I be if I can't fix? Besides, there's Monique. She's watched my back on more than one occasion."

Sinner nodded and looked away, being careful to avoid looking at the slight glint of light he saw in one of the nearby windows. Probably nothing, but quite possible a sniper; he marked it and broadcast the location. "I could get you a few Mark 5 AARs."

The Tinman looked at him silently, as if measuring him up. "I need twenty."

"What you kidding? For you to point out some guy in a friggin' bar? That's top of the line Imperial hardware we're talkin' about. They retail legit for fifteen hundred a pop. I can get you one for that shit… and with that I'm being generous."

"My life's worth more than one Mark Five. I'll give you fifteen-grand for the lot plus finger the guy for you."

"Forty and finger the guy."

"Thirty."

"Deal," Sinner said, standing up straight and spitting on his palm. The Tinman responded in kind and took Sinner's hand. The Tinman moved to let go, but Sinner held his grip for a moment longer, smiled and leaned in close. "And you know you're dead if you get the wrong guy."

Across the river, on the opposite side from where D'Ascoine was watching the meeting through the eyes of the gamepariah, Chrom kept the Tinman in her sights until she received the second all clear from Sinner. She turned off the sights, stowed away her rifle, and made her way to the rendezvous point.

High above them on board the *Hunter*, D'Ascoine relaxed their final backup. He smiled as he watched the Tinman's people pack up and leave the area. The blast from the ship's laser turret would have blown up half the building that the man Sinner identified as Blade had been poised in. A bit of overkill perhaps, but it would have ensured that Sinner got away neatly.

Fran was nervous. She stood naked in the centre of the cylindrical chamber waiting for what ever it was that DuZhod was going to do. Just being naked like that was disconcerting enough, she'd never been all that comfortable with her own body, not to mention the thought of others, even doctors, staring at her. That, combined with the intensive metabolic scanning she was about to receive, was nerve wracking. Even without nanosurgery, she was entering a world of freaks.

How many times had she seen the bone chilling visage of the prole-savs wandering through the dockyards, hooked on their constant connection to a cyber-intellectual world? She shivered at the thought of gamepariahs and other forms of the murmuring millions, trapped by their addiction to sending emails, mind messages, sim-conferencing, digital downloading, gaming and the thousand other forms of the constant chatter of the connected. She was sick to her stomach, swallowing belches that tasted of acid. She jumped at a loud thudding noise. The lights came on and a robot rolled into the room.

"Please open your mouth," it said in its pre-programmed politeness.

Fran complied and the medical drone extended a swab into her mouth, scraping the insides. It drew a drop of blood from her left ring finger, then plucked one of her long brown hairs from the top of her head. She rubbed the painful spot as the drone thanked her and returned to its alcove.

"That is the end of the invasive procedures," the same voice said. The lights in the room then turned to a neon-blue bathed hue. A white lined grid was suddenly projected upon her body. She looked down at it, cocking an eyebrow.

"Please stand perfectly still for a moment." The computerized voice echoed through the chamber.

A layer of bright white light then descended through the room, followed by a bright red light and the sounds of four more such scans that she couldn't see. Individual squares of the grid briefly turned solid white in a random sequence. Her body became decorated like an alternating chessboard. A few buzzes and knocks sounded around her, and then came the more physical processes.

She was asked to run in place, a treadmill appearing below her. She was asked to perform calisthenics, which proved both physically and mentally uncomfortable as she bent over and bounced her way through the varying exercises. The room grew icy cold, then steaming hot. She wondered what purpose all the exercises and temperature changes might have been, but assumed it was to measure her body at different extremes.

In the end, the whole process took approximately four hours. Along the way, she was in fact at no point aware of the most important element of it: the point where the DuZhod released the cloud of nanobots into the air that Fran unknowingly inhaled.

CHAPTER 46

The two teams raced out of the entrance tunnels, with blue smoke billowing from the methane engines and nothing but a warm buzz coming from those vehicles fuelled by biofuel cells. This was the main event, the Seventhnight Sealed Entrance Team Duel. Eighteen vehicles barreled onto the great oval track of the Binghouse Circuit Maximus Arena, traveling at speeds over one-hundred and sixty kilometers per hour. They had not yet completed one full circuit when three mid-sized motorcycles and a light motortrike from one team cut off from their group and entered into the great armored maze that lay in the center of the oblong racetrack. Their opposition's counter-parts, three light and two heavy bikes peeled away from their formation and also entered the maze. Shortly afterwards bullets, grenades and other firepower started to fly.

Gunnery Sergeant Andrea Chrom eyed the combat with disgust, then returned to scanning the cheering arena crowd for potential threats and dangers. Thus far, there had been four 'duels' previous to what the Tinman had said would be the Big Fight. These bloody and explosive matches had done their job and warmed up the alcohol and drug fuelled crowd into a cheering and chanting frenzy. It was a gladiatorial death rage, and voluntary or not, it churned Chrom's stomach.

Born into poverty herself, Chrom could see the appeal of fast cash and instant fame that the arena gave, but money and fame did not give one self-respect. As a kid she hadn't understood that, but when the Empire arrived to her homeworld, they gave people options, and gave her a sense of worth. She had joined the Marines, escaped poverty, and built a future for herself. She hoped one day some of these toughs might do the same, and knew that the best way to help them do so was to take out the Federalist trash. Finding the Ankh was a big step to finding the Dalang and his scumbag terrorist followers.

As of yet, however, the Ankh had not made an appearance; or at least the Tinman had not spotted him. So she kept scanning the crowd and watching the games. Chrom wished that Sinner had pulled this duty, but he was hooked into the different media feeds of the arena, hacking and riding the system so that once the targets were IDed, he would be able to track them. D'Ascoine was also in attendance, but elsewhere in the crowd. Right now it was her, Tinman and the woman named Monique walking through the throng, searching for a figure that only the other two knew. The Gunnery Sergeant was left to cover their backs and watch the death matches with disgust.

The first match was a general admission amateur melee, an open door event where men and women tried to win two grand and maybe get onto the pro-circuit by fighting in low-end vehicles provided free of charge. The second was a team matched pro-am combo of five teams of two, one professional and one amateur who fought each other until death, surrender or escape. The third combat, which involved the most skilled driving according to Leftenant D'Ascoine, was a sealed entrance grudge duel between two roadsters who had decided to settle a debt of honor in the media circus before them. By that point the crowd was warmed up for the main event: the sealed door team fight to the death that they were watching now. Two of the motorcycles had killed each other in the maze, while the five circling cars of one team closed in on the three cars and van of the other. The vehicles dodged mines and slicks that the teams were laying down on the track.

"Got him," Monique said. At first Chrom thought she was referring to the fight. "He's in the second level business-class boxes, heading towards the bar area."

Chrom looked at the solid mirrored implants that covered the woman's eyes and followed her gaze across to the more elite viewing sections of the arena. The distance was far too great for Chrom to see unaided. The woman clearly had highly enhanced optics in her visor.

"Can you broadcast the signal?" Chrom asked, wishing once more that Sinner was here.

"Do I look like a wirehead to you?" Monique responded, keeping her eyes on the target.

Yes, Chrom thought to herself, but said nothing. The lower tech level of Lai-Jung Prime did not provide discreet appearance options for individuals with commlink implants. Instead, native wireheads tended to look more like typical media cyborgs with external reception antennae and a part-robot look, often highly stylized as a fashion accessory.

"Point him out to me," Chrom said, and put her electronic binos to her eyes with as much stealth as possible. There were more than a few individuals with binoculars of one type or another in the crowd, but they all had their eyes fixed securely on the match. Chrom felt completely exposed and obvious as she eyed the spectator box. "Second level, he's in the bar now."

"Where's the bar?" Chrom asked.

"Third rank of windows from the left. He's the really tall thin guy, funny lookin' face."

Chrom moved her binos up two levels, then counted panes of glass until she came to a bar filled with suits. It was very crowded.

"Which one… I need more to go on."

"Tall guy, looks like an offworlder, white suit, lots of pictures or something woven into it,"

Around her, the crowd was screaming. She was jostled by enthusiastic fans as more death was dealt in the maze. On the track the two circling sets of autos closed in.

"Don't see him."

"See the black girl in a red-dress?" Monique said. She hadn't taken her eyes off the target despite being jostled by the throng, "She's talking to some guy in a peach colored set of fake arena armor."

"Yeah, I can see him for sure."

"Two people down the bar, really tall thin guy. Funny-lookin' face."

"Got him," Chrom picked out the target. He was an ectomorph, born in low or zero gee, not common in a small backwater like Binghouse. "He's just put down his drink… he's now talking to someone, now picking up some snacks…."

"Yeah, that's the one."

Chrom pressed a button on her binos and took a series of digital images and tried to discretely jack a dataline from her PAD into the optical viewer. She showed the image on her PAD to the Tinman who nodded: it was Ankhenatun. She uploaded the image to Sinner as she turned binos to the match. A second later he had established a live three-way link with her and the Leftenant.

"*We've got our target, Bravo Echo. You get my photos*?"

"*Yep*," Sinner replied, "*Now, use your rangefinders and send the feed direct.*"

Chrom turned back to the box, found him again and pressed the second button on her binos. An IR laser rangefinder fired at her target. The beam was refracted by the bar's windows, but with the blue prints of the arena already loaded into his systems, Sinner was able to extrapolate the position of the man known as the Ankh and lock the hi-jacked security systems into tracking him.

"*Got him*!" Sinner announced.

"Can we get in there?" Chrom asked, "Get closer?"

"What? Dressed like this?" the Tinman asked. He was clad in a typical set of road armor, Monique was wearing leathers over a pbc cat-suit and Chrom wore baggy street pants and a sleeveless T-shirt. They were not dressed for mixing in the business class bar.

"*It's alright, Sergeant,*" D'Ascoine said, "*I can enter the bar if need be, but the Chief has him on all systems. We need to position ourselves for him to leave in case we can't track him on the other city systems.*"

Chrom communicated the announcement to the two mercenaries she accompanied. Keeping a window open to Sinner's feed, they made their way to an area where they could more readily cover the exits from the business area.

In the arena, the combat came to a head. The team with five cars was catching up to the team with the van and close range weapons had begun to eat away at each other's armor. Suddenly, the leading team spread from a diamond formation into a staggered line. A cloud of smoke and a slick oil-like substance was sprayed from the rear of the van and two mid-sized cars that flanked it.

As the other vehicles raced through it, struggling to maintain control, the lead team performed a remarkably well synchronized bootleg turn at high speeds. They fired as one into the on-coming team. The compact car in the lead exploded almost at once. Within seconds, the second team's cars were all dead, and an enormous cheer filled the arena when the other vehicles, including the van, entered the maze to finish off the remaining enemy bikes and trikes.

"It's very rare for a van to go into the maze," the Tinman said as they waited, "This is a great show. Even the orbital media's picked it up."

Chrom fought back her disgust, forcing herself to smile and nod in response. She had a target to follow and hoped she would soon leave this repugnant display.

Sally's bright blue eyes sparkled as she looked at Alex teasingly over her cup of coffee. She sat crossed legged on the hotel bed, her pale and lightly freckled skin glimpsed out from beneath the bathrobe. Her ginger hair was still tussled from the night before, and a smirking smile graced her lips as if she were a naughty child. Under normal circumstances she would have been fetching.

"It is not funny," Alex said with irritation as he tucked in his shirt.

"Oh I think you'd see it was, if you were in my place," Sally replied.

"You are not supposed to know where I am."

"My explanation gave you plausible deniability," she responded and took another sip of her black coffee, "Besides, my family has a number of business interests in this system, and it is becoming a very popular stopover among the in-set. The who's-who crowd all find Lai-Jung so delightfully barbaric, what with their gladiators and roadwars and all."

"That is not the point, Sal. I have just started to win the approval of my crew and now you're here? How do you think that is going to look?"

"Like I'm wild about you."

"Or just wild."

"That too." She stopped smiling, put her coffee cup down, and spoke seriously. "Look, Alex, I needed to see you, alright? There are things we need to discuss."

Alex stared at her silently, then shook his head as a slight smile appeared. "What am I going to do with you?"

"Make mad and passionate love to me?" she answered, smirking once more.

Alex glowered at her.

The DuZhod watched Fran trying on her new gear. As she adjusted the fit of her helmet, they adjusted the signals from the nanobots whose web was woven through her nervous system. When the reception from Fran's helmet and interface box was perfectly synchronized with the tiny robots, the Colonel smiled. So did the rest of the local hub of the Interactive.

In one sense, the Colonel had not even lied to her. He had merely omitted some facts and exaggerated others, though that subtlety was irrelevant. The DuZhod did not really care what any one individual thought. They only considered the importance to the Interactive, and less so, to the Ministry of Justice. Now the MoJ had their spy onboard the *Hunter*: a spy that would allow them to observe Fotheringday's investigation and, more importantly, Ripper's Raiders as a whole. What was more, the DuZhod had obtained the measurements and memories of a full natural, something the Interactive had not had in a very long time: it all worked beautifully into its collective plans.

"So you want to keep the ships on those routes, even though I've shown you the increased risk," Hammond said as he stared in disbelief at the Hierarch.

"It's the risk that helps make those routes the most profitable," Sir Richard responded. He was looking out the front viewport of his starship's lounge. Below them was the curving blue and white horizon of Lai Jung Prime.

"What about the attempt on your life?"

"A message, that's all," Sir Richard said. Turning, he smiled at Hammond before moving to the wet bar. Hammond followed two paces behind.

"One hell of a message."

"It's a sign of our success," Sir Richard said. Pouring a drink, he handed it to Hammond before filling one of his own.

"Attitudes like that could end up getting you killed."

"Attitudes like that will end up making both of us rich."

"Things aren't always about money, Ritchie." Hammond took a sip of his drink, then a large swallow.

"I have news for you, Kyle," Sir Richard said as he leaned against the bar, "It's never about money, it's always about power. The money just helps."

Hammond shook his head and took another drink. Sir Richard rattled the ice in his glass and chortled to himself. They turned in unison to stare out the viewport.

"I might need to borrow this ship again," Hammond said, his eyes followed one of the shuttles leaving the orbital.

"It will have to wait," Sir Richard said, a smile touching the corner of his mouth.

Hammond turned to look at him and stared in silence for a moment before turning back to the view port. He rattled the ice in his glass.

"So tell me, who's the girl you've been running around with?"

Sir Richard turned to give Hammond a long, cold glare.

CHAPTER 47

Alex walked through the comfortable entrance courtyard of the Hotel Therese and made his way immediately towards the poolside restaurant. He climbed the marbled staircase and came to the series of umbrella tables that nestled along the uneven rows of sun-loungers. Ivy covered walls and pillars lined three sides of the courtyard. The fourth looked out over the Old Quarter of the resort city of Rehan and the sea that lay beyond it. A large immaculately clean pool lay in the center of the courtyard, gentle mosaic patterns upon its floor. Its far end abutted against the open view of the sunrise, a handful of morning swimmers breaking the calm of the waters.

Alex stopped in the courtyard, took in the view, and then made his way to a cozy corner table next to the patterned towel and book he had covertly scanned for. He sat overlooking the pool and sky beyond, breathing in the fresh sea air as it wafted over the city. Noting the rosy colored hues of the sky as the sun slowly rose, a part of him yearned to enjoy this for what it was, to take the long rest that surely he deserved. Thoughts of his mission quickly drove such dreams from his mind however, and he scanned for any potential problems.

"Do you care for anything, sir?" a white clad waiter asked.

"Yes, a glass of water, a carafe of coffee and a pain-aux-chocolate if you would be so kind," he responded. It felt odd to be out of uniform, though he knew that had he dressed in anything but the faux-linen khaki jacket and light weight trousers he would have appeared out of place.

When the breakfast arrived, he smiled, nodded to the waiter and gratefully took a sip of the coffee. Casually, he cast a glance across the swimmers in the pool as if it was the first time he had paid them any notice. Out of them all, his eyes lingered for only a moment more upon the strong smooth stokes of the woman in red swimsuit. Alex doubted anyone noticed; most everyone there also spared that swimmer the occasional glance. He sipped his coffee, enjoyed his pastry and took in the view of the city.

He waited about fifteen minutes before he watched Samantha extract herself from the pool, casting the wet of her blond hair to one side, and wringing it briefly before walking towards him. The one piece red swimsuit highlighted her curves, emphasized her breasts and revealed the smooth golden tan of her skin and strong tone of her arms and legs. Glistening with water as she approached, she greeted him with a slight smile, nod and barely audible "morning" as she passed him.

Picking up her towel from the lounger two seats away, she began to pat herself down. A tall blended juice and a coffee were delivered to her as she did so. As she spread the UV cream across her long shapely legs, Alex became aware of exactly how attractive his Executive Officer really was. It was a thought that he did not feel overly comfortable with.

"*Good morning, Lieutenant,*" he broadcast to her, using a scrambled low strength tight beam communications link from his PAD to hers.

"*Good morning, sir,*" she responded, "*I'm sorry that I called you all the way down here, but I thought it would be best to meet face to face, exchange ideas and such.*"

"*No I perfectly agree. What have you found so far?*"

"*Well to be honest, not much. I've made solid contact and have seen Quarry on numerous occasions, but as of yet neither I nor the Nest have identified anything unusual. Certainly nothing to tie him to the Wayang,*" she said using the codenames for Sir Richard and Corporal Bowman, "*Both my direct observations and our planted surveillance devices have only shown him engaged in legitimate business and socializing.*"

"*Keep at it, Samantha, he was always a very good intelligence officer, and if he is in fact involved with the Wayang, he will be skilled at keeping it secret. Lots of intermediaries and the like.*"

"*Understood, but….*" She stopped spreading the cream and stared at the horizon. Her thumb was running over her forefinger.

"*Yes?*"

"*To be honest, Alex, he seems completely legitimate. What makes you think it's him?*"

"*I am not certain, but in two cases where information was compromised, Quarry was in the perfect position to do so. He also has direct business interests in the system with the anomaly that first raised your suspicions. It is a lot of coincidences, too many to ignore, but I hope I am wrong.*"

"*So do I.*"

"*Are you becoming personally involved, Lieutenant?*" Alex fought the desire to look at her.

"*No, sir. He just seems like a nice man.*"

"*He is nice man, a man I consider a friend, but nice is different than good, Lieutenant.*"

"*My position is not compromised, nor am I biased. It's just I don't see evidence of collusion.*"

"*Good, but we must be certain.*"

"*Understood, but… well… permission to speak freely, sir?*"

"*In private meetings, Samantha, I will always need you to speak freely,*" he said, affording her a look.

"*I wondered if it's possible that your previous relationship with Quarry, and its tie to the* Slipper, *could be biasing your view of the mission,*" Samantha said, leaning back in the lounger and stretching with her arms above her head. The sun glistened off the sun screen.

"*It is possible,*" Alex said, looking away and crossing his legs, "*and is one reason why I have you doing this investigation. I trust your analysis of the situation far more than my own.*"

"*Understood,*" she looked towards him for a moment, "*I'm sorry if it seemed that I was doubting you, Alex.*"

"*No apologies needed, if you think we are wrong I want to know it: I could well be overcompensating. I want your opinions, Samantha. I need them.*"

"*Thank you, sir,*" she said looking away and blushing ever so slightly. She picked up a book. "*As for other news, has Falcon begun tracking his target?*"

"*Indeed. Hopefully it will prove fruitful. As for Eaglet and I, we have been scouring the records and found there was a brief increase in underworld violence that occurred shortly before a marked increase in Quarry's corporate income.*"

"*Quarry mentioned that diversification into other business interests had significantly increased his company shares and earnings.*"

"*He said as much to me some months ago, but I would have expected a loss for at least two years. Still, hardly damning is it?*"

"*No. It isn't,*" Samantha said, then remained silent for a moment as she pretended to read her book, "*Personally, Alex, if Quarry is involved I don't think I'll be able to find any evidence of it by snooping around the edges. I'll need to access some of his private files, preferably those on board his ship.*"

"*Too risky. If you are blown while on board that ship, retraction would be impossible.*"

"*Sometimes risks are worth it.*"

Fran fought back the dizziness as she toggled from the virtual world back into the real one. She was impressed by the increased speed and power of her new interface, but she was also having problems adjusting to the bombardment of new sensations. She was often nauseated and felt phantom itches or tickles. Both the Colonel and, more importantly, the

Commander had told her such a period of adjustment was normal. It took a bit of time for her brain to adapt to the new inputs, but she wanted to get on with it.

Fran reached for her PAD and connected it into the large, briefcase-like interface machine sitting in front of her. Multitudinous wires led from the armored device designed to be carried as a backpack, to the user interface skullcap she wore. Despite the increased capabilities that it gave her, she still felt uncomfortable wearing it. Not only did she fear cyber-addiction, she suspected the helmet made her look like something from a parody of pre-space-flight science fiction movies. Still, the device definitely helped get the work done faster.

Fran toggled back into cyber-space and the VR library that waited for her there. She turned to retrieve the data from her PAD, but discovered it was still being virus checked in quarantine. She decided to busy herself with other work.

Opening mental windows, she noted the pile of data to be reviewed, but her eyes went to the relaxation icons that appeared. Their presence infuriated her. There was the nagging desire to screw off; play some game or watch the inbuilt media entertainment instead of working. The concept that such facilities were always available made it more difficult for Fran to concentrate. She could see how people could become addicted to them, and lose themselves in a cyber-reality. She decided to delete the icons from her interface. Even then, there was something else that bothered her.

She knew that if she wanted to she could be "closer to anyone than ever before" by sharing thoughts and even feelings, but she didn't want other people to read her thoughts or worse yet, access her fantasies. While she was unconnected, her mind was her own, but once she put on her helmet, she was linked into a world that was shared by others.

What if the Skipper became aware of her feelings towards him? What if she accidentally broadcast them or someone hacked into her head? Sinner could do it, she was pretty sure of that. He said he was a goa, and goas could hack into any system and ride them like they were their own bodies. Couldn't he do the same with her? The whole concept freaked her out.

"*Why am I even jacked into this thing?*"

Because it helps me do my work and I want to be the best Tech around, she answered herself. She thought of Fotheringday's comment how if she could be both a natural and wirehead she would be the perfect Intelligence operative. She eagerly returned to work. Before she knew it, the quarantine was over and she had access to the archives.

"*Okay, so let's look at the files. I'm sure I'm missing something here. Where are the systems with increased terrorism or piracy over the past few years? Alright, there are about twenty of them. Damn, nothing new. So, think like the Skipper. What other activities would indicate stuff?*"

She called up the records on terrorist activities. Again no clear correlation.

"*Smuggling?*" The answer showed an overlap in some systems where smuggling activities were identified and terrorism had increased. She smiled as she looked at the chains of star systems formed on the charts.

"*Navigational archipelagos,*" she realized, and in the back of her mind she noted something, another pattern that looked familiar to her. She stared at it trying to figure it out.

"*Excuse me, Miss?*" a voice sounded next to her.

Startled, Fran turned, uncertain whether the sound came from the real world or the virtual one. A MoJ clerk stood next to her in the formal hall of the Archive space.

"Yes?" she responded in both the real world and the virtual one.

"*You're leaking,*" the man responded as if that would mean something to her.

Fran looked around and realized that she was attracting the attention of a few of the other readers in the archive room. Looking up, she came to the embarrassed realization that the stellar map she was observing had not been projected into her private space, but rather into the shared space of the archives library. She was mortified both by the irritation this would have caused the other readers and by the fact that she was broadcasting her own sensitive research to anyone in the room.

Had she also been broadcasting her thoughts? Fran turned a deep red and immediately switched channels. She blurted out effusive apologies and the man left her alone in agonizing embarrassment.

In the real world she wanted to vomit while in the virtual one she retreated into the privacy of her own interface room. Swallowing acid belches, she tried to return to work, overlapping the queries and looking at them. This time, she ensured she could not broadcast anything.

Okay, there's kind of a link between smuggling, terrorist activities and piracy. Shocker. But there's something else that's missing. What? What? She looked at the search parameters to see what she might have been missing.

"Oh, duh!" She said out loud as she read the definitions used by each of the different services and realized her mistake. In Naval Intelligence "terrorism" was broadly defined: any insurgent activity that involved interstellar transport or was engaged in within the confines of inhabited bodies such as planets, moons or space stations. It was based on a media definition and generally used by the Navy to define elements that were and were not within their remit.

However, both the MoJ and Imperial Army Guardian Intelligence used a more refined definition: acts of terrorism were those carried out against a civilian population. Guerrilla attacks, the sporadic and/or clandestine attacks by insurgent groups against military personnel, were not so defined. Since she was querying MoJ and IAGI databases, no Federalist attacks on military targets would be included in her search. She added the search term into the query.

"*I'm sorry*," Mr. Miller said as he suddenly appeared in her private space, "*those records are restricted access and cannot be viewed outside the archives themselves.*"

Growling with frustration, Fran returned to the library space and, ensuring that she had placed a privacy bubble around her, reran the query. It took minutes to get the results, but when she did a much more distinctive pattern formed: gaps were filled in, branches were formed, information came together. The routes between the stars looked like a tree, but what was more, it looked like a tree that she had seen before. She leaned back and stared at it, trying desperately to figure out why the pattern looked so familiar.

"Holy shit," she said aloud when she realized where she'd seen the pattern before.

CHAPTER 48

After the arena, tracking the Ankh became much easier. Sinner used the city's communication and security systems to follow the man across town. The justifiably paranoid and omni-present police and private surveillance systems of the city allowed him to maintain constant contact with the target. They hacked the Ankh's communications, bugged his room, and followed him on video surveillance for three days.

The Ankh was clearly dodgy as hell, but he was also quite careful. He walked among a mélange of the privileged and the lowlifes, welcomed warmly, but seldom in the company of any one group aside from his bodyguards for very long. He never spoke business in public, and whenever he arranged for a meeting it was in a windowless room with no security systems. As a free-city in a free-port, Binghouse had many such rooms. D'Ascoine's team watched him enter and leave them time and again, but they could never record any of the meetings despite their high-tech sonics. Sinner suspected that the Ankh had access to high-tech solutions of his own, probably Federalist in origin.

What they learned for certain was that Ankhenatun was an offworlder – born as a free-trader in Imperial space, with long thin features like so many who had grown up without gravity. His pock marked face and knobbley knees, however, were the result of a disease he had encountered as a child on a world his family had traded with. No one knew why he hadn't had the scars body sculpted away. He was clever, well connected, and despite their best efforts, he remained elusive. They were not even able to determine for certain if his shady dealings were with Federalists, not to mention with the Dalang.

Even so, by the time Alex was meeting with Samantha, it had become obvious that the Ankh was getting ready for a big meeting. D'Ascoine's Team Falcon knew where and when the meet was scheduled, but had problems figuring out how to bug it. A series of elaborate plans for breaking and entering or posing as businessmen were proposed, but each seemed flawed. After hearing several such schemes, Alex decided to meet with his tracking team. It meant putting off an urgent request by Fran for a briefing, but finding the link between the Ankh and the Dalang took priority.

He met D'Ascoine and the others in the low-grade hotel that they were operating out of. The walls had peeling and stained wallpaper, and no holoprojectors. Alex had expected D'Ascoine to lodge a complaint, but as the hierarch TOMO explained the situation, he seemed surprisingly non-plussed by the rooms. Indeed, he even seemed mildly interested as Alex presented a solution.

"Plant a sleeper-bug," he said after they gave him a full report, "The Leftenant should book the room before the meeting, and plant a recording device in a sealed set, timed to go off at a given time. At this tech level, the hotel bug-sweepers won't detect it while off, and the targets won't pick up a give-away signal because it doesn't broadcast. You go in and collect it after the first meeting is done."

"What cover should I use when having the meeting?" D'Ascoine asked, a broad smile appearing on his face, "An autoduellest? I would rather like giving my hand at that, after all I am..."

"You don't use a cover, Leftenant," Alex said. D'Ascoine's face fell.

"You are an Imperial hierarch," Alex continued, "Our rival intelligence agencies know you are in system, and probably our prime suspect does as well. What is more, everyone knows that you are a racing fanatic. Book into the hotel as yourself, reserve the meeting room for two hours before the Ankh needs it, and 'meet' with the Gunny there. Together, you plant the bug, leave and go to the Arena to watch some fights."

"Won't they get suspicious, sir?" Chrom asked, a frown appearing on her brow.

"It is possible, Gunnery Sergeant, but I doubt it. Leftenant D'Ascoine is well known on the Imperial celebrity race tracks, and the local blood sport is exactly the kind of thing he is likely to go see. Am I correct, Leftenant?"

"Without a doubt," D'Ascoine said, his pout having reduced at the suggestion of watching an arena fight.

Sinner didn't say a word. He remained silent with his arms crossed, and gave only a single nod at the end of it.

"Now, I've got to return to the Orbital," Alex said, "and if I am to remain discreet, that will take at least two days. Carry on."

A day into his convoluted trip back, Alex received a coded message telling him that the operation was a success. Team Falcon had recorded a criminal meeting and now had a new target to follow, one they suspected might even be the Dalang himself.

Samantha looked at herself in the mirror, smoothed the line of her floor length white dress and smiled. Normally she cursed whatever power, man-made or divine, that had burdened her with such large breasts. *I had thought mandellans were supposed to have been designed for combat*, she would say to herself, *but 'these' clearly get in the way of everything.* Without proper and customized support, they bounced painfully when she ran, jumped or performed most of the kind of action that were normally expected in a combat environment. They were also almost certainly responsible for the frequent dull backaches she had.

Obviously the designer of the mandellan genetic cocktail was an adolescent boy who wasn't breastfed, she thought, but she knew that most other mandellan women were not nearly so large in the chest. In truth, she had almost definitely inherited the trait from her mother's side of the family. Aunt Anne was even larger than she was.

Tonight, however, she did not so greatly object to what man or nature had endowed her with. The image that gazed back at her from the mirror looked particularly appealing in the white, well made, off-the-shoulder dress. Normally, clothes did not fit her so well. They either made her look like she had a huge stomach or that she was falling out of the top. This designer, however, one recommended by D'Ascoine of all people, had fitted her perfectly.

Samantha fumbled with her make up, having to remove her lipstick not once, but twice. Sinner would no doubt have given her grief over her nervousness, but fortunately the Chief would never know. Unlike most mandellans, she had only been to two formal receptions, one six years ago, and the other years before that. Tonight, however, she would be attending the Imperial Ambassador's Reception at the Embassy. The fact that she would be going as Ainsley Dumachelle rather than Samantha Smith eased her concerns about social and political ramifications of the daughter of the Grand Egalitist attending any social function. In fact, she thought she might even enjoy the evening. That was assuming, of course, that she could pull off her mission.

"*Nest, this is Osprey,*" Samantha said, "*Quarry is due any minute. I'll sign off when we get to his ship to avoid detection.*"

"*Osprey, Nest,*" Bowman's voice sounded, "*Copy that.*"

"I am sorry it took so long for me to get back," Alex said as he stepped into the MoJ debriefing room and gestured for Fran to sit down, "I needed to take commercial flights if I were to keep our people covert. Now, what was it that you needed to speak to me about?"

"Of course, sir," Fran said as she sat back in her seat. She felt her stomach lurch as the Skipper came in. She wasn't used to Officers apologizing to her. "I hope I didn't call you away from something urgent. I didn't mean to…."

"I needed to get back for tonight's event, anyway," Alex said as he sat down, "Which reminds me, we must keep it brief, I am expected at the Ambassador's reception in short order."

"Of course. sir," Fran said, her stomach knotting painfully as she turned on a series of graphs and star charts, "I did a crosscheck between Anti-Imperial activities that were not defined as terrorism by the MoJ and the Army and I thought I recognized the pattern. So, I looked at the trade routes used by Sir Richard's company and found that over eighty-five percent of the systems where the Cameron-Inglesie Corporation did business also showed signs of a strong guerrilla presence."

"Curious," Fotheringday said, "but not proof of collusion."

"No sir, but when I compiled a sub-query of the first data already selected, comparing dates of ships from the Cameron-Inglesie jumping into system to the dates of the guerrilla attacks, the results generally correlate pretty closely."

Fran highlighted one graph, and Alex leaned forward to study it. He remained quite for a very long time. After a moment, the muscles in his jaw began to pulse.

"Guerrilla attacks occur after Cameron-Inglesie ships arrive in the system in more than fifty percent of the cases?" He asked, the color draining from his face.

"Normally within a week of their arrival. It's not constant. Attacks sometime occur when no Cameron-Inglesie ships have been to a system."

"It would not be constant," Alex said, and swallowed as if his mouth were dry, "Weapons may not always have been available, ammunition might sometimes last longer than expected, and so forth."

"Here's the clincher, sir," Fran said, torn between pleasure that the CO seemed to agree with her theory, and concern that he looked like he might throw up, "Whenever there was a big increase in guerrilla attacks, or a particularly heinous bombing or something, there has always been a Cameron-Inglesie ship that arrived in the system before it. Always."

Alex looked at her for a moment, a grinding noise coming from his teeth. "Always?"

"Yes, sir," she said.

"Nest? This is Eagle," Alex said, glancing up in the way of someone opening a comms line, "Tell Osprey to abort the operation."

He remained silent for a moment before closing his eyes and hanging his head. His color turned a pale shade of green. "Oh, Bloody Hell."

CHAPTER 49

"Why now?" Alyiar asked as he walked across the broad tarmac. He avoided looking at Wylde as he zipped up the jacket of his corporate security guard uniform. They'd barely spoken in two days and Alyiar didn't want to start now.

"Because the Dalang said it was time," Rubo said as he adjusted his shoulder holster, "I'd have feckin' well thought you'd be happy."

Alyiar grunted. Over the past two days, Rubo had seemed to take Wylde more deeply into his confidence, and if anything had been cutting Alyiar out of it. Alyiar knew where that road led, but there was nothing he could do: not if he wanted to keep serving the cause.

"This is big, Al," Wylde said, beaming ear to ear, "We're moving up in the world."

Alyiar wondered if Wylde was happy to meet the boss or relieved that Rubo's suspicions were focused on himself. He couldn't figure out how Wylde had managed to get the finger of doubt pointed, but in one sense it didn't matter. Regardless of who was suspected, Alyiar didn't think it was a good idea to let a possible traitor that close to the Dalang.

"What happened to the cell structure?" Alyiar asked, allowing himself a sideways glance at Wylde, "Need to know and all?"

"The Dalang has decided he's got bigger plans for you," Rubo said, "Says it's time you two move up the ladder."

They headed towards a series of ships clustered together on the landing area. Three were simple planetary vessels, technically boats not ships. The other two were proper starships, capable of interstellar jumps. Each was emblazoned with a different corporate logo.

"It seems a funny time to do so," Alyiar said, casting another sidelong glance at Wylde, "What with the MoJ looking at us, not to mention the pressure from the other Networks."

"The Dalang knows what he's doing, boyo. Don't you forget it."

They walked into the cluster of vessels, moving around them without concern; their security uniforms gave them clearance to be close to the ships. Wylde looked very pleased with himself. Alyiar wondered if the son-of-a-bitch had the other Federalist groups following them, ready to take out their leader.

They walked in silence until they came across a starship with the bright orange and white logo of the Cameron-Inglesie Corporation. Rubo headed up the ramp into the ship's cargo hold. Wylde and Alyiar followed. Once inside they passed through a series of huge airlocked compartments, all of them empty. Their feet beat a steady tattoo that echoed through the cavernous bays.

"So the Dalang's here?" Wylde asked, "on this ship?"

"He will be shortly," Rubo said as they came up to an airlock that didn't open. Rubo gave a quick smile to Alyiar. It was the first one that his leader had given him in days. Alyiar grew worried, and primed his implants for action.

Rubo punched a code into the keypad by the door. When it slid open, he gave a grand gesture for his men to enter first. Inside, the cargo bay was immense and dimly lit. Great metal arches cast odd shadows across the flat floor. Water dripped from the external airlocks echoing across the chamber. Alyiar nodded for Wylde to proceed.

"Is he in Binghouse or are we going to pick him up?" Wylde asked, stepping into the empty hold.

Alyiar moved to follow him, but Rubo put a restraining hand on his chest. Alyiar gave a questioning look to his leader. Rubo's face was deadly serious. He held a remote control in his hands.

"Rube?" Wylde asked, turning around with a smile. Seeing Rubo's expression it changed into a look of confusion, then a grimace of pain. A scream started to escape from his mouth, but was quickly cut off, becoming a gurgle.

Wylde's face began to boil. His hands raised to his head as the skin was eaten away. It was just like what had happened to Bolyiacov, only Wylde was alive.

"Feckin' well betray us to Hectoro will ya' boyo?"

Wylde fell to his knees. His arms telescoped out towards Alyiar, but whether it was meant as an attack or a plea for help he couldn't tell.

"Ya' damn well near got us all killed," Rubo said, tattoos spreading across his face, "and worse yet, betrayed the man with the best chance of winnin' this war."

Wylde took half a step forward and fell to his knees. The metal in his skull now showed and as the left half of his body grew longer, the right contracted. He collapsed, falling face forward, his extended arms hanging over the edge of the airlock. Rubo stepped forward and kicked them back inside.

"Come on Al," Rubo said, pushing the key pad.

"How long did you know?" Alyiar asked, still standing as the metal and ceramic body deteriorated behind him. The airlock door slammed shut.

"I suspected someone was sellin' us out to the rival Feddie networks for a while," Rubo said, putting a hand on Alyiar's shoulder, "and I sure as hell knew it wasn't you."

Alyiar looked at the remote in his leader's other hand. A muffled explosion sounded from behind the door.

"The twisted feck thought the Dalang had lost sight of it all," Rubo said, still holding the device, "Thought we were betraying the cause. Now his feckin' masters can spend their days wondering whether he was whacked or just betrayed them too."

"And Bolyiacov?" Alyiar asked, his body remaining tense, "She wasn't a traitor."

"That was Hectoro," Rubo said, turning to face Alyiar, "or one of the other feckin' core Federalist groups who can't seem to deal with the fact that the Dalang is winning the war they're losing."

Alyiar stood perfectly still, his eyes locked on the remote in Rubo's hand.

"Bolyiacov died because of our little friend back there," Rubo said, his eyes following Alyiar's gaze, he went to his own hand, then back to Alyiar. He dropped the remote in his pocket. "And because she was lazy. If she'd changed form more, she wouldn't have drawn attention."

Alyiar looked Rubo back in the eye. He turned on a pre-programmed trusted smile. Rubo nodded and turned.

"Come on boyo, let's put this behind us. There's a new day ahead."

"Where are we really going?" Alyiar asked, still standing where he was.

"Not far," Rubo said over his shoulder, "We've got another job to do, and afterwards, the Dalang really does want to meet you."

The Ambassador's Reception was held in a grand hall at the distal end of the great spinning cylinder that was the Imperial Orbital complex. One end of the hall looked out into the enormous central axis park with its waterfalls and curving gardens; the other provided a full view of Lai-Jung Prime's horizon highlighted by small zigzagging stars and giant swords of light. The engines of varying ships, some headed to the planet, others to different orbitals, and some to the edge of the system or beyond. Lai-Jung was a busy system.

Alex could not look at those lights without feeling anxious. One of those coming from the planet carried Samantha; he hoped. There had been no communication from her since she had left the hotel with Sir Richard. Using the different surveillance systems, Bowman had watched her board Sir Richard's yacht, but had no contact since then. Alex kept telling himself that everything would be fine. Samantha was an experienced operative and Sir Richard had no reason to suspect her. What was more, there was still nothing directly tying Sir Richard himself to the Dalang, just his company. He kept reminding himself of that.

"You're not focusing," Sally said, drawing his mind from the ships back to the reception. She wore a very stylish green dress, shimmering and alluringly translucent, highlighting her feminine athleticism, and hinting at her sensuality. Alex saw many of the other celebrants blatantly surveying her lithe figure. Sally clearly found their responses entertaining.

"Sorry," Alex said, sipping the sparkling drink she handed him, "Work."

"Try to keep focused on the here and now, will you darling?" she said with a gentle smile.

As members of the Imperial hierarchy in system, both Alex and Sally had been invited to the evening. D'Ascoine's attendance was also requested, but much to the Army Officer's chagrin, Alex had again given him other duties to perform. He and his team were following up on a lead they had obtained from their surveillance of the Ankh. It was the only thing that made Alex relax.

If Team Falcon's target was the Dalang, then Sir Richard was in the clear; he couldn't be in two places at the same time. At the moment, D'Ascoine and the others had an eye on their suspect, but Sir Richard was with Samantha on his yacht making their way to this very reception. Of course, that didn't mean that D'Ascoine and the others were on the right track, nor did it mean that Sir Richard might not be involved with the terrorists in another function, nor that some other permutation was in play. The possibilities were endless.

Alex tried to take his mind off of the mission and studied the Ambassador's reception instead. It was for a new trade delegation arriving from one of the small stellar states beyond the Imperial Fringe. The new nation's rise was in no small part due to the economic growth of the Sophyan Empire. By comparison to the representatives from the Empire, or even its client states, the delegation's early stellar technology seemed quaint at best. Indeed compared to the conspicuous display of wealth and development that was the Empire itself, it had the appearance of barbarism. That was, of course, the diplomatic corps' intent: welcome representatives of other worlds with grace and on equal footing, and let the technological wonders of the Empire speak for themselves.

This form of contact, the initial reception of a culture into an Imperial environment, was carefully staged in association with the Imperial Astrographic Service. The cultural specialists of the IAS ensured that the effect was not too overwhelming: that could lead newly re-emerging cultures into a xenophobic spiral rather then lure them into the Empire. Alex knew that Samantha had very specific views on the topic; she had been such a specialist before she had joined Ripper's Raiders. That background had certainly proved useful in the past, and he hoped it was helping her at the moment. Alex checked the time. Sir Richard's ship was running late.

"You're grinding your teeth, dear," Sally whispered, "I'm going to get you another drink."

She was gone before he could stop her, and Alex was left to look around the room. There were a scattering of other members of the Imperial Ruling Classes among the guests, as well as a proper balance of uniformed members of the Imperial Services. Representatives from both the Empire's local corporate and regional mega-corporate interests mingled with them, doing business and generally networking.

Alex's eyes were drawn across the hall to the clusters of Naval black, Marine red, Army Assault green and Army Guardian grey throughout the room. Others mingled more freely: the military stuck to themselves. He wished he were free to join them.

Of the Imperial uniformed services, only the dress whites of the Imperial Astrographic were properly mixed in with the mélange of business suits, foreign dress and alien attendants. It had the appearance of a natural gathering of interstellar elites, but Alex had no doubt the attendance had been carefully planned, balanced and organized by diplomats and the IAS Contact division. They had elaborate formulas designed to create the perfect combination of Imperial and non-Imperial assets that would best facilitate the assimilation of whatever new growing state this trading delegation represented. He suspected that Samantha would have been excellent at such a task.

"Here we go," Sally said, coming to him with an alluring smile and carrying two sparkling drinks. Soon she had launched into a discussion of the new nation's dress sense. She bubbled on, focusing on the aesthetic rather than the cultural.

How much of you is façade? Alex wondered, gazing into her eyes as she chatted about some irrelevant detail, *Have you played the dilettante so long that it has taken root?* But he said nothing, simply listening to her babble.

"*Quarry has landed,*" Bowman's voice broke through the comm systems. Alex opened a mental window and tuned to the frequency that Bowman was sending. For the moment, there was only a sealed airlock door.

"*Eaglet,*" Alex opened a channel to Fran, "*any news from team Falcon?*"

"*That's a negative sir,*" Fran responded, "*Last report noted that operation is still in play.*"

Alex tried to appear to be looking around the room, but his attention was focused on the mental window showing the airlock docked to Sir Richard's ship. Alex was concerned with D'Ascoine's mission, of course. It held immediate danger, particularly for Gunnery Sergeant Chrom, but backup was readily available. If something went wrong with Samantha, however, it would be very hard to support.

A green light appeared above the airlock door and Alex held his breath. When the door slid open, he heard Sally chastise him for grinding his teeth, but ignored her. A moment later Samantha emerged from the ship on Sir Richard's arm and performed a brief gesture of self-preening. It was the signal they were waiting for: everything was going according to plan. Soon they would arrive to the ball.

Alex shut the window, turned to Sally, and let loose a sigh. She gave him a look of strained patience. He smiled, leaned over and kissed her cheek. She cocked an eyebrow in response, but he also noted her blush. Folding her arm in his, she gently led him across the room with her accustomed grace. They flitted between conversations, talking to one of the trade delegates here, chatting to an Imperial Diplomat there. Knowing Samantha was all right, Alex began to actually enjoy himself.

"I don't know, Alex," Sally said as they found themselves momentarily alone, "There are times where I wonder if the acculturation process is really fast enough. I mean, assuming that our great mission as a state is to return cultural exchange, civil liberties and Sophant rights to the galaxy, don't you think that perhaps there are one or two cultures that need to be thumped a little harder?"

"I assume you are speaking of the gladiatorial combats of Lai-Jung?" Alex asked, pleased to be speaking to Sally the intellectual rather than Sally the celebutant.

"No, though that is not a bad thought. I was in fact referring to the…." Sally's comments drifted off as Alex watched her eyes suddenly drawn across the room. Her delicately arched eyebrows frowned as Alex received a rare glimpse into her mind.

He followed her gaze and saw the couple entering the ball that had drawn her attentions. The man was dressed in the artifacts of an Imperial Hierarch, but it was the woman that drew most people's attention. She wore a long, tight and low cut white dress that managed to walk the difficult line between tasteful and revealing. She swayed with a powerful grace, silken blond hair falling about her shoulders, a bright, anticipatory smile on her face. Alex felt both relief and an unexpected thrill at her appearance.

"Her pictures don't do her justice," Sally said, her large blue eyes shifting between Alex and Samantha.

"Jealous?" Alex asked turning to his girlfriend with a bemused smile.

"Should I be?"

Samantha allowed herself to be led across the room by Sir Richard. They stopped frequently, chatting here and there as he was greeted by numerous partygoers. He played the part of the socialite well, but each time he spoke, Samantha could tell the air of the cold businessman beneath the pleasant façade. He smiled broadly, speaking longer to those with whom he had some economic tie and quickly cutting himself loose from those who did not. All the time, he took pains to introduce her, and she became uncertain if it was out of deference to her or the desire to show her off as a trinket.

"I'm sorry about all this," he said as if reading her mind, "I have to greet people, and then we can spend a little time just enjoying ourselves."

"Richard I understand," she said with her best winning smile, "this is work for you, I get it."

"I know you do," he said with real warmth in his eyes, "and I–"

His face froze for a moment as he looked over her shoulder, but Samantha could not read whether it was shock or horror that filled his mind. Following his gaze she saw Alex standing with a striking redhead in a very alluring dress. It took Samantha a moment to recognize her from the images on his desk.

"Do you know them?" she asked, turning back to Sir Richard. It took all her self control to stop her finger from picking her cuticle.

"I do," he said distractedly, then a smile returned to his face, "Come, let me introduce you."

As he led her across the room, Samantha realized that Alex was right: Sir Richard was an astute operative. Had she not seen his unguarded moment, she would never have guessed that he was disconcerted by Alex's presence. Samantha just hoped that her own façade would hold up to seeing her commander with his girlfriend: a woman who shouldn't even have known they were in system.

"Alex! Lady Symbletyne!" Sir Richard greeted, "Imagine seeing you here!"

"Ritchie," Alex responded with an equally natural smile as he extended his hand, "I was hoping you might be around."

"Please, allow me to introduce Ms. Ainsley Dumachelle," Sir Richard said with obvious pride. Alex took Samantha's hand as if they had never met, "Ainsley, this is Lieutenant Commander Lord Alexander Fotheringday and Lady Sally Symbletyne."

"It's an honor," Samantha said, gracefully taking the hand of each.

"A pleasure," Alex responded, while Sally gave little more than a smile and a nod.

"So what brings you two to my corner of the Empire?" Sir Richard asked.

"Different things," Alex responded, "Sally is here on pleasure."

"As ever," she added with a giggle.

"And I am afraid it is duty that brings me in system; bit of file searching for the fleet you know. Yourself?"

"Business calls me to Lai-Jung quite a bit. I tend to live on board the yacht more than I do on the estates."

"Still one of the spaceborn then."

"Mmm."

"And you, Miss Dumachelle?" Alex asked politely.

"Also business, I'm afraid."

"What business would that be?" Sally asked.

"I'm an actuary."

"Oh, dear, all that maths makes me dizzy."

"It's just a trick," Samantha said, taking a drink from a passing tray.

"Now, enough work," Sir Richard said, "I'd like to hear more about…"

"Oh drat!" Sally said looking down at the ground, "I've spilled my drink. I say Richard, be a darling would you and come with me to get another."

Sir Richard paused for a moment, as if torn between leaving his date in the hands of a rival and taking that rival's date away, but etiquette gave him little choice and he soon found himself walking away with the leggy redhead.

"Does she know?" Samantha asked with surprise once their respective dates were out of earshot.

"No," Alex responded, "she's just Sally."

"What is she doing in system?" Samantha said, tilting her head as if intrigued by idle chit-chat, "You didn't tell her where you were being deployed did you?"

"Of course not," Alex said with irritation as he stepped out of the way of a passing diplomat, "She took the fast boat to Billanobia to buy some antiques, and then stopped over in Lai-Jung to take in the parties."

"What a coincidence."

"Hardly. She figured out that there was a good chance that this is where I was being sent, and came here with a gaggle of her friends."

"Cunning. She doesn't seem the type," Samantha said, glaring at a man who was staring at her breasts. He looked away.

"Excuse me?" Alex gave her a sharp glance.

"Nothing."

"My girlfriend is not quite your affair, is it Ms. Dumachelle."

"No, of course not," Samantha suddenly blushed, "I'm sorry."

"Anything to report?" Alex asked. His smile had returned and he gestured with his drink to the trade delegation. They were speaking to one of the Imperial businesswomen.

"Nothing," Samantha said, turning to fully look at the foreign dignitaries, "I was able to surreptitiously gain access to some of Sir Richard's personal files, but at first glance I saw nothing suspicious. Full analysis may prove otherwise."

"And the navigational records?"

"No chance to check those at all yet. There is a full serving staff on board, two of them lurked around me quite a bit. Perhaps on the trip back."

"I think not. Fran identified a direct link between Cameron-Inglesie and the Wayang Network. I am going to end the operation."

"Does it show a link between Sir Richard and the Dalang?" Samantha asked. Feeling her finger pick her thumb, she clenched her fist to stop it.

"No."

"Then we need more proof," Samantha said with a nod and a smile, "Solid evidence one way or the other Alex, remember what you said?"

"Not at the risk of your life Lieutenant."

A waiter passed with a plate of gold wrapped appetizers. Alex took one and nodded a thank you.

"The mushroom hautes are quite lovely," Alex said. Placing the gold ball in his mouth, he gestured for Samantha to follow suit. She did, waiting for the server to leave.

"If Sir Richard is guilty we have to prove it beyond a shadow of a doubt," Samantha said, once they were alone again, "but if he's innocent, we owe him the chance to prove that too. I owe it to him, and so do you."

Alex stood staring at her for a moment, then turned away to look at their returning dates.

"Be careful, Samantha," he said.

"You two look terribly serious" Sally said, bounding into the conversation with her customary bravado before draping herself across Alex's shoulders, "What are you…? Oh, my dear Ainsley, you seem to have cut your thumb."

CHAPTER 50

"You've grown quiet," Samantha said, "Is everything alright?"

She sat on the large curving couch in the observation lounge of Sir Richard's yacht, looking out the viewport towards the gently curving horizon of Lai-Jung. One of the moons hung above the blue green world with its streaks of cloudy white. Under other circumstances, it might have proven romantic. Samantha suspected the course had been chosen because of that, but Sir Richard had not yet tried to take advantage of the circumstances. Instead he stood staring out the window, drink in his hand.

"Sorry," Sir Richard replied, "Old phantoms."

"Does it have to do with that mandellan Naval officer we met?" Samantha asked.

"Yes, I suppose so. We had served together some years ago, he was quite promising. So was I back then, but, let's say that a mission went bad. Proved to be the end of my career you see. People died, people were blamed, but it was his mistake. Now he has a high profile posting in a high profile fleet, and what am I?"

"A very successful business man, a hierarch, and a man of influence."

"When you put it that way," He sat down next to her. "Enough melancholy, did you enjoy the reception?"

"I did," Samantha said with a well practiced bright smile.

"Mmm, yes, the Ambassador always throws the most wonderful parties."

"I agree. Thank you very much for inviting me."

"My absolute pleasure my dear," he moved closer, his leg touching hers. A warm passionate kiss was soon followed by gentle caressing hands.

Oh joy, she thought, *how do I get out of this*?

Rain spattered off the stray dumpsters and air-con units in the dark alley. A yellow light set in its wire cage cast long shadows down the night hidden shaft. A single darkened figure lurked beneath a fire escape, half sheltered from the rain, keeping to the dark. A navy-blue hood was pulled over her head, her strong black arms were bare, grey arena armor hung on her legs. She stood silently, calm and patient; she was used to waiting. Her dark eyes caught movement in the main street, watched it pass. It wasn't her target.

A drop of rain traced the long pale scar on Chrom's cheek. The Gunnery Sergeant brushed it off, barely noticing what she was doing. She stood ready, waiting and anxious; not because she was afraid, but because of what she was supposed to do. It reminded her of when she was a stupid punk-assed kid. Chrom had spent years shaping that kid into something she was proud of. Now she was here lurking in the alley like the kind of petty crook she'd once been, and she didn't like it one bit. Still, what she'd become was a Marine, and Marines did what ever it took to get the mission done.

"*Kite, this is Peregrine,*" D'Ascoine's voice signaled in her head, "*Bravo target is moving your way.*"

"*Copy that, could you provide me with a diagrammatic*?" Chrom sent, her eyes focusing on the street beyond the end of the alley. A moment later a simple vector map was overlaid on her vision, showing a blinking icon moving down the line drawing of the city. She opened a window, watched Sinner's broadcast of the CCTV data he was hijacking and saw the man in the tan business suit making his way towards her position. This was the third meeting that the same man had had with the Ankh. In the last one, there had been talk of what would appear to be arms shipments, and the Wayang Stalkers. They decided to follow this new contact: a man who could even prove to be the Dalang.

She waited patiently, watching him move ever closer. *Hell, if we'd had this kind of surveillance back in the day,* she chuckled to herself. A rat shuffled out of a dumpster, looked at her, and then carried on its way like she wasn't there. *Bad ass rat.* She kept waiting. The rain fell a little harder. The map told her that the target had reached the end of the alley. Chrom stuck her right hand into her pocket and slipped on the micro-needle, but still waited.

When she saw him with her own eyes, she shut down the projected map and camera and launched into action. She barreled out of the alleyway and ploughed into the target like rail freight. Her right hand locking around his throat, she used her momentum to swing him towards the alley from which she had emerged. The suddenness of her actions caught him by surprise, but he was quick to react. His hand flew to break the grip on his neck, his leg moving behind her knee in an attempt to trip her, use her own force against her.

He's military trained, she thought, but she knew his moves. She had taught them to others. She countered his defense and shifted her weight. He slammed into the wall, cracking his head against the cold hard surface.

"Gimme your fucking wallet!" she shouted, spittle from her mouth hitting his face. She pressed a knife against his side. He was scared, sure, but the look in his eyes said that this man had seen danger before, he was evaluating his present position, coming up with the proper tactics.

Chrom did not wait for him to act or react. She did what any junked-up street kid would do. With a cruel brutal speed, she jabbed the knife into the man twice, but what seemed thoughtless violence was calmly calculated. She made certain to aim where the stab would do the least damage; she was an artist with a knife. She felt the slight resistance as she pierced the skin, saw the horrible wince as the man felt the dull blade penetrate his side, felt the warm rush of blood. She grabbed his wallet and ran off down the street.

She hadn't gotten two blocks before she heard a shout followed by footsteps. As expected, he had been tailed by a security detail. They were good. Sinner hadn't caught sight of them. She heard the speed of their feet increase to a drum roll pace; they were serious cyborgs.

Chrom ran half way up a cinderblock wall, and flipped over the top. She dashed and darted down different alleys with the practiced ease she had learned as a child dodging the cops, and perfected with her Marine training. She serpentined through the maze of backstreets they had scoped the previous day. She could hear her pursuers gaining. One of them had a heavy Archon accent.

"*Shit*!" Sinner's voice sounded in her head, "*They just jumped that wall in one leap. They're Wayang Stalkers Gunny*!"

"*Meet me at the bravo extraction point*," D'Ascoine ordered. In the distance there was the squeal of tires.

Slipping down another side alley, she was in new territory, she hadn't had a chance to memorize the bravo route as well as the alpha. She listened to the Chief coordinate both her and D'Ascoine's paths and launched a projected map in the corner of her vision. She scaled a chain-link fence like a pro, hurtled a high wooden fence, and saw an approaching van cut off the end of the alley. The door slid open, she rolled in, and the door closed. The timing was perfect, the vehicle didn't change speed, any surveillance systems that Sinner didn't hack and might have caught the pick up would not even have noted there was a person in the alley as the vehicle passed. It had seemed to work like a charm.

"Well done, Sergeant!" came D'Ascoine's unexpected praise.

"There's blood, you hit?" Sinner said with a concern that somewhat surprised Chrom. He was quickly checking her for wounds.

"Nope," Chrom responded, "not mine."

"Report?" D'Ascoine asked.

"You sure?" Sinner said, digging through her wet cloths to be certain, "there's a lot here."

"I'm sure, it's the target's," Chrom said, "I ambushed the target as planned, and think I placed both trackers."

"I'm gonna check anyway," Sinner said digging through her cloths and examining her for any signs of injury.

"You *think* you placed the trackers?" D'Ascoine asked, turning from the driver's seat to spare her a glance from the road.

"Sorry, sir," Chrom apologised, ashamed of her less than professional report, "I mean that I made contact with the target as expected and placed the sub-dermal tracker on him by grabbing his throat and injecting it with the micro-needle. He resisted with some skill, suggesting a military background, but I still managed to inject the more robust transmitter with the knife implanter. I have every reason to expect that the wounds inflicted were superficial and that he will not be kept in any medical facility once he is stitched up."

"There's no wound here," Sinner said.

"Told you."

"Good work, Sergeant," D'Ascoine said as they rounded another corner.

Sinner looked down and closed his eyes, "Both signals are sending. We've got the target."

Samantha slipped out of her quarters, pulling the white robe around her bare shoulders as she went. Sir Richard had been a complete gentleman, or an *almost* complete gentleman; a fact that made what Samantha was doing all the more difficult. She thought of her parents, of the newborn sister she would never see, and she found her resolution. *Besides,* she thought, *if he has nothing to do with this, then this will prove his innocence.*

She walked down the corridor and into the lounge. The wine glasses remained where they had been. One was tipped over with a small pool of wine, just as they had left it.

PAD in hand, Samantha opened the sliding glass door to Sir Richard's office and slipped inside. She touched the control, closing the door and switching the see-through walls to one way transparencies. That by itself might raise suspicions, but not as many as someone seeing her rifling through his things. She walked to the desk, jacked the datapad directly into the i/o port and activated Sinner's latest cracker program. Once it was launched, she opened a comm channel to the surface – something linked to insurance rates.

The cracker broke into the system and delivered a worm into the network. It was slow to unwind, but would eventually use the yacht's own commsystem to send the ship's entire datamatrix to the *Hunter.* Sinner, Fran and Alex had all assured her that it was undetectable, but she knew that in truth there was no such thing.

The door to the lounge opened and a pair of stewards walked in. Their eyes went immediately to the one-way mirrored wall, then each other. Samantha watched them as they stared at their reflections. She felt her heart in her throat: all she was armed with was her bathrobe and there was no way out of the office.

"With a woman like that in his bed you would have thought," one whispered.

"He's dedicated. Come on."

The two of them left, leaving the wine glasses where they were. Samantha cocked an eyebrow, but returned to her work. She had to finish before Sir Richard came looking her.

Once the worm had hacked the system, Samantha decided to take advantage of her access to the system. It was dangerous, but might be the only chance she had to ensure that the information she had worked so hard to get was in fact obtained. Using the manual control panels, and hoping she was dodging all the security checks, she obtained access to navigational charts. She searched for the one record she knew the ship should not have, but it was there.

Hidden deep in the matrix of star charts and gravitational data, there was a 0.05% correction to the data for the Inglesie system. Samantha felt herself grow cold, and nauseated. She had the immediate desire to take a shower.

She also noted other data, more information than was present in the naval database. *Someone has been to that location in this ship*, she thought, and then saw the reason why the correction had proven so interesting. A small astrological body lay in that position, an asteroid or comet that had escaped the orbit of the Inglesie sun. She would have to look at the data more fully to examine its full nature, but the records on the ship showed that additional corrections had been made, the course of the asteroid had changed ever so slightly and that someone had made corrections to that course – more than once.

What is out there? Why did somebody go to the effort of removing the data from the Naval database? Why return so many times? Samantha heard the door open.

"Ainsley?" Sir Richard's voice sounded behind her and she turned around to face him. He stood behind her wearing a dark red robe and an expression that could have been either confusion or suspicion. "What are you doing here?"

"Oh, sorry," she said, pulling the slipping shoulder of her own robe back up, and clutching it closed at the breast, "I had just wanted to check on the updated stock review. I know, I know, I obsess too much about work."

"I suppose it's admirable," Sir Richard replied as he walked over to her, "Though I had somewhat hoped that the evening might have distracted you a bit."

"Oh gods, Richard, it did!" she responded, moving deftly in front of where she had placed her pad and yanking the jack from the ship's i/o port behind her back, "But some of us have to live in the real world you know. If I don't keep on top of these things, someone else will."

"I suppose, but one night in a world of dreams won't kill you will it?" he came up to her as she dropped her PAD into the bathrobes' pocket. His hands fell on her hips, then slid to the terry cloth belt and pulled free the knot there, "Just one night?"

She swallowed hard and forced a smile as his hand slipped under the robe and across her smooth skin.

CHAPTER 51

"There was no other information in the system worth mentioning sir," Samantha said. She seemed despondent, a bit removed. Alex wasn't surprised, he felt the same way.

They had gathered in his quarters back on board the -*Hunter*. Alex sat behind his desk, D'Ascoine and Samantha in their usual seats, while Chrom stood 'at ease' behind them and Sinner leaned against the door jam, arms folded. Elsewhere on the ship, Bowman was on watch and Fran was still doggedly reviewing files, certain she was on to something.

"I think what you found was quite enough," Alex said, "Thank you, Lieutenant. You did an excellent job."

"Thank you, sir."

"We now know Sir Richard's private yacht has been to that system," Alex said, "Fairly damning, but circumstantial. Someone else could have taken the ship. We need something more solid if we are going to condemn an Imperial hierarch."

"You don't still think he could be innocent do you?" Samantha asked. Alex couldn't tell if her face was hateful or hopeful.

"It doesn't matter what I think," Alex said, "It matters what a court thinks. Besides, I have gone off half-cocked before, Lieutenant, and as you may recall, that ended rather badly. Now, your report Leftenant?"

"After I planted the recorder in the room that this Ankh fellow kept using," D'Ascoine said, failing to notice Sinner shaking his head, "I noted one individual who appeared more often than the others. I designated him the Bravo target. When he mentioned arms shipments, I decided to have the Gunnery Sergeant put a tracker on him and see where he led us. She managed to do so, though the target was injured in the scuffle, but when he was, who should appear but two of the Wayang Stalkers. They took him to the starport and boarded him onto an orbital shuttle. It was registered to the Cameron-Inglesie corporation."

"Sir Richard's company," Samantha said.

"Indeed," Alex said, "Where is the shuttle now?"

"We 'borrowed' some of the 253rd's surveillance setups and I've got an eye on it," Sinner said, ignoring D'Ascoine's indignant stare, "I can track the shuttle as long as it stays in system, but as for now, it's just sitting on the tarmac at Binghouse."

"Excellent," Alex said, turning next to the Gunnery Sergeant, "Any ID on the Bravo target?"

"Not yet, sir," Chrom said, remaining in her professional stance, "We're still doing checks, but he was unmistakably greeted as a senior on board the ship."

"Do you have the recording ready to view?"

"Yes, sir," Sinner said before D'Ascoine could respond. The Army hierarch gave the CPO a strained look that Sinner chose to ignore. "Unfortunately, Bravo the terrorist stayed out of view of the cameras. As you know we had a bit of a hard time placing them where they wouldn't be detected, and this guy? He stuck to areas out of sight, like he thought maybe he was being watched."

"I understand," Alex said, "The Wayang are very professional."

"You ain't joking," Sinner said, then turned one of the holowalls in the captain's cabin over for the purpose.

The image of a windowless room immediately filled the wall. Taken from an odd angle, the faces were not clear, the image was far from ideal, but the sound was very good. One of the men seemed to hang to the corners where he was least likely to be noticed. He wasn't a pro, but he was clearly very well trained in avoiding surveillance; the other was not as good.

"I think that's it," one man said.

"That voice is the Ankh," D'Ascoine said and indicated the less skilled of the men.

"There are two other ships that might've checked in," the Ankh continued, "but they're late and you know what these people are like."

"Yes I do," replied the second voice, who D'Ascoine identified as the Bravo target. Alex was sure he'd heard the voice before. "I know it all too well. Which reminds me, the people we're supplying with weapons should be using them to focus on hierarchs and the wealthy."

"Hey man, once the weapons move on from me, I can't control how they're used."

"You can pick your clients with more care," the Bravo target said, shifting to a new set of shadows, "Now let's see, we can send out a series of combat rifles with this lot, and of course a number of guided missiles."

"And me?" asked the Ankh.

"The usual."

"It's becoming more dangerous."

"You're becoming more greedy," Bravo said, "This is for the revolution you know."

"For you it's for the revolution," the Ankh said, "For me it's to eat. We on Lai-Jung are not so affected by your glorious cause."

"You and your world are more tied into it than you think you are," Bravo responded, "Still, you've earned your cash."

They watched the Bravo target take a case from beneath the table and open it on the desk. His face was still unseen, but there was something, not just in his voice, but in the way the man moved that seemed familiar to Alex. *Someone from 253rd? Someone from the Raiders? Where do I know this man from?* Bravo began to count out the money.

"...A hundred and twenty, two-hundred and forty, three-hundred and sixty..." the count continued on, raising in groups of twelve. A chill crept down Alex's back.

"...Four hundred and eighty, six hundred, seven twenty..." the base twelve count continued on, and Alex put a face to the voice.

Alex did not notice the door chime ring until Samantha pointed it out to him. Even after he let Fran in, he remained only half-aware of what she was saying. Instead he watched the back of the man on the screen.

"I knew we were still looking for the name of the navigator on the *HMS Reichmann*," Fran was saying, unaware in her excitement that he wasn't listening, "But I realized that the records we were looking for were probably also sent across to the MoJ's Anti-Imperial Flying-Squad as part of standard procedure, you know? Because the *HMS Reichmann* was involved in anti-insurgency actions. Well, they weren't, but they were sent over to the Guardians. So I found the listing and the name of the navigator. I know that we don't really suspect him anymore, but I thought it'd be good to cover all the bases. So, basically, that's it. I'm sorry to have interrupted you. I guess it seemed kinda important at the time."

Alex gradually became aware of Fran. The room was silent. Fran swallowed hard and blushed. Alex was still fighting the urge to vomit.

"What's the name?" Samantha asked, stepping in where Alex should have been leading.

"Hammond," Alex responded before Fran could form the words, "Lieutenant Kyle Hammond, my former XO and present employee of the Cameron-Inglesie Corporation."

CHAPTER 52

Alyiar closed his eyes and shuddered. He was in another cargo hold, but it wasn't where he was that bothered him. It was where they wanted him to go.

"I know it's a lot to ask," the Dalang said, "but I need you're help. I can hack those systems, but I need someone to ride the equipment. I need someone who can edit a realistic sim. You're the best."

Alyiar looked up at his leader: the man who had changed his life, changed the revolution, and indirectly saved him from being a cyberjunkie. He wasn't at all what Alyiar expected.

"You can do it, boyo," Rubo said. He stood off to one side smiling at Alyiar the way he used to. It was almost as if he hadn't killed Wylde, or Bolyiacov.

"I need you, the Cause needs you," the Dalang said, putting a hand on Alyiar's shoulder. He didn't look anything like the extreme ectomorph who was the basis of the Wayang Stalker form. Even with the bandaged side, he looked like a wealthy businessman or corporate drone. He looked like an Imperial.

Alyiar looked from the great leader of the Wayang to the man who had recruited him, and killed his friends and comrades. He saw the small bulge of the remote in Rubo's pocket. Closing his eyes, Alyiar bowed his head.

"Okay," he whispered.

"You're a good man and a true revolutionary," the Dalang said, a proud smile spreading across his face.

Something wasn't right with this shuttle, it should have taken off by now. Sinner panned around to a different view, but still the ship sat unmoving. He switched to a higher EM spectrum, but nothing looked unusual.

"Why would someone board a shuttle and then sit there for twenty hours?" Fran asked in both the real and virtual worlds.

"No idea," Sinner said, toggling down the image to a window in his vision.

They sat in engineering, their stations both tuned into surveillance systems. Fran wore her funny new head-gear. That was something else that just didn't seem right.

"Chief?" Fran said, intently staring into space like a true cybernaut, "I keep picking up this tiny little blip on the EM scans, it's no big deal. I'd say it's a stray signal or something, but it repeats every twenty minutes."

"Exactly twenty minutes?" Sinner sat up in his chair.

"No… every nineteen minutes and twenty-two seconds."

"Oh crap." Sinner said. He immediately opened a line to the Tinman.

"They faked me out, sir," Sinner reported, "The ship took off hours ago. If it wasn't for Fran here we'd still be watching a friggin' sim."

"That's not really…" Fran started, but was silenced by a stern look by Sinner. It wasn't fair. He was taking the whole thing on his shoulders, and she was just as much to blame. She'd seen the repeating spike in the signal earlier. If she'd said something they might have been able to track the ship.

The Skipper looked at them in silence. He wasn't angry, he was disappointed. That was far worse. The whole crew was gathered in the mess-lounge, Fran and Sinner stood 'at-ease' in the middle. It made her feel like she was on trial. She stifled a burp.

"And Sir Richard?" Alex said, turning to Samantha, "When did we lose him?"

"The last we know for certain is that his ship was en route to one of the orbitals. Our surveillance routines told us he docked, but the records from the orbital show he never arrived," Samantha reported. Fran had never seen her blush before.

"From what we can reconstruct," Samantha continued, "it looks like they received a transmission and altered course about halfway through their transit. Once we knew that, it took us a while to find it again. It seems the yacht docked with our rogue shuttle and headed out of system a few minutes later."

"Have they jumped yet?"

"No, but they will shortly. It took us this long just to find where they had gotten to. Even if we contact the 253rd or the MoJ, they're beyond reach."

"Any indication of a struggle?" Chrom asked.

"No," Samantha said.

"A well run hijacking would leave no trace," Alex said, "and the Wayang are experts at that."

"You think it's possible Sir Richard was kidnapped?" Samantha asked sitting up a little straighter and moving to the edge of her seat.

"Possible yes," Alex said, "Our first conclusion was that the Navigation officer on board the *Reichmann* hid the information, that officer was Kyle Hammond. He was also XO on the *Renfield* and could easily have sold us out. Sir Richard may still be involved and dirty, but he could know nothing about this."

"But the navigational records were on his ship," D'Ascoine said, crossing his legs and cocking an eyebrow.

"He could have leant that ship to Hammond," Samantha said, "He told me that he let trusted executives use it for important business deals. They had served together in the past."

"You are right," the Skipper said, "and the same could be said about the correlations between the increase in terror activities and the arrival of Cameron-Inglesie ships. Our theory about the Dalang being in the company is still valid, it's just that he sits a lower level."

"Isn't it possible that it was Hammond who was set up?" Fran asked. Everyone looked at her like horns had sprung from her head, "I mean, they faked us out with one sim-recording."

Sinner blinked as his eyebrows shot up and Bowman flashed her a bright smile.

"I saw the man face to face," Chrom said.

"They're shape-shifters." Fran shrugged.

Bowman's smile broadened. Chrom and the Skipper both nodded. Samantha was about to speak when a bell chimed through the ship.

"The yacht just jumped," Sinner reported. Alex grew pale.

"What do we do, sir?" D'Ascoine said, coming to his feet, "we can't track it now."

"Sir Richard has had his life turned upside down once because of a man who worked for him," Alex said, slowly standing and straightening his uniform, "If he is innocent, he's been kidnapped and we need to rescue him."

"And if he's guilty?" Samantha asked, standing along with the rest of the crew.

"Then we need to capture him. Either way, one of those men is the Dalang, responsible for the death of the passengers and crew of the *Silver Slipper*, not to mention the countless deaths caused by the Wayang Cell. We must bring whoever is guilty to justice."

"How do we do that?" Fran asked, then blushed at her breach of protocol.

"We go to the coordinates," Samantha replied, looking at Alex, "We go to the location of the anomaly."

PART V

The Puppet Master

CHAPTER 53

"*It's a large asteroid or a small moon,*" Samantha said, wearing her standard avatar dressed in a Naval uniform, "*Or at least it used to be. Now, it's a rogue: a free floating body with a large debris field traveling at a very high velocity.*"

The *Hunter* had been delayed in leaving Lai-Jung by a sudden interest in their work by the 253rd's Liaison Officer, Lieutenant Corduroy. Samantha had thought they should ignore the request for their presence, but Alex feared that if they did they would tip their hand. Sir Richard had served with Corduroy and the Dalang had access to Naval patrol schedule; even if the Dalang was Hammond, it would seem there was some form of collusion going on. They couldn't risk it in case Corduroy was involved, so they lost three days pretending to cooperate with the local fleet. Now, after sixteen days of transit to the anomaly, the *Hunter* stood in the middle of a vast emptiness. There was no local sun to provide light, and only one object immediately visible to either the eye or the sensors.

"*And why would our terrorist friends care anything about it?*" D'Ascoine asked.

The crew were at their duty stations, but had gathered virtually in Samantha's navigation space, giving the impression they were floating in the interstellar depths. Hovering before them was a single misshapen planetoid that was ever so gradually receding away from them. Sinner's polar bear form was picking its nose, a sure sign that he was only partially paying attention. The others seemed more focused. D'Ascoine's egoistic portrayal of himself hovered in full dress uniform with his arms behind his head.

"*Good question*," Samantha said, her real body's stance at odds with her avatar's earnest smile, "*Perhaps it's a weapons' stash or smuggler's dead drop*."

"*Or a secret pirate base*," D'Ascoine broadcast a stage whisper to Fran, whose avatar blushed.

"*Another possibility*," Samantha said to D'Ascoine as if his suggestion was not intended to be humorous.

"*Any sign of activity or construction*?" Alex asked. As ever, his avatar was dressed in Naval blacks.

"*No sir*."

"*Oh, I see, an invisible secret pirate base*!" D'Ascoine said, this time to all, "*Well done*!"

"*Sometimes your lack of understanding of the astrographic process astounds me, Leftenant*," Samantha replied, then caught the disapproving look from Alex and adjusted her tone, "*If that rogue body has a Federalist installation, then we hardly want to use active sensors to find it. That would do little more than announce our presence. As a result, we can only use our passive arrays, so unless they start broadcasting or sending up ships, we need to get a lot closer before we can see any activity*."

"*How long will it take for us to approach the planetoid*?" Alex asked, standing with his hands behind his back.

"*It's traveling very fast. Since we can't use our fusion rockets without giving ourselves away, it will probably take almost a week to approach using our reaction drive. Still, the closer we get, the better our data will be*."

"*Then I suppose we get started*," Alex said, "*Duty stations one and all*."

Alyiar shivered as he looked down at the large Rendethi sleeper ship on the launch pad; the one that Rubo had thrown the Meridothite out of. The six remaining Wayang Stalkers were scattered around the bunkroom over the reception bay, chatting, moping, lurking. Six was all that remained of the once mighty shape shifting urban guerrillas, but the remaining Wayang cells were safe. The sectional fighting with the other Federalist groups had been particularly hard on the Stalkers, but Rubo had said that their sacrifice had kept the rest of the network intact. Privately, Alyiar wondered how many of his fellow Stalkers had been eliminated by Rubo as Wylde and Bolyiacov had been.

The others were unaware of the 'security' measures taken by the head Stalker. Even Alyiar hadn't been told that Bolyiacov's death was at the hands of their leader, but he knew it just the same. She had proven a liability because she kept using the same shape, so Rubo whacked her. Alyiar wasn't sure how he felt about that: Wylde had betrayed them, but Bolyiacov had just made a mistake. Then again, the MoJ had been following her. She could have compromised them all.

The thought of it all made Alyiar want to hide, to just go back into the Virtual world and lose himself to a totally different cyber reality. He repressed another tremor as it ran through his body, and fought the horrible desire to drop back into the network and find the simworlds he craved. Across the room Rubo was talking to one of their comrades. He was smiling, laughing. At that moment, Alyiar hated his leader more than he had ever hated the Empire.

Alex and Samantha performed yet another course correction to match speed and direction with the drifting moonlet. The surface of the body was now fully visible to the ship's optics. Covered with methane and hydrogen ice, the rogue was spider webbed with fractures and cracks. It was not spherical and had a hundred kilometer wide halo of ice chips, snowballs and meteors that accompanied it on its long journey through interstellar space. The *Hunter* had matched and surpassed the body's velocity and course well enough that they could launch their satellites and get a better view. Even so, it would take a few more hours of observation to ensure that their transit would be properly coordinated.

Samantha watched her CO. Concentrating on the relativity data in front of him, he seemed completely unaware of her observations. He was focused and professional, so different from what she had first thought of him. Still, she suspected that the clenched jaw and tiny line on his brow were not just due to his concentration. She could empathize with a sense of betrayal.

"Alex?" Samantha asked after a moment, "Have you ever wondered about Eleanor of Allevi?"

"How do you mean?" he asked looking up from his files and smiling, "Do I think we will catch her? It would be fairly unlikely, but I must admit I have daydreamt about the possibility when I was a young Ensign."

"No, I mean about the case against her. It reminds me of this case. Eleanor of Allevi has always denied that she or her faction supported terrorist activities, and denied that she was even supporting rebel groups before she was declared an outlaw."

"Somehow I doubt very strongly that the Federalists would have gained much support in the Core Sectors if they admitted to planting bombs and killing children."

"True, but still, do you ever wonder if it's possible that the Federalists are telling the truth? That they focus only on military targets and that the rest is Imperial propaganda?"

"To what end?" Alex asked. He pushed aside the projection of his files and faced her.

"To create a sense of a threat," Samantha said, "To build fear and political strength that goes with it."

"If that is the case, then we should look to see who has the most to gain from the threat. Would not that be our own Admiral? Lord Rippavitch? After all it is the threat of terrorism that rallies people to the Hegemonist cause."

"Are you suggesting Admiral Rippavitch is conspiring with the insurgents?"

"No!" Alex said, throwing his head back and laughing. It had been a long time since she'd seen a true smile on his face. "I am suggesting that there is no conspiracy. That everything is actually as it seems. There is no need to invoke a conspiracy when someone is really setting off bombs."

"Maybe they are all just fringe groups and splinter cells. Radical extremists like this Dalang character."

"In which case, they are still part of the cause, and while Allevi doesn't embrace them, she doesn't denounce them either."

"True, true," She said blushing, "I must sound ridiculous."

"On the contrary," Alex said, "I think you sound like someone who actually considers her opinions. I respect that a great deal."

There was a melancholy smile on his face, wistful and sad. It was the first time she had really seen him unguarded. For a moment, she felt just a tad less alone.

"Do you think he's guilty?" she asked, "Sir Richard?"

"I'm trying to stay objective, but believe me, if he is involved, Ritchie knows every element of what's going on. He will be in it for the money and power, and would never leave details to chance. As for Hammond, I have no idea why he would be involved."

"Belief in the cause?"

"Perhaps, but sadly not every supporter of democracy has the moral fiber that your father did. If they did, we would not be here."

CHAPTER 54

Fran sat in the lounge, rubbing her eyes and struggling to clear the headache that had begun during another long session in virtual space. After Samantha had made certain that the satellites were properly deployed, the crew of the *Hunter* got the long drawn-out process of surveying the surface of the planetoid underway. Much of that work needed the skilled and experienced attentions of the XO, who was supported in her efforts by Sinner. That left the rest of the ship's standard maintenance and engineering work to Fran, who struggled to fill the shoes of the Chief Engineer. It was not easy. Despite her DuZhodian interface, she still found it difficult to maneuver the repair drones. She particularly struggled with the nanobot controls, and occasionally became nauseated by the unnatural interfaces with the world of the microscopic. Still, it was markedly easier than before.

Fran took a long sip of her coffee, closed her eyes and listened to the soft music she had chosen to help her relax. She was off duty and needed the time to get her mind into the actual world rather than the information bombardment of her new computerized reality. She knew she should eat, but her stomach was still a bit sensitive.

After two sips, she began to think that coffee was not the best idea. She put it down and returned to rubbing her temples. When warm hands grasped her shoulders, she initially jumped, but as the strong fingers released the tension that had built up between her shoulders, she felt herself unwind at once.

"Oh gah, Bowman, that is so nice," she said relaxing.

"I'm pleased you like it, but I'm afraid it's not the good Corporal," D'Ascoine's voice sounded behind her.

"Oh shit, sir, I am so sorry," she erupted as she moved to stand up. The Leftenant's hands held her in place.

"Shush, you've been working hard Fran," he said, and she noted the use of her first name, "Relax. You deserve a bit of pampering."

"But, sir, I'm not–"

"Consider it an order," he said, his hands kneading her muscles once more. Gradually, she relaxed under his command. At first his touch was comforting, but after a prolonged silence, it seemed a tiny bit arousing and inviting. She pushed those thoughts to the side when he spoke about the mundane activities that filled their lives.

"So, how are you progressing with your new interface?"

"Oh, it's good sir, though I admit it seems a bit, well, it still seems a little strange to me."

"Really? How so?"

"Oh, you know," she said, trying to focus on his question and not his hands, "seeing things through other eyes and different angles. It's hardest when doing the sort of goa work that Sinner does, but even the more normal stuff you know? Just being so tied up with a machine and seeing a world that isn't really there? It's like, I don't know, it takes some getting used to."

"I suppose it does," D'Ascoine said, his fingers gently tracing the lengths of her muscles, "You know, when I was a lad, training in the use of interfaces, I was taught a series of exercises to assist me in getting used to them. I don't know if they would work with your non-invasive systems, but I would happily show them to you if you're interested."

"Anything that might help me do my job better." Fran felt gases move about her stomach.

"And your combat practice?"

"Well, sir, I'm still not very good at it. Not enough strength. I don't think the Empire would remain safe if it came down to me coming to the rescue."

"Then perhaps we should take a little tumble eh? Maybe I could teach you a thing or two," he said, his hands sliding gently along her arms.

Fran felt a sudden tremble of excitement, and looked up to the officer smiling down at her. His face was very close to hers. He moved closer, close enough to kiss her, then pulled away slowly, his finger tips gently tracing up the line of her arms, one gently brushing her breast. His hands slipped back to her shoulders, and the comforting kneading they were doing there.

Was that an accident? Fran wondered, *What's happening? What would I like to happen*?

D'Ascoine was a very good looking man, and he had always been nice enough to her, but something warned her about him. He was dangerously predatory; but then again, that was part of the appeal.

He's an officer and a hierarch. You're just imagining it, why would he take any interest in you?

His hands moved from her shoulders to the very top of her pectorals. Fran felt a rising warmth within her. She wondered if he knew how close to her breasts his hands were getting. She could feel his breath in her hair, a tickle of breeze in her ear. She turned to face him with a quizzical look. He smirked in response and moved a hair's breadth closer.

He's going to kiss me! She thought, and a mixture of pent-up desire and warnings flooded thorough her mind; desires for D'Ascoine, desires for Fotheringday, desires that existed for no other reason than the fact that she had been cooped up in a ship and faced imminent danger. He moved closer still, she moved a fraction further away, and then he pulled back completely.

It took Fran a moment to realize that the alarm in her head was not the only one sounding. She blinked as she looked around the room. The Captain had sounded the summons to an all-hands meeting in the lounge. D'Ascoine was already some distance away from her by the time the others entered room and Fran felt a touch of irritation at the Leftenant. He had pulled away from her at once, moving quickly, as if he feared being caught doing something naughty. She felt cheapened.

"You alright?" Bowman asked as he sat down next to her.

"Yeah. Sorry I was just.... Never mind, I'm fine," she responded, but the Corporal continued to give her a long stare. Across the room Sinner was glowering at D'Ascoine.

"Thank you for coming," Fotheringday said as he and Samantha entered the room, "As you are aware, we have been covertly examining the surface of the planetoid for more than three days and as of yet seen no indications of pirate or indeed any other form of human activity."

"Perhaps we're chasing shadows?" D'Ascoine said with a smirk.

Bowman discretely signaled with his eyes. Following his gaze, Fran looked down and realized that her jump suit was not properly fastened. She felt the blood rush to her face as she strove to covertly redo her suit.

"That remains possible," Alex responded, "But the remarkably well documented nature of this rather insignificant ice fragment does raise some questions that need to be addressed. To that end, I am organizing an EVA reconnaissance mission to the surface, see if it identifies anything we cannot see from orbit."

"When do I get started?" D'Ascoine asked.

"Sir, with all due respect to Leftenant D'Ascoine," Samantha said, "I have more experience in Naval reconnaissance. He is a fine troop commander, but this is intelligence gathering and requires knowledge of different ship systems–"

"And with no offense to the Lieutenant, sir," D'Ascoine interrupted, "I have considerably more combat experience than she does."

"This is a recon mission, Leftenant, not an assault," Samantha said.

"If your theory is correct it could become an assault, and if you're wrong there's no data to gather. Personally, I–"

"You both have excellent points," Fotheringday interrupted, "but I am afraid that in this instance, I will be taking command of the landing party. I have more intelligence gathering experience than either of you, and I have more than a little background in Marine combat. What is more, should there be a fight on the surface, the more guns the better, eh Gunny?"

"Sir, yes sir," Chrom said. Fran thought she saw just a hint of a smile beneath the Gunny's professional demeanor.

"Besides," the Skipper continued, "Ms. Smith is more than capable of taking command of the *Hunter* should something go wrong. What is more, she is far better able to perform SIGINT and surveillance, while keeping the recon team in communication than either you or I."

"Aye, sir," the two officers responded in unison. Fran wasn't certain, but she thought that she noticed the Lieutenant blush ever so slightly at the compliment.

"As for an assault," Fotheringday continued, "Our primary mission is the gathering of intelligence. It is more important that we provide the information we already have obtained to Ripper's Raiders than either gaining more information or freeing a single citizen."

"Who will make up the landing party, sir?" Gunny Chrom asked.

"The TOMO and Marine contingent, of course, myself and Able Technician Harpur," Alex responded, then looking back to D'Ascoine he added "Leftenant D'Ascoine will keep an eye on our tactical situation, and that will allow the rest of us to focus on reconnaissance observations. AT Harpur will assist in those tasks and provide any on-site technical support or hacking that is required."

"Sir, if I may?" Sinner spoke up.

"I know, Chief," the Skipper said, "You are far more experienced with intrusion and tech work, but I need you to stay on the ship with the Lieutenant. I do not want to risk her having to take the ship back to Lai-Jung without at least one combat experienced crew member."

"Actually, sir, I was going to ask if you wanted to bring the drone."

"Oh of course," the Skipper responded, "Yes, I would Chief. That will give us access to your knowledge and more firepower should we need it. Now, Leftenant, if you could see to the details of the landing party?"

"Aye, aye, sir," D'Ascoine responded, his voice slightly peevish.

As the room cleared, Fran watched D'Ascoine saunter back to his quarters. She could not help but feel somehow violated. She began to wonder if she really did like her Tactical Officer after all.

CHAPTER 55

The space-taxi slid from the hold with its cargo of the combat drone and landing party attached to it. As pilot, Alex was the only one with a proper seat. The rest clipped themselves to its rocket-like length. When the taxi was five meters away from the *Hunter*, it changed its configuration from its compact torpedo shape to one better suited for zero-gee operations. The torpedoesque length of its body split into six equal parts, simultaneously pivoting and extending until the vehicle resembled some form of six limbed cephalopod or aquatic arachnid with small engines on the ends of its limbs. Alex fired the thrusters and carefully piloted the taxi into the debris field surrounding the former moon.

He steered as best he could to avoid the micrometeors and the largest of the dust clouds, but a certain amount of impact damage was unavoidable. They had all put on an extra covering of ablative armor to protect from the debris field, though it didn't take long for that layer of protection to begin eroding away. Even so, Samantha confirmed via a line-of-sight communication that the particle cloud made it nearly impossible for her to track them. That gave Alex some relief, if even a skilled astrographer was having difficulty following them, then a half-trained terrorist would never see them.

As the taxi approached the tiny moon, Alex spun it around and gently decelerated. He allowed the ship to slowly descend until the vehicle was about fifty meters above the jagged surface of the planetoid. Giving a slight angle to the rockets, he fired them to keep drifting towards their destination. They passed over rocky protrusions and plains of ice, bobbing up and down like a jellyfish with each use of the engines, until at last they approached their designated landing zone.

In total it took three hours for the landing party to reach the LZ. Throughout the transit, the crew remained plugged into the taxi's supplemental life support system, reserving their suits' forty-eight hour supply of air for as long as they could. During their final descent, Alex twisted the thrusters once more, further slowing the approach. As the sled drifted down to a distance of two meters, the Marine force with its Army officer and Naval Able Technician attaché jumped off and formed a perimeter around the gradually descending vehicle. They moved quickly, both to ensure cover and to gain a safe distance from the touchdown.

As the taxi came in contact with the surface, its latent heat instantly turned the frozen nitrogen, hydrogen and other elements into gas. Shards of ice and rock exploded like fragmentation grenades causing the vehicle to lurch upwards. Alex launched the grapplers into the icy surface of the moonlet ensuring that he was not suddenly rocketed back into space.

When the taxi was finally anchored, the landing party stripped off their micro-meteor coveralls and unhitched the combat drone. They set the robot to operate via its onboard AI. It only had the intelligence of a well trained dog, but the debris field made any Line-Of-Sight comms link sporadic at best, and even a randomly modulated broadcast signal was too great a risk at this point. Thus, they let the robot guide itself, sporadically uplinking to the *Hunter* to keep them informed. After all, Sinner could always override the AI and control the drone directly.

Once they were on the march, everyone quickly fell into position. The microgravity of the moonlet made for a difficult passage, but they knew the heat from their maneuvering jet-packs could give away their presence. As a result, they walked through the treacherous canyons and valleys of rock and frozen gases.

Bowman and D'Ascoine took point, keeping slightly ahead of the rest of the squad and moving stealthily over the broken terrain. Each occasionally slipped out of formation to one side or the other, ensuring they were fully aware of their surroundings. The others walked in a diamond formation. Chrom, dressed in her OST-1012, took the lead, followed by Alex and Fran trekking in a rank of two. The combat drone took up the rear-guard position. They searched the landscape for signs of activity, keeping a distance of about five meters between them at all times.

"Why are we so spread out, Sir?" Fran asked via a laser comm link.

"So no one can kill us all with a single grenade," Alex said as he realized that there were still gaps in her training, "Now let us try to keep our chatter to a minimum eh?"

"Aye aye, Sir," she responded. Her voice hardly sounded encouraged by the answer.

The group's passage across the surface was far from easy. Where possible, Alex kept them close to the tectonic cracks and impact craters that scarred the small moon's surface. The broken terrain provided cover but also made for the most difficult transit. Even so, at times they had to cross open expanses of plain, which made Alex feel extremely exposed. Eventually, they came without incident to the location they had thought the most likely place for an enemy hiding zone. He gave the order and they spread out into a line to search in earnest.

They reconnoitered for hours, looking for footprints, tool marks, or any other clear evidence of activity. As they entered into a series of naturally formed gulley-like cracks in the frozen surface, they found several suspicious looking piles of rubble. Alex, however, did not have the experience to determine whether or not they were natural or man-made.

Maybe Samantha would have been a better choice to lead this party, he thought, *After all, she does have more experience in exploration. I imagine she would have immediately known if these were natural or artificial…*

His thought was interrupted by a fast burst signal from Bowman, who was searching off to one side. Surprised, Alex followed the maze of crevices to the position that he knew the Corporal should be in. Turning the corner he saw why Bowman had summoned him.

The narrow gulley had suddenly opened into an enormous canyon. Constructed into its side was an immense man-made structure that clearly descended below the surface of the ice. It was built into one of the great tectonic cracks in the surface of the moon, with several immense hydrogen glaciers looming over its well hidden position. As might have been expected, most of the base was underground, but an extensive system of pipes and ducts ran throughout the fjord-like valley. These had been built haphazardly, giving the impression of a great metal vine system that twisted and turned throughout the crevice. Towards its bottom, they clustered around a landing pad, giving it the look of an enormous flower. The pad was large, easily able to take a two-thousand ton vessel. Even his first glance told Alex that it was built upon hydraulic lifts, and that meant that it was likely to have quite a considerable ship bay underneath it.

"I say, what do you know?" D'Ascoine broadcast over the tight beam communication line, "It really is an invisible secret pirate base."

Alex cast him a disapproving look before continuing to scan the landing pad. There were three starships sitting on it. One could readily be identified as a thousand ton Rendithi sleeper ship; a passenger vessel of one of the Empire's constituent alien worlds. Another looked to be a three-hundred ton cargo freighter that had been reconfigured for combat. It was a crude and brutal conversion, but done well enough to threaten commercial shipping. Sitting side-by-side they gave all the signs of being a pirate ship and its prey.

The third ship, sitting slightly to the side, was considerably smaller than the other two, but of clear Imperial origin. Using his suit's telescoping vision Alex zoomed in on the orange markings of the smaller ship and noted its registration. He checked with his implants to be certain, but he had known the answer long before: the ship was Sir Richard's personal yacht. Aiming his line-of-sight comm at the position he knew one of their recon satellites would be positioned, he sent a quick burst communication to the *Hunter* explaining what they had found.

"So, they're here," Samantha said. She sounded resigned.

"So it seems, though we still do not know if Sir Richard is involved or merely a victim. Indeed, Fran might have been right when she suggested the sim of Hammond with the Ankh was a fake. We need to know more. Standby for additional communications and prepare to jump in case of an emergency."

Signing off, Alex used direct short range laser comm to give the order to the landing party. At once they began recording what they could. Using both hand held sensors and suit recorders, the landing party both filmed and took static images of what they observed. Infrared to ultra-violet sensors recorded information that extended far beyond what they could see, the radio and X-ray sensors furthered those senses even more. All of the crew except Fran, who was untrained in the procedure, used their weapon's range finders to record the exact position of different portions of the base. They were careful not to target any of the constructed surfaces directly; they could easily be covered by a web of detection sensors. Instead, they targeted observable rocks and surfaces in the vicinity of the constructions knowing that they could create a reasonable facsimile later.

Meanwhile, Fran paid particular attention to the constructed surfaces, ducts and piping, recording her mental notes into her DuZhodian computer. It was clear to her that a great deal of hydrogen mining was being conducted, and some of the surface installations that popped up between the maze of piping were obviously portions of the refining process.

"Sir," she communicated to Alex during one of their laser link-ups, "They're creating fuel reserves, more than enough for this installation."

"I would guess that they could keep about thirty to fifty ships fuelled from what they have here," he responded.

"Perhaps more," Fran suggested, "The caves around that far facing could only be due to a fairly intensive mining operation,"

"Well spotted, Harpur," Alex said.

They moved slowly across the edges of the crevice, keeping to cover and remaining out of sight. It was a slow and painful process that took more effort to remain undetected than was spent recording the information. The knowledge of the base's presence was more important than anything they could discover in addition. They spent a total of four hours on the reconnaissance before Alex gave the order to return to the taxi.

"Sir?" D'Ascoine said, opening a private laser link to the Captain, "Aren't we going to try an assault?"

"No, Leftenant," Alex responded, "I know we have the element of surprise, but this base is large, and there are doubtless too many individuals here for us to take out."

"Will we destroy it from orbit then?"

"No, that Rendithi vessel is clearly a prize ship, and they may well still have the passengers on-site. Rendithi fetch a good price in outworld slave-trading and body parts. Besides, there may be key information inside. We will bring our intel back to the fleet, and recommend this as a primary target for a raid; one that I would think you would be well positioned to lead."

This seemed to please D'Ascoine, but Alex felt more than a pang of guilt. He wanted to rescue the Rendithi, who had done nothing to deserve such treatment. A part of him was appalled at the idea of leaving civilians behind to be sold into slavery, not to mention the potential that one of his friends might also be captive. He wanted to prove which of them was innocent and save them. He wanted in some way to redeem himself for the part he had played in the *Silver Slipper* incident, and bring the person responsible to justice. Yet the calculating part of his brain told him it was a lost cause. The base was large; if they attacked, they would be hopelessly outnumbered.

No, Alex had to remember his primary mission: to gather information and present it to the 12th Fleet. If they acted too soon they could tip their hand and reveal what they had already uncovered. That would allow the terrorists to abandon the base, cover up any connections between Cameron-Inglesie Distributors and kill any survivors from the Rendithi ship. While a life of enforced servitude may not have been a good one, it was still a life. Alex had been responsible for too many civilian deaths already. As for Sir Richard and Hammond, each had once pledged their lives to protect the innocent; one of them betrayed that oath and the other would understand his choice. At least, that is what Alex kept telling himself.

CHAPTER 56

Samantha spent most of her time searching for signs of activity, either on the surface of the planetoid, or in the area of space around it. Staring at the readout and listening to static, she kept her attention acute by keeping her mind active. She performed odd calculations and side observations that did not distract her from watching the monitors.

The first few hours passed with her focusing solely on the issues at hand. By the time the landing party had started back towards the space taxi, however, she had mapped as much as she could of the planet surface. To fight her waning concentration, she decided to determine how an astral body that had been drifting through interstellar space for eons still managed to have a debris field. After all, the ice and rock should have either formed a ring or been drawn to the rogue moonlet's surface after a few million years.

She determined the relative speed and direction of the rogue as compared to the surrounding stars, then moved on to examining other aspects such as the fissures and tectonic cracks. Most individuals would have needed to focus their attention, but Samantha performed it in the back of her head while still keeping an eye on the sensors. As the problem continued to elude her, however, she became absorbed by the question.

Fascinating, she thought as she narrowed down the possibilities, *but even so, there still remains too great an amount of debris in orbit to be explained by that.* She entered the data into her survey program, calculated errors using the navigational system, and finally found the answer. *Of course! The debris was created when they made the base!*

Samantha was still congratulating herself on the cleverness of her calculations when she noted a sudden burst of electromagnetic signals from the surface. Examining the frequency, she realized that it was in the radio-communication bandwidth. She ran a quick search program through the sensor logs to see if any similarly strength signals had been detected during their stay. When the ship told her that five such bursts had been detected over the past few minutes, she cursed herself.

Oh, that's just great Sammy-girl, she said to herself, *you're so smart you figured out where the debris came from instead of performing your damned duties!*

She turned the ships optics to the location where the signal originated from and searched for a source. It didn't take her long to find it.

"Eagle One, this is Nest," she said, opening a line to Alex.

"Copy, Nest, this is Eagle One, go ahead."

"Eagle One, we have hostile personnel on the surface and heading your way. They emerged from airlock designation four and are approaching your position along the same crevice you are following. ETA your position, two minutes, or less. Repeat ETA two minutes or less."

"Roger that. Is there any sign they are aware of our presence?" Alex's voice sounded calm and in control. Samantha felt a sparkle of admiration. Surface side combat at near absolute zero was an extremely dangerous business.

"Negative, Eagle One, from the looks of them, they're a maintenance party."

"Repeat I …" static "… copy."

"No sign of intentions, but they appear to be a maintenance party."

"Roger that, good work Nest, keep us appr…sd of the situation."

"Affirmative. Nest out." Despite the praise, Samantha felt far from proud at her work and she had a bloody nail bed to prove it.

Chrom positioned herself within the rocky nook she had identified. The timing could not have been worse. They were half-way down a long crevice that, while providing good cover from outside observation, left few places to hide should someone decide to travel along it. Before the enemy had been detected, the Skipper had judged it worth the risk of following since it was by far the stealthiest route across the most exposed portion of the surface. The odds of someone coming out of the only entrance close to it seemed remote. Long ago, however, Chrom had noticed that life has a tendency to beat the odds, especially when it was most inconvenient.

Moving into a crack in the ice, Chrom was careful to ensure that none of the heat bleeding systems of her suit were anywhere near the icy surfaces. The landing party remained in a comms blackout. With the enemy so close, the Skipper feared that any radio bursts might give away their presence. Instead, the squad took positions that allowed each of them line-of-sight with at least one other member of the team. Due to the size of her suit, her position had the least number of other contacts, excluding the combat drone of course. It was the drawback of the big assault suits: they were not as easily camouflaged. She stood with weapons ready, as did the rest of the unit, waiting for the maintenance team to pass.

They could have easily taken out the Feddies, that was not a question. They were well armed and had surprise, but the Skipper wanted to avoid conflict. That made sense to

Chrom. Their mission was to gather information, not to engage the enemy. If they attacked the maintenance team, they would give away their presence and the terrorists would know that they had been discovered. By the time Ripper's Raiders, or even the 253rd showed up, the base would be long abandoned, and the Dalang would have had the chance to destroy all evidence connecting him to the crimes.

Chrom didn't need this explained to her. It was the basic premise of recon, even if it didn't seem to sit well with D'Ascoine. So they waited and watched and prayed the Feddies would pass them by. She sat in the dark, lights off, passive arrays on, searching to see signs of the enemy and hoping she wouldn't.

According to the XO there was technically a trace of atmosphere on the rock, but for practical purposes it was far too thin to carry sound. As a result, the first real indicator of the approaching enemy was when she saw the lights of their suits hitting the path in front of her. She held still and watched them go by.

There were eight of them walking in a double column. They were dressed in standard EVA suits and armed with lasers; a solid zero-gravity choice of weapon for non-professionals. None of them had their weapons drawn; they were burdened with construction gear. Slowly, they walked by Chrom's position, until one of the last pair dropped something he was carrying and bent over in Chrom's direction to pick it up.

Chrom remained completely motionless as he bent over, and thought for a moment that she would pass unnoticed. Then the Feddie straightened up and paused, looking straight at her as if trying to determine if she were part of the outcropping of rocks. When he dropped his load and suddenly stepped back, Chrom knew he knew the answer. Her arm flew straight out, her right waldo-grip in a knife-hand position. The powered arm smashed through the faceplate of the terrorist, carrying straight on into his skull. The game was up.

Behind him, his paired team-mate turned towards the sudden movement, oblivious to the motion behind him. Bowman stepped forward, swinging the blade of his zero-gee cutlass-hook through the man's radio antennae. He smoothly reversed its momentum and brought the edged hook back through the man's air-hoses. A cloud of gasses erupted as the terrorist fell struggling to the ground. Bowman stepped back as the escaping warm air from the suit came in contact with the frozen hydrogen and caused it to explode through sudden heating. The Federalist's body flew several hundred feet before it slowly drifted back down to the low gravity of the moonlet's surface.

Seeing the activity, Alex pushed forward toward the figure closest to him, sonic drusus in hand. The micro-vibrations running through the single crystal blade allowed it to slice smoothly through the top of the helmet and skull of the first person he encountered. Capturing the momentum of the swing, Alex twisted, tumbled and thrust the short-sword through the chest plate of the second. He gutted his second target with ease.

Fran had never been so frightened in her life; she saw the combat going on around her and froze. She didn't know what to do. Across from her hiding spot, she saw D'Ascoine rush from his position and thrust the bayonet of his AAR-5 through the head of a terrorist. He quickly withdrew it, and opened fire on two others. The fact that the slugs were launched by magnetic field rather than by gunpowder explosion meant that there was no recoil, nor any latent heat in the bullets. The few stray rounds that missed their targets hit the surrounding rocks and ice, but did not cause explosions. The same could not be said of decompressing suits of those that the Leftenant had killed. In a moment the air was filled with fragments of rock and ice.

The explosions threw the last remaining terrorist to the ground at Fran's feet. She saw the sudden, shocked and frightened look in his eyes. He wasn't much older than she was, and she could read the horror in his face: *This can't be happening, not like this….* She fought back the rising bile as she fired a single round through his visor and into his head. She trembled, her own face frozen in disgust, guilt and fear. Fran Harpur had killed a man face to face. She fought back the tears as she sounded out the all clear.

"Blast!" Alex said as he looked around, "Nest, this is Eagle One, did they get off a signal?"

"That's a negative, Eagle One," Samantha's voice sounded from the ship. They were using LOS comms relayed through the micro-satellites for the moment, "You kept them quiet."

"Roger that. How long until their next check in?"

"No idea, sir. Most of their comms appear to have been ground chatter to one another. If they follow standard military protocol, between eighteen to twenty-eight minutes."

"We're at least an hour from the LZ," D'Ascoine said, "We won't be able to get back to the taxi before their next check-in. Should we use our thrusters packs to maneuver to the ship? If they EVA across the surface there's no way they would be able to catch us."

"Agreed sir," Chrom said, "but they'd probably detect us. They could launch their own taxis, fighters, or even missiles. We can't out-run those."

Alex continued his concentrated silence. It had been a simple recon mission. Had he pressed it too far yet again? Would it have been better to simply report what they had found? Now everything was compromised. If they ran back to Lai-Jung, the base would be abandoned by the time they returned in force. If they attacked they were outnumbered. Then there was Sir Richard and Hammond. One was the Dalang, the other would soon be dead. Most of all, there was the ship load of Rendithi civilians….

"We're not going to out-run anything," Alex said with sudden certainty, "We're going to take the base."

"Brav-oh!" D'Ascoine said.

CHAPTER 57

Alex finally had time to think while Harpur worked on hotwiring the outer airlock door. As they had traversed back to the base, he ordered Samantha to stay in orbit, but to jump back to Lai-Jung and notify Alterande High Command if the assault team was captured or killed. It didn't go down well, but in the end she reluctantly agreed. Now he only had to worry about assaulting the base, keeping his people alive, rescuing the Rendethi - and a friend - and of course bringing the man responsible for the *Silver Slipper* and a thousand other attacks back to justice. Assuming they could get inside the airlock.

Alex's palms were sweating as he watched Fran pick the lock. She was noticeably agitated, and her nervousness added to Alex's own. He suspected that the airlock would only be large enough for either a team of four people or one person and the drone. The drone was the best piece of combat gear and sending it in first would mean only one person's life would be risked. Unfortunately, that person would have to be Fran, she was the only one capable of hotwiring the locks. Even if Sinner rode the drone, it just wasn't set up for the kind of detail work that would allow him to perform a manual bypass. As a result, putting Fran in with the drone would leave them with the least combat experienced team member on point with a low-grade AI in a first contact situation. The other option, however, risked four people's lives instead of one. As the airlock slid open, he remembered what happened on the *Slipper* and made his choice.

"Leftenant, take in your fire-team," he ordered, "Harpur, work the lock. All units prepare to switch over to short range radio frequencies. We need to keep in constant contact."

Alex picked up their sensory feeds as the Marines poured in. Chrom took the middle position, Bowman took the left, D'Ascoine the right. All had their weapons aimed at the far door. Fran slipped into the side of the chamber, tools in her hands instead of weapons. She smoothly removed the cover of the inner cycling controls and hotwired the sequences again. It took considerably less time than before. The outer door shut and Alex was left to watch their feeds.

With the drone still on autopilot to his side, Alex monitored D'Ascoine and the others through the displays inside his helmet. He felt uneasy not leading from the front, but he knew that despite his cross-training, the Marines were more experienced in ground combat than he was, even D'Ascoine, whose armored cavalry background was still based on planet-side action. All the same, each second that passed raised Alex's heart rate.

Chrom stood at the ready; the Rapid-Fire Rail-Gun at her waist poised to send hundreds of rounds per second into the doorway. To her right the Leftenant looked primed for combat, to her left Bowman stood reliable and set to go. Both had their AAR-5's trained on the inner airlock door, prepared to either pull the trigger or fire the Armor Piercing High Explosive grenades chambered in their launchers. Beyond D'Ascoine she could see the young Able Tech Harpur working away at the electronic locks, taking what seemed to be an age and a half to open the inner door.

"A little speed, my dear," D'Ascoine said.

Fran seemed to ignore the comment. It took her less than two minutes to run the cycle. When the inner-door opened, it revealed an empty junction with a stairwell leading deep into the ground, and long corridors sloping away to the left and right.

The Marines moved by the numbers, D'Ascoine rolling out to the right side, Bowman the left, while Chrom covered them before moving forward to peer down the stairwell. She upped the acoustics, IR and other passive arrays, looking for signals bouncing up or down the stairs. There was no sign of movement.

The Leftenant made a sharp pointing gesture at Fran, who stayed by the airlock. She fiddle with some wire and cycled it while Chrom and the others held their positions. A moment later, the CO entered with the drone running on auto behind him.

"AT Harpur," Fotherinday said as he stepped into the hall, "I want you to leave a motion detector at this junction. We will head down the right corridor towards the main base. Go."

D'Ascoine and Bowman took the lead, walking side by side down the wide corridor with Chrom giving them cover from behind. Behind her, her sensors showed Fotheringday and Harpur walking abreast, with Sinner's drone taking rearguard. Thus far, the Gunnery Sergeant saw no indication anyone knew of their presence.

"Sir," Harpur said as they began to trek down the long hallway before them, "I'm picking up a wireless system. Do you want me to try to hack it?"

"Can you do so without giving away our presence?" Alex replied.

"I'm pretty sure, if I do it now, sir, but it'll be impossible if they find us first. They'll lock out the system, maybe even shut down the wi-fi. If I get in first I might be able to override those commands."

"Very well," he said looking Fran in the eye, "do it, but be careful."

Fran adjusted the commands on her breastplates and initiated the DuZhodian interface. She entered her interface room: a quiet space modeled on her bedroom at home. Posters of pop-stars from four years ago were displayed on the holowalls, the smell of her mother's cookies wafted gently in the background. She felt herself stumble as the virtual world clouded her vision.

"*Fah*!" she said. She hadn't wanted to fully enter the VR world. She quickly opened a window into the real world in front of her in order to stop herself from tripping.

Keeping half-an-eye on the real world window, Fran's virtual self walked through her virtual bedroom door and entered into the clean efficient work space she had created beyond it. She immediately adjusted the frequencies, making certain she was using the proper bandwidths before attempting to hack the terrorist's system.

She readied a century of phreaker-worms, viral-dragons and other hacker programs, including one special firmware-assassin that she and Sinner devised during their transit to the moonlet. They had built it after examining the files on the Wayang Stalkers that the Skipper had taken from the MoJ, and she was particularly proud of it. Once she set that in an easily accessible place, she opened a new series of windows in her mind to review the information. When she was ready, she closed out her view to the virtual universe and saw the small hovering monitor windows super-imposed upon her vision within the real world.

She studied the spikes and troughs of the different radio signals being broadcast through this portion of the base. As they turned a corner in the real world she identified the programs that were most likely associated with innocuous systems controls. Adjusting her secondary frequencies to those, she launched one of Sinner's hacker programs. It pretended to be a maintenance drone cycling through the different comms networks for further instructions. In fact it, was entering random passwords on different systems and looking for backdoors left by second-rate programmers and systems engineers. It didn't take her long to find her way into the personal entertainment system of the base.

Performing both random and systematic searches through the user files, she was able to find out hints and notes from about two dozen users who had thought they had cleverly hidden clues in case they forgot their passwords. Once she had that, she hacked directly into other systems in no time. Within five minutes she had access to over twenty-percent of the base's computer files.

"Sir? I've got a general map of the facility."

"Well done, Harpur," Alex replied, "Squad hold your positions."

He received the 3D image from Harpur and immediately began to review its layout. The base had been built haphazardly, with contours that fit the crevice, and tunnels running at strange angles. At present, they were some distance from the center of the base, out along what appeared to be a spur of the corridor systems designed to access the upper edge of the crevice. It linked into the ice mining shafts about two hundred meters ahead, and eventually ran into a series of junctions that lead to the main body of the base. By toggling on and off different layers of the map, Alex noted that the more sensitive elements of the computer network were not broadcast this far out. They would need to get into the central body of the base before they could download any sensitive information. Looking at the time display on his helmet, Alex noted that they only had ten minutes before they had estimated that the maintenance crew they killed were due to report in. It would take them at least that long to get to the sensitive areas. It was going to be close.

"Right, Ladies and Gentlemen, here is a map of the facility," he said, risking a randomized broadcast communication to the ship to include Smith and the Chief in the link, "We have to get to these areas here as fast as we can without tripping any alarms."

"We'll have a problem once we get to those areas, sir," Sinner said, "They're gonna be a lot more likely to pick up your signals in there."

"Understood, Chief, but it is a risk we will have to take. Move out."

Alex broke the link to the *Hunter*, and had his team continue their march as quickly and quietly as possible. They mostly traveled along straight doorless corridors, but from time to time they came to junctions. There Bowman or D'Ascoine would extend the snooper cameras from the wrist of their OS-745s and look round the corner before they would turn and move as quietly as possible down the tunnel. They made reasonably good time, though Alex was growing uneasy about the number of unexplored corridors they were leaving behind them. Still, he saw little choice but to continue into the base, even if that meant they could get cut off from behind.

They moved deeper, and hadn't come across a terrorist despite Alex's fears at the size of the base. He was just allowing himself to smile when a door opened ahead of them and a woman carrying a PAD stepped into the hall. She stared dumbly at the heavily armed and armored individuals for a moment before her chest erupted with blood and she flew backwards with the force of Bowman's bullets.

D'Ascoine moved immediately towards the still open door, and seeing three individuals in the room, opened fire with his AAR-5. The bullets flew noiselessly down the barrel of the gun, spurred on without flash or recoil by the electromagnetic current before tearing into the room and the technicians therein. None of them had the time to raise the alarm. The only sounds made were the brief gasps of pain and surprise, and the thud of stray rounds imbedding into the walls.

"I don't see any security cameras," D'Ascoine said as the others joined him.

"It won't take long for them to figure out we're here now," Chrom said.

"Sir?" Fran interrupted, "There's a hardline data point over here."

Alex looked up and down the corridor and compared their position on the electronic schematics that Fran had provided earlier. With a long hallway that had sub-corridors approaching it on either side, the room was a death trap. If they were caught there, they would be trapped and the enemy could send reinforcements to surround them at their leisure. It was a completely indefensible position in the midst of enemy territory. Put against this was the fact that it was now only a matter of time before they were discovered, and the information junction that Fran had discovered was exactly what they had entered the base to find: a way into the main network. He cursed silently.

"How long will it take you to hack?"

"That depends upon their secure systems sir."

"Sir, this position is very vulnerable," Chrom added, "and if this is a major maintenance area–."

"I am aware of the risks, Gunnery Sergeant."

"Skipper, I brought along a grade four comms-uplink," Fran said, "If I plug it into the data port, I could hack it while we're on the move. I know using broadcast comms might give us away, but if staying here is a concern.... Besides, if I'm using our comms and linked into a hard port, I can't be thrown out of the system if they shut down their wi-fi."

"If we do that," Bowman said, "we might as well link the drone back to the ship and let Sinner help Fran while he rides it."

Alex risked contacting the ship and asking for confirmation.

"If I'm riding the drone," Sinner said, "I can't spend much time hackin' the system, but Fran could, and she's good enough. It should work sir."

"Right, get to it Able Tech. And good work."

"Captain?" Samantha's voice entered the link, "Piggybacking a signal like that requires that a lower rate of frequency modulation is used. That'll raise the likelihood of your broadcasts being detected."

"That's a chance we'll have to take."

It only took Fran a few seconds to link the communication device into the data point and camouflage it. Less than a minute later she and the Chief had set up the relay link through the drone. Once that was done, she allowed the DuZhodian device to overlay the command prompts and data feeds as translucent text over her view of the real world. Letters, symbols, icons and graphs streamed as pale blue projections over her vision, making it difficult both for her to move along the corridors and to concentrate on hacking the system. She cursed herself, knowing that Sinner could probably have done both without a problem. For the first time, she realized the appeal of getting the kind of implants that Prole-savs used to autopilot their bodies. That thought sent a shiver down her spine.

After a brief reconnaissance of the non-secure systems and a comparison to the broadcast network she had already penetrated, Fran customized a few of her programs and launched a series of viruses, worms and tunneling dragon attacks on the network. The rest would take time and concentration, luxuries that she did not have. Still, she was glad that they were trying to be stealthy, otherwise she would have tripped.

Alyiar was ignoring the conversation occurring between arguing terrorcrats around him. He knew he shouldn't be, that he should feel honored at being included in the discussion. At the moment, however, he couldn't care less. These people were using him and his comrades the same way the hierarchs used the rest of population. Maybe Wylde had been right; the Dalang and his cronies had betrayed the cause. Alyiar didn't know, he just knew that the only people he trusted were his fellow Wayang Stalkers – excluding Rubo of course.

Alyiar figured that if he was going to help them, he would have to find the access codes to their Stalker Implants. He would have to close the backdoor that Rubo had used to activate Wylde's self destruct. He figured those codes must be somewhere in the base's network. That's what he told himself anyways. That's what he used to justify the fact he was spending hours checking out corners of the base's network. A part of himself hated the very concept that he had even glanced at the base's comms system, told him it was just an excuse to return to the cyberworlds. Either way, curiosity had eventually gotten the better of him. Now he had lost hours to browsing the network while, outside, disembodied voices argued about pointless things.

"Personally, I don't care what the Council says, this tactic is working."

"The tactic doesn't fit with their strategy."

"It ain't their strategy that it don't fit with. It's their feckin' agenda."

Ah… Rubo's here, Alyiar thought as he careened through the gaming systems. On the side, he noted someone had opened up a new entertainment sequence that used an unusually large bandwidth. He wondered what it was.

"It's interfering with other Federalist operations."

"They're afraid because we are more successful than they are."

"He's right. They've always been more interested in their feckin' agenda than in–"

Skimming across the network, Alyiar looked at the new game system. It didn't seem all that interesting. Just some puzzle piece without much of a sim running in it. Alyiar liked sims better than the simple mind-teasers. He was about to close it up when he saw the amount of computing power the game took. Something didn't seem right about it. He was about to investigate when he realized Rubo was shaking him.

"I said, on your feet!" Rubo said, looming over him in his Stalker form. There was a yellow light blinking in the corner of the room, "Get your feckin' head in the game! Go down and get ready to blow the Sleeper ship, just in case."

"What's going on?" Alyiar asked, blinking himself back into the real world.

"Probably nothing," Rubo said, picking up an assault rifle, "but best to be safe right? We don't want none of those bugeyes or fancy boys getting' away do we?"

In the end, they were never quite certain what alarmed the base to their presence. The time for the first maintenance crew they had killed to report in had passed, but the alarm could equally have been raised by someone coming across the second group they had killed in the room, detection of their radio signals, or even their passing by an unnoticed security camera. All they knew for certain was that, just as they were coming into the direct broadcast range of the more secure computer networks, they met enemy resistance at a t-junction.

The firefight did not last long. Chrom opened up with the Rapid-Fire Rail Gun, literally cutting in half the three Feddies who came up behind them. Meanwhile, Bowman launched a fragmentation grenade down the right side of the t-junction, and D'Ascoine down the left. The sound of their explosion muffled the screams that followed. The team ran quickly towards the intersection and fired around the corners, finishing off the few walking wounded who remained.

After that, there was no point in using stealth. The operation became a standard Marine assault: maximum speed, maximum force. Sinner rolled to the lead, taking point. Chrom followed behind him since she could fire over the top of the drone. Alex took the left flanking position behind the Gunnery Sergeant, while D'Ascoine took the right; it allowed them opportunity shots around the Gunny. Harpur remained one step behind, focusing on the virtual world while Bowman took up the rear guard. From time to time they were forced to go in single file, but wherever possible, they tried to go with two people abreast to maximize their firepower.

They sped down the corridors, smashing in doors and firing on anyone who could pose a threat. Behind them, Bowman paused to set the occasional wire and grenade trap. Fran had to stop her cracking attempt and cover him while he did. Working quickly, he set a grenade to one wall with a rapid-stick epoxy pad, looped a wire around the pin and strung it to a second pad on the far wall. Fran tried to stop her hands from shaking as she aimed down the hall. She worried she would miss or not react fast enough should someone come around the corner. But Bowman was a professional, and did not take long.

They were up and running after the rest of the landing party within moments, allowing Fran to return to her attempts to hack into the system. Focusing on the computer, she tripped and fell. Tumbling through the low-g environment, she smashed into a wall with enough force to bloody her lip and sprain her wrist. Glad that she hadn't fallen outside where the heat of her suit might have caused an explosion, she waved off the helping hand offered by Bowman and managed to regain her feet.

A few seconds later she completed the switch in her hacking tactics from the low level stealth assault, to an out-and-out combat crack that used every systems hacking, cracking and smashing program in the book. It would announce that she was trying to break into the system, but Fran figured they suspected that already, and that it was only a matter of time before they started deleting files. Behind her, in the real world, she heard the blast of one of the booby trapped grenades behind them going off.

Alyiar was extending the docking arm to the Rendethi ship when the claxons sounded. A moment later, the combat lighting went on and he knew something had gone wrong. Linking into the comms network, he searched for the Wayang Stalkers channels. He linked in, watching Rubo and the others slide their way down the narrow ventilation shafts. How many times had he done that himself? Worming his way through ship's lifesupports as he made ready for combat. Closing his eyes, he opened the sensory links. He felt the metal sliding around them as they extended and contracted their way through the shafts towards whatever ambush they were planning. A sudden thud ripped him out of it. The docking arm had sealed on the side of the Rendethi Sleeper ship.

"Get a grip," he muttered to himself, "set the explosives and make sure the captives are secured."

Alarms were sounding and the lighting had turned red. Alex knew their best bet was to hit hard and fast. Thus far all they had encountered were small security teams running to respond to an uncertain problem. That wouldn't last. Alex needed to take advantage of the element of surprise while he had it. He had to act before the enemy could set up a proper defense.

They had to hack the system, download the data, rescue Sir Richard or Hammond, and most importantly, save the Rendithi captives. He just hoped the prisoners were all in the same place. If they could secure data and the hostages, they could leave the base and destroy it using the *Hunter*'s nuclear arsenal. Until they had at least saved the civilians, however, he and his team were stuck there: a small group of combatants outnumbered and possibly outgunned in the heart of an enemy base.

"Got it!" Fran shouted, "I'm in their system, sir!"

"Well done, Harpur," Alex said, "Initiate a general download, link me into their security system and then begin navigating through their files. Look for the sensitive materials: personal files, ship logs, anything like that. Once you start downloading those, let me know and–"

Alex was cut off as gunfire suddenly hit them from the rear. Bowman was knocked down by the force of the bullets. Fortunately nothing penetrated his armor. Alex spun around and launched three APHE grenades down the corridor. As each armor piercing high explosive round struck its target it erupted, tearing the men in their inferior combat armor apart. Shrapnel and flechettes ripped into others and the sound of screaming wounded filled the hall.

Other armed men quickly took their place; the insurgents were mounting an organized defense. Two more grenades and a hail of bullets ended the rear assault, but the sudden appearance of a Light-Anti-Tank weapon rising to the shoulder of a terrorist caused Alex's heart to skip a beat. Bowman, however, deftly countered that threat with a single shot that detonated the round in its launcher.

Fran looked around as the smoke cleared. It wasn't a pretty sight, and in the back of her mind she wondered why she wasn't sick at seeing it. She wondered obliquely if it was because of the DuZhodian device or simple adrenaline. Either way, she began to follow the orders she had been given before the attack.

"We need to press forward quickly down this hall," the Skipper started, but was suddenly cut short.

Fran looked up to see a long, thin, tattooed figure drop on the CO from the ceiling. It was impossibly fast and snakelike in its movement. She froze as others fell from above.

Gunshots sounded around her, and the world moved in slow motion. She saw Fotheringday grapple with the gun in the figure's hands, saw razor-like nails extend from its long curving figures, fangs snatching at his visor. It moved with lightning speed, and the Skipper struggled desperately with it.

She was vaguely aware that the others were also locked in combat, but for the moment all Fran could see was the Skipper.

Move, move, move, she repeated to herself, but her body seemed frozen for hours before at last it responded.

Fran leapt forward, jumping onto the back of the horrible ectomorph with the arabesque tattoos. She grabbed it from behind, hoping to slow its motion, but that was not her real attack. It worked.

"*Feck off!*" the creature screamed, and twisted its form.

Fran found herself flying to the side of the hall, but she had done what she wanted. She'd identified the frequency it was communicating on. In her mind's eye she activated the firmware-assassin she and Sinner had written. The effects were almost immediate. The Wayang Stalkers instantly became as limp as rag dolls as their implants were taken over by the program.

Alyiar screamed as he watched his last remaining comrades flop powerlessly to the ground. He knew what had happened immediately. The girl, the stupid horrible little girl had somehow accessed the backdoor in their implants: the broadcast access route that Rubo used to kill Wylde. Now they were trapped in their bodies, perhaps paralyzed and watching through empty eyes, or perhaps trapped in some virtual hell, unaware of what had happened. It made little difference. The Imperial bastards didn't wait to see why their enemies were suddenly helpless, they just killed them. Guns, knives, and hands, it didn't matter; the Wayang Stalkers were slaughtered. All at once Alyiar was the last of his kind.

Looking around the Rendethi Sleeper ship, an anger grew in him that surpassed any hatred he had felt before. He hated the Imperial pigs who had killed his comrades. He hated the Dalang whose words he now knew were empty, nothing more than a way to manipulate good men and women. He hated the stupid girl whose program had killed the last of the people he cared about. Most of all, he hated himself for having fallen back into the virtual addiction, for having failed his comrades, for having lived.

"*The Dalang wants to be sure none of the captives escape?*" he said. His bones grew, his skin shifted, and arabesque tattoos twisted and twirled across his skin.

"*I can make sure that no one escapes. No one.*"

Alyiar's long thing legs carried him towards engineering and the fusion engines that lay there in. The explosives he had set would kill the Rendethi, but little else. He went to ensure a trap that left no survivors at all.

CHAPTER 58

As they came to the door, the combat drone focused all its weapons forward and rolled up to less than a millimeter's distance from the hatch. Chrom took up her well practiced position behind it, the long magnetic barrel of her Rapid Fire Rail-Gun pointing at the door, shoulder mounted rockets at the ready. D'Ascoine threw his back against the wall to the right of the door, Bowman did the same to the left. Both were ready to roll around the corners and open fire on whatever lay inside. The Skipper held the rear guard, and Fran focused her attention on the security systems, but held her gun ready.

Chrom hoped that it would not come to the Able Tech adding to the fight. Not only would that mean things were desperate, but because the girl just wasn't up to a real fire-fight. Still, Fran had heart and was good at cracking the systems. Chrom was impressed with how she'd been feeding the enemy false intel and countering the automated assaults launched by the base's security system.

"Ready Sir!" Leftenant D'Ascoine said. Chrom focused.

"Go!" Fotheringday ordered.

The door opened to reveal a less than pleasant surprise. Beyond was an exceptionally large room, filled with people –

exactly the kind of thing that caused a Marine's blood to run cold in a boarding operation. Yet training and experience overrode thoughts and fears. There was a momentary pause as Chrom looked, knowing this was in part a rescue mission, knowing that they could be civilians. She saw guns, she saw lines of people, she saw weapons being handed out, and she perceived that she faced a room filled with enemy combatants. The process took less than a second, but in the adrenaline rush of combat, her indecision felt like minutes. Fortunately the muster point of insurgents had been caught off guard. Chrom opened fire, an action echoed by Sinner.

A stream of bullets raced down the electromagnetic barrel of her RFRG, slicing in half the stunned men and women in front of her. Simultaneously she gave a mental command and launched two of her shoulder rockets. They flew three meters through the door, then curved in opposite directions, disappearing out of sight before rocking the entire base with the shockwaves of their explosions. Chrom's IR-sensors shutoff with the overload of heat from the blast-furnace that had once been the dining hall before her.

Sinner's reactions were only a second behind the Gunnery Sergeant's. His view through the drone's sensors was a compiled mixture of sonar, optics and EM spectrography data that told him fifty-six people were in the room, two of whom were plasma gunners. He targeted them with his RFRGs, and let the drone's automatic systems sweep the rest of the room with its fusion cannons. The plasma gunners erupted as the armor piercing rounds penetrated their heavy combat armor, but Sinner could not see the results. Like the Gunny, the drone's sensors were also momentarily overwhelmed.

D'Ascoine and Bowman each swung around their corners and fired into the room, careful to keep to as much cover from the wall as possible while avoiding Sinner and the Gunny's lines of fire. They each launched a flash-bang followed by a series of fragmentation grenades. Sinner rolled the drone forward into the room, pivoting his weapon arms in each direction and spraying the chamber. Bowman and D'Ascoine sent short neat bursts into the few individuals who remained in the room. Chrom followed.

The enemy had only fired three shots in the entire combat: two hit the walls, the other killed one of their own. Fotheringday and Fran backed into the room after the "all clear" was given. No matter how much false intel Fran was feeding them, the sounds of combat would tell the enemy exactly where the landing party was. Now they really had to move fast.

Alyiar kept a voice channel open to the base command center and listened to the chatter coming from it. He had lost the Imperial intruders in the maze of false data being fed to the security systems, but the explosions told him they were still on the base. As long as that was true, they wouldn't escape. Still, the Dalang needed watching. Alyiar had no desire for the terrorcrats to escape the end he had planned for them, so he listened in on them while focusing on the Rendethi ship's fusion engines.

"They're on sub-level sixteen!"

"What the hell are they doing there?"

"It's false data...."

Alyiar agreed with the assessment, not that it would matter for long. He adjusted the controls on the plasma injectors until they shined bright red.

"Send an assault force to sub-level sixteen!"

"I'm telling you, they've hacked the network, they're not there!"

The ground shook and a deep rumbling noise followed. A series of explosions sounded nearby. The lights on the landing pad dimmed momentarily before the back-up power kicked in. Alyiar smiled. Even if the base lost power, his plan would still work. He looked at the ship's instruction texts hovering in front of him and did the opposite of what they said. Still the Dalang and the others argued incessantly.

"Where the hell was that?"

"Not sub-level sixteen."

"It was in the main dining room!"

"That's on this level!"

Arguing was all that they had done since he had met them. On board the Rendethi ship, an alarm sounded. No one on the base would have heard it.

"I warned you. You! Stand up! I'm taking over this terminal."

"What are you doing?"

"You know what? You're great at wrangling deals, and laundering money and organizing the set up, but sometimes your lack of combat training really shows. There we go, the assault team, main dining room."

"How did you–"

"Ten years in NavCom teaches you something. See that? Four of them and a Combat drone, and look, see the gold laurel? Two nobles, one of them with green markings, Army, any guesses as to who the naval officer is?"

"Damn it! Fotheringday! Assault Team Four, belay my previous order! Get to the Launching Bay now!"

That caught Alyiar's attention. He didn't want them getting to the launch bay yet.

"Launch bay? Why not here? They–"

"Listen, I'll give you the fact that you have more experience in combat, but I'm the Intel officer. Trust me, on this one. I know Alex, and he'll target the launch bay. Now, is there anything you can do to slow them down?"

Alyiar began speeding up his sabotage. Just a few more minutes and he would get the engines to go nova.

"Maybe. In fact, it's just possible that I can stop them in their tracks. Where the hell did I save that little program I wrote?"

Fran was halfway across the large dining room when the world became a blinding white light and her skull was filled with a sharp cutting pain. Her hands flew to the sides of her helmet, she stumbled and fell writhing on the ground. *Feedback*! The thought somehow managed to fight its way through the agony. Blind, Fran tried to slap the surface of the DuZhodian device she wore slung around her side, desperately trying to kill the connection.

"Halt!" Alex gave the order as he noted his AT's reaction. It took him a moment to recognize the signs, but when he saw her slapping the computer at her side he knew a Feedback Assault program had been launched and he ran to her. He flipped up the kill button cover and hit the big red button twice, but Fran kept writhing. Her hands were now back to desperately clawing at her helmet.

"Chief! Harpur has been assaulted by a Biofeedback Killer. I've tried the kill button but the systems still working. Please advise. Chief? Sinner!"

No response came. Alex looked up towards the drone and saw that the combat robot now stood perfectly still, red blinking lights indicated that it had begun going through a cycling system.

"Bloody hell," Alex whispered, before shouting an order just as the killer robot began to turn, "All hands! Open fire on the Combat Drone! Now! Now! NOW!"

"Clear path between Bridge and Engineering!" Samantha shouted as she slid down the ladder into Gunnery Control. She squeezed through the still opening airlock and ran as fast as she could past the living quarters, through the next hatch, and into the mess/lounge. Hurdling the furniture, she clipped her foot on the top of the sofa and fell sprawling across the floor.

"Guh – mother fuck," she muttered, skidding to a stop. She could hear Sinner's screams through the bulkheads now. She scrambled to her feet and bolted in his direction. The screams were horrible, like a scalded child or a pig being ineptly slaughtered.

She pounded past the armory, unaware of the string of obscenities flowing from her mouth that would have made the Gunny blush. By the time she reached Engineering, the screams had stopped. Her curses became a desperate repetition of denial.

"No, no, no, no, no!"

She burst into Engineering Central Control to find the drones physically severing the connections between the Chief's G-couch and the rest of the ship. All comms to the Chief had already been cut, the redundancy systems ensured the ship's safety. At the moment, however, Samantha didn't care. Her eyes were locked on Sinner, whose features were contorted in a silent scream. Whatever virus, worm or other nasty that was attacking him was shooting horrible feedback into his implants. She had little doubt it was lethal.

She thanked God Sinner's couch was open, and rushed to his side. His back was arched, his muscles frozen in contraction, his eyes staring widely into space. Samantha ripped through his pockets, desperately looking for the emergency PAD that he kept for such circumstances. Her mind flew wildly, trying to remember which pocket it should have been in. They had practiced this a dozen times. *Why can't I remember what fucking pocket it's–*

She found it, pulled it out and slipped the optical connector into the i/o port on his wrist. Still cursing, she pressed her thumb against the PAD's surface. As the device powered up, she shouted into its speaker, "Penguins, penguins, toffy-covered penguins!"

The PAD came to life and began to force Sinner's implant to perform an emergency restart from its backup. Samantha hoped, prayed, begged that it was going to work. She stood and stared, waiting.

After a moment, she remembered her duty and attempted to access the ship's IS through her implants. A moment of panic struck when she could not, but the fear quickly passed.

She had forgotten broadcast comms were automatically cut off when anyone on the ship was hacked, infected or the like. She crossed over to Fran's workstation and began to type in manual commands.

There was no sign that the assault had breached any part of the ship. As per protocol, any system that could possibly have been compromised had been isolated and deactivated. Redundant systems were noted as running; the ship was as safe as it could be. Toggling windows, she checked on comms to the surface. Nothing. The lines were dead.

"Fuck," she said, turning back to Sinner. His body had finally stopped contorting, but his grey complexion and glazed over eyes seemed worse. Her heart pounding, Samantha stood perfectly still until she saw that his chest move. When she realized he was breathing, she let loose the lungful of air she hadn't realized she was holding.

Looking back to the monitor, she saw that comms to the surface were still dead. Engineering was in quarantine. She would have to go to the bridge to fly the ship, but Sinner could die if she left him alone. Then there was Alex and the rest of the crew down on the base. She knew she had orders to jump out of system if she thought they were compromised, but they might still be fighting down there. They might need her help. Samantha looked back to Sinner, and knew she had to make a choice.

"Well this just sucks."

It was an eventuality that they had not heavily trained for, so there was a delay in the reactions as the crew registered what the Skipper had ordered. Everyone except Gunnery Sergeant Chrom, that is. Experience had made Chrom well aware of the dangers of having a remote controlled robot in their midst. It was the very reason why the Marines still used people as ground forces: robots could be hacked.

She opened fire before the drone had a chance to target her, launching all of her remaining shoulder mounted rockets and depressing the trigger of her RFRG. Then she gave a mental command to drop-fire the smoke aerosols. It was classic Marine style, first take out the enemy then worry about defense.

Even as the stream of Chrom's bullets began to tear into its armor, the Combat Drone opened fire. Its lasers reflected off the OST-1012's armor, but the room was quickly filled with streams of armor piercing rounds from the robot's RFRGs. Fortunately, whoever was controlling the device was not a great aim. Chrom's own railgun hit home before the robot's fusion cannons came on line. The drone rocked backwards and fired wild. Even so, the room shook as the bolts of energy exploded into the far wall.

Then Chrom's rockets hit their mark. The room was quickly clouded with Chrom's smoke screen whose mirrored particle compound blocked the drone's optic ER sensors and providing cover from lasers. More explosions rocked the base as first Bowman, then D'Ascoine pelted the last known position of the Drone.

"Cease fire!" D'Ascoine gave the command when the Drone stopped firing. When the smoke cleared, charred pieces of drone littered the hall.

"Sound off!" Alex gave the command.

"Eagle Two, clear, but damaged," D'Ascoine said.

"Eagle Three, clear, but damaged, not injured," Chrom said.

"Eagle Four, clear," Bowman replied, but nothing followed where Eagle Five should have sounded. Equally there was no reply from the *Hunter*.

Alex was not surprised by the silence. He looked down and saw that Fran was still conscious, her face wracked in pain and her hands desperately clawing at the sides of her helmet. He began unlocking the helmet, confused as to why the kill button had not stopped the Feedback Assault. Once powered down, the DuZhodian device should not have sent any signals. It would have been different for most anyone else, since their implants could have been infected, but Fran was a natural. According to Colonel DuZhod, the device had no implanted components. Alex knew that Fran would never have agreed to it.

"Leftenant? Gunny? What is your status?" Alex asked as he broke Fran's helmet seal and threw it across the room.

"I'm afraid I've been hit, old boy," D'Ascoine replied, Alex looked up to see the shattered remains of the TOMO's combat helmet on the ground and blood trickling down D'Ascoine's forehead. "Nothing that serious, but still…."

Alex looked back at Fran, she had stopped writhing. She rolled onto her side and vomited, then placed a trembling hand on the ground in an attempt to steady herself.

"Corporal Bowman, examine the Leftenant's wounds." Alex ordered, turning his attentions to Chrom. Much of her ablative armor had been removed from the laser assault, and a serious scorch mark blazed across her left leg. Dents and small holes riddled the front of the OST-1012 armor.

"I'm fine, sir," she said, "The armor took all the damage, the leg was grazed by one of the plasma bolts, but not a direct hit. The suit will limp but I won't. None of the rounds penetrated the outer armor. I'm out of rockets, but fully operational."

"Delighted to hear it, Gunnery Sergeant," Alex responded. Looking at Harpur he saw her hold up her hand and nod, signaling she was okay, though clearly still unable to speak.

"Corporal Bowman, report."

"The Leftenant has some shrapnel in the scalp. Bits of helmet sir, but nothing seems to have gone into the skull."

"As I said, sir, just a flesh wound."

"Still, watch yourself," Alex said, "and you keep an eye on him as well, Corporal. Now, Harpur?"

"I'll be," she started, but her own coughing interrupted, "I'll be fine sir."

"Give yourself a dose of medi-drug, you too, Leftenant, and both of you break out your bubble helmets," Alex ordered. The flexible plastic bubbles would seal their suits and provide protection against gas or the vacuum of space, but gave no defense against bullets, shrapnel or any other assaults on the wearer's head.

"Sir? I could wear my helmet," Fran pointed out as she pulled the folded clear plastic bubble from the pocket on her right thigh.

"No, the effects of the cyber-assault stopped when we took off the helmet," Alex said, "I fear the virus might have infected the DuZhod interface firmware inside it; the programs that allow the transceivers to broadcast into your brain. It's not worth the risk. Now, we have got to get out of here on the double. Ammo count, if you will."

They took turns checking their rounds as they made their way out of the wrecked dining hall. Alex cursed at the result. They were running low on ammo, half of their fire-power was now destroyed, two of his people were wounded, and they had lost the element of surprise. On a different front, it was clear that the intel download had been interrupted before all the information had been gathered, and they were still some way away from freeing the captives. Added to all this was the fact they were out of communication with the *Hunter*, and, of course, had still not found the Dalang. All told, things were not particularly good.

Though Alex's assessment of their position was correct, he had been wrong about the helmet's firmware. The fact that the feedback assault ended when he removed the helmet was coincidence. The attack had stopped because the anti-virus software in the nanotech computer network implanted in Fran's nervous system had finally been able to neutralize the assaulting program. Since, however, neither she nor Alex knew that the implants had been installed, his observation had made sense. Had Sinner been there, he would have noted the fault in the logic, but the Chief would never find out the details of that attack.

CHAPTER 59

Alex took point with Bowman at his side. There were hundreds of drawbacks to putting the CO in the line of fire, but with the drone gone, D'Ascoine and Harpur using bubble helmets, and Chrom's armor damaged to the point of near-uselessness, there wasn't much of a choice. Besides, morale was a key factor now, and having the ranking officer lead from the front would boost spirits.

Behind Alex and Bowman came Chrom, whose suit's added height allowed her to shoot over their heads. Next was Fran, the most vulnerable of the lot of them. She tried to use the keyboard and pop-up monitor of the DuZhod computer, but had limited results. Her link into the hardline network had been severed, and everything but their line of sight communicators was being jammed. Even so, she tried to re-hack the system, or at least identify a new data point where she could try to break back into their main network. She said that every now and then she thought she saw a ghost image in her mind of what was displayed on the monitor, but Alex suggested that was some hallucinatory residual effect.

D'Ascoine took up the rear, walking backwards and occasionally leaving booby traps in their wake.

Every few minutes Alex tried to raise the ship, but whoever was jamming them was good enough to ensure that no such contact could be made. Whatever else was happening, he hoped that Samantha had kept the *Hunter* safe and was preparing to jump away. Harpur had managed to download and transmit about half of the base's data before the ECM assault had taken over the drone and broken their contact. Now, it was Samantha's duty to return that information to Ripper's Raiders, ensuring that they could track and shut down this operation.

He hoped she would follow those orders. She would make a fine commander, but she was attached to her crew. He worried she might undertake a foolhardy "rescue" rather than staying on mission. Of course, maybe putting the lives of the crew first wasn't such a bad thing. Maybe if he had... Alex drove such thoughts from his head. He didn't have time for self-doubt or questioning, at least, not at the moment.

It didn't take them long to make their way to the launch bay, and the lack of resistance they met gave Alex some hope that they had managed to wipe out much of the base's compliment in the Dining room. Even so, he did not let his guard down, nor did anyone else. They passed through an observation lounge and saw the three ships on the launch pad. The personal yacht and armed merchant both had the markings of Cameron-Inglesie Distributors. Behind them, the rest of the bay was blocked out by the enormous shape of the Rendithi Sleeper ship.

"Sir?" Fran said, "I think there's a high level data point in the cargo bay on the level just below us. If these diagrams are still valid, then I'm sure I could regain access there."

"How long would it take you to crack the system and download the rest of the data?"

"I don't know, sir. The cracking won't take long, but the download depends on how much info is in the system. About as long as before I would think."

"We will give it a shot, but rescuing those Rendithi is now our prime objective."

"Well, if the diagrams are right, sir, there should be access to the landing pad through that bay."

"Sir?" D'Ascoine said, sounding somewhat surprised, "What about the Dalang?"

"We will get what we can, Leftenant, but this base has been compromised and we can ill afford to think that the terrorists are fools. We will get the Rendithi out of here and Sir Richard, or whoever is captive, if we can. Then, if the *Hunter* is still about, we will nuke the site. The loss of any additional intel will be regrettable, but not as regrettable as the loss of civilian life, or ours for that matter. Now let's move out! The plans that our intrepid Harpur has obtained show a stairwell in the corner that should lead down to the cargo bay."

Alex noted that Fran smiled at his compliment; a smile that broadened when the plans she found proved correct. He was glad to see it, especially after she had been the focus of an attack. He was very pleased with Harpur; she was made of stern stuff.

They went down one level to the bottom of the stairwell and made ready to enter the cargo bay. Bowman sent his fibre-optic probe around the corner of the slightly opened door. After a second, he quickly withdrew the probe and backed up fast.

"Take cover!"

As they dove out of the direct line of the door, it burst asunder. Fire and fragments of airlock cut through the bottom of the stairwell. The sound of gunfire and ricochets immediately followed and they were all forced to crouch behind the little cover that the battered doorframe gave them. Alex was just about to order a retreat up the stairs when he heard the sound of clinking metal coming down them. He looked up and saw several small objects bouncing down the steps.

"Grenades!" he shouted, and covered his head.

The blast collapsed the bottom flight of stairs, burying Sergeant Chrom in a pile of rubble. Fortunately the ordinance available to the terrorists was not as high quality as that carried by Imperial personnel. The Federalists above them only had fragmentation grenades, and the stairs had blocked most of the blast. Only Bowman had been hit by the burning shrapnel, and the anti-personnel rounds could not penetrate the heavy armor of his OS-745. But the Corporal's armor could not stop the bruising and concussion, and he was momentarily dazed.

Alex was the first to react. Rolling onto his back, he saw movement two flights up and launched his AAR-5's flash-bang grenades towards the target. Explosions and screams followed, telling him that the terrorists above them had been temporarily stunned by the bright lights and concussive noise of his attack.

"Cover me!" D'Ascoine ordered, wholly inappropriately, and threw aside the twisted remains of his combat rifle.

Before anyone could react, the Leftenant was on his feet: the long, heavy, army FAP-17 pistol in his right hand and the more compact PPL-110 Naval issue handgun in his left. Alex watched in horror as his so-called Tactical Officer charged into the enemy kill zone through the doorway with his handguns blazing. There was no way in which Fotheringday or anyone else could provide suppressing fire. He fully expected to see the bloodied and charred remains of his third in command come flying back through the door.

"You stupid son-of-a-bitch," Chrom muttered as she watched the army officer run to certain death. Covered by rubble and debris, the Gunnery Sergeant kept her wits about her as she watched events unfold from the feeds she was receiving from the other members of the assault team. She had been splitting her attention between the small windows of information she obtained from her squad after the stairwell collapse. As a result, when she saw her troop commander charge into the line of fire, she knew he only had one chance, and that was simply because the combined audacity and stupidity of the charge had caught the enemy off guard. Unfairly cursing the entirety of the Army, the officer corps and whatever divine force had put this fool in command of her, Chrom reacted with a response that proved the faith that her superiors had placed in her was well founded.

The Federalists barely had time to notice the gallant and foolish officer charging into their sights before their attention was ripped away by the mammoth figure of an OST-1012 rising from the rubble of the collapsed stairwell, dust billowing out from her like smoke from a demon. Neither did they have time to target the new menace before it opened fire with the RFRG, sending a stream of high velocity armor piercing rounds into the open space of the cargo bay. The few Feddies who didn't duck for cover, targeted the threat of the Gunnery Sergeant instead of the bravado of the Leftenant. Most of those were sliced in half by Chrom's deadly volley, but some bullets bounced off her ten-twelve, and an Armor Piercing High Explosive grenade was launched into the stairwell. Chrom saw it and threw herself on top of the Captain as it exploded at the back of the now shattered staircase. The still undamaged rear of her ten-twelve stopped the blast, saving both her and Fotheringday from certain death.

What saved Fran was a combination of inexperience and the slight concussive daze that came from her lack of a protective helmet. Temporarily deafened by the explosions and seeing an officer charging into the fray, Fran simply followed D'Ascoine into the killing zone, firing her own AAR-5 as she charged. A small figure in the smoke, no one noticed her in the slightest. When D'Ascoine paused for a second in the center of the room, Fran tugged on his arm and led him to the data point that she had somehow remembered as the purpose for their coming to this bay in the first place. Fortunately, it was positioned by a door and within a slight alcove that provided reasonable cover for the two of them. D'Ascoine opened fire, while Fran stared blankly at the outlet. After several seconds of dazed gawping, she remembered why she wanted to get to the data point and jacked the DuZhodian device into the wall.

"Are you alright, sir?" Chrom asked as the smoke cleared.

"I'm fine, Sergeant. Yourself?" Alex asked, checking the views and status monitors on all of his crew. He was shocked to find them still alive.

"Nominal," she replied, and rolled off her CO to take cover behind the rubble and target the enemy through the doorway.

"Corporal?"

"Uninjured, sir."

Checking the feeds from his crew, Alex noted that Bowman had one of the upper doorways covered, and that D'Ascoine and Harpur had managed to take cover in an alcove. He moved to cover a second open doorway above them, and called for all his units to sound off and give status. They were now separated, trapped, and running low on ammunition.

Their only advantage was that Harpur had somehow managed to get access to a data point. Working without the aid of a direct interface, she was madly typing commands into the DuZhodian device, desperately trying to re-hack the system. D'Ascoine had taken her combat rifle and was harassing the enemy with it, but none of their fire presently had much effect. The Federalist defenders had erected a wall of armored riot shields across the cargo bay, giving them reliable cover from all but the Gunny's weapon. Even so, she had to target the RFRG on a single shield for almost three seconds before even her rounds penetrated, and she was running low on bullets. Alex cursed as he realized that it was only a matter of time before the enemy could bring enough firepower on them to take advantage of their predicament.

"Corporal, on my mark, you and I will fire our remaining APHE grenades at the shield wall, then we'll aim over the wall, dropping grenades behind: a flash-bang each and three fragmentation grenades before we head back to cover. Gunnery Sergeant, take advantage of any holes we make."

"Roger that."

"Sir," Bowman added, "I'll have to reload my grenade magazine."

"Understood, let me know when you are set," Alex said, hoping that D'Ascoine would catch on to the strategy. The Leftenant was out of their line of sight, and signal jamming stopped them from using the broadcast signals. When Bowman gave the word, Alex nodded and began the count.

"Three, two, one.... MARK!"

Alex and Bowman both rolled around their respective corners and unloaded their heaviest remaining munitions at their attackers. Alex fired three armor piercing high explosive grenades into the shield wall, Bowman managed two. They then both fired grenades over the shield wall.

The APHE grenades had the desired effect, punching holes through the armored shields, breaching the wall and giving Chrom targets for her deadly RFRG. When the flash-bangs went off, however, Alex was disappointed. While screams of eye-blinding pain did come from many of the enemy, many others clearly were unaffected by the blasts.

Flash-suppressors! Alex cursed. When the fragmentation grenades went off with a similarly limited effect, he realized that some of the defenders were dressed in combat armor.

The breach of the shield wall gave Chrom new opportunities, however, and where the defender's combat armor was proof against a few fragmentation grenades, it was no protection against the munitions of her RFRG. There were only a few gaps in the shield wall, but the sudden death that followed was almost enough to break the enemy morale.

Almost, but the crew of the *Hunter* could not keep the assault up for long.

"Fuck! Out of ammo!" came the devastating report from Chrom.

"Corporal! Suppressing fire," Alex ordered.

He and Bowman rolled back away from their walls, laying down a range of fragmentation grenades and flash-bangs; firing as they could into the rapidly filling holes in the defense wall. Chrom used the brief covering fire to unhitch her empty RFRG and pull out her lightweight Mark 4 combat rifle. Designed as a backup for heavy-weapons specialists such as herself, it had no grenade launcher and only a single clip, but was easily carried without encumbering the wearer. She opened fire once she was free of the heavy accelerator rifle, but it had little effect.

"Ammunitions check," Alex ordered.

"Bullets: two APHE clips, four AP clips," Chrom began, "three fragmentation hand grenades, three flash-bangs, and two fuel-air hand grenades."

"I've got three clips of APHE rounds, one normal sabot, two flash-bangs mag-launcher grenades, two frag hand grenades and that's it," the Corporal reported.

Alex checked his own supply, saw he had plenty of bullets, but no grenades of any sorts left. He reported this to his crew and tried to define a tactic to use while keeping up his suppressing fire. Running through the weapons they had left, no clear tactic came to Alex's mind. Bullets alone would not win the day. Hand grenades were powerful enough to penetrate the heavy armor of the Feddies, but his team didn't have enough to make a difference. The fuel-air grenades could bring down the whole cargo bay, which would kill his own people along with the enemy. Still, that would serve a good last ditch response if all else failed; after all, there was no chance the Wayang would let them live even if they surrendered. The best hope remained in Fran and her attempts to crack her way into the base's controls.

Alex was issuing orders to conserve ammo when there was movement on the landing above them. Bowman turned quickly and threw one of his hand grenades onto the overhanging platforms. Rubble and body parts fell, but bullets were soon firing down at them. Alex was just about to aid Bowman in returning fire when he noted the airlock door behind the remnants of the enemy shield wall opening. *Blast! Reinforcements!*

Stepping though the airlock into the combat filled cargo bay of the base, Samantha held down the trigger of her heavy laser and swept the rear of the enemy position. Lingering smoke from the grenades and gunfire highlighted the four centimeter diameter beam as it cauterized its way through combatant after combatant. Here and there, the beam diffracted off those clad in combat armor, sending bright flashes in strange angles, but Samantha ignored this and continued cutting a trough of burning death through the backs of her enemies.

It had not been easy for her to leave Sinner alone and at death's door, but in the end she couldn't abandon Alex and the others. Neither could she let a whole shipload of innocent civilians die at the hands of terrorists. She had EVAed straight from the ship to the base, gambling that the on-going raid would distract the enemy. She won that bet, and now coldly cut a slow fiery path into the backs of the men and women who sullied the name of democracy.

For five seconds Samantha hosed down the enemy line, cutting in half no less than fifteen of the enemy. By the time the survivors realized that they were being attacked from the rear, it was too late. When they turned to face her, she met them with another devastating attack.

Samantha adjusted the focus of her laser to its widest setting and fired off a series of single shots. The broad-beam attack would not even have caused second degree burn in unarmored targets, but the intensity of the light was more than enough to overcome the flash suppressors. Blinded and screaming, the few terrorists who managed to get off shots hit nothing but wall.

Stepping backwards out of the room, Samantha tossed three APHE grenades into the room and took cover behind the doorframe. As the detonations sounded, she slipped the laser into its battery backpacked holster and pulled out her pistol and drusus. Stepping back into the room, she finished off the enemies in front of her with a slow and steady ruthlessness that spoke of the hatred in her soul.

"Eagle One, this is Osprey, the cargo bay is clear," Samantha reported, her own communications overwhelming the radio-jamming of the enemy.

"All hands take cover!" came Alex's fast and clear response.

Bowman and Fotheringday raced rapidly out into the room while Chrom pulled a large grenade from her ammo belt and threw it hard up the stairwell. The sergeant leapt out of the staircase and dove for the ground.

The powered arm of the OST-1012 helped the Gunnery Sergeant to throw the fuel-air grenade forty meters up before it activated. It sprayed a fine mist of particles and flammable liquid for two seconds before igniting the combustible mix. The resulting explosion was vast, and the following implosion ripped down the superstructure of the stairwell, collapsing portions of the base, and filling the landing with rubble. There was no longer any concern of an assault from that front.

"I say, old girl, I never thought I'd be so glad to see you!" D'Ascoine said, breaking radio protocol.

"I thought I ordered you to return to Lai-Jung if we were compromised?" Alex said as he looked up toward his Executive Officer.

"Those were your standing orders, sir." Samantha began, but did not get a chance to finish her explanation.

Alyiar smiled as he watched the combat unfold. He smiled as he saw the Dalang and his terrorcrats desperately attempting to defend against the Imperial bastards, he smiled as he saw each side think it was about to win. None of them would win. He would.

He turned to the fuel controls of the Rendethi ship and adjusted them fully. Little green bars of light shot upwards, becoming yellow, then orange, then red. When more of the ship's safeties engaged, he flicked them off. Claxons sounded through engineering, gases suddenly vented through places in the ship. Lastly, he pulled a physical lever that was the very final defense.

"*You are all alike*," he said as the fusion reaction began to careen out of control, "*traitors to the people you swore to defend, or free, or liberate. Now, you will all die.*"

A white blinding light filled his mind, but there was no pain. No agony, no burning. Alyiar was glad. He didn't mind suffering himself, but many of the Wayang soldiers who still fought were simply duped as he was. Many of the Federalist regulars fighting the Imperial bastards were innocent of anything but fighting for a cause. He didn't want his comrades to suffer.

CHAPTER 60

"*Why am I still alive?*" Alyiar asked. The white light had continued far longer than it should have. Nuclear reactions took place near the speed of light, he shouldn't have been able to think.

Slowly, the light faded. He was in a small brightly colored garden. A fluffy pink bunny hopped its way along the grass. Neon colored flowers lined the path. A bright green hedge lined a garden. A cold horrible chill ran down Alyiar's spine.

He looked down at his long ectomorphic hands. They were slowly shifting back to mesomorphic proportions, the black spiraling tattoos gradually fading. From somewhere deep in his memory, his body was returning to its original shape: the shape it had before he was recruited. A moment later, he was a teenage boy of no more than fifteen.

"*Checkmate.*"

The gruff man's voice came from behind him. A girl's laughter followed. Alyiar spun around. He saw an opening in a softly colored hedge. He followed a path through to another garden as a bird with glowing blue plumage flew overhead.

A polar bear sat at a table playing a game with a cartoonesque teenaged girl. They looked up at him and smiled. The girl giggled. Alyiar thought she looked familiar.

"*Checkmate*," the bear said. The girl laughed. They were on a loop.

"*A signature*," Alyiar said as he walked over to them, "*The fuckers left me a goddamn signature*"

Projected on the table was an image stolen from his own eyes: the ceiling of the Rendethi engineering room. The girl giggled. Out there, in the real world, he was laying limp and motionless on the floor of the sleeper ship. Here, trapped in a virtual world, pastel colored tears began to roll down his digital eyes.

"*I was infected when Rubo and the others were.*"

"*Checkmate*," the bear said.

The girl laughed. Alyiar screamed.

Fran was kneeling on the ground, typing madly into the DuZhodian device when she heard the airlock open behind her. Up until that point, only two things had mattered to her, cracking the network and the strange way she was doing it. She had known that if she could gain control of the security systems, she could do far more to help the fight than her pathetic efforts with a gun. So she focused her mind despite the screams, explosions and desperate combat occurring around her.

It had proven easier than she imagined, but hacking the network had still remained hard. On more than one occasion she had nearly managed to crack the system when someone had countered her. Whoever was working the defences was good, not as good as Sinner or Lieutenant Smith, but better than she was. That had made Fran focus even more greatly, so much so that she barely noticed that some of the code was being written while she was concentrating on other algorithms. It even took her a moment to realize that some of the windows she had opened appeared to be hovering in the air, and not held within the confines of the screen built into the DuZhodian device. It was as if she was still receiving signals directly from the odd machine. A part of her shuddered at the realization that such a thing required implants, but her consciousness repressed that knowledge to deal with once they were safe.

Instead, Fran became so absorbed in her task that she did not notice Lieutenant Smith entering the room, nor even the ground shaking blast as the fuel-air grenade went off. What she did notice was that whoever was countering her programming seemed to stop. That made her hacking that much easier. The small part of her mind that was aware of the world outside her virtual reality attributed the disappearance of her nemesis to having been killed in the explosion.

When the gunfire suddenly stopped, however, she looked up from her monitor to see Lieutenant Smith speaking to the Skipper in the middle of the room. Gunny Chrom was picking herself off the floor while Bowman was securing the rest of the room. Fran smiled and refocused her attention on hacking, then she heard the sliding of the door. Before she turned to look, she felt the hard probing metal of a gun barrel press against the soft plastic of her emergency bubble helmet.

"Don't move," came the voice behind her.

She decided to obey. To Fran's side she could see D'Ascoine drop the AAR-5 and slowly raise his hands as a combat rifle was similarly pressed against his head. Gradually he sunk to his knees.

"I suggest you tell your people to drop their weapons, Alex," a voice said from behind her, "This is a detonator, and if I let go, the Rendithi ship will explode."

"On your knees, Lord D'Ascoine," the other man said.

Neither one was in armor or even a pressure suit, but both were armed, and both seemed deadly serious. Fran raised her hands from the keyboard and in her mind's eye stretched out her consciousness, trying to connect into her shipmates' comms systems. To a mixture of horror and relief, she found it worked. She opened windows that showed images from her crewmates' combat video systems and suppressed a shudder. Dread filled her as the certain knowledge that DuZhod had penetrated her brain with nanobots sank in. She drove out the thoughts of tiny spider-like robots running through her skull, and concentrated on what the views of her shipmates told her.

Only two men had entered the room, one held the rifle at D'Ascoine's head, the second held a detonator in one hand and pressed a pistol to her head with the other. Though she had never seen them in person, Fran immediately recognized them both. Her own captor was Sir Richard Al-Escobar, while the Leftenant was held by Kyle Hammond. Fran listened as she focused her attention on Sir Richard, his pistol and most of all, the detonator. It was a dead-man's brake, the kind of device that was triggered if the wielder released their hold.

This totally sucks, Fran thought to herself, but immediately returned her attentions to the virtual universe, searching out some way to direct the base's defense systems against her captors.

"*Unless you want to get shot, I suggest you stop right now*!" a broadcast voice entered her mind. She noted that Hammond afforded her a quick glare. She shrugged in response. Looking to D'Ascoine, she saw that he was pale and trembling. She felt a new fear rise up inside in response.

"Both of you," Alex said, the feeling of betrayal sinking deep into his soul. He had always suspected it, but had hoped that one of them had not been part of the conspiracy, "You are both the Dalang."

"Actually neither of us are," Sir Richard said, "The Dalang is a computer program created by Hammond here, but I suppose as far as us being in command of the Wayang Insurgency, you do have a point."

"You bloody bastards. How many people have you killed?"

"Every war has casualties, Alex," Hammond responded.

"Not every war deliberately targets civilians," Alex said.

"Neither do we," Hammond said.

"What about that Rendithi Sleeper?"

"Them?" Sir Richard responded, "They're not even human. A small price to pay for freedom from tyranny."

"You're disgusting," Samantha said, "You just justify your actions as it suits you don't you, Richard? Those are sentient beings on that ship."

"Ainsley?" Sir Richard paled as he recognized her voice.

"May I introduce Lieutenant Smith, Imperial Naval Intelligence," Alex said, baiting his one-time friend as he tried to buy time, "you didn't really think a woman like that could fall for a man like you did you?"

Sir Richard looked like he might vomit. For a moment, Alex thought he was going to shoot Fran or release the detonator, but he didn't. Instead he began to sneer at Alex's XO.

"You bloody Imperialists with your bleeding heart sympathies and your anthropomorphisms," Sir Richard said, shaking his head, "You think anything that speaks has the same rights? A bloody computer can speak, that doesn't mean that it has a soul."

"Actually, Richard, I'm more of a Egalitist myself," Samantha said.

Chrom stood primed and ready for action. To her side, she noted that Bowman was similarly examining the situation, judging the distance to his rifle, his hand hovering near the butt of his sidearm. Chrom, however, had an advantage in the wide array of sensors and heightened reflexes of her OST-1012. She used all of her suit's active systems to try and find a weakness in the hostage takers. A combination of radar, sonar and different optic sensors gave her a full 3D image of the scene unfolding around her. She looked desperately for some opening she could take advantage of, but the deadman's brake held her at bay. She timed the speed at which her suit enhanced reflexes could react, compared them to the time it would take to release the trigger, and realized that she could do nothing from where she stood. So instead she listened as they droned on.

Leave it to the fucking hierarchs to have a political debate in the middle of a combat! Chrom thought as she triggered her suit's injectors to send a blend of combat drug and amphetamines into her bloodstream.

"Egalitists!" Hammond said, tapping the muzzle of his gun into D'Ascoine's head, "You sit back and use Sentient Rights as an excuse to let the rest of humanity suffer the yoke of tyranny."

"Federalists are somehow better?" Alex said, "The Egalitists stay within the law, they don't commit murder to force their will upon the majority."

"And neither do we!" Hammond shouted.

"What do you call piracy?" Samantha asked, noting that Sir Richard had grown very quiet.

"Oh, we may disrupt trade, but we target those vessels that support the repression of the masses!"

"And how did the *Silver Slipper* fit into that?" Alex asked, "What about all those people you helped to kill. They weren't all aliens, nor were they carrying weapons. They were men, women and children simply trying to live their lives."

"What are you talking about?" Hammond asked.

"The *Silver Slipper?* Have you killed so many people that you don't remember them? Or hadn't Richard recruited you by that point?"

"Of course I remember the *Silver Slipper*," Hammond said, confusion on his face, "But–."

"Hah!" Sir Richard said, slowly shaking his head, "Don't you get it Kyle? He's blaming the *Silver Slipper* episode on us!

You think we betrayed you. Oh, how rich. How ironic. Alex you egotistical sod, we didn't plan the *Silver Slipper.* And here's another little news flash for you. I didn't recruit Kyle, Kyle recruited me! As far as us planning the failure of the *Silver Slipper* mission, neither one of us were even involved with the Federalists then. No Alex, we were loyal and true Naval officers when you launched that little disaster."

"You lie very convincingly, Richard," Alex said, but he had known Richard Al-Escobar for a long time; he sensed the honesty in the man's words.

"He's telling the truth, Alex," Hammond said, "It was the *Silver Slipper* that made me realize how unjust the entire Imperial system was. Here I was, a lowly commoner who had worked his way up through the ranks only to have his chance at command taken away from him when a hierarch wanted the post, but I could handle that. Hell, I was even loyal to you, and defended your actions all the way through the trial. But then, when the trial was over, you ponced on with your life and career while everyone around you was punished for your mistake."

"What are you talking about?" Alex said, "I ensured that no one other than myself was disciplined for that action."

"Oh, yes, and what a disciplining it was eh? A real slap on the wrist!" Sir Richard said, punctuating his words by hitting the gun into Fran's head, "Look at you now! CO of a highly prestigious Intelligence team in the most coveted fleet in the Empire!"

"I spent two years on a cargo vessel," Alex objected. It sounded flat even to him.

"Two years?" Hammond continued, "How horrible for you. What you, with your family's wealth to fall back on? What ever would you do? Leave the Navy and have to be content with your vast wealth and ruling your corner of the galaxy? My career, Ritchie's career, everyone who served under or above you, we were ruined! Poisoned by the paint of your brush! Ritchie was posted in a port to a position below his rank, while me? I had the joy of serving on board a

Systemboat tender. You have no idea how thrilling it is to load munitions onto defense boats. I even got to be told by my CO that I would be lucky if I rose to the rank of Executive Officer on a cargo ship! That's when I realized how intrinsically unfair the whole thing was. No Alex, we didn't ruin your career, you ruined ours!"

"And that justifies your acts of piracy?" Samantha said, taking a step forward, "The fact that you even view that episode in terms of your careers rather than the lives that were lost speaks of something, don't you think?"

"It doesn't matter," Alex said. He felt a horrible sinking in his heart as he realized they spoke the truth. He tried to put his personal feelings of failure aside. "No matter how you justify it, and regardless of whether it was even right or wrong, it is over now. You are trapped. Even if you were to get away, your lives are ruined, your ill gotten gains will be confiscated. You are done. Unless, of course, you can offer us any larger fish."

"Betray the cause to save our necks? You really don't understand the common folk do you?" Hammond said, but Sir Richard glanced in his direction.

"Immunity from prosecution?" Sir Richard asked.

"Unlikely," Samantha said. Alex noted her hand twitched.

"You don't know what I have to offer."

"Ritchie,." Hammond said with warning, taking his eyes off of D'Ascoine for a moment.

Alex looked at Sir Richard and realized his former commander and friend knew something of value. Ritchie knew the intelligence community too well, he knew bluffing would only ensure harsher interrogation. What was more, despite Hammond's talk of commoners, Sir Richard was still a hierarch. Regardless of their democratic rhetoric, the Federalists were still elitist in their own way; he might have made high level contacts.

"What do you have to offer that is bigger than yourself?" Alex asked with irony, "Eleanor Allevi?"

"Oh, Alex, it's bigger than that," Richard said, his smirk returning.

"You son-of-a-bitch!" Hammond said, and suddenly shifted his aim from D'Ascoine to Sir Richard.

Chrom watched D'Ascoine very carefully. At first she feared he would do something courageously stupid; then she saw he was pale and trembling ever so slightly.

As Hammond grew excited, he tapped the muzzle of his gun into D'Ascoine's head. The TOMO flinched with each blow. For a moment, Chrom thought that the Army Hierarch would cry. Then, Hammond switched his aim from D'Ascoine to Sir Richard.

"Oh fuck," Chrom muttered as she saw the realization of freedom come into D'Ascoine's eyes. A heartbeat later D'Ascoine leapt into action and dove for cover as best he could. Chrom froze, her eyes still on the detonator.

The sudden leap by D'Ascoine was enough to cause a momentary hesitation in Hammond. That was an opportunity that Sir Richard was not going to let pass. He had seen the motion of his comrade-in-arms, and known that Hammond was enough of a zealot to ensure their mutual death in the name of the cause. Sir Richard was a pragmatist. He had not helped create the Dalang, nor joined the 'Federalist cause' for freedom or civil rights or any of the nonsensical excuses that Kyle used to justify his actions. Sir Richard had joined out of a desire for power. He was not going to risk his life for some foolhardy idealism, and he knew that Hammond was fully aware of that. Kyle was going to kill him unless he acted quickly. Fortunately, he had already planned for such a standoff.

As Kyle Hammond was distracted by the sudden motion of D'Ascoine, Sir Richard raised his gun and fired twice. The first round went into Hammond's chest, the second into his skull. What happened next, however, surprised Sir Richard totally.

Fran sat quietly fighting down her fears as she carefully watched the events unfold. She knew her duty, and she had known what she would do from the moment that she realized the two might turn on each other.

When she felt Sir Richard's pistol leave her head and target Hammond, Fran spun around and grabbed the detonator in Sir Richard's hand. She clasped both of her hands over the hierarch's grasp, and ensured that he could not release his grip to detonate the bomb. At once, the others sprung into action. Chrom leapt across the room to tackle the surviving terrorist, Alex and Bowman both grabbed for their weapons, and Samantha drew the laser from its holster, but it was Sir Richard who responded first.

Feeling the sudden grip on his hand, Sir Richard turned his weapon back onto Fran and pulled the trigger. A pink cloud erupted from her bubble helm. Red globules formed in the low gravity, creating a momentary arc that trailed after her falling form. It did not take long for Fran's face to be obscured by the blood that filled her helmet.

Inside the shattered remnants of her skull, the DuZhodian nano-bots sent a backup to the computer-like central control box. Then they began to devour the network and implants that they had made before finally self-destructing. No one would ever know that they had intruded into her body, but the system would download all it observed next time it came into contact with any member of the Interactive.

The rest of the crew was already set in motion. Chrom was fast, the first to react, the first to move. She knew her mission and had prioritized her objectives: save the Rendithi, obtain data, and protect her crewmates. She cringed as she watched herself fail in two of these even as she reached her target. Fran died just before Chrom's own hands were clasped around the detonator and the force of her momentum pulled Sir Richard wildly. At once Sir Richard's head exploded with fire as it was suddenly struck dead in the center by Samantha's laser.

Alex froze and stood staring for a moment. Harpur was dead, her body sprawled like a broken doll. So were Hammond and Sir Richard, and with them whatever secrets they had fought over. He supposed it was possible that the information was in data they had managed to retrieve, but he doubted it. The rest had probably been deleted by this point.

He looked towards Samantha, whose shot had either been exceptionally well aimed or particularly unfortunate. There was a deep seated fury in her eyes as she stared at Sir Richard's corpse. As for Alex, his eyes were drawn back to Fran.

"I've neutralized the detonator, sir." Gunny Chrom's announcement pulled Alex from his thoughts.

"Secure the perimeter," he heard himself order. He felt dead.

D'Ascoine came to his feet and responded with the Marines. Samantha simply walked over to Harpur, Hammond and Sir Richard's bodies. Smoke still rose from Richard's neck, while pools of blood flowed from the other two.

"Dirty fucking bastards," Samantha said with utter hatred in her eyes, "They used a cause to justify their means, but they were no freedom fighters. They were nothing but murders, betraying everything that they say they stood for."

"Indeed."

EPILOGUE

Mr. Robert T. Harpur and Mrs. Hela Green
HabUn 47832
Springfield Enclosure
Highfield Park Arcology, Lyndeswurl PLC
Carlowth Subsector
Sophyan Sector
Day 027, Year 34(IC)
Dear Mr. and Mrs Harpur,

It is with the greatest sorrow and deepest sympathy that I write to inform you of the death of your daughter Fran. Of all the duties one faces as an officer, the hardest is this, the informing of the family of a shipmate that their child has passed on. In this case, however, it is especially so due to the fondness that I, and the whole crew of the *HMS Hunter* felt for your daughter. Fran was a remarkable young woman, which you no doubt knew. She had a promising career within the service and I was intending to recommend her for Officer's Candidate School at the end of the mission that took her life. Yet, I had more than respect for Fran's abilities: I liked her, as did the whole crew. She was bright, cheerful, and a joy to be with. We shall all miss her greatly.

I am afraid that at this juncture, matters of security do not allow me to discuss the manner of her death, though in due course I believe that these restrictions will be lifted. I can say, however, that Fran not only died in the line of duty, but she died a true hero. She willingly and willfully placed herself at risk to literally save the lives of thousands of defenseless Imperial citizens. No doubt that is of little comfort, but perhaps I can provide some solace by giving you my word as an officer, and an Imperial hierarchy, that her death was sudden and painless. Other than that, I know that no words that I can offer will ever lessen that sorrow, nor reduce your loss. I am so terribly sorry.

With Deepest Sympathies,
Lord COM Raiden Alexander Parviz Fotheringday, INI
Eorl of Hammonrie
CO-HMS Hunter

It was the third time that week that Hela had read the letter. She slowly put it down and looked at the varying other materials in the communiqué. There were press reports telling of the destruction of an insurgency network, the taking of a terrorist base, the rescue of a Rendithi sleeper ship, and the loss of a brave young Able Technician whose name was withheld until her next of kin could be notified. There was a letter informing her that her daughter had been selected to receive the Emperor's Bloodcast Imperial Nova with Trinary Cluster (posthumous), the highest award in the Empire, for actions above and beyond the call of duty. With it was an invitation to the ceremony on Sophya where Hela and her husband would be given the commendation for their daughter's heroism by the Emperor himself.

None of this meant much to Hela Green. She tossed it aside to look at the holo-images and streaming videos that her CO had also included in the package. Feeling empty and numb, hollow and dead, Hela looked through the images of her daughter and waited for the tears to flow, but they would not. Gods how she wished they would. It was not that Hela did not feel the grief, she did. It was tearing her up inside, eating at her heart like a horrible cancer. Sometimes all she could do was sit and stare, sometimes she just performed the duties like an automaton. Yet she could not cry. She had too much to do, too many people to tell, too much information and too many feelings to process. So she clung to her grief and let it devour her.

Her daughter was dead, her precious little Francie was gone. Hela would gladly have traded every one of those Rendithi lives, or whole worlds of men and women, just to see Fran one more time. No medals, no ceremonies, no pride would ever make that right. Her darling little daughter was dead.

Samantha stood with Sinner on the balcony of her apartment, staring out at the mixture of city lights and forested hills beyond them in the failing light of the evening. She was out of uniform, wearing a set of light shorts and a sleeveless shirt ideal for the muggy weather that hugged the town where she kept her small place near the port city. Sinner wore a light T-shirt and some cargo pants; regardless of the heat, he avoided shorts like the plague.

"So they were both the Dalang." Sinner asked as he took a slug of his beer.

"That's how it seems," Samantha answered, staring out at the lights, "The diatribes were given by a low grade AI running a sim of the Dalang. That's why they sounded so unoriginal, they were just auto-synthesized from other speeches."

"And Hammond served as the Linking Agent?" Sinner asked as he took a slug of his beer, "the liaison with the core Federalist network, while Sir Richard ran this particular cell?"

"Pretty much," Samantha answered, swirling the beer around in its can. Her mind was on other things. "But only after the *Silver Slipper* incident. What we found in the files matched what they said in the end. Hammond was turned first, out of a sense of injustice as to what happened while serving under Alex."

"Alex?" Sinner said with a smirk as he leaned against the railing, "How long you and the Skipper been on a first name basis?"

Samantha sighed, and stared him in the eye. Things had not been the same since the mission to the base, since she had chosen the civilians and the rest of the crew over his life. He said he understood why she had left him. He said that the civvies and the mission had to come first, but both of them knew it wasn't that simple. She had left him to die and that had changed everything. Sinner shook his head and looked away.

Samantha sipped her beer before continuing. "Hammond recruited Sir Richard shortly there after. Richard was the key, not only did he have access to intelligence from three different fleets, he could also provide an extensive transport network through his family's company. His merchant ships served as both cover and as a conduit for smuggling and piracy, while he kept the Federalists informed of Naval operations against them."

"So why did he leave the fleet?" Sinner asked, still staring out to the city. In the distance a siren wailed.

"Greed and power," Samantha said, "Hammond was a true believer, but Sir Richard was simply self-serving. He didn't care about the cause, he was trying to play both sides against the middle. He was interested in profit and prestige, and simply used revolutionary rhetoric to make himself feel better, if that. It was probably just a form of advertising."

"You think he was really gonna turn to state's evidence?"

"Without a doubt," Samantha said, looking Sinner straight in the eye, "That's what led to the final conflict between Hammond and Al-Escobar. Hammond was dedicated to the cause, he saw the Skipper and what happened at the *Silver Slipper* as perfect example of what was wrong in society. He wanted to fix it at any price, even his own life, but he knew Richard would never make such a sacrifice."

Sinner grunted and nodded as he took another deep drink of his beer. Standing side by side, they continued to look out across the city. The siren had faded.

"What about the Skipper, huh?" Sinner asked, "What was the verdict?"

"He's what he says on the label," Samantha said, turning her back to the city she smiled, "a good officer who fell victim to an excellent trap."

"He didn't sell his crew up the river? 'Cause you know it sure looked like it."

"No, I think he honestly thought he'd made a deal to take the fall himself," Samantha said nodding, "When Van Trappinni started to come down on me for having taken out Sir Richard, Alex came to my rescue. He stood up for me, took the blame himself and said the whole thing was on his shoulders."

"And you sure he didn't cotton on to the fact that the whole thing was a pantomime huh? I mean, you keep saying he's good."

"Oh he is," Samantha said, "but I'm better. So's Van Trappinni. No sir, if I hadn't know it was an act, I would have thought the Ripper and Van Trappinni were going to have my laurels for that one, but Alex stood up and was willing to take the bullet. He passed that test hands down."

"Well, that's good to know." Sinner pounded the last of his beer and let loose a prideful belch.

"You want another?" Samantha asked. Her smile was more relaxed.

"Naw, I gotta get going," Sinner said, "I promised Chrom and Bowman I'd meet them in about an hour and I'm gonna be late already."

"Really?" Samantha said.

"You want to come?" Sinner asked, but for the first time, Samantha felt that the invitation was more polite than heartfelt.

"No thanks," she said as they walked into the apartment, "I should get some personal stuff done while I'm in the city. But have one for me would you?"

"You bet," Sinner said as they walked to the door. Stopping as he opened it, he looked at her intently. "You okay Sammy?"

"Fine. I guess there's just a lot on my mind right now."

"Okay," Sinner said, but didn't sound convinced, "You know where to find me."

"Always," Samantha smiled. The two hugged and she watched him go down the stairwell before closing the door. She let her shoulders slump ever so slightly as she turned back to her empty apartment.

It was sparsely furnished, with few personal effects other than the occasional piece of understated artwork or indigenous artifacts of some alien race. A lifetime spent on-board ships had not given her much time to worry about buying decorations or furniture, and the past few years of intelligence work had encouraged her to keep little evidence of who she was in the places she lived. A part of her yearned to change that, but as with so many things, Samantha repressed those desires.

She felt empty, with no sense of reward. She had joined the Navy in search of revenge, a desire she had never suppressed. For five years it had worked, kept her striving towards her goals, but now she was beginning to question what she had really accomplished. The Empire was no closer to establishing her father's vision of a true democracy for all sentient beings, and those responsible for her parents' death were still killing innocents. What was more, with each mission she learned something that put her need for vengeance into deeper conflict with her father's ideals; particularly this last one.

Give it time, she told herself, *stay the course and see what's revealed. You can only fight one evil at a time.*

Taking another swig of beer, she found only backwash. She looked into the empty can, wondering how many of the evils that she hated were being supported by her own decisions. The emptiness remained as she returned inside and pulled another can from the cooler. The sun was down, the horizon dark. Samantha sat on the white sofa and turned on a holovid to wrench her mind away from the turmoil caused by her rational mind. It didn't work.

It was the first new thing that had happened in the garden for a very long time. Even the view from the game table had long since turned into nothing but the image of a prison ceiling. The fluffy bunnies seemed to scamper from it, though the bear and the girl kept on their irritating loop. Her giggle had gone beyond irksome. So when it started, Alyiar turned to watch.

It began with a subtle sparkle in the corner of the garden. The twinkling lights quickly evolved into a swirling mass of shining pixels, and Alyiar could tell something was fundamentally different from what he had seen before. As the human figure formed, he knew that this new presence went far beyond a representative avatar. He felt it in his very core.

Slowly, the visual representation took shape: a broad and muscular man who glowed with a golden aura. Streams of data flowed in and out of him like rays of light, small subroutines drifted and flitted in orbit of him like casually swimming fish. Some of these approached Alyiar, touching him briefly before flitting away. The man himself appeared almost divine: heroic and bald with mirrored eyes that reflected Alyiar's own twisted and torn image of himself. A gentle and amused smile appeared on the god-thing's face.

"What have we here?" The man's voice penetrated into every pixel of his being. "Zhis could be quite interesting."

The man reached out his hand and a light spread out from the golden avatar's palm to Alyiar's chest. For a brief moment, the last of the Wayang Stalkers felt pure euphoria. He smiled, filled with happiness. Then the flitting subroutines descended on him like piranha and tore into his soul.

"It's good to have you back," Sally said slipping her arms around Alex's neck.

"It's good to be back," he responded, closing the door to the apartment behind him.

"I would have preferred it if we could've just met alone," Sally said with a coy teasing smile as she nestled her body closer to his.

"I needed to meet with some of the other ARAG commanders," Alex said with a smile, "and I wanted to show you off to them, make a lasting impression. Networking is important."

"I taught you well," she smiled before stepping on her toes and kissing him, first softly, then with more passion.

"You give good incentives. Come on. Let's go to bed."

"Well if you put it that way." Sally leered at him, and let her embrace fall. Kicking off her high heels, she led him across the apartment.

Alex followed Sally into the bedroom, watching her pert bottom as her hips swayed like a house cat's. He threw his coat on a chair, closed the door and sighed. Leaning against the far wall with one foot against it, Sally stared at him. Her deep blue eyes shown with expectation, and a small knowing smile was on her lips. Even after he was certain the ECM was running, Alex remained silent.

"Well?" Sally asked eventually.

"I am in," Alex responded as he continued to undress, "You can tell the Director of the OSA that the Emperor has his mole inside the 12th Fleet."

"Do they suspect anything?"

"Of course they do," Alex said in a condescending tone as he unbuttoned his shirt, "They are trained professionals, they will always suspect something, but I've passed the first hurdle. Of course, now I am truly in the Ripper's camp, my father will never speak to me again."

"He will, when your real mission is complete," Sally said, "It's only a matter of time before this is all over. Then everything will go back to the way it should be, our agency will make sure of that."

"Indeed." Alex replied, but with the knowledge of his own guilt, he knew nothing would ever be the same.

AFTERWARD

For those who may not be aware, "Wayang" is the Javanese word for the art of Shadow Puppetry, and "Dalang" is the term for the puppeteer. Wayang is one of the most beautiful art forms that I have had the honor to see, often depicts or is inspired by religious themes, and frequently used as a form of social commentary. In this book, this wonderful and inspiring type of theater is portrayed in the same sort of bastardized light that democracy is. It is done so to reflect the way that things can be corrupted to service the ends of individuals and ideologues, and in honor of the way the art form has frequently been used to make cutting comment on society.

If you would like to learn more about the beautiful art form of Wayang, there are many sources on the internet and available in the Library. I first came across it in the 1982 film, *The Year of Living Dangerously*. It intrigued me enough to seek out a real performance as soon as I could, and believe me when I say that seeing Wayang portrayed live by a real Dalang makes anything you could see on a screen appear as blasphemy.

To this end, I hope that readers will understand and accept the intention of my portrayal of Wayang as literary commentary on the misuse of philosophies, art and ideas as a whole, rather than take it to imply any negative concepts to be associated with this wonderful art form or the culture that produced it.

ABOUT THE AUTHOR

Tom was born in Vancouver B.C. Canada in 1966 to an American mother and a British father. He has a Doctorate in archaeology from the University of Oxford and has worked throughout Europe, the US and bits of Latin America, specializing in concepts of spatial analysis, gender and identity. He lives with his wife and son in the Pacific Northwest.

For the past several years, Tom has reviewed and written about Speculative Fiction, Mysteries and Espionage on his blog *The Archaeologists' Guide to the Galaxy* (www.sophyanempire.wordpress.com).

He has numerous academic and technical publications. This is his first novel.

www.ingramcontent.com/pod-product-compliance
Lightning Source LLC
Chambersburg PA
CBHW071632260626
47170CB00001B/69

9780988543607